Do Not Disturb

LAURENCE GELLER

This novel is a work of fiction. Names, characters, places and events are the product of the author's imagination, and any resemblance to actual persons, living or dead, businesses, organizations, characters, events or locations is purely coincidental.

©2006 by Laurence Geller

10 09 08 07 06
                        1 2 3 4 5

ISBN (hardcover): 978-1-56625-308-6
ISBN (paperback): 978-1-56625-300-0

The Library of Congress has catalogued the paperback edition as follows:

Library of Congress Cataloging-in-Publication Data

Geller, Laurence.
  Do not disturb / by Laurence Geller.
     p. cm.
  ISBN-13: 978-1-56625-300-0 (pbk.)
  1. Hotels--Fiction. 2. Hotelkeepers--Fiction. I. Title.

  PS3607.E45D6 2006
  728'.373092--dc22

                                        2006015902

Volt Press
a division of Bonus Books, Inc.
9255 W Sunset Blvd., #711
Los Angeles, CA 90069
www.volt-press.com

Cover Design: Lai Shan Mui
Cover photo: Macduff Everton
Author photo: Sandro

Printed in Canada

In memory of Eric Bernard,
a true hotelier

ACKNOWLEDGMENTS

With appreciation and gratitude to Dr. Tony Marshall for the inspiration, Dick Marek for his patient editing and mentoring, Pam Bernstein, who became a wonderful friend; Jon Mindes, whose endless preparation was the work of scribes; Mary Ellen Viskocil for her disciplined administration, which brought it all together.

Special thanks to Tanya, Guy, and Misha, who hid their amusement at their father's foibles, and to Ruth, whose encouragement, support, and motivation led me to, and through, an adventure into the unknown.

"The penalties of defeat are frightful."

Winston Spencer Churchill

PROLOGUE

Kestrel Hotel, Union Square, San Francisco
2001

It was the same bench. The same damned bench in front of the same damned hotel where twenty-eight years before he'd sat up all night plotting to build the best hotel chain ever—at any cost. Then, he was full of hope, energy, and ambition. So he took the chance, took on the risks. Now, he was filled with a foreboding sense of defeat, faced with ruin, humiliation, prison—perhaps even death.

The thought of prison was worst of all. It wasn't the degradation; he could survive that. For a man who had valued freedom above all other things in life, being cooped up in a cell seemed unbearable. And jail would afford him no protection from his enemies. They could reach inside any prison; kill him at will whenever they felt like it.

Memories of the beating he'd sustained in Berlin swept over him. They had chosen not to kill him then, preferring instead to merely terrorize him. Well, it had worked.

"Andre Bouchard was right," he muttered. "I flew too close to the sun."

A cop approached. "You all right, Mr. Ritter?"

"Yes, Charlie, everything's fine. It's just such a nice night and I've had a lot on my mind. Fresh air always helps me sort things out."

Charlie continued on his way, but something told him to keep a watchful eye on Rolfe Ritter, chairman of Kestrel Hotels. It was the least he could do for a man who had done so much for San Francisco.

Gradually, Rolfe's vat of self-pity emptied and his mind cleared. He knew what he had to do. Now. Now was the time to do it. The decision made, it was as though an axe had been removed from the center of his brain.

*****

"Good morning, Mr. Ritter." Every member of the graveyard shift stood at attention as he crossed the familiar lobby.

"Good morning." He nodded, acknowledging each one.

He took the elevator to his penthouse suite, changed into a sweatsuit and well-worn Nikes, and stretched. It was the same routine he'd followed for twenty years; he found it oddly comforting today. Then, in the bedroom, he took out the nine-millimeter Glock he'd carried with him since Berlin, checking to make sure it was loaded and the safety catch on. He slipped it into the waistband of his Lycra running shorts and tucked his sweatshirt over the protruding handle. Nobody would notice it. He would present the same picture as always: Rolfe Ritter out for his morning run.

Back in the lobby, he could feel the hotel's energy rising, as it did every morning. The polishing finished, the marble floor gleamed. Fresh flowers were arranged in each of eight enormous urns. The chandelier sparkled, and the lobby furniture, recently upholstered, was as inviting as ever. The concierge, cashier, receptionists, and bellhops were all in their appointed places. The Plaza, the Connaught, the Imperial, the Ritz: none of them, in Rolfe's eyes, outshone this flagship Kestrel.

"Have a good one," Lennie, the doorman, said. He had been with the hotel since it had reopened, in 1974.

"Everything good at home?" Rolfe asked. "Wife and kids?"

"Fine. Thanks, Mr. Ritter. Enjoy your run."

He ran toward the wharves as he always did, letting the rhythm of his stride relax him. He inhaled the smells and sounds of the Embarcadero: coffee, fish, baking bread, and, near Ghirardelli Square, chocolate; the cacophony of traffic; the voice of a solitary singer who every morning belted out Puccini's "Nessun Dorma."

Usually, he liked to speculate on what was happening in the houses along Marina Boulevard; today he paid them no notice as he passed by. His strides even, he ran past warehouses and deep into the Presidio, now nearing his destination.

A foghorn's sigh beckoned Rolfe's attention to the Golden Gate Bridge nearby. Smelling the salty sea hanging in the air, he could almost feel the water's spray on his face and for a minute considered stopping to enjoy it. No. He must press forward. Into Fort Point he ran until he reached the end of the running path.

He halted and stared at the bay, turned gray in the breaking light. The Golden Gate loomed overhead, its top obscured by the fog. The Point was enchanted, he thought.

Looking out over the bay as he caught his breath, self-pity once again washed over him. To lose this beauty, to never see or smell this magnificent place again, to never run or love again or feel joy or satisfaction—that is what his enemies had wished for him all along. Now, they had triumphed. They'd left him no other choice.

He took the pistol from under his shirt and, with a kind of exaltation, released the safety catch, brought the Glock toward his face, and closed his mouth over the barrel. He thought of the loved ones he'd leave behind—Momo, Susan, Ron, his mother—and those who had already passed on, Mike, Josh, his father. Would the living miss him? Not for long. Would he see the dead on the other side? Probably not.

His trigger finger tightened. One second more. The pressure increased.

The sound of the gunshot under the bridge sent gulls flying through the morning sky toward the Kestrel.

Book One

*"To perceive a path and to point it out is one thing,
but to blaze the trail and labor to construct
the path is a harder task."*

Winston Spencer Churchill

CHAPTER 1

1944

Day and night melded into one in the bowels of the buildings occupied by Section III of British Military Intelligence. A maze of offices snaked their way through anonymous-looking adjoined buildings nestled in a secluded side street off London's High Street, Kensington.

The process of intelligence gathering and analysis droned on. The clattering of typewriters, the streams of people, the hush that fell over the office when an operation went wrong, the rivers of code-named and security-stamped files and the cryptic looks and whispers of those with access to them . . . all came together to make Margaret Summers feel like a denizen of a netherworld, one so removed from wartime London that she often wondered whether she'd stepped through Alice's looking glass.

At age nineteen and against her father's wishes, Margaret had left the safety of his Northampton home, joined the army, and fait accompli, confronted her tyrannical father with enlistment papers clutched in her hands. Recognizing that his rule over his only daughter was over, Jack Summers telephoned Bruce Radcliffe, his late wife's brother, for help.

A glowing introduction from her uncle, General Bruce Radcliffe, persuaded Colonel Michael Riverstone to hire Margaret as his personal secretary. Now, two years later, Riverstone was as grateful for the referral as she was. Margaret made his job easier.

* * * * *

Section III was responsible for intelligence gathering in Belgium, Holland, Luxembourg, Northern Germany, and Eastern France. Riverstone's role as one of three department heads meant he'd been assigned a range of activities, all currently aimed at providing intelligence support for the much-anticipated and now imminent Allied invasion of Europe. A quiet, slim, sandy-haired

1

man, Colonel Riverstone had been a professor of European history at Balliol College in Oxford and was among the first to echo Winston Churchill's warning against pandering to Hitler. When Churchill was proved right, Riverstone received his call-up papers and soon joined the intelligence team in London.

Riverstone relished the challenge of being an integral part in the creation of an intelligence network throughout Nazi-occupied territory. Agents provided his London-based team with information on troop movements, train schedules, command changes, factories converted to arms and munitions production, and the construction of military bases. Target after target was identified for Allied bombers or local saboteurs. Information, Riverstone knew, would be the key to victory when the invasion came.

* * * * *

Within a short period of time, Margaret and Riverstone had developed a strong partnership. Now, he depended on her.

Her long, wavy, ash-blond hair highlighted her cheekbones, milky complexion, and emerald-green eyes. With the beauty of her face combined with a figure that her height and uniform only enhanced, Corporal Summers was invariably approached by the foreigners who constantly roamed in and out of Section III. She went out with many of them, and sometimes, in the heat of their ardor, these men allowed details of their covert activities to slip from their tongues. Always, Margaret passed on their indiscretions to Riverstone.

Despite their interest in her, Margaret rarely dated the same person, foreign or English, more than two or three times. She set her boundaries, and they had no choice but to respect them. Her reputation remained pristine. Margaret Summers, an English rose at the age of twenty-one, was still a virgin.

* * * * *

Corporal Summers was focused on typing Riverstone's report on unusual German troop movements along the Rhine when she felt, rather than noticed, the presence of someone standing in front of her desk.

"One moment," she said without looking up.

"'How do I love thee? Let me count the ways,'" a voice boomed out. Heads turned. "I love thee to the depth and breadth and height / my soul can reach, when feeling out of sight . . .'"

"'. . . for the ends of Being and ideal Grace,'" Margaret finished the passage from one of her favorite poems by Browning, astonished at herself. She looked up. The man had the body of an Olympic skier, the stance of Hercules, the intense gaze of Laurence Olivier in *Wuthering Heights*. He wore the dress uniform of a foreign army, which one she couldn't place, and sported a cane, which added strength rather than weakness to his posture. To her, he seemed three-dimensionally superimposed against the whole office.

"What can I do for you, Mr. Browning?" she asked.

"'Fly away with me! Leave your cruel father and join me in a life of rarified love bequeathed to but a few mortals,'" the stranger quoted the last line of the poem. Then he winked at her. Winked! "Or you can tell your boss that Major Willem Den Ritter is here."

Transfixed, she swallowed, stood, and opened the door to Riverstone's office. "Colonel, there's a Major Den Ritter to see you. He doesn't have an appointment. He just sort of appeared."

"Wim!" Riverstone shouted. "No appointment needed, Maggie! Just wheel him in."

Margaret turned to find Den Ritter perched on her desk, reading the report in her typewriter.

"Stop!" she said. "That's classified."

"Really?" He unfolded his body and, using his cane for support, ambled toward Riverstone's door. "'Love me Sweet with all thou art feeling, thinking, seeing—'"

Feeling blood rush to her cheeks, she closed Riverstone's door behind Major Den Ritter.

* * * * *

Wim Den Ritter's smile vanished the instant the door closed. In the poorly lit, windowless room, the odor of cigarette butts predominated.

"Gott Verdommett, Mike, you can't just ground me!" he said. "There's work to be done."

"It's for the safety of your network," Riverstone said calmly. "You're crippled."

"Bullshit!"

Riverstone glared. "Let me remind you, and heed me well, you're an officer under my command, not a law unto yourself. I issued you an order. It is not negotiable."

"But you need me, now more than ever."

"I need you alive. Look at you. You're barely able to walk. The Germans know who you are. And you know too much. If you're caught—"

Den Ritter held out his hands. "You need information, and I can get it. I may not know what you're up to, but I'm no fool. I know the invasion isn't far off."

Riverstone shrugged. "You'll be valuable here, analyzing information, much of it from your own network." His voice softened. "Get healed, for God's sake. After we've landed in Europe, we'll need you to help put the Continent back together again."

"I'm a field man, Mike! I'll wilt in a miserable box like this."

"There's nothing more to discuss," Riverstone said and turned his attention to the papers on his desk.

Den Ritter limped through the outer office without a glance at Margaret. She looked at his receding back. My God, she thought. What happened in there?

* * * * *

The next morning Margaret was the first to arrive at the office and went to the file room where she found a manila folder in the cabinet marked PERSONNEL: FOREIGN. She sat down at a desk and opened it.

Den Ritter, Willem

Major, Royal Dutch Armed Forces, Serial # 37982814.
Codename: The Kestrel

Born 1912, Amsterdam, Holland. Only child.

Father deceased 1928.

Honors student in high school.

Extracurricular activity: Acting.

Sports: Speed Skating.

1932-35: Attended University of The Hague. First Class degree in European Languages.

1936: Joined Amstelveen Bank in Amsterdam. Promoted to assistant manager, 1937.

April 1938: Enlisted Royal Dutch Armed Forces. Accepted for Officer Training. Showed exceptional analytical skills.

October 1938: Promoted to Second Lieutenant and assigned to Military Intelligence.

January 1939: Selected as part of elite infiltration group. Demonstrated remarkable ability in problem-solving. Note to file: Had difficulty accepting orders and respecting chain of command.

1940: Given codename, The Kestrel, Promoted to First Lieutenant. Sent to Berlin to form network of undercover agents.

Supervisory reports indicate Den Ritter's mastery of language and acting skills allow him to impersonate German officers.

1941: Seduced wife of General Von Planten, officer responsible for logistical support for German regiments besieging Stalingrad. Through her, accessed circle of officers in German High Command.

1941: Obtained plans for German Special Forces operations within USSR to support the German invasion. Note to file: Her Majesty's Government provided plans and materials to Soviet High Command, enabling them to frustrate all planned German raids.

1941: Special commendation for heroism behind enemy lines. Promoted to Captain.

Margaret rubbed her eyes. Was Den Ritter too good to be real? she wondered. A comic-book man of action, a fantasy? There was more.

1943: Promoted to Major.

February 1944: Assigned to find out where the German High Command believed Allied invasion would land. Infiltrated Field Marshall Rommel's headquarters in France. Betrayed by his mistress, Brigita Laufler, fled arrest and was shot twice in the thigh before escaping through a sewer. Used his own network to reach Rotterdam, and from there to a fishing boat rendezvousing with submarine H.M.S. York Minster.

May 1944: Released from Claremont Military Hospital, Surrey. Assigned to Section III, London. Posted inactive for any work in enemy territory. Awarded King George Medal for Valor, and Royal Dutch Military Cross. Note to file: To send him back to the field might compromise underground operations in Germany, France and Holland.

The file, for all its details, told her nothing of the man. Margaret felt empty. What sort of man would risk his life so often? He was handsome, charming—perhaps too charming—a rogue hero. But what made him tick? How did he think? How did he feel?

"Doing a little light reading?" Colonel Riverstone was standing over her; she had not heard him enter.

She blushed. "The Den Ritter file."

"Ah, you suspect he's an enemy agent?"

"Not at all. I was curious about him after I heard the two of you shouting at each other."

"We were merely having a discussion. And you don't have to sneak around looking for files. If you want to know something, just ask me."

"All right, I'm asking."

He looked at her fondly. "He's one of the bravest men I know—and the most foolhardy. For God's sake, don't fall for him. He'll break your heart."

"Of course I'm not falling for him," she said. "I told you, I'm just curious."

* * * * *

"Learn to win a Lady's faith
Nobly as the thing is high
Bravely as for life and death
With a loyal gravity."
                    I dedicate myself to learning—W.D.R.

The card bearing the handwritten inscription was attached to a single red rose that lay on Margaret's desk. Standard operating procedure, she thought. Still, she was flattered. He'd probably talked his way into the office late last night and delivered the rose himself. Colonel Riverstone had seen it, she was sure, and blushed again. Yes, she would hear from the Dutchman again. What was the best way to tell him she wasn't interested?

She didn't have long to wait. A week later, she left the office at 8:00 P.M. to walk the blacked-out streets to her West London flat.

"Be careful," a voice said behind her. "It's dangerous for a woman to be alone this time of night."

She gasped, turned. There he was, leaning on his cane, eyes vividly blue, just as she remembered.

"I'll walk you home," he said, "It's on my way."

"How do you know where I live?"

"I'm an intelligence officer."

"Then you're intelligent enough to know your hotel is in the opposite direction from my flat."

"Aha! You've been checking up on me." Despite the gruffness in his voice, she could tell he was pleased.

"Colonel Riverstone's orders."

"Why don't I believe you?" he said, taking her arm.

"Believe what you like," she said, feeling foolish.

They walked through Kensington until they reached a café near her flat. She accepted his invitation to tea.

* * * * *

"I left school at fifteen," she said. "Took a secretarial course, worked for a local solicitor. Grimly boring, but it enabled me to look after my father."

Wim cocked his head to one side and lifted an eyebrow. "There's more."

Lots more, she thought, reflecting on the pain of her adolescence. "Dad wanted me to spend all my time with him. He was angry Mother had died and took it out on me. He made every decision—what I should wear, what time I should come home, what I should eat for dinner—and blew up if I dared challenge him."

Wim leaned forward. "What about boyfriends?"

She grimaced. "I wasn't allowed."

"No wonder you like Elizabeth Barrett. And you too ran away."

She nodded. "To London. Dad's still furious."

"And now you have boyfriends by the carload."

"Occasional casual dates. Generally, I'm too busy with work."

"'Too busy for love.' Now, that would make a nice song title."

Though they'd finished their tea, neither moved to get up. He gestured to a waitress. More tea appeared.

"If it's any consolation, I fly solo too, by choice. In my line of work, I can't afford to care about anyone. It could make me lose my edge, do something stupid, compromise my comrades, or end up dead."

"But you're not doing dangerous work anymore."

He glanced at her. She realized what she had said and busied herself with the tea, astonished at her forwardness. For God's sake, don't fall for him. He'll break your heart.

"We seem to have led parallel lives," he said. "In my case, it was father who died when I was young and my mother who brought me up alone. But she didn't try to hold me back. She couldn't. Besides, she's always been incredibly self-sufficient herself. When the war started, I tried to get her to come to London with me, but she stayed put. 'Fight your war,' she said. 'I can take care of myself.' So I did; haven't seen her in two years. But I know she's safe. Woe betide any German who tries to get in her way."

They sat silently for a while, and when Wim took her hand, she did not pull away. Again, Margaret felt her cheeks flush. He looked at her intently, as if probing deep inside her soul, and she had to look away, out onto the empty street through gaps in the windows' blackout covering, to avoid his piercing gaze. He is an actor, she reminded herself, a lady-killer, surviving by living out lie after lie. How would she ever know if he were telling her the truth?

As she took a sip of her tea, it suddenly occurred to her that she had no idea of how long they'd been talking. She looked at her watch. "I must go," she said, releasing his hand and standing. "I have to be back at work in a few hours."

Wim stood, laid some bills on the table, and helped her into her coat. "I'll escort you home," he said. She didn't protest.

They walked silently to her flat, their footsteps and the occasional brushing of their coat sleeves against one another the only sounds passing between them.

Watch out, she warned herself, he can see into my heart.

* * * * *

Over the following weeks, they explored the Inner Circle of Regent's Park and wandered through the rose garden, Wim telling her the Latin name for each species. Later that day, as he rowed them under the bridges and willow trees, he delighted in admitting to her that he had made up the names.

She introduced him to Gilbert and Sullivan, and they became regular visitors to the Savoy Theatre. After the shows, they dined at the theatre's namesake hotel and danced until the band started to pack up their instruments.

Piccadilly Circus became their regular meeting point, and they would wander through crowds of uniformed Americans, Australians, New Zealanders, Canadians, and Poles, blending in with their British counterparts. They danced at Romano's, drank tea at Lyons Corner House, watched a rerun of *Arsenic and Old Lace* at the Empire Cinema, Leicester Square, and the Cole Porter musical "Something for the Boys" at the London Coliseum.

Wim, the foreigner, was the leader of their expeditions; she followed gratefully, seeing the city through his eyes—its beauties and its dangers. Though she felt increasingly confident in their relationship, uncertainty remained.

In late spring, they picnicked in Holland Park. Wim spread a blanket on the lawn near the empty bandstand, and Margaret unpacked the food and wine she bought with the last of her ration coupons. With the chicken pie and Stilton cheese eaten and the remains of the fruit carefully stashed away, they lay on their backs, savoring the sun.

"Umm," she said. "Perfection."

He rolled onto his side, leaned over and kissed her. His hand touched her breast. She moved it away. "Don't."

"Why not?" He sat up.

"You know why."

"It's bloody ridiculous!"

"Not to me. Not until I marry."

His frustration welled over. "You may well be a virgin for the rest of your life!"

"If necessary."

His tone softened. "Look, we want each other. I'm damn near out of my mind."

"No!"

"No one will know. What's the difference?"

"To me, all the difference in the world. Don't pretend you don't understand. You just don't want to accept it."

"But I love you."

It was the first time he had said it, and it angered her that he had chosen this time and this purpose to tell her.

"No," she repeated.

They lay on the blanket without speaking as the dusk turned black.

* * * * *

Her doorbell rang in the middle of the night. She sprang out of bed, conscious of rain pelting the window, a reminder that the air raids had blessedly stopped terrifying the city. "Who is it?"

"Me. Wim."

She opened the door and gasped. His uniform was drenched, his hair plastered to his skull. But it was his face that shocked her—drained completely of color, while his red rimmed eyes were totally bloodshot.

She led him to her tiny sitting room, the first time he had ever been there, and settled him on the sofa, where he sat shivering, shoulders slumped, staring numbly ahead. She unfastened his jacket and gently eased it off his shoulders. In his eyes she saw a look of unutterable sadness.

She knelt on the carpet in front of him and took his hands. "Tell me."

"It's Beatrice."

"Beatrice?"

"Beatrice Vermeij, the wife of my closest friend at university,

Jan Vermeij. I recruited her as part of my Dutch network."

"What happened?"

"She was caught by the Gestapo. Mike told me."

"And?"

"They gave her electric shocks to make her give up names in our network. When that didn't work they cut off her fingers one by one. She still wouldn't talk, so they let her bleed to death."

Envisioning the horror, Margaret felt cold. "How did Mike know?"

"One of the Gestapo in the interrogation room was a mole, part of the network. He was powerless to stop them without giving himself away. For all I know he helped in the torture."

Wim's body shook, and his breath came in great sobs. "Jan never knew about her work with us. Mike's going to tell him she was rounded up and executed in a reprisal for some resistance attack."

"Oh, God," she cried. "I'm so sorry. My poor darling, so, so sorry." She kissed his tears. "Let me get you out of these wet clothes." She led him to the bedroom, where she removed his shirt and toweled his torso.

"Hold me," he whispered.

They lay together on the bed. She could feel his heart pounding, or was it hers? He kissed her gently, and then again more firmly, and then again and again, and when his hand found her breast, this time she welcomed it.

When dawn broke, while her exhausted lover slept soundly, she got up and stared at the bloody sheets, her mind racing. Had she been a fool? Was the story about Beatrice even true? Would he disappear now they had made love, as she'd heard so many other soldiers did? Yet, when she looked at him, none of the questions mattered, not for now.

So this is love, she wondered.

* * * * *

Preparations for D-Day energized Section III. Margaret worked sixteen to eighteen hours a day. Riverstone lived in the building, sleeping on a cot in the corner of his office.

Wim Den Ritter had a permanent office now, and he provided analysis of and often surprising conclusions to the varied pieces of intelligence coming in from all over Europe. He had moved into Margaret's flat. Far from disappearing, he was with her always, and as their love grew, so did their hunger for one another.

But one morning, Wim said, "When the invasion happens, I'm going to France. I don't know how long I'll be away or when we'll see each other again."

"Oh!" was all she could say. Would he go behind the lines again? Would he be captured or killed? The pain at the mere thought was too great, unbearable.

"Say you'll marry me. Marry me now."

She dropped her coffee cup on the table. Its contents flowed over the newspaper and onto the floor.

"Does that mean yes?" he asked.

"Of course! Of course! Of course!"

There was no doubt now, only joy … and terror. God only knew how long he'd be away, when, or whether, he'd come back. He was fearless. Risk-taking was his life.

Dear God, don't let him die, she thought.

* * * * *

One week later, in a chapel off Holland Park Corporal Margaret Summers became Mrs. Willem Den Ritter. The simple ceremony was attended by an astonished Bruce Radcliffe, his wife, Mary, their sons Percy and Robert. Mike Riverstone was best man, and Margaret's sullen father, Jack, gave her away.

After only ten days of wedded bliss, Major Den Ritter was assigned to the Allied Invasion Forces in France. Not long after V-E Day, he returned, unscathed, to Margaret, a woman half-crazed with jubilation.

CHAPTER 2

1946–1956

Immediately upon receiving word that his mother's health was failing, Wim and Margaret prepared to leave London immediately. Riverstone arranged early demobilization for them both; their time with Section III had come to an end.

"I'm not going back to Oxford," Mike told them at a farewell dinner. "Too much politics and pettiness, and after all we've been through, too much boredom. I'd sooner watch traffic jams."

Wim understood his boss's restlessness. "What will you do?"

"Spying, it appears, is a growth industry. A new combined-intelligence arm is being formed within the civil service, reporting directly to the prime minister. I've been asked to join it, and have decided to become one of the worker bees. Can you believe it? Me, a bloody civil servant." He chuckled. "Wim, why don't you think about doing the same in The Netherlands? The Dutch government's going to need people like you."

Wim frowned. "I hadn't planned to stay in Holland for more than the few months, just until to Mother is well. I'd be frustrated as a caged tiger doing routine work at some bank. Don't you think, darling?"

It was true, Margaret knew. She said simply, "It's worth investigating."

* * * * *

Where were the rolling hills of England? Margaret wondered. The land around Haarlem, where Wim's mother lived, was flat and uninspiring, dotted only with an occasional canal or windmill. The house itself was a horror. The garden was overgrown with weeds, the gate was broken, and paint peeled off the window surrounds.

Inside, everything seemed brown, and the heavy oak furniture was heavy and forbidding. Eerie rays of dust-filled light forced their way through dirt-encrusted windows to illuminate faded portraits of Wim's ancestors. The walls were paneled in dark wood; a wooden staircase led upstairs to rooms, Margaret was sure, of more wood. Even the bed, she guessed, was uncomfortable.

And the kitchen! Good heavens! The terra cotta on the walls had cracked, and the floor was filthy and rutted. The hanging pots were thick with grease, the smell of ancient fat permeated the walls, and a patina of grime was so thick Margaret's fingers turned black when she touched the shelves.

Margaret was put off by the decay. Wim seemed unfazed by it and pleased to be home.

"Mother is elderly and has been ill, and she had no help during the war," he said matter-of-factly. Then he added, "We'll get it cleaned in no time."

His mother was at the hospital, they discovered on arrival. They would sleep—Margaret shuddered—upstairs and visit Wim's mother first thing in the morning. Meanwhile, she took some comfort from Wim's evident pleasure in being home and tried to qualm her disgust.

* * * * *

Wim's mother passed away five days after their arrival. She never regained consciousness, so there had been no reunion of mother and son, no greeting of the new daughter-in-law. While Wim sat by his mother's bedside holding her hand, Margaret strolled the corridors and the depressing streets outside.

"She's gone," Wim said when Margaret returned from one of her walks. "Her hand went limp, and that was it."

He seemed unperturbed. If Wim had felt anything profound for his mother, he did not show it then. Dry-eyed, he gently kissed the top of his mother's head—more of a tribute than any show of affection—and left the room.

* * * * *

Sophia Den Ritter was laid to rest in the graveyard behind the local Lutheran church she had attended for decades. There were fewer than twenty mourners: a handful of women in their late seventies and early eighties, evidently Sophia's friends, and some neighbors whom Wim had not seen since the outbreak of the war. Her brother had long since died, and his middle-aged daughter, whom Wim had not seen since childhood, did not recognize him. Margaret thought her dispirited and sullen.

Only one man was of Wim's age. Short and stocky, he walked

up to Wim when the brief service ended, his red hair blowing in the afternoon breeze, and hugged him affectionately.

"Darling, this is Jan Vermeij," Wim said. "Jan, my wife, Margaret."

Recognizing the name, Margaret's eyes widened, but she said nothing.

Though sadness lay deep in his eyes, Jan Vermeij had a definite spark. To Margaret, he seemed the only person in attendance, other than her husband, who seemed still alive.

"Jan and I were at university together. I cribbed all my notes from him," Wim said. "He was in England during the war, claims he was doing something important in military intelligence, but he won't tell me what. Personally, I think he was guarding a WC outside Manchester. Be careful of him, he can be quite wicked. Whatever you do, don't believe a word he says."

Margaret offered her hand; he pulled her into his arms.

"She's beautiful, Wim," he said, stepping back to appraise her. Then, his eyes twinkling with merriment, the sadness temporarily gone, he said to Margaret, "What I want to know is how a scoundrel like him ended up with a dish like you? Why, I've half a mind to steal you away from him myself."

"Not a chance!" Margaret said, as she slipped her hand into Wim's. "You see, I'm hopelessly, completely, endlessly in love with this scoundrel."

Jan pretended to be piqued. "Then offer me a drink to soothe my sorrow. I haven't seen the old house in years. Still as depressing as ever?"

"Worse!" Margaret laughed.

"Then I'll need at least two drinks." He stepped between them, allocating an arm to each, and off they marched. "I've got the feeling we'll be seeing a lot of each other, and"—he winked at Margaret—"you might as well know up-front, I'm every bit the reprobate they say I am."

* * * * *

"I suppose you heard about Mike Riverstone's new position," Jan said as he sat with Wim and Margaret on their porch.

"Indeed," Wim nodded, and took a swig of scotch.

"I've accepted a similar position for our government," Jan continued. "I'll be in charge of counterespionage. Should be fun, sorting out who's doing what to whom. Want to come work for me?"

"No way. I'm taking Margaret back to England. Riverstone

suggested I work in intelligence, too, but I've got to settle down sometime. The banking life's for me."

"You're mad! You'll be bored out of your mind in a month."

Wim sipped his drink thoughtfully. "So you think there's something I could do for you? Something meaningful?"

"Meaningful? Why, man, there's going to be a whole new Europe, every day a different alliance, a different threat. We'll need every good man we can get."

"It's Russia, isn't it? The 'different threat' you're talking about."

"Russia and China. Communism. We're going to have to take sides and be careful how we do it."

"And a gimp like me—?"

"Should be square in the middle of it. You've already got your networks. I'll bet half the men who worked under you would want to do it again."

"I'd better do it fast." Wim was ablaze. "Start in Germany. Move quickly on to Austria and Czechoslovakia. We could coordinate with Riverstone. He'd be as happy as a bear in a honey tree."

"Exactly! I'll call him tomorrow. Maybe you and I should—"

Margaret stopped listening. They had forgotten about her, these two men who both claimed to adore her, one of whom she could not live without. She turned to look at the forbidding house behind her. It was here she would stay during those many times he'd be away, and in danger. In her heart, the dread she had managed to briefly forget rose with sharpened talons, and she stared at her husband with cold rage.

* * * * *

"Jan was Beatrice's husband, wasn't he?" Margaret asked as they were preparing for bed.

"Yes. Thank God you didn't say anything. He must never know the truth. Do you promise me?"

"Of course I do."

* * * * *

Wim was often away, but Margaret had learned to make the best of solitude during her years in London and now turned to learning Dutch and making friends in her new neighborhood. Her primary occupation, however, was rejuvenating the gloomy mansion.

"I called it Bleak House the other day, and Wim was furious," she wrote to her father. "But by the time you get here, it will be different. When are you coming? Sometimes I think that if I don't hear an English accent, I'll go mad."

She hired men to scrape the floors and walls and to redo the fireplace in the sitting room, decorated the rooms in bright pastels, bought new, more comfortable furniture, replaced everything in the kitchen, planted a garden, festooned the bedrooms with prints and posters, and filled the library with new books.

When Wim returned from his third trip "East," she took him on a tour of their refurbished home.

"Well, what do you think?" she asked when he had finished his inspection.

He hugged her. "You're a genius! You've taken a Dutch dungeon and transformed it into an English country home."

"Our home?"

He looked at her, surprised. "Of course."

"Forever?"

"For the foreseeable future. Why do you ask?"

"Because I'll have to do more remodeling."

"Why? Each room is perfect."

"Did you notice the small room next to our bedroom? The one I had set up as my study?"

"Yes. It will be good for you to have a private space of your own."

"But it needs to be changed."

"How so? It looks wonderful and—"

"—to a nursery," she interjected.

She watched as his expression changed from puzzlement to comprehension.

"Yes, Wim. You're going to be a father."

* * * * *

In the blossom-filled spring of 1948, Rolfe Michael (named after Wim's grandfather and Margaret's former boss) was born to Willem and Margaret Den Ritter of Haarlem, Holland.

Mike Riverstone, not waiting to be asked, announced, "Given that I'm responsible for bringing you two together, it's only right that I be the godfather." And so it was agreed.

Margaret's joy was tempered by her ever-present fear that Wim would be killed. How could I bring up Rolfe alone? she wondered. The feeling exacerbated whenever Wim disappeared on one of his assignments.

"Don't worry, I'll be back soon," he'd tell her. And he did return, each time with perfume or a blouse for her and a toy for Rolfe.

But with each trip, her fears increased. When she tried to talk about her fears with Jan or Mike, they pooh-poohed her. Their reassurances only made her more nervous. When Wim was away she couldn't sleep, and her irritability transmitted itself to Rolfe, who took to tantrums as a way of getting what he wanted when his father wasn't home.

When Wim reappeared, however, the boy would rush into his father's arms and follow him about the house, reluctantly leaving his side only when Margaret forced him to bed. Father and son were closest when they explored the maze of Amsterdam's streets. At each bridge, canal, or square, Wim would describe how he'd played there as a child, and Rolfe would listen as though to his own adventures, staring at his father with rapture, trusting him completely.

Jack Summers had grudgingly accepted Wim as Margaret's husband, and with the birth of Rolfe, the rift between father and daughter healed. Jan Vermeij, Wim's best friend, gradually became Margaret's close friend too. Only the subject of Wim's work was taboo; for everything else, Jan dispensed advice.

"Ignore the local women's gossip," he told her. "You're as alien to them as if you'd come from outer space. Let Rolfe play with their kids, but don't expect them to like you. Before they married—and even after—they all wanted Wim, and it's their frustration in you landing him rather than any of them that shapes their attitude. It's nothing personal."

A widower, Vermeij would often visit accompanied by his son, Pieter, six years older than Rolfe. The two boys detested each other from the start, and tolerated the relationship only for the sake of their parents. Pieter seemed to derive satisfaction from torturing Rolfe, which he often did when his father was out of earshot. Given the difference in their ages, there was no way Rolfe could retaliate.

Wim taught his son to swim in the lake behind their home. When he was six, accompanied by Jan and Pieter, he took Rolfe to the Haarlem municipal swimming pool and, with his son's hand squeezing his in unadulterated fear, dragged him up the slippery metal staircase to the five-meter board. Rolfe tried to back away when he realized what his father wanted him to do. His father's grip was like iron.

"No. Please, Dad, no," Rolfe implored.

"Jump. Jan is waiting in the water. Jump."

Terrified, he looked everywhere for help. The only face he registered was Pieter's, sporting a smug look of self-satisfaction as he stood, arms crossed, at poolside. Reluctantly, Rolfe shifted to the edge of the platform, and now free of his father's hand, he closed his eyes tightly, held his breath, and stepped off into the air.

Suddenly, all fear evaporated. He was flying. The water rushed toward him and parted. He bounced to the surface in exhilarated glee, ignoring Jan and swimming to the edge of the pool unassisted. Grinning ear to ear, he clambered out of the pool and headed toward an even higher board.

"Dad, can I do it again?" he shouted, relishing Pieter's dismayed look. "Only this time, I'm jumping from the ten-meter board."

* * * * *

From time to time, Mike Riverstone would come to Holland and speak with Jan and Wim. Other times, Jan and Wim huddled alone. Margaret and Rolfe were always barred from these meetings, each fostering a growing resentment that neither of them dared voice for fear that Wim would vanish forever.

When Wim was gone, Rolfe did not know enough to worry, and he had no real cares. Both his mother and father clearly loved him dearly, and his place in their hearts and in life was secure.

Until the summer of 1955.

* * * * *

It was a special day. Rolfe's parents were taking him to the circus! He and his mother would meet his dad after work, and the three of them would drive to Rooseveltlaan Park, where they'd see animals, acrobats, trapeze artists, jugglers, and best of all, clowns. Rolfe had studied pictures of them and knew all about their antics. During the entire week before the big day, he had pretended to be a tightrope walker, using the lines between the kitchen tiles as his make-believe rope, steadying himself with the kitchen broom.

Throughout the afternoon, he badgered Margaret with questions: "Will the clowns throw buckets of water over me?" "Are the lions really fierce?" "What if they escape?" "Can I have candy floss?" "What if the trapeze breaks?" "What if the bareback riders fall?" And incessantly, "Is it time to go yet?"

Finally it was time. Hand in hand, mother and son walked through the cobblestone streets from the bus stop in Dam Square toward Wim' office. Rolfe's questions kept coming—"Will there be lots of elephants?" "Can I ride one?"—but Margaret had long since stopped listening to her seven-year-old's babble, and simply hurried along as he pulled her toward their destination.

They arrived a few minutes early, and so sat on a low wall near Wim's Citroen, which was parked alongside the canal. As they basked in the summer twilight waiting for Wim to join them, Rolfe became anxious. "Are we late?" he asked, afraid they would miss a single moment of the circus.

"Hush, darling," Margaret said. "There's plenty of time."

Rolfe watched the office doors intently, willing his father to appear. It worked! "There's Daddy! He's coming now!" he shouted and stood up on the wall, waving his arms. "Daddy! Over here!"

Rolfe watched as Wim said goodnight to the security guard and strolled down the deserted street toward them, smiling in the special way he had when there was an adventure to share. Rolfe's heart filled with love. Surely he was the luckiest boy in the world to have such a tall, handsome, strong father on such a night. Surely he had never been so happy.

Rolfe heard the roar of an engine and looked past his father toward the source of the sound. A car. Black, huge, louder than any lion, was bearing down on Wim from behind. Rolfe tried to shout, but his throat was so tight no sound came. He saw his father turn, heard his mother scream, and then all sound was eclipsed by the thump of metal against flesh and the sight of his father being catapulted into the air, arms flailing as though he too were a clown.

In a moment, all was silent. The car sped away, its work done, and his father lay against the red-stained brick wall, blood streaming from his head and mouth. The quiet lasted only a second. His mother's howl, an eerie sound like a wounded animal in agony, filled the air, and as if in a dream, he watched her run to his father and collapse at his side.

Rolfe wanted to run to join her, but his feet wouldn't move; he simply stood, his body weaving awkwardly, as he'd seen drunken people stand. He felt as though he were watching the scene from a vast distance. He could scarcely breathe, and gasped to take in air. The inhalation of air brought a rush of adrenalin and life back to his legs, and he ran toward his parents, weeping and saying over and over, "Daddy-daddy-daddy-daddy," like an infant just learning to talk. As he neared them, in utter despair he screamed, "DADDY!"

His mother, on her knees, turned to him, her face twisted into a cruel shape he'd seen in pictures of witches in his fairy tales. "Stay away," she croaked. Then this woman he didn't recognize, speaking in a voice he'd never heard before, waved her arms at him, as if to say, "Shoo! Shoo!" He stopped in his tracks and stood rigid as a tin soldier, hurt to his core. His father's eyes were open, staring but not seeing, as though blaming him. Rolfe whimpered and, unable to look any longer, stepped back, vaguely aware of movement in front of his father's building.

The security guard ran up to his parents and leaned over both of them. Eyes widened in horror, Rolfe realized that his mother's cream-colored dress had turned bright red with blood. She threw herself on top of Wim and began to kiss his bloody lips. Her howls wails had turned into soft little cries, like that of hungry baby birds in the trees by their pond.

"It's no use, Mrs. Ritter," the security guard said. "He's dead. I've called an ambulance."

Dead! Somewhere deep in his heart, Rolfe already knew it, but the word penetrated his consciousness, shocking him into fully grasping the reality before him, of where he was and what had happened.

The security guard pulled at his shirt. "Come on, son. There's nothing you can do here."

"No! Leave me alone. I'm staying here. Let me go." The sound of his voice startled him, and he struggled to get free, but the guard held him fast. Rolfe beat on the man's arms with his fists, but the man held him firmly, and he finally let himself go slack.

An ambulance arrived. Two blue-uniformed men climb out and lifted his father onto a stretcher. His mother, her lips smeared with his father's blood, as though she had run amok with her lipstick, was now standing. When his father's body was placed inside the van and the back doors clanged shut, she finally moved toward him.

But this was not his mother. This was a madwoman with wild eyes come to take him to a place of even greater horrors. He shrunk back against the guard, and it was only when Margaret took him in her arms and he felt her familiar hands caressing his hair, heard her beloved voice telling him she loved him, smelled her familiar perfume beneath the metallic stench of blood, that he knew his mother had returned.

He also knew that from that day forward he would never feel

safe. He knew that the roar of the lion-car, the howls of his mother-witch, and the sight of his father-clown turning somersaults in the air would forever burn in his brain.

* * * * *

After a sufficient amount of time had passed since Wim's funeral, Jan Vermeij paid Margaret a visit. They sat in matching chairs arranged cozily before the newly restored fireplace in the lounge—the room she'd furnished with Wim in mind, imagining the two of them sharing enjoying it together, forever.

"You have to start thinking about yourself," he said. "Wim is gone. Nothing's going to alter that fact. You've got to accept it and get on with your life."

"I need to know why, Jan. Why was he killed?"

"We're investigating, but so far, we have no solid clues," Jan said, choosing his words carefully. "All I can tell you is that Wim was working on some serious matters."

"Such as? I've got a right to know."

"You know the rules. I can't discuss this with you. Aside from the obvious rules and security risks, it could put you in danger."

"Who the hell do you think you're talking to? I worked in Section III, remember. Wim told me about his job every day. Do you really think I'm just a stupid woman whom you can calm down with a few soft words? You should be ashamed of yourself!" Margaret slammed her hand down on the arm of her chair and leaned forward, her face now inches from Jan's, her breath jagged with rage. Through clenched teeth she hissed, "I want specifics. Motives. Most of all, names." Her eyes narrowed. "Then I want to kill them."

She sat back and silently stared into Jan's face, daring him to speak the truth she'd demanded. She could tell he was trying to decide how much to tell her.

Finally he spoke. "Wim was convinced that we have a foreign agent working at a senior level within the Ministry of Foreign Affairs. Probably a Russian. He was obsessed with the idea, concentrated on nothing else. He told me he was getting close. Then..." He shrugged.

"Is that who had him killed? The KGB?" She gripped the arms of her chair. "What's his name?"

"Believe me, I don't know. I wish I did. As far as who was actually in the car, we have only sketchy eyewitness reports to go on."

"What reports?!"

"A secretary who was working late saw the car hit Wim and noted the license plate number. The number is not registered. Either she wrote down the wrong number, or, more likely, it was a fake plate."

"That's it?"

"No. We found a man who feeds the birds every evening. He was at the wall."

"I didn't see him."

"He was there, I promise you. He told us he'd seen the same black car cruising past our offices for a week. If he's right, then the killers had been planning this for a while."

The explanation only increased her unease. "There must be more. For God's sake, Jan, tell me!"

"Calm down, and I will."

"Don't you dare tell me to calm down! It wasn't your husband who was murdered. It wasn't your son who was left fatherless!"

"Have you forgotten that it is my wife who was killed by the Germans, and that it is my son who has been left motherless!"

Margaret bit her lip with embarrassment. "I'm sorry. I'm so sorry. Of course, you and Pieter have suffered too."

"We all have. And still are. Wim was my friend too, Margaret."

"Yes. Yes he was," she said softly. "Go on. Please tell me about the bird man at the wall."

"He provided descriptions of the two men in the car: a bulky man in his forties and a slim teenager. No one in our office matches either of those, so if it was a double agent from our office who killed Wim, he used accomplices."

Margaret started to interrupt, but Jan held up his hand. "Before you ask, yes, we have police artists working with the witness to come up with sketches. Yes, we've alerted Interpol, and we'll check the sketches against their files. If that doesn't help, we'll print the pictures in the papers, here and throughout Europe."

She felt disappointment settle over her like a too-heavy coat. "It's not enough. What else?"

Jan looked at her without expression. "If—and it's a big if—these two men were hired to kill Wim in order to protect the spy, they were paid by a foreign government and were probably out of the country before the night was out."

"Meaning, you'll never find them?"

"Meaning, we may never find them."

Her body seemed to crumple in the chair, making her look suddenly small and frail. "Damn you. Damn you," she growled. "Wim would be here had you not talked him into that job. It was your fault. You killed him. I'll never forgive you."

* * * * *

"That's everything I know, Mike. Everything Jan told me," Margaret said, clasping the receiver tightly to her ear. She'd woken early and phoned him at his London flat; he had become her buoy, her lifeline.

"I can't call Jan," he said. "He'd think the British government was meddling. All I can do is poke around here, see what I can find out."

"Oh, would you?"

"Sure, but I doubt there's much more I can dig up. My guess is the traitor is Russian and the killers KGB. If so, then Jan's correct: They're long gone."

His words tore into her heart. "What do I do? How do I get revenge?"

"Forget revenge. It'll eat you alive. There really is only one thing you can do: Start fresh, build a new life for you and your son. I'll support you in any way I can, but it's up to you, Maggie. You and Rolfe."

* * * * *

Margaret's loneliness made for interminably long nights. Sleep, with its horrific dreams, became her enemy, so she stayed awake to memories that were worse than her nightmares. She withdrew further and further into herself. Only her need to look after Rolfe kept her going.

"Is Daddy in heaven?" the boy kept asking.

"Yes, darling."

"I miss him."

"I know, sweet boy."

"Why, Mummy? Why?"

"I don't know. I don't know."

Nightmares disturbed Rolfe's sleep too. In his dreams, he watched powerless as his father was hit by the car and thrown against the wall, and he would wake up screaming, the smell of his father's blood in his nostrils, the face of a witch glaring at him from above. Then he would go to his parents' bedroom, hoping, always in vain, to find his father. Sometimes he would crawl into bed with his mother. Often, in her own grief, she would reject him and send him back, alone, to his own room.

* * * * *

One glorious summer's afternoon months later, Jan took Rolfe to a local confectionery where he fed him a "Knickerbocker Glory" sundae.

"I want to tell you about your father," Jan said. "You're old enough to know."

Rolfe sat expectantly in front of him, the long-handled spoon frozen in mid-air.

"He was a hero," Rolfe said flatly.

"You bet he was! He found the bad guys, never let any of them get away. After the war, too, when we worked together at the ministry. One time Wim discovered that a man from the Rumanian Embassy had stolen information from us. By the time your father figured out his name, the man was already on a train bound for Germany, where he planned to hand over the information to another spy. Your father jumped on the train just as it was leaving the station. He pulled the emergency handle, and the train stopped. Wim went through it car by car. When the spy saw him, he opened the carriage door and leaped out. To this day, I don't know how he did it, but your father chased him down. The spy pulled out a gun, fired, but missed. When the police arrived, your father was sitting on the Rumanian examining his bloody knuckles. 'Do you need help?' a police officer asked. 'Indeed I do,' your father said. 'I've lost my bloody cane, could one of your men find it for me?'

"Your dad's code name was 'The Kestrel,'" Jan added. "He was the bravest man I ever knew. Above all, he was a great patriot, always fighting for good. Never forget that."

No, Rolfe thought, I never will. "What's a kestrel?" he asked.

"It's a kind of hawk, or falcon. Tough, fearless, and mean. It can stay in the air forever, flying against the wind. When you grow up, you'll be the next Kestrel."

The boy nodded in agreement, his heart pounding with excitement. But an unwelcome question nagged at him: If I'm so tough, why didn't I try to stop that black car?

Rolfe determined he'd be the best spy in the world. The Kestrel name would live on. He'd be like the hero in the book that he and his mother read together, *The Scarlet Pimpernel*. No one would know who he really was.

* * * * *

Rolfe's grandfather journeyed to Holland to try to talk Margaret out of her depression. "Sell this bloody mausoleum and come home," Jack Summers ordered.

She refused. This was the place where she had loved Wim, where Rolfe was conceived and born. "Rolfe and I love you very much," she said, "but this is our home. I won't leave it."

"Then go back to work. You're bi-lingual, and you've got excellent skills. Any business would want you," her father advised. "At least close down some of the house to reduce your expenses. This place has more rooms than a bloody hotel."

In bed that night, Margaret played over their conversation. "More rooms than a bloody hotel." Precisely.

* * * * *

At sunrise the next morning, she called Jan.

"Hold on," he said, chuckling. "You're talking too fast."

"Buy me lunch today, and I'll shut up right now."

They met in the lobby of the Amstel Hotel.

"You look radiant," Jan said. "Who is he? I'm going to hate him."

"Not a man," she said. "A plan. I know what I'm going to do."

Over lunch, she told him. "I'm going to make our home into a hotel, a unique hotel. Look at all the businesses coming into our area. Think of all the corporations making Holland their headquarters." She had neglected her food.

"I can't make it a real hotel, it's not large enough," she went on. But it can be the finest bed-and-breakfast in Haarlem. We're close enough to Amsterdam so that people can use it as a center—or a retreat. Elegance is what I'll feature: fine wines, fine food, gorgeous rooms. I'll subscribe to all the international newspapers, create a small version of a London gentlemen's club. If guests need secretarial work done or arrangements made, I'll do it."

She stopped for a moment, then took Jan's hands. "What do you think? Am I crazy? Tell me the truth."

The truth, he thought. It's a wonderful idea, but was she up to it? She had become cold since Wim's death; would that same coldness infect the hotel? He had difficulty sorting out his emotions toward her: friendship, guilt, love of some kind, frequent irritation, constant frustration. Would a hotel bring her closer or take her further away?

He answered carefully. "It sounds great, and I think you'll make money, but I warn you, you'll be a slave to it. Do you have any idea of the work it would take? Not only now, while you're getting it started, but also once you get it running?"

"I've thought about that," she said, removing a sheaf of notes from her handbag. "See. Here's the staff I'll need, the changes I'll need to make to the house. I'll use Wim's life insurance money. The banks will give me a loan, and I've got Wim's pension to fall back on. I can manage it. I know it!"

"What about Rolfe?" he asked, looking over her notes and marveling at their thoroughness. "Will you have enough time for him?"

"Rolfe will help with the hotel when he's not in school. I'll be there, in our home, any time he need me. As he grows, we'll work side by side."

"And me?" he asked.

"I can't do it without your help. I know how busy you are, but you've got to promise me you'll pitch in. Otherwise, I won't go ahead with it. You were Wim's best friend. Be mine. I need you, Jan. More than ever."

"Just try to keep me away! Watching you pull this off will be about the finest entertainment our little city has to offer."

CHAPTER 3

1956–1964

It's gloriously alive!, Margaret thought, strolling for the fiftieth time through the rooms of the completed hotel; it's as though I've splashed sunshine on the walls. She had decorated each of the ten guest rooms in a different blend of soft pastels, florals, and chintzes. The beds featured extra-thick mattresses, over-stuffed duvets, deluxe feather pillows, and hand-carved mahogany headboards. Each room was named after a different flower or tree, announced on ornamental signs fixed to the door; Willow was Margaret's favorite. Fresh tulips would await each arriving guest.

She had redesigned the sitting room to include sitting nooks, furnished with leather sofas and club chairs. Bookshelves were filled with classics, current bestsellers, and the latest magazines. A large rosewood and silver antique sideboard served as a cocktail bar.

Hung majestically over the fireplace was a large portrait of Wim in his major's uniform. Margaret had it painted in oils from a photograph of him that reminded her of the day he'd first appeared in her office.

When Margaret allowed Jan a tour, he followed her through the rooms in awe. The place is an extension of Margaret, he thought, her self-confidence and pride evident at every turn. Her hand was everywhere, from the dressing table accessories to the long-stemmed crystal wineglasses in the lounge. She's beautiful and talented, he concluded. Amazing. I want her to know she's loved. But it's too soon for both of us.

"The house is wonderful," he said. "Stunning. More magnificent than I could have imagined. What are you going to call it? It needs a name."

"Ten," she said, "The numeral '10,' because it has ten guest rooms."

"Perfect."

* * * * *

Hotel 10 soon became a landmark in Haarlem. Most of the regulars came from Great Britain and the United States, but all nationalities, save for Germans and Russians, were welcomed.

Some of the guests were attracted to the owner, and made fruitless plays for her. Some of the rejected suitors became friends. Others were never allowed back.

Most evenings the talk in the drawing room was of business and politics. Young Rolfe liked to take in the multilingual conversations and was generally indulged. The guests had no concern about a pre-adolescent boy, but Rolfe was learning and remembering, information he knew would be invaluable once he became a full-fledged spy.

Mike Riverstone was a frequent visitor. He too listened and learned. Having never married, he treated his godson as his own, invariably turning up with armfuls of presents. One was a plastic Luger. To Margaret it looked scarily real, and she urged Mike to take it back, but he refused.

"It's a good replica," he told the boy. "Standard German Army issue. Your father used to carry one when he was impersonating German officers."

"Was he a good shot?"

"Excellent."

Rolfe's favorite present was a crystal set radio. He sat entranced while Mike and Jan assembled the pieces. When they switched it on, men and boy whooped with glee as a scratchy broadcast from Radio Hilversum filled the air. Rolfe imagined setting up the set in a hidden place and receiving secret messages from headquarters. Just which place and whose headquarters he was unsure.

Uncle Mike impressed on him the same message he had drummed into Wim: Facts are friendly.

"Never forget anything about anyone. It's like having money in the bank," he told the boy. "Remember: information is key. Knowledge is power."

* * * * *

Rolfe became part of the 10 staff. He helped set up breakfast in the morning and served drinks in the evening, clumsily at first, but soon with the adeptness of a seasoned bartender. He cleaned up, took messages, and helped his mother escort to bed someone who was "over-emotional," as she termed a guest who'd had too much to drink. He hurried home from school so he could assist with setting up the evening meal before his bartending chores, wanting to make sure everything was as nearly perfect as his mother desired. As he grew older, he earned tips for one personal service or another, like sneaking a guest's lady friend in and out of the house, hidden from his mother's disapproving gaze. Mindful of Uncle Mike's admonitions, he wrote down the names of the guests for whom he provided these special favors, concealing them in his schoolboy diary. One entry was typical of many:

> April 11, 1960
> Easy day at school. Miss Klemp was ill, so we had no math class. No homework!
> Mr. Prager, who comes from Basel (where there are bears!), is a regular guest. Mother calls him "Oo-li"— what a funny name. He asked me to help him bring a friend to his room this evening. Mummy is very strict about allowing visitors in guest rooms, but I did it anyway. She'd be furious if she knew!
> I waited until about 9:00 P.M. Mother was in the lounge; when I heard her put on the gramophone, I opened the kitchen door and let in Mr. Prager's lady friend. She had lots of hair and wore too much perfume. I used a newspaper to fan the smell out of the kitchen. I took her up the back stairs to Mr. Prager's room.
> Just after midnight, Mr. Prager woke me up. I took the lady downstairs. She had on no makeup, and her hair was messy. I locked up after she left the kitchen. Did they have sex? I wonder. She wasn't very pretty. When I have sex it will be with someone beautiful.
> Mr. Prager gave me twenty guilders. A lot of money for a few minutes' work!

* * * * *

By age fourteen, Rolfe had grown into a tall, handsome young man. At least his mother told him so and so did many of the guests. At school, he was interested only in languages and managed to do just enough of the other work not to attract the wrath of his strict Lutheran teachers. He was fluent in Dutch and English, could read and write German, and had more than a passable knowledge of French, though he found the accent hard to master.

He had developed a fascination for all things American. Uncle

Mike made increasingly more trips to the United States, and each time reported back on the glories of Washington D.C., the excitement of New York, the charm of Boston. He was working with his counterparts in American intelligence—"The Cousins," as he called them.

Rolfe fantasized about being in these strange places himself, working secretly with other spies to thwart the Russians, who were by then the world's enemy.

"My friend from the Dorchester arranged for me to stay at a hotel called the Waldorf Astoria in New York," Mike recounted after one of his trips. "I've never seen anything like it. The lobby is always packed with such well-dressed people, I felt embarrassed to be seen there in my rather plain clothing. I stayed on the thirty-fifth floor—imagine. You're closer to the clouds than the ground."

"Did you see any movie stars?" Rolfe asked.

"Charlie Chaplin."

"Wow!"

"Where did you go next?" Margaret asked.

"Washington. That's where I spent most of my time. I stayed at a lovely hotel called the Hays Adams—more your style, Maggie, only larger. Every statesman in the world stays there. It's like the Audley in London. I had lunch with the general manager, Henri Le Mesurier, imported from France. He was put in charge of the hotel four years ago—had to be more of a politician than a manager, he told me. Knowing Le Mesurier is like knowing the president of the United States! They have lunch with the same people."

Rolfe lay in bed that night too excited to sleep. America!

* * * * *

Margaret worried that Rolfe was drifting through school. "He's more interested in 10 than his studies," she complained to Jan.

"Mike will be here at the end of next week," he said. "Why don't the three of us have dinner with Rolfe and give him some guidance?"

* * * * *

Coincidentally, Bruce Radcliffe showed up and became part of the conspiracy—at least that's the term Rolfe would have used to describe the meeting. They ate at Benissimo, an Italian restaurant Rolfe liked, but this night he had no interest in food.

His mother's eyes darted nervously around the table, never catching his. A bad sign, he knew. Her expression took on the serious look that portended trouble. "You're nearly sixteen," she said.

"It's time for you to start thinking seriously about your future."

In fact, Rolfe had been thinking about little else for the past few months. Ideally, he would become a spy, following Mike's and his father's paths. But he had lost interest in the crystal set, and the toy Luger sat unnoticed on his bedroom shelf. Lately, he had felt his confidence slipping, even though Mike and Jan reminded him how much he was like his father. His nightmares were visiting him with redoubled ferocity. If spying meant death, he did not want to die. If intelligence meant murder, he failed to see what about that was so smart. Maybe there was another way to prove himself worthy—to his mother, to the memory of his father, to himself.

As the voices of his mother, his uncle, his godfather, and Jan swirled around him, a previously half-formed idea took solid root in the boy's mind.

". . . career in government," his mother was saying. "Your language skills, your intelligence, your background, they'd all be useful. . . ."

Rolfe said nothing. He dug his fingers into his legs.

"I don't mean intelligence work," Margaret continued. "I've lost one man to it and couldn't endure losing another. But the diplomatic service—ah, that's a different matter. You'd be posted all over the world, could even end up as a British ambassador. Bruce could get you started once you've finished university. Couldn't you, Bruce? And you, Mike?"

Both men grunted assent, but Rolfe had difficulty concentrating. His mind flashed back to the source of his nightmares. Mother pushed me away then, he thought. She's doing the same thing now.

He drew in his breath, forced a smile. "I always believed I'd be just like Dad," he told the expectant group. "Do something exciting. But now I don't want to do that at all."

Rolfe could see his mother staring at him. He avoided her eyes.

"What is your decision then?" Mike asked.

Another breath. Another smile. "I'm going to be a hotel manager."

"Never!" his mother shouted. Her face had turned white.

"Why not?" he asked, risking further fury. "You do it, Mom. It's because I love 10 so much that I want to do it." His brain was clear, his words came easily. "Only I'm going to manage hotels all over the world. Who knows? One day I may even own one."

There. He'd told them. He sat back.

"Forgive me," Bruce said, "but I think you're cut out for something better. A hotel manager's a whore—forgive me, Margaret, but it's true. You don't want to be working for other people; you want people working for you."

"Agreed," Mike said slowly. "A diplomat can change the world. Wouldn't you want to do that?"

Not particularly, Rolfe thought. If his father couldn't change it and Mike couldn't either, how could he? Peace, he knew, was only a slice of time between wars. Hadn't his father been killed in peacetime? Wasn't Mike always talking of the impending war with Russia, as though it were sure to come?

"I've made up my mind," he said emphatically, speaking with more calmness than he felt. "I don't want a career in government. Governments are hollow."

"True!" Mike laughed. "How did you become so wise so young?"

"Because he's learned to think for himself," Jan said. "You really are your father's son—a contrarian." Then he addressed Margaret solely, as though Rolfe weren't at the table. "If that's what the boy wants to do, I see nothing wrong with it. It's an honorable career, all the better if he ends up owning a place, a profitable one. You haven't done so badly, my dear. And if, in a while, he decides he doesn't like it, then it's not too late to change. When he's finished his grammar school, he can easily get into the Hotel School at the University of The Hague and get his degree in hotel management there."

Rolfe's heart was pounding. "I don't think that's right for me, either."

"Not right?"

"No. I want to learn from the bottom up—starting immediately."

"What in heaven's name does that mean?" Mike asked.

Was there a twinkle in his eye? Rolfe wondered. Was he enjoying himself?

"It means I should go to France to learn the kitchen, and later to England or maybe Switzerland for restaurant service and then the front desk. That's the way hotel managers have always done it. It's much better than learning some dumb theory at a school."

Margaret had taken this all in silently. Rolfe watched her stand, turn, start to leave. "Where are you going?" Jan asked.

"Home," she said. "I won't listen to anymore of this. Rolfe, when you've come to your senses, we'll speak again." She wheeled on Rolfe's godfather. "This is your fault. All that talk about the managers at the Waldorf Astoria and the Hays Adams. 'Just like the president.'" She slapped Mike, hard, across the face. "How dare you!"

Rolfe felt blood rush to his cheeks and an emotion he had never acknowledged before: rage at his mother. "Mother—"

"Don't Mother me! You can be anything you want. Do you think I brought you up to be a hotel manager? Are you crazy? You've seen the life I lead, attached to that place twenty-four hours a day. And it's only ten wretched rooms!"

"Then maybe you should hire a general manager," he said icily. "But don't look to me."

"I have an idea," Bruce said gently. "I know the manager of the Plaza Athénée in Paris. Why don't I see whether he'll take Rolfe on for a year as a kitchen apprentice." He grinned. "Maybe the heat of the stoves will take the steam out of him."

"Good idea," Mike said.

"Great idea," Jan echoed.

"No!" Margaret sat back down. "I forbid it."

Now it was Rolfe's turn to stand. "Sorry," he said. "I'm going. I'll wait till I'm sixteen; then neither you nor anyone else can stop me."

She clutched at him, her hands like claws. He looked at her in disgust. "Goodbye, witch," he muttered under his breath, and left the restaurant.

It was the bravest action he had ever taken.

* * * * *

He walked for hours, trying to exhaust himself so he could sleep. When he got back to 10, only the light in the foyer was on, and he used the back stairs to creep to his room, the same silent route upstairs the lady friends had taken.

His door was unlocked. He immediately saw a shape on the chair in front of the window, a human form hunched under what looked to be a blanket. He stifled a cry, approaching carefully. Moonlight lit his face even as it darkened the silhouette in front of him.

"My men have different ways of deserting me," his mother said. "One gets killed; the other seems intent on killing me."

Heartbeat slowing, he switched on the light. Margaret was staring at him through reddened, unblinking eyes. She was dressed in her nightgown, her hair hung over her shoulders like the hood of a cape, and her breathing was rapid. How old she seemed, how helpless. She held out her arms. "Don't go. Don't do this to yourself ... and to me."

For an instant he yearned to accept her embrace, to comfort and be comforted. But the image of her turning from him at the side of his father's corpse thrust itself unbidden into his brain, and he made no move toward her.

"I'm sorry I talked to you that way at the restaurant. Of course you're free to choose any career you want. But at least stay until you're eighteen. Then, I'll let you go without a fuss, I promise. Or I'll retire, and you can have the hotel."

She was making an effort, he knew. He could feel her need and was touched by it. But it was too late.

"My chance is now," he said, surprised by his coldness. "Besides, I don't want 10. I want to make my own way, live my own life."

"And sacrifice mine?" She was crying now—he couldn't remember when he had last seen her tears—and he was shockingly aware of her frailty.

"You have Jan and Mike and Grandpa. Aren't they enough?"

Her silence was his answer. Wim, he thought, that's who she really wants.

The realization made him gasp, and he knelt in front of her and awkwardly put his arms around her, feeling sorrow, guilt, inadequacy—and resolve. Whatever doubts he might have had about his future course had vanished.

* * * * *

Three weeks after his sixteenth birthday, he was on a train from Amsterdam to Paris, where he was to begin work as the lowest form of existence in the Plaza's kitchen, a *commis de cuisine*.

CHAPTER 4

1964–1965

Self-conscious in his spotless chef's whites and starched hat and carrying the knives into which he'd painstakingly carved his initials, Rolfe nervously descended the two flights of stairs from the staff entrance to the kitchen—a trip into the inferno. White hats surrounded him like a forest of tall mushrooms. Orders bombarded his ears, shouted across the kitchen in a patois he'd never heard, always preceded by the command, "*Ça marche.*" Cauldrons of stock bubbled in one corner, belching clouds of steam into the kitchen's already fetid air. The open stoves spouted fire, as chefs in every area sautéed, fried, boiled, steamed, and poached.

Rolfe's nose was assaulted by a variety of smells, while his eyes took in meats, fish, and vegetables, some familiar, most he'd never before seen. Pandemonium, he thought. I won't last a week. I'll be sent back to Holland in shame. Bet that will make Mother happy.

"Ritter, come with me," A small man wearing a bloodstained apron prodded Rolfe's shoulder. "Monsieur le chef is ready to see you."

The famed *chef de cuisine* of the Plaza Hotel, Monsieur Hervé Toutlemonde, a man barely five feet tall but wearing the highest chef's hat Rolfe had ever set eyes on, stood at his desk in an office off the kitchen. A pencil-thin moustache adorned his cherubic face. His kitchen whites were immaculate, and the linen scarf around his throat was tied as neatly as any Windsor knot. In his thin girlish hands he wielded a one-meter ruler.

"So, Ritter, you want to be a chef."

No, I want to be a general manager, Rolfe thought, but did not correct the little man, who had launched into a speech.

"The Plaza is the best training ground in the world. If you work like a dog and do everything you're told without hesitation, we'll train you to be worth something to us, and to yourself. At least, you'll be able to find your way around the kitchen. If you disobey, you'll be fired in an instant." He whacked the ruler ferociously against the desk.

"This hotel is famous for delivering the best food, wine, and service. There is no room for mediocrity, only excellence." The ruler slammed down again. "Attention to detail, every minute of the day. No exceptions. No excellence, no job. Do you understand?"

It was hard not to. Rolfe nodded.

"You'll start in the larder. Next, soups and vegetables; then, on to fish; and then, if you're worth something, meats and sauces. By then we'll know if you have any talents and where they lie. If you're very good, we might let you work in pastry."

Toutlemonde left his office, motioning Rolfe to follow. A giant of a man walked toward them.

"This is your new *commis*," the chef said. "Work him hard."

* * * * *

"My name is Jean Le Favre," the giant bellowed. "*Chef garde-manger*, in charge of the larder." The immense man appraised Rolfe. No sympathy here, the boy thought. "Your hours will be eight in the morning until the lunch service is complete, then five-thirty in the evening until after dinner service. Some days you'll need to come in at five in the morning to help with breakfast. You will work six days some weeks and seven days others—off days are earned. And you'll do exactly and only what you're told."

The chef gazed at Rolfe with disdain, "I suppose you can't even peel and chop an onion. Watch me."

He brandished a paring knife. In seconds, an onion was peeled without a blemish on its opaline skin. Le Favre cut it in half, and in a blur cut each section into what seemed to Rolfe at least a hundred slices, stopping just before reaching the end of the half. He turned it ninety degrees, then slashed three horizontal cuts across the onion and sliced again. A mound of tiny onion cubes fell on the chopping board.

"That's how you do it. Get to work."

By the end of the day, Rolfe's fingers were raw. He had peeled, chopped, and sliced so many onions and carrots, so much celery and garlic, his exhausted mind recoiled at the memory of it. After changing in the sweat-reeking staff locker room, he shuffled up the long hill to the staff hostel, realizing as he walked, I stink like an onion.

His home was a cubicle on a floor of seven other like-sized cells, each curtained off from the next, furnished with an iron bed, locker, and scratched nightstand on which stood a weak light. All the commis shared one grubby bathroom. At least he had a bit of privacy, he reflected as sleep washed over aching bones.

Unfortunately, there was no privacy. The curtains of the cubicles left little room for imagination; every sound carried, and each grunt, groan, snore, and fart was shared. A continuously squeaking bed meant masturbation, its lonely end signaled by a barely audible sigh.

Along with Rolfe, the quarters were occupied by a Frenchman, an Italian, a Portuguese, a Spaniard, an Austrian, a jovial German, and a taciturn Swiss; pidgin French was the common language. They had different reasons for being at the hotel—some simply needed a job, others aspired to become chefs themselves. Only Rolfe, it seemed to him, wanted to be the general manager of a hotel as great as the Plaza.

After two months, he felt part of the kitchen's symphony and ready to display his newfound skills. He was moved to soups, where he spent twelve-hour shifts stirring and gratinating. He wrote to his mother, picturing her, while he wrote, as she had been when he loved her—when he was a little boy.

> *One of the chefs told me that every time a guest checks out, the toilet seat in the bathroom is removed, taken to the cleaning room where it is thoroughly sanitized and sealed in a plastic covering before being reinstalled, so it always seems like new. Not that I recommend that for 10!*
>
> *Some things haven't changed here for a hundred years, even though the place was taken over and used as offices by the Germans during the war and by the Americans afterward.*

Her letters were always terse. The only solace he got from them was the *Love, Mother* at the bottom of the page.

Eventually, he graduated to the saucier's section at the stoves, where his and two other commis' hands were persistently bloody from handling slithering meat, game, and fowl. From time to time Rolfe would lift his head from whatever he was working on to see his peers in similar positions, their faces illuminated by flames. It was as if a macabre group of devil's helpers were toiling in the eerie light.

On rare occasions, he was assigned to assist one of the chefs in carving the roast of the day on the high, domed, silver gueridon carving trolley, which was wheeled from dining table to dining table. For this chore he had to change into clean clothes and keep absolutely silent.

> *It's a treat,* he wrote his mother. *At first I felt like an actor performing on stage. But then I realized I was invisible to the guests, merely part of the ambiance. Now it's easy. You should see the way the chef pockets the tips he gets for giving "special attention" to certain guests— larger portions, choicest cuts. And he never offers me a centime. A commis de cuisine is the lowest form of life. But in the end, it doesn't matter to me. I'm not going to spend my life carving beef, lamb, pork, and duck for fat cats.*

* * * * *

The general manager's assistant, Chantal Le Peron, often came down to the kitchen to collect lunch for her boss; when she did, Rolfe's chest tightened. She was in her mid-twenties, he figured, and her auburn hair was cropped short in the current Paris fashion. She had a button nose, green eyes set off by a touch of eye shadow, round, discretely rouged cheeks, full lips, and a body—oh, a body—that would make Aphrodite jealous. She mostly wore tailored suits that accentuated her flat stomach and rounded hips, but sometimes she'd wear subtly hued, contour silk dresses that swirled with every step and let him imagine the flesh beneath them.

At night, it was his bed that often squeaked. He would think of her body, particularly her wonderful breasts. He could picture himself playing with them, Chantal crying out in pleasure as he gently bit her nipples. Some nights his fantasies were so vivid he would wake believing she was in his arms, and become morose and frustrated when she was not.

His disappointment was acute on the days she did not come to the kitchen. Did she know of his obsession? he wondered. He thought of making love with her—he, a virgin; she immensely experienced. Why, she'd ridicule him!

The Kestrel had been a renowned lover; he'd heard many whispers of his father's prowess. Had Wim Den Ritter ever flinched at the prospect of a beautiful woman? Quite the contrary. Well, then, he would be bold as well. But where to start? How to attract her attention?

When she next visited the kitchen, he slipped out a side exit and waited for her in the corridor leading back to the executive offices. Soon she appeared, carrying a tray. He bumped into her.

"Sorry—"

The tray shook in her hands, but did not fall. "No you're not," she said unsmilingly. "You did that on purpose."

"Really, I didn't." He tried to take the tray from her, but she held on to one side while he held the other.

"There is no need to pretend, Mr. Ritter. See, I know your name, just as I'm sure you know mine. Rolfe Ritter. R-R. Just like Rolls Royce. Are you as good a ride as a Rolls?"

He was utterly nonplussed. What was she talking about? How had she learned his name? And why? How could she know he'd learned hers? He saw flickers of amusement in the turned-up edges of her mouth.

"Well," she said. "Can I let go? Are you going to carry the tray for me?"

"If you want."

"I do." Her fingers brushed his as she released the tray. He had to grab it to keep it from falling. They walked together down the corridor.

He looked straight ahead, afraid to tip the tray, but was conscious of her green eyes—they were shining.

"If you wanted to meet me, why didn't you just ask? There was no reason for this subterfuge." Her voice was melody to his ears.

"I didn't have the nerve."

"Then you have to learn courage, don't you?"

Was she laughing at him? Had he made a fool of himself? He felt hideously self-conscious.

"Tell me," she said. "Why would you think I'd not be interested in meeting a good-looking young man?"

He had never considered his looks; he was who he was. But Chantal's question aroused a pleasurable excitement. She thinks I'm attractive!

"By your behavior," she went on, "I'm guessing you think I'm good-looking too."

"You're beautiful," he managed, blushing.

"Then say so."

They had stopped by the door marked: Executive Offices: Jacques Bergeron, General Manager.

"I just did," he said.

"Yes, but I had to pry it out of you. Say it again, with conviction."

He summoned passion. "You're the most beautiful woman I've ever met."

"That's better. Now, hand me the tray and go back to the kitchen. It would not be good for us to be seen together—the general manager's secretary and a commis."

He let her take the tray and stood unmoving, staring at her.

"Run along," she said, her hand on the doorknob.

He walked backward, still staring, until he tripped over his own feet, and then he turned and, her laughter ringing in his ears, stumbled toward the kitchen.

* * * * *

Two days later, days spent trying unsuccessfully to interpret what had happened, she palmed him a note as she was leaving the kitchen:

Fouquet's on the Champs-Elysées. 5 p.m. tomorrow.

She knows my schedule, he marveled. Tomorrow is my day off.

* * * * *

He arrived fifteen minutes early, ordered coffee, and sat with his eyes closed, reliving that single touch of her fingers. If she wanted dinner, particularly here at Fouquet's, he could not begin to afford it. If she wanted him to be funny or intellectual or to speak of world events, he'd trip over his words as he had over his feet. As good as a Rolls Royce? He wasn't even a pre-war Citroen.

She thinks I'm attractive! That phrase alone kept him from bolting.

At 5:15, he looked again at the crumpled note she'd given him. He was at the right place, Fouquet's, and he'd been there in advance of the appointed time. Now, it was well past five o'clock. Had she changed her mind? Was he being stood up? Could she be that cruel?

He stopped a passing waiter. "Check, please."

"Certainly, sir."

Within two minutes, the bill was staring up at him from its saucer. As he reached into his pocket for his wallet, her voice stopped him.

"Leaving so soon, Mr. Ritter? Have you another appointment?"

He looked up. She was wearing a green sheath dress, gold earrings, and a beret. A single diamond hung suspended by a gold chain from her flawless neck and brushed against her breasts. He averted his eyes from it.

"May I sit down?"

"Of course. I was afraid you weren't coming."

"Just being fashionably late. It's how Parisian girls are supposed to behave."

He felt stupid. "I didn't know."

She ordered a glass of champagne. "Won't you have one too?" He hesitated. "It's my treat."

"In that case," he blurted, surprising himself, "let's have a bottle!"

She applauded. "Perfect! You learn quickly. I've heard that about you."

He felt his shyness evaporate. "What else have you heard?"

"Oh, this and that. One thing's for sure, you're different from the other commis—from most of the others in the hotel, for that matter. I saw your references. You have some important friends. So my guess is you don't intend to stay a kitchen boy forever."

"I intend to be a general manager."

"Oh, ho! Quite an ambition. At the Plaza?"

"Wherever. But I have to tell you, I have a way to go. I'm only seventeen."

"Sixteen. Remember, I've read your file." She grew serious. "Don't lie to me, Rolfe. Not ever. You can only impress me by being who you are, not somebody you think I want you to be." She sipped her champagne. "I, of course, have the option of lying to you. It's a woman's prerogative."

He realized how much he was enjoying himself. She's flirting, he thought, the revelation a sunburst. "Then tell me how old you are."

"Fifteen. You see, already my first lie."

"Do you have a boyfriend?"

"No. That's my second little white lie. Actually, Georges is in America on business—he's a banker—and I thought, while he's away, why not have some fun."

"And you picked me." It seemed too good to be possible. "Why?"

"Because I think you're the most beautiful man I've ever seen."

Her mimicry of him made him laugh. What difference did why she'd chosen him make, he thought. All that matters is that she's here with me.

"Oysters?"

The question startled him out of his reverie. "If you want. Anything."

"They're supposed to be an aphrodisiac. Let's see if it's true."

She ordered a dozen for each of them; they were served nestled in a bed of ice. As he spoke of the heroism of his father, he watched her tilt her head back and slowly slide each oyster down her throat. The way her breasts moved as she swallowed fed his fantasies. Another bottle of champagne magically appeared. When he picked up his glass, his hands were trembling, and he hoped she hadn't noticed. Actually, she was staring into his eyes with an expression of—what? He couldn't define it, but it quickened his pulse.

The oysters gone and their glasses empty, she called for the check, paid it, and stood, swaying a little with the effects of the wine. He stood too and took her arm, which she brought next to her body so he could feel her warmth.

"Time for bed," she purred.

He looked at his watch. "But it's not yet eight o'clock."

At her signal, a cab pulled up. "Precisely. I'm not finished with you tonight."

* * * * *

Her apartment building was near Neuilly. He followed her through ornate wrought iron gates and up a marble staircase to the second floor, standing silently by as she opened two locks on the door.

Inside, while she found and lit two candles, he took in the room. The ceiling was high and creamy white, its molding a delicate diamond pattern. Double windows overlooked a courtyard. A soft green couch stood against one wall, fronted by a teak coffee table on a white throw rug. There was a ceramic bowl on the table, filled with fashion magazines. Chairs covered in the same fabric as the couch made up the rest of the furniture. A lamp stood by each, but she made no move to turn them on. In the candlelight, he looked at a poster for a Raphael exhibition at the Louvre on one honey-colored wall and a reproduction of a Raphael painting of a farm girl on the opposing wall. He made out a fireplace and walked over to study the photographs on the lintel above it: pictures of Chantal and what he took to be her parents; a shot of Chantal with a man standing with his arm around her, both in ski clothes, her head against his shoulder. Georges, the man, he supposed, who enabled her to afford this apartment.

Chantal had put on the record player; Edith Piaf singing "Non, Je Ne Regrette Rien." She took his hand and led him to the couch. He was conscious of the beating pistons of his heart.

"I've got to tell you something," he said. "I've never been with a woman before."

She lay down and pulled him beside her. "You'll see that honesty pays. Relax, you beautiful boy. Tonight I'm your guide."

* * * * *

He awoke to the aroma of fresh brewed coffee. He stood and raised his arms above his head like a champion. What a fantastic night! What a fantastic woman! He squirmed at the memory of how he had come while she was fondling him, how she had laughed gently and quickly brought him to the precipice again and again until he could hold himself back for her. Hour after hour, she gently guided him to ways that would please her. Everything was new, everything wonderful. They cried out often, wet with desire.

For breakfast they ate smoked salmon and caviar. Even at 10, this was too elegant for anyone but the very richest customers. Here and now, Rolfe thought it fitting.

"Why do you keep working?" he asked, licking a final beluga egg off the side of his mouth.

"Because I need the money."

"But you're rich. You must be, to afford all this," he gestured toward the table.

Again, she laughed. He was getting used to the music of it, falling deeper into enchantment.

"Oh, I didn't buy any of this. They were presents."

A flutter of jealousy. "From whom?"

"Le Favre, for one. I flirt with him all the time. Last week I told him how much I loved smoked salmon. Two days later, there was a package of it on my desk. The quail eggs you so cavalierly spurned were from Monsieur Toutlemonde. As for the caviar, a new supplier was waiting to see the general manager. I told him I had tasted caviar only once and was sad because I liked it so much but could never afford to buy it. The next day—" she shrugged, and then laughed again at his expression. "It's only flirting. Don't worry, I'm not a whore. My body belongs to Georges, and now to you. So from now on you can be my supplier."

"But I've no money."

"You mean you've never taken anything from the kitchen?"

"Of course not!"

She came to his side and put her hand on his penis. "It's time for you to learn."

* * * * *

That evening, he cooked two of the Plaza's finest steaks while they sipped Beaujolais from a crystal glass he recognized from the hotel's restaurant.

"Tell me how you did it," she said.

"Easy. I told Le Favre I'd been given an order for two filets from the carving chef. I cut them myself, put them in a kitchen drawer until I took a break, and then wrapped them in cheesecloth and hid the package under my apron until I got to the locker room. When I changed, I taped a steak to each leg, walked past security, and *voila!* Filet mignon for Mademoiselle."

She clapped her hands in delight.

Over the next several weeks, they dined on the finest the Plaza had to offer. In return, Chantal showed him how to pleasure her in many different ways in many different positions. She liked to dress up, sometimes as a nurse, sometimes as a schoolteacher, and brought him sex toys he'd never seen before. Each game and each toy produced the same result—and their hunger increased.

"Above all," she said, "in sex and with people: be single-minded in your objectives. Enjoy what you're doing. Give your partner what she wants most, and keep even more for yourself."

* * * * *

Besotted, he wrote to his mother, telling her about Chantal. She arrived a week later to see for herself.

The three met at Lipp on the Left Bank. Margaret was silent for most of the meal, asking only a few questions of the girl, seeming to enjoy her son's chatter and enthusiasm. The two women kissed cheeks as they parted, but Chantal was uneasy.

"I don't think she approves of me," she said when the couple got home.

"Nonsense. How could she not love you?"

"Because she's a cold bitch."

"Chantal!"

"Yes, a bitch who thinks only of herself. Watch out. That woman doesn't care for you, only what looks good to her society friends." She paused. "My own mother was like that. . . . No wonder she was horrified you took a job as a commis."

"She got over it."

"She says she has. Read her face, Rolfe, not her words."

* * * * *

"She's too old for you."

This was his mother's greeting when he met her alone in the Plaza dining room. His anger flared. "It doesn't matter to either of us."

"It will to her, if it hasn't already. You're still a little boy, and Chantal's a young woman who likes men."

"We're in love!"

"You're in love . . . yes, with sex, not with her. As for her, you're just a game, a *bouche amusant* until her man comes home."

Why did she have to be this way? Disapproving of everything he did, every pleasure he enjoyed?

"You're just jealous. You can't stand that I have another woman in my life besides you."

"Oh, there will be many women. There were in your father's life too. But he came back when he needed me, and so will you."

"Never!"

"Give it time." Her calm was ominous. "We'll see who's right."

"I want your blessing," he said. "Chantal and I are going to get married."

If he thought to shock her, he was disappointed. Her scornful laugh resounded through the restaurant. "Well. You must send me an invitation."

A waiter approached. "I don't think we'll be staying," Rolfe told him, his fury intense. "My mother has to take an early flight to Holland."

* * * * *

"It's too risky. What happens if someone catches us," Rolfe asked when Chantal locked the door to the hotel laundry at six-thirty one Friday evening.

"No one will catch us. The laundry is partially closed for the weekend, you're on a break, and I'm not officially here." She untied Rolfe's apron and unbuttoned his chef's jacket. "Besides, the risk makes it more exciting. You'll see."

* * * * *

I did see, he thought, half an hour later as he stared into the flames of the salamander searing the turbot. The smell of freshly laundered linen on the sheet-folding table where they'd made love lingered in his nostrils, the persistent drone of the clothes dryers still hummed in his ears. He felt his hair for the remains of the flying lint, as he remembered trying to quiet Chantal as she noisily came.

"Ritter, where's my bloody fish?"

"Coming, chef!"

* * * * *

Every day, there was a new demand. It was getting increasingly difficult, and dangerous, to please Chantal. Finally, he balked at presenting her with a gift of one of the Plaza's silver caviar dish.

"You decided not to do what I asked you?" Chantal's voice was at its most ominous. "Who suddenly put you in charge?"

"But it's wrong. Surely you see that."

"What I see is a teenager who's frightened to do the little favors his lover asks."

"Or who only takes lawlessness so far." He was sick of fighting, sick of her. She must have sensed it.

"You're right," she said. "I've given you sex, but I'd like to give you more. You're a good boy, Rolfe, and I don't want to be as mean as your mother."

He had told her about the fight in the restaurant. Now, he wondered what she was up to. "Give me more, how?" he asked.

"You'll see. And you'll be pleased, I promise you."

That night, though, she made him sleep on the couch.

* * * * *

"I've spoken to my boss, Monsieur Bergeron, about you," she told him the next evening. "Told him how ambitious you were, what a good job you're doing, and that Toutlemonde thinks you're a rising star."

He was still smarting from their argument the night before. "Thank you."

"He was impressed, and in my presence called his friend, the general manager of the Latimer Hotel in London." She grinned. "It's part of the Audley chain. A great place. Park Lane. Very posh. There's a position for you there."

Rolfe looked at her with suspicion. Her face and voice were as innocent as a schoolgirl's. "You're incredibly lucky," she continued. "They're giving you a job in the Grill Room. You should make the most of it."

He could feel her urgency. She wants to get rid of me, he thought, and he was so dismayed he could barely grasp what she was offering.

"I'm not going anywhere." He tried to bring her toward him, but she pulled away. "I'm staying in Paris with you."

"My darling Rolfe. We agreed from the beginning that you had to focus on your career. And what could be better than the Latimer?"

Nothing, he knew, but the knowledge hurt. "What about us? The future?"

She stared straight ahead, without looking at him.

"Let's get married. You can come to London with me."

Now she turned to him. Her eyes were expressionless. "Georges is coming back at the end of the month. I intend to live with him, and I am giving up this apartment. Let's make the most of the rest of our time together. Come on, I'll take you back to Fouquet's."

"Chantal!"

"No regrets. Please. No bitterness. Champagne and oysters!"

"You don't understand—"

"It's you who doesn't understand." She went to get her wrap. "I need an experienced lover, a mature man, not a boy who wants to be his father and needs his mother's approval. I told you, everything has a price. I got what I wanted; you learned how to please a woman, and on top of that, you got a big step forward in your career. All square, no?"

It was as though she had cut a hole in his chest. He gasped with pain. Body shaking, he brushed past her into the bedroom, put his few things in his duffel bag, and walked toward the door.

"Fuck your oysters," he said. "If that's the way you feel, I'm leaving. There are plenty of women out there who will appreciate being loved."

She ran to him and kissed him on the cheek before he could push her away. "True," she said. "And when you grow up, they'll find a fine lover in you. Who knows. I may even come back one day."

If you did, he thought, I wouldn't let you get within a mile of me.

* * * * *

A week before Rolfe was due to leave, he took the metro to Gare du Nord and bought a train ticket to London via Calais and the Cross-Channel ferry. Then he wrote his mother:

> *Dear Mother,*
> *Believe it or not, I'm off to London. I'll be working in the Grill Room of the Latimer Hotel—quite a step up from commis!—and after that—who knows.*
> *I'll be close to Mike, of course, so you needn't worry about me. He already knows I'm coming. And if you feel like visiting, maybe I'll have enough influence at the Latimer to get you a discount.*
> *I hope all is well with you. Please give my best to Jan, but not to Pieter. (I'll never forgive him for bullying me when I was a child!)*
> *Rolfe*

He decided not to mention Chantal. His mother had been right, but he didn't want to give her the satisfaction of knowing it.

The few friends he had made at the Plaza gave him a small farewell party and promised to stay in touch, though he knew they wouldn't. The next morning, he took his meager belongings and went to the lobby. Just outside the door, Chantal was standing next to a waiting taxi, its doors open.

"Taxi?" she said.

In the short weeks since their split, he had forgotten how radiant she was. Seeing her now, memories of their nights together crowded out everything else in his mind. Had Georges left her? Had she decided that he, Rolfe, was her favored lover after all?

"You're coming with me," he said, not knowing whether he actually wanted her to.

"No, darling. I simply saw from the duty logbook that you were leaving, and I've come to take you to the station. I want us to part as friends."

In the taxi he wanted to kiss her one last time, longed to hold her body close to his one more time, but he held himself back. He wanted to show her he had restraint and was focused completely on London. He was too proud for her to know that it wasn't that simple.

They arrived a few minutes early and stood awkwardly by the entrance gate, with Rolfe willing the clock to move faster toward the departure time. A whistle blew. The train was announced. Chantal cupped his face in her hands and kissed him. Before stepping back, she thrust a small package into his pocket. Astonishingly, there were tears in her eyes.

"Remember," she said. "Focus on your objective. Never forget how small the hotel business is. You'll come across the same people time and again. Learn everything you can about them. The knowledge will be worth a fortune."

Knowledge is power, Mike Riverstone had said, and turned to her to tell her, but she was already making her way out through the crowd.

In the train, Rolfe opened the package. Chantal's gift was a leather-bound diary with his name engraved in gold letters on the cover. On the front page she had written: *To my beautiful boy. Never forget me. C.*

Well, he would have to forget, though he doubted it was possible.

CHAPTER 5

1965–1967

The Latimer Hotel's Grill Room, overlooking Hyde Park from its Park Lane perch, had earned a reputation for serving as fine a mixture of French and English cuisine as London had to offer. That, combined with an outstanding wine list, the discretion of its management, and the well-trained staff, made it popular with diplomats, bankers, and businessmen—the staid rich, as Rolfe thought of them.

Reservations were hard to obtain, with tables by the windows bargained for daily. Rolfe wrote his mother about how the head-waiter, a portly man from Bath, used a "magician's handshake."

> His empty hand starts its journey toward a guest and comes back with a tenner. Amazing.
> "This is theatre. The kitchen and the back of the house are backstage, and the front of the house—the restaurant and public areas—is the stage. The staff are the actors, and our uniforms the costumes.

Rolfe thrived. He was popular in the kitchen, where the chefs quickly recognized one of their own. It didn't hurt that he bribed them with packs of cigarettes to ensure he got his dishes quicker than his colleagues. In two months, he was promoted to station headwaiter in charge of five tables and the team that ran them. At last, he discarded the symbols of his lowly status—the cumbersome white apron, the white jacket—and sported a crisp black tailcoat. He looked good. So good, in fact, that he attracted the attention of David Murtoch, the Latimer's general manager.

One evening Murtoch, who deserved the credit for turning the property into one of London's most prestigious hotels, called the headwaiter over to his window table.

"Who's that young man at section three?" he asked.

"Name's Rolfe Ritter. We may have a winner in him, Mr. Murtoch."

Murtoch watched as Rolfe went about his duties. He noted the effortless way the young, multi-lingual man served guests and the easy manner with which he anticipated their needs. He was especially intrigued by the way he discretely charmed guests into buying more than they expected: a serving of beluga caviar, the sautéed fresh *foie gras* with fresh morels, a harlequin soufflé, a Romeo and Juliet cigar, or a "special" armagnac—"our general manager's favorite."

"A winner for sure," Murtoch told the headwaiter as he left. "Push him as fast as you can. Let's see what he's got. Meanwhile, send him to see me at three o'clock tomorrow."

* * * * *

"He's running a few minutes late," Murtoch's secretary said. "Why don't you wait in his office?"

Rolfe scrutinized the room. On the wall behind the desk was a framed certificate from L'École Hotelière Lausanne: David Paul Murtoch was a graduate in good standing. He took the easy way, Rolfe thought. I wonder what silver spoon he was born with.

A framed picture on a side table showed Murtoch in army uniform with a group of other officers. Pictures of Audley hotels adorned one wall, a large picture of the Latimer another. Murtoch's desk free of clutter, an old lawn bowling ball with holes drilled for pencils its only decoration.

"Sorry I'm late, Ritter," a voice behind him said.

Rolfe spun around. Murtoch was a spare, lanky man in his forties with thinning, immaculately cut brown hair, a reddish nose, and a sallow, unhealthy complexion beneath his tan. He wore pin-striped gray trousers, black jacket and waistcoat, a gold fob watch chain, a crisp white shirt with separate starched collar, a silver tie with a tight Windsor knot, and a red carnation in his lapel button. His shoes were so polished they reflected the ceiling light.

"Sit down," Murtoch said, indicating a chair across from his at the desk.

As he seated himself, Rolfe noticed that he was being equally appraised.

"I've heard good things about you." The general manager took a file from a desk drawer. "You did well in Paris, and your headwaiter here thinks you have potential." His smile showed imperfect teeth. "What do you think of the Latimer?"

"I like it very much, sir—the staff, the guests, the operation, my boss. Every day I learn something new."

"Including how to give the right answer." Murtoch stretched comfortably. "Why don't you tell me about yourself—your background, your ambitions."

Rolfe described life at 10, how hard his mother had worked after his father had passed away and how he had striven to help her. Sensing genuine interest from across the desk, he found it easy to be candid. "Someday, I want to become a general manager myself, sir. Like you," he admitted. "But I know that means hard work and study."

"A noble goal, if I do say so myself." Murtoch took his watch from his pocket. "For now, our time is up; I've got other obligations." He stood and extended his hand. "I have an idea. . . . Why don't we finish this talk over an early supper. Monday's your day off, I believe. Let's do it then."

* * * * *

They ate at Wheeler's, a fish restaurant in Soho. Murtoch was a genial host, regaling Rolfe with stories of his boarding school days in Scotland, his time at the École, and his adventures in the Army Catering Corps. Rolfe listened with increasing puzzlement. Why had this man asked him out? Was it only to hear himself talk? It's as though I were a guest at the hotel, he thought, and not his employee.

Murtoch signed the bill with a flourish. "I know you live in South Kensington," he said. "I'm in Knightsbridge; it's on your way. Why don't we drop by my flat and have a nightcap before you go home."

* * * * *

Rolfe sank into the overstuffed pillows on one of two peach-colored loveseats placed opposite each other in Murtoch's living room. The ceiling was faux Tiepolo, white clouds drifting across cerulean blue, and the ground underneath was a lush green carpet from which the divans seemed to grow. On the rose granite coffee table between the two divans stood a silver tray with three crystal decanters containing, Rolfe guessed, scotch, cognac, and gin.

The harmonies of a Debussy string quartet filled the room. Murtoch brought over two Waterford crystal snifters, half-filled them with brandy, and sat next to his protégé. "Cheers." He lifted his glass. "To your success and our friendship."

"Thank you, Mr. Murtoch."

"Please. Outside of work, call me David."

"David." The cognac slipped down his throat too easily. The atmosphere seemed to him eerie, like a humid day before a thunderstorm.

"People in the hotel will be jealous of our friendship and the fact that I've singled you out as a promising star, so let's keep this to ourselves." David's hand lingered on Rolfe's arm. "You're intelligent, charming, attractive. You'll go far." His hand moved down to Rolfe's thigh and squeezed it gently.

Homosexual! Rolfe knew the word but had never met a homosexual in his life. Panic rose; he fought an urge to bolt. "Please don't," he said weakly.

"It will be all right, I promise," Murtoch whispered. He leaned forward.

He's going to kiss me. Rolfe's stomach rebelled, and he could taste bile in his throat. Yet he let the older man's hand stay where it was, powerless to move, his brain on fire. Everything has a price, Chantal had said. He wanted advancement. Murtoch could help him on his way. But would the price be too steep? It seemed a bargain, an easy calculation. He had endured the fires of the Plaza, the reek of the hostel. God, he had seen his father killed! What was about to happen was nothing more than a physical act. How bad could it be if he kept his mind abstracted, hung on to his own essence? He put his hand on top of David's and turned his face toward the general manager.

The decision would haunt him forever.

* * * * *

Rolfe lay awake, listening to David's rhythmic breathing at his side. His head throbbed mercilessly. He hadn't imagined the physical pain, but the humiliation was worse. He had slept with a man, been used by man. Ashamed, embarrassed, repelled, he relived the sex time and again. His ass was sore. His mouth tasted of David. He closed his eyes. Shame overwhelmed him. As quietly as he could, he rushed to the bathroom; his knees cold against the marble floor, he put his head over the toilet and retched sturgeon, brandy and remorse until he could bring up no more.

* * * * *

He tiptoed back to the bedroom. David was sleeping on his side, curled against a pillow the way Chantal slept. Rolfe had planned to run, no matter the consequences, but now he reconsidered. How bad was it really? If they had sex again, it wouldn't be nearly as painful—in time, he could get used to it. Meanwhile, David could teach him to run a hotel, not just a kitchen or a dining room. He could introduce him to people he had no hope of meeting on his own. It could save him years, maybe decades, in his rise to the top. Maybe his initial plan would work after all.

Asleep, David looked vulnerable, benign. To win a war, Rolfe thought, a man had to be battle-tested. If he ran now, it would mean the battle was too tough for him, that he hadn't the stomach for it. Yes, that was the way to look at it: a battle in a war for independence. His father had fought a thousand battles, each one more dangerous than this. Why was he balking at repeating a simple physical act? He had experienced its consequence: self-loathing. Repetition would not exacerbate that emotion. He could not undo the initial act. That being so, why not go forward, use it for the rewards he envisioned?

He felt cold. His hands were shaking. Fighting back tears, he slipped into bed beside David, careful that no parts of their bodies touched.

* * * * *

They had breakfast in the kitchen. Murtoch wore a blue silk dressing gown; Rolfe was dressed in his jockey briefs and shirt, held closed by a single button. Only a few weeks before, he had sat like this in Chantal's apartment.

"Last night was wonderful," Rolfe said. "You were gentle with me, and I'm grateful. You guessed it was my first time."

Murtoch kissed Rolfe's palm, his stubble rough against the flesh. "You're the most beautiful boy I've ever seen," he said. "Next time will be easier, I promise."

Rolfe looked down. "It's going to be difficult serving you in the restaurant."

"Nonsense. You'll never have to serve me again. I'll put you in the management-training program. You'll start immediately. That way we can spend more time together without anyone knowing we're lovers."

Only two people were accepted into the program each year, a virtual guarantee of a future management position. Rolfe brushed his new friend's lips with his own.

* * * * *

Two days later, dressed in pinstriped trousers, a gray waist-coat, black jacket, crisp white shirt, and pearl-gray tie, Rolfe started at the front desk of the Latimer Hotel. Later, he would spend two to three months in each of a variety of departments.

He started to keep a diary in the book Chantal had given him.

* * * * *

Infrequently at first and then with regularity, Murtoch took Rolfe to dinners with his "friends": bankers, businessmen, celebrities, prominent physicians, a diplomat, an architect, a bishop in the Anglican Church.

The diary filled with names, places, indiscretions.

February 23, 1966:
Bishop Atherton brought a young man named Mark to dinner at Robin Calloway's house. David told me Mark is well known to the group—he's slept with several of them. David swore he wasn't among them, but I wonder. The bishop drank half a bottle of port and fondled Mark at the table. Robin tried to say something, but the bishop told him to mind his own business. David finally called a cab and helped Mark get the bishop into it. Afterward, the conversation got bitchy. I wonder what they say about David and me behind our backs?

* * * * *

March 17, 1966:
David and I had dinner at the Coq d'Or (how fitting!) with Andrew Denton, an MP, and his friend David Penforth, also an MP. I had never met them before. They'd just come from the House of Commons and were in fine form, joking about fooling their wives and meeting in the House for, as Penforth described it, "a quick grope." It made me feel sick. When I told David so after they'd left, he told me I shouldn't judge others by the way we conduct our relationship. "These men are under a lot of pressure, leading double lives," he explained. The thought of England being led by such men is terrifying!

* * * * *

It didn't take long for Mike Riverstone to find out about Rolfe's affair with Murtoch. He called Jan in his Amsterdam office.

"That's the story," the British intelligence officer concluded.

Jan was shocked. "I wouldn't have thought Rolfe was queer for a second."

"It's true, I assure you. What do we say to Margaret?"

"Nothing. She'd be devastated. Probably fly to London to drag the boy home."

"Then what do I say? After all, she made me responsible for him while he was in London."

"Do what we've been trained to do and have been doing for more than twenty-five years."

"What's that?"

"Lie, of course. Just lie."

* * * * *

One advantage of mixing with David's friends, Rolfe realized, was that he was getting inside information on their businesses, many of them public companies. While his salary was small, he had almost no expenses, and he was able to buy and sell a few shares through a stockbroker his grandfather had recommended, never mentioning the transaction to David.

What Rolfe didn't know was that the stockbroker called his grandfather. "The lad's uncanny," he told Summers. "He seems to know what's happening well before anyone else."

Rolfe's grandfather told the stockbroker to buy and sell the same stocks as Rolfe, only in far greater quantities. He put away the profits for Margaret and his grandson.

The stockbroker also bought and sold the stocks, only he kept everything he made for himself.

* * * * *

"If you're going to be a great hotelier, you're going to have to dress the part," David said.

"I can't afford it."

"Nonsense. Leave it to me."

Rolfe was soon wearing Saville Row suits. Other gifts followed: ties, gold and enamel cuff links, a signet ring for the little finger of his left hand, a cashmere overcoat, and, on Rolfe's nineteenth birthday, a gold Patek Philippe watch.

Though his relationship with Murtoch, he learned that, while some of the men his mentor consorted with were brilliant, others were run-of-the-mill, having achieved their status not through brains, aggressiveness, and ingenuity, but through inherited wealth, family connections, or the network established at schools like Eton, Winchester, and Harrow. Take, for example, Sir Charles Sinclair, the chairman of the country's leading manufacturer of airplane parts. Rolfe found him a bully, always determined to have the last word, yet much of what he said Rolfe knew from reading the *Times* and the *Daily Express*. Captain of industry? Rolfe thought. I wouldn't let him captain a rowboat on the Serpentine.

"What do you think of Sinclair?" Rolfe asked Murtoch, as they dined alone for a change.

"A good man," Murtoch said. "Bright. A fine leader."

If David thinks Sinclair's bright, then how clever is David? Rolfe couldn't help but wonder. David was one of the top general managers in London, and if he was on Sinclair's level, then how far could he, Rolfe, go?

Don't be stupid, he told himself. Without wealth, family connections, or education behind me, who am I kidding? How far would I have gotten without David? A wave of shame and humiliation washed over him every time he asked himself that question.

He vowed that David would be the first and last man he'd ever go with. A stepping stone, that's all. Never again. Sex with David was a business transaction. Emotionless, mechanical, and repugnant, it gave Rolfe no physical or emotional satisfaction. Sexually, he was frustrated, felt unfulfilled. He needed to be with a woman, but he knew he had to be careful with his female co-workers. Of course, he couldn't think of touching any of the guests, despite the frequent innuendos and occasional blatant offers. Nor could he dare risk David hearing of any "indiscretions," but Rolfe had to have sex, real sex, with a woman.

On the nights he didn't see David, Rolfe started frequenting clubs and pubs in South Kensington and Earls Court, where he met available young women whom he'd take back to his bed-sitter for the night. He never saw any of these women twice.

Riverstone quickly learned of these trysts. It made him feel more at ease about his godson.

* * * * *

"I've pretty much learned everything I can at the Latimer," Rolfe told David. "What's next?"

The general manager seemed piqued by the question. "What do you want to do?"

"You've built up such a strong team, there seems to be no suitable open position for me here. What about department head in one of the other hotels in the company? Besides, being around you all day and trying to hide my feelings is difficult. I can't act that well."

The older man was mollified. "I'll think about it," he said.

* * * * *

"Mr. Ritter? This is Mrs. Green, Monsieur Bouchard's secretary at the Audley Hotel. He'd like to meet with you at ten tomorrow morning."

Rolfe gave a little whoop when he hung up. The Audley itself. One of the premier hotels in London. The Hays Adams Hotel in Washington was its equivalent, Mike had told him. And Bouchard? Even Murtoch had called the Swiss general manager the best.

He dialed David, told him of the meeting. "What's it about?"

"Bouchard's got an opening. I've recommended you. But be careful. The man's a stickler for tradition and politeness."

* * * * *

In a hotel that seemed to Rolfe a palace, he was in the office of its monarch. "Good morning, sir. Thank you for seeing me."

Bouchard shook his hand. "Sit down. David Murtoch speaks well of you; your file speaks well of you; your colleagues speak well of you. But you're very young."

Rolfe smiled. "I can't help that, sir." His glance fell on a picture of Bouchard welcoming Queen Elizabeth II to the hotel.

"Why do you want to work here?"

"My mother runs a small hotel in Holland. She's been here and thinks it's the finest hotel in the world. I remember her speaking of the Audley when I was still in grammar school, and I've wanted to work here ever since."

As amusement passed over Bouchard's face, Rolfe realized the man had seen through his lie.

"Tell me more about yourself," Bouchard said.

Rolfe did. Finally, the Swiss hotelier opened a manila folder on his desk. My file, Rolfe thought. I wonder if David can arrange to let me get a look at it.

Bouchard lifted his eyes from the papers. "When I was your age, I was offered a senior position at Delmonico's in New York City. 'This is your one opportunity,' the general manager told me. 'Fail, and your career will be a failure evermore. Succeed and—" he indicated his office—" 'success will follow you for the rest of your life.' This is your opportunity, Ritter. And I don't think you'll fail either. You start next Monday." He stood.

Rolfe, so filled with elation he was afraid he might dance, stayed seated. "Thank you, sir. I won't let you down, I promise. But one thing, sir. What's the job?"

"Good heavens, didn't Murtoch tell you? You're the Audley Hotel's new front office manager. Congratulations."

CHAPTER 6

1967–1968

His godfather looked old, Rolfe thought. The British spy scandals, the Cold War, and the Arab-Israeli Six-Day War had aged him grievously.

Over dinner at The Mirabelle, on Curzon Street, the young man chattered on about his job, the outdated practices at the hotel. "They have so many staff they're falling over each other. It's chaos. Do you know they still build their own beds, make their own mattresses—each one with 967 individual springs?" Rolfe was clearly comfortable in the restaurant's classically elegant surrounds, displaying an enthusiasm that Riverstone would impart to Margaret.

"The demands of the guests are wild," Rolfe continued. "We even have a Japanese lady staying with us who likes to bathe each morning in thirty-six pints of unpasteurized milk! But once I figured out that to each of them I was merely an indentured servant, the job got easier. I've learned to deal with the demands of presidents and royals, to say nothing of fulfilling every religious, ethnic, dietary, and decorative whim—and I've begun to enjoy myself.

"It's only when one delegation doesn't want to check out and another insists on checking in that havoc occurs. And your government's protocol boys don't help. You can't imagine how many times I've been told I was about to be sent to The Tower and then beheaded."

Riverstone played with his fork. "But you're comfortable there? Well-liked? Part of the Audley 'family'?"

"I think so."

"Good. I'm proud of you. You enjoy working for Bouchard?"

"Absolutely, though he's left me pretty much alone."

"A mark of trust. How would you like to work for me as well?"

"What?"

Riverstone spoke softly; Rolfe had to lean in to hear him. "Your father provided invaluable information to me during the war. How would you like to do the same for me now?"

"You mean work in intelligence?" The idea was difficult to grasp, but with enlightenment came a shock of joy akin to the elation he'd felt after he first made love with Chantal.

"Precisely. I can't promise you anything in return, only the satisfaction of doing something useful for your adopted country."

My father's footsteps, Rolfe thought, barely listening. Strange. Exciting. "Go on."

"Before I do, there's something I need to ask." Mike chose his words carefully. "I know you've been David Murtoch's lover for a couple of years. I know you've been picking up girls in South Ken. Are you bisexual?"

"I don't understand."

"It's a bloody simple question. Are you bisexual? Yes or no?"

"No." He could feel blood rush to his face. His uncle knew! The sin that shamed him, the act of a pervert. He had been found out. Riverstone's eyes bored into his soul and saw everything.

"Then what the hell are you? You've got to be a sexual something. After all, you're sleeping with the man."

"I'm not homosexual," Rolfe said grimly.

"You two are fucking—there's no question of that; we have photographs. Let's have the truth."

"I—I—" Rolfe felt betrayed, violated. He saw no sympathy in Riverstone's eyes. "Yes, I'm sleeping with him. But it's not what you think." How lame he sounded.

"What do I think?"

His godfather's sarcasm pummeled him. "You think it's an affair, but it isn't. It's business."

"Really?"

"I'm using him to get ahead. How do you think I got the job at the Audley?"

"How convenient."

"It's the truth, I swear it. I'm using him like Dad used women. I wanted to get ahead. David came on to me, and I took the opportunity." He stared into the cream tablecloth. "I hate myself for doing it, but I have no idea how to get out of it and keep my job."

He stopped trying to fight back the tears, and looked plaintively at his godfather. "I'm so ashamed of myself. Look what I've become. I try to hide it, but I hate myself more each time I see him. I told myself I could control things, and now it's taken control of me. I'm no different from a prostitute. That's what I've become, a bloody whore." He paused to stem a sob, and then let his words rush out. "I don't know whether I'm any good at my job or whether I got it simply because I'm Murtoch's bum boy. I can't have a real girlfriend. Every time I look in the mirror I realize what a freak I've become. I'm trapped. I can't leave him."

"Actually," Riverstone drawled, "there are worse ways to make one's way in the world. It was really quite enterprising of you."

Rolfe used his napkin to dry his tears and stared at his godfather in amazement. Enterprising? Did that mean Mike forgave him? Or that Mike was just as much a whore?

"Anyway," Rolfe said, "it's what the Kestrel would have done. But I need sex, real sex, and I can't risk David finding out. That's why I go to the pubs and clubs, isn't it?—to pick up women." He paused, horrified. "You haven't told my mother?"

"Of course not." Riverstone chose not to mention Jan, who might indeed have told her. "Your father might or might not have slept with a man to get information, but certainly not to get ahead in his career. He was fighting a war; you're fighting to get ahead personally. There is quite a difference."

True, Rolfe acknowledged to himself. But it didn't mean his father wouldn't have used the same tactic had be been in his son's position. It was a different fight, different circumstances. Yes, Dad would have done the same, he told himself defiantly.

"You've been spying on me," he said to his godfather. "What are you going to do with those photographs?"

"Nothing, I promise you. We took them because we wanted you to work for us, but we needed to make sure you couldn't be blackmailed. It's a relief, really, to know you're straight."

It didn't soothe Rolfe's resentment, but he chose to keep quiet. The idea of working for Riverstone was too attractive. "Are you satisfied now? I assure you, I'll sleep with Murtoch as infrequently as possible and no other man. That's a promise. And if you can know of a way for me to get out of it . . ."

He thought of Chantal. "If necessary, I have an expert witness who'll swear I'm straight."

"The French girl. Yes, yes. Don't look so surprised. I know about her."

"Jesus, Uncle Mike!"

"Okay, I'm a bastard. But I'm good at my job. Let's go back to the subject. Had you answered my questions differently, our conversation would have ended. But I believe you. So let me ask again: Are you interested?"

He was aware he had passed a crucial test. Joy returned. "What kind of work would I be doing?"

"Provide me with information. Simple as that. I want to know the names of important people who make reservations at the Audley, when they're there, who comes to see them, their sexual peccadilloes—that sort of thing."

"You mean spy on them."

"Precisely. The Audley's a diplomatic hub. You're at the center of it."

It would be an adventure, Rolfe thought, and it might come in handy to be owed a favor from Her Majesty's government. If the information was useful to Mike, it might be useful for him, too. "I'll do anything I can."

"Capital! But I must be sure you're really committed."

"I assure you—"

"I want information on Murtoch's friends as well. Dates, times, places, who they're with, how they act, what they say."

Was he saying, Go on with David? Use him more? Rolfe blanched. "Impossible. They're David's friends, and they trust me. I can't betray them."

Riverstone shrugged. "So be it." He signaled the waiter for the check.

"Wait," Rolfe said. "Why do you need the information on them?"

"Some of them are in sensitive positions. We want to be certain they can't be compromised. Others are influential. We must ensure they influence the right people. We won't use the information indiscriminately, but it will help to have it." He signed the check. "What do you say?"

Rolfe swallowed. "You'll have it."

* * * * *

The tasks were small at first. He'd tell Mike when a certain guest or that guest's visitor arrived and left the hotel. Sometimes he'd let one of Mike's agents into a guest's room when its occupant was away. Once he persuaded a diplomat to use a limousine instead of a cab, the limousine being driven by a man from Intelligence.

Rolfe enjoyed it. "I've done everything you asked," he told Mike over the phone. "Even given you chapter and verse on David's friends. I'd like to do more."

"Too risky. If anything happened to you, your mother would

murder me."

"Then I'll be careful. But this is penny ante stuff. Big deal that the Swedish foreign minister likes teenage Asian girls. Give me something with substance."

Mike was silent. Then, "You know, you sound just like your father."

* * * * *

During the next two weeks, Rolfe was given lessons in the use of micro-cameras, making molds of keys, planting listening devices in telephones, lamps, pictures, and cocktail cabinets, and installing tracking systems in briefcases and cars. He learned to pick locks.

Colin, his instructor, a seemingly benign, freckled man from Bristol, was particularly demanding. "I've never been inside a nick and never will," he announced proudly. "And if you do what I say, neither will you." He opened his suitcase and took out four different locksets mounted on wooden stands and a small brown box which he opened. "The keys to the bloody kingdom." He pointed to an assortment of bent wires and needle-nose pliers laid out neatly in the box. "These are your best friends, so mind you, treat them nice."

For three hours each evening, Rolfe struggled to learn the skills.

"How many times do I have to tell you? It's done like this, not like that. Be gentle, for Christ's sake. Pretend it's a bloody woman, not a bag of cement."

Rolfe's excitement overrode his anxiety. His mastery grew. His hands became deft, his brain clear.

"You could rob the Bank of England," Colin said when Rolfe graduated.

* * * * *

The first job was easy: making molds of the master keys for the hotel. Now Mike's people could go in without further help when Rolfe told them where and when. Soon, though, the job got more complex.

"I've got something important for you," Mike said. "The Syrian government is sending a high-level delegation to discuss economic aid. I think it's a cover. They're financing some terrorist groups, and I want to find out what they're up to. They'll be staying at the Audley for a week. We need to know everything we can: how often they receive visitors, what those visitors say—that sort of thing. You'll need to plant the bugs. Don't get caught."

* * * * *

The Syrians had taken five rooms and one suite. The day after they arrived, Rolfe copied their files and registration cards, including their passport numbers, and then let himself into the Royal Suite, where the head of the delegation was headquartered. Damn! The Syrian had taken his briefcase with him. He planted listening devices as he'd been instructed and bugged the other bedrooms, feeling like the Invisible Man.

Downstairs, he saw a member of the delegation in the bar, talking to a blond-haired, vaguely familiar man dressed in a blue suit and Dunhill tie. Their heads almost touched as they bent over the table; the large man's fingers absently toyed with his glass. Rolfe rushed back to his office, took his tiny camera, and returned to the bar. The two men were still conversing.

Rolfe placed himself deep into the corner alcove, hidden from the two men, and snapped a roll of film. Then he went behind the reception desk, where he had a view of the doors to the bar. Twenty minutes later, the two men walked to the elevators.

"Brian," Rolfe asked the operator as soon as the elevator returned. "On which floors did the gentlemen get out?"

"The Arab gentleman on the sixth, Mr. Berchtold on the fourth."

Berchtold. He had stayed at the hotel before, Rolfe remembered. He found the Austrian's file and wrote down the details: passport number, address in Vienna, amount of deposit, dates of his previous visits, rooms he'd stayed in. He put the information and the roll of film into an envelope, and late that evening, he handed it to the night porter at Riverstone's office.

* * * * *

"Your boy did well," Gerald Logie told his boss the next afternoon.

"How so?"

"He's shown us why the Syrians are here. Franz Berchtold is an old acquaintance." He handed Riverstone a picture.

"Looks familiar," Mike said. "But I don't place the name."

"That's because Berchtold's an alias. His real name is Lazlo Moricz. He's an Hungarian arms dealer who fronts for the Soviets with some of their third-world clients."

Riverstone banged his palm down on his desk. "I remember! Bad news."

Logie nodded. "My guess is the Syrians want weapons that can't be traced in order to give them to terrorist groups, and that the Soviets are more than happy to oblige."

"We'll keep watch on Moricz. If the deal looks like it'll go through, maybe we can stop it."

* * * * *

Riverstone and his godson walked down Old Bond Street toward Piccadilly. "Your work has helped," the old man said. "I'm grateful. Now, I want you to plant bugs in Berchtold's room and to get more information on him and, if possible, the Syrians."

"I'll do my best."

"I know you will. But listen to me carefully. Don't take any risks, none whatsoever. They can't know you're watching them. These people are killers. Understand?"

Wasn't what he'd been doing dangerous too? Rolfe wondered. He'd already proved he would not be caught. "Yes," he said. They walked past the windows of Aeroflot's offices. Rolfe imagined himself slipping in and out of shadows, seeing but not seen, obtaining secrets no one else could find.

* * * * *

By morning, he had an idea he thought might work, but it would be risky. He decided not to tell his godfather what he planned to do.

At 2:00 A.M., Rolfe set small fires in several of the emergency stairwells, organizing them so the alarms would ring for thirty minutes.

Some of the staff herded the upset and angry guests into the downstairs lobby, while other staff members looked fruitlessly for the source of the problems. Naturally, they were following the orders of the night shift's duty manager, Rolfe Ritter. Once the irritated Syrian delegation, surrounded by their security detail, was assembled in the foyer, Rolfe ran upstairs and let himself into the Royal Suite. He picked the lock on the briefcase, photographed the documents inside, and relocked it, and then quickly repeated the operation in the next room. By the time he got to the third room, the alarm had stopped.

His stomach churned. He had taken too much time! Voices in the corridor carried into the room. A key turned in the lock. He froze. Shit.

The door opened. Rolfe smiled pleasantly at the dark-skinned, bearded man who entered.

"Who are you?" the Syrian demanded.

"The duty manager, sir," Rolfe said blandly, as though it was the most natural thing in the world for him to be in the room at this time. "We're sorry for tonight's disturbance. The staff and I are going from room to room to make sure your beds are freshly made and not smelling of the smoke."

The Arab stared at Rolfe, who was busily plumping up the pillows. "The English are completely mad," he said aloud in Arabic. Only the walls understood him.

* * * * *

"Can you spare a few minutes to come to my office?" Mike Riverstone asked his godson over the phone.

It was an unusual request. Mike rarely met with him while Rolfe was on duty. Still, he wasn't surprised. The material he'd sent over last night must have been explosive.

"Be here in an hour," the intelligence officer ordered.

* * * * *

"It's a lovely day," Riverstone said, brandishing a paper bag. "We're going to St. James Park to feed the ducks." They walked across Birdcage Walk and sat on a bench under a willow by the side of the lake.

"It's one of my favorite places," Riverstone waved his arm first to the left toward Buckingham Palace and then to the right where Victorian government buildings sat in Whitehall.

Rolfe fidgeted impatiently. Why had he been summoned?

His godfather opened the bag and took out half a loaf of bread, throwing torn handfuls into the water. Moments later they were surrounded by ducks and swans.

"Tell me how you got your information," the intelligence officer said.

Rolfe did, satisfaction evident in his voice. "I was exhausted when it was over, sat at my desk shaking for half an hour afterward. When that Arab walked into the bedroom—God!"

"Pleased with yourself, are you?"

"I think I did well. Didn't I give you what you wanted?"

The bread ran out, and the waterfowl drifted away. Riverstone crumpled up the paper bag and dropped it into the waste bin behind the bench. "Did you remember my instructions?"

"Of course."

"Well, if you did, why in God's name did you ignore them?"

The words were bullets. Rolfe reeled back.

"Don't you realize how stupid you were?" Mike's voice rose. "What would have happened if you'd been caught or those fires had gotten out of hand? Not only would you be fucked, but you'd have implicated us as well. Do you understand the diplomatic implications had that happened?"

"But you wanted information."

"Not that way. Do you know how stupid I would have looked? I trusted you. Then you risk embarrassing me, the department, and the government at the same time. What the hell were you thinking?"

"Excuse me, sir. I didn't get caught."

"You will the next time."

"I did it for you. You told me it was important. I didn't want to let you down."

"Then, why didn't you clear the plan with me first? It's because you knew I'd veto it, isn't it>"

The day suddenly chilly, Rolfe sat shamefaced, motionless.

"You think you're the next Kestrel? Your father disobeyed instructions and took unnecessary risks, but it was war, he was a professional, and he knew what he was doing. What are you trying to prove? That you're better than he was?"

Riverstone put a hand on Rolfe's arm. His tone softened. "Jan has filled you with claptrap about your father. God knows, Wim had his share of blemishes. Don't try to emulate him. You'll get yourself killed. And if you ever want to do anything for me again, I need your assurance that you'll obey orders. Otherwise—"

Rolfe acknowledged the threat. "I promise, Uncle."

Still, he thought, it had been exciting.

* * * * *

Six Syrians sat on one side of a conference table in a secluded Hertfordshire mansion. Lazlo Moricz sat on the other, flanked by two Russians: Nickolai Zagoskin, the Soviet commercial attaché and secret KGB resident for the United Kingdom, and Yevgeny Popov, Zagoskin's aide, not yet thirty years old but already trusted and admired. By the end of the meeting, a deal was struck. The Syrians would buy arms from Moricz; the Hungarians would buy them from the Soviets. Profits all around.

"I didn't like that fire the other night," Moricz said. "Nor the way they chased us downstairs like cattle."

"Yes, and the staff is crazy," one of the Syrians said.

"How so?"

"When I went back to my room, there was the manager there remaking my bed. I've heard of good service, but this seemed too much."

Zagoskin's glance took in all of them. "Did anyone else have their beds remade also?" he asked casually.

A chorus of shaking heads gave him his answer.

As his limousine left the mansion, Zagoskin turned to his aide. "Popov, find out who that manager is. Dig into his background and report back. I don't like what I just heard."

* * * * *

Zagoskin put down Popov's report and shook his head. His aide waited anxiously for a reaction.

"Another Den Ritter! This time the son. Listen, Yevgeny, here's what to do."

CHAPTER 7

1968–1969

Although exhausted, Rolfe picked up his pen and diligently wrote his diary notes.

September 16, 1968:
Occupancy today was 94%, a record for this date.

Three governmental delegations here at once, each more difficult than the next. The South Africans are demanding but pleasant. Besides, they know how to tip!

The Moroccans brought their own chef to cook for the president. The kitchen in his suite is inadequate, and the smell of herbs stunk up the corridor. In the end, we had to let him cook in the main kitchen, but he acts as though the whole place were his, and our staff hates him. Uncle Mike wants to know who's been seeing them. There are so many, it's difficult to keep track. But what Mike wants, Mike gets.

The delegation from Yugoslavia is the main problem. Last night, our head porter brought in eight prostitutes for a party in the foreign minister's suite. I sent Mike the name of the agency the porter used and the amount paid. Those women weren't cheap! At 1:00 A.M., I went up to see what was happening. Five men, all very drunk, were in the suite, the minister in his underpants. Three of the women were stripped down to their bras and panties. When I peeped into the bedroom, a couple was making love. I told them politely that this was against hotel rules. The protocol equerry agreed they'd have the women gone in an hour. To mollify them I sent up more champagne and caviar. The tip was £250. Not bad! But they don't care. It's their government's money.

David's complaining that I'm not spending enough time with him, but what chance do I get? Besides, it's a relief to have a legitimate excuse to be away. The man is suffocating me. Each time I see him, I feel worse about what I've done—and continue doing.

* * * * *

Late one night, Rolfe photocopied each page of his diary. The next morning he the stashed originals in a safe deposit at one bank and the copied pages in a safe deposit box at a different bank. Each month he repeated the process with new pages. Information. It was an investment in the future.

* * * * *

"Have a good evening, sir. It's a nice night for a walk."

"Thank you, Harold. I'm looking forward to it," Rolfe told the doorman. He walked toward Grosvenor Square, preoccupied. He thought about how the Audley Group was becoming mired in its own past and that he saw no future in it for himself. On top of that, Murtoch was becoming too insistent they live together. It was time to move on. But how, and to where?

He suddenly became conscious of a car gunning its motor behind him and of a dark shape bearing down on him. He wheeled around. Two men were in the front seat; he could see the fury in their eyes. They meant to kill him! Transfixed, he braced himself against the inevitable impact.

Invisible hands yanked him backward off his feet. His head thumped on the pavement; he yelled out as pain spiked through his body and his vision was obscured by tiny suns of red and yellow. When he could see again, there was only the blackness of the night. No one was near him; the car had disappeared.

* * * * *

Two hours later in his darkened bedroom, he lay on sweat-soaked sheets, his head and heart pounding, his mind screaming with memory. "Daddydaddydaddydaddy," he moaned in his sleep. Each time he closed his eyes, he saw his father swirling in midair. When he opened them, his mother's witch face was before him, her face smeared with blood, glaring at him with blazing eyes. He bolted awake and dialed a number.

"Uncle Mike, I need you. Now."

"Ah," his godfather said. "I was wondering when you'd call."

* * * * *

"What do you make of it?" Riverstone asked Logie as soon as

he'd hung up.

"I'd say your boy's got a problem." Logie had reported directly to his boss once his men had pulled Rolfe to safety. "Looks like tailing him was a good idea."

"An essential idea. Those fucking fires. Any security man worth his salt would have known they were suspicious and found out who set them. The question wasn't whether Rolfe would be attacked, but when."

"Now that it's happened, it proves my point," Logie said.

"Which is?"

"The Soviets and Syrians are up to some real mischief. Now that we know that for sure, we'd better get your godson out of London before they finish him off. The further away, the better. We can protect him for a while, but not forever."

* * * * *

Rolfe and Riverstone were sharing a bottle of Chablis at a table on the lawn of the Riverside Inn in Bray, barely conscious of the late afternoon sun reflecting off the meandering Thames.

He had explained to Rolfe the role Logie and his men had played in literally pulling him out of harm's way. "I'm virtually positive the KGB is behind it," Riverstone said.

A waiter placed a candle in a glass globe on the table. Shadows flickered across the intelligence man's face, making him look as sinister as the scenario he was presenting. The KGB! It was almost certain they had been behind his father's murder, and now, Rolfe thought, they're after me.

"I'm too bloody frightened to sleep," he said. "And when I do drop off, I have nightmares."

"I can't say I'm surprised." Riverstone was infuriatingly calm.

"What should I do?" Rolfe urged. "You got me into this. Get me out."

"I got you into this? Is your memory failing you?" Riverstone retorted. "At any rate, you must leave London, that's for certain."

"And where can I go? Amsterdam is too close and too obvious; they'd find me easily." A vision of being mowed down by a car on the same street as his father made him tremble.

"A lot further away than that," Riverstone said. "The United States, for example. If need be, our cousins in the CIA could look after you."

He hadn't envisioned America, but of course! That's where the hotel industry was booming. All the innovation happened there. It would be perfect. Away from danger. Away from David. A professional step up. Maybe this would work out after all. "Can you help with a job?"

"I can pull a few strings, but it's got to look like you made the arrangements alone. Otherwise, sooner or later we'd be tied in, and that would be as bad for you as it would be for us. You should try to get work there yourself. And try not to involve Murtoch, would you? From what I hear, he can turn nasty when he's crossed."

And he can be oh so helpful when he has to, Rolfe thought.

* * * * *

"I've been thinking about my future, about my career," Rolfe said, his head in David's lap. "I've been at the Audley for almost two years. There's nothing more I can improve. It's time to move on."

Murtoch twisted away, forcing Rolfe to sit up. "Move on where?"

"Away from London."

"Good God, no!"

"I wouldn't consider it, except that I'm worried about us, too. We're together so much. Inevitably, there'll be gossip that could damage your career."

"It's a risk I'm prepared to take." David could barely control his irritation. "You want to get away, don't you?"

Rolfe said nothing.

"Well? Where would you go?"

"The United States."

David jumped up, his face crimson. "I won't have it."

Rolfe had anticipated his response. "You know it'll be good for my career. I'll be back in a year or so, and we'll be together again. I need your help and support. Please don't let me down now."

"We won't be together again, and you know it," the older man retorted. "I don't want you to go, and I certainly won't help you do it."

"Be realistic." Rolfe struggled to keep coldness from his voice. "If I'm successful, it will reflect well on you—after all, you've boasted that I'm your protégé, your great discovery. You and I both know we mustn't part angrily. It wouldn't be good for either of us, nor for your friends or the Audley—it would be difficult for everyone."

"I can't believe it!" Murtoch exclaimed. "You're blackmailing me."

Rolfe saw fear in David's eyes. This was going to be easy. "I only meant to suggest I'd be upset if we parted badly."

The older man cupped the Dutchman's face in his hands and kissed his closed mouth. Rolfe watched him recoil at the frigidness of his lips.

* * * * *

The five general managers in the Audley Group were having their monthly meeting with the chairman, Sir Alan Germaine.

"How's young Ritter getting on?" Murtoch asked André Bouchard during a lull in the conversation.

"Well. Very well. No one can say he's bound by tradition, but he's energetic, bright, and ambitious, and our guests like his style. He's cut staff and costs, while making made improvements. Some of his innovations have netted us a healthy profit. I'll tell you one thing: I've never seen anyone better at persuading guests to upgrade to suites or more expensive rooms."

It was important for Sir Alan to hear Bouchard's praise, but Murtoch felt as though a knife had lodged in his heart.

* * * * *

"You said this is personal. ... What is it?" André Bouchard asked as soon as Rolfe sat down.

"Sir, I've never been as happy anywhere as here. You took a risk by giving me this opportunity, and you've taught me more than I could have imagined. I don't know how I can ever repay you." It was clear to Rolfe that the Swiss was waiting for the caveat to drop. "However, I've been here almost two years and don't know where to go next. I'd appreciate your advice."

Bouchard let out a slow, angry breath. "Go next? What are you talking about? You're only now beginning to make yourself useful. You're staying here. Don't be ungrateful. You're making a fool of yourself. We'll discuss this again in a couple of years."

Rolfe thanked his boss and returned to his office. The conversation had gone exactly as David had predicted.

* * * * *

Two days later, Murtoch sat in Germaine's Berkeley Square office. "I won't waste your valuable time, Sir Alan, but I have a sensitive problem and need your guidance." Germaine beckoned him to continue. "Do you remember that at our last meeting I asked André about Rolfe Ritter, his front office manger?"

"I do indeed. He spoke highly of the young man."

"The lad's only twenty-one. I've been monitoring him since I discovered his abilities as a waiter in the Grill Room."

"You've always had an eye for spotting talent. Go on."

"Ritter came to see me recently, concerned he may have upset Bouchard. Apparently, he said it was time for him to move on—within the organization, of course—and tried to get André's advice about the next step in his career."

"And how is that a problem?"

"There's no place for him. You have fine people in every post. However, I know you want to develop your people. The hotel business is full of fine managers, graduates of the Audley's on-the-job training. It reflects well on the group."

"What do you suggest?"

Murtoch twisted the knife Bouchard had lodged. The pain was so great he could barely speak. "You have friends in the United States, owners of fine hotels. Maybe one of them has a management position for one of our rising stars."

Sir Alan lit a cigar. "I'll think about it."

* * * * *

"Ritter speaking. How may I help you?"

"My name's Steve Westerman, calling from San Francisco. How are you?"

"I'm fine," Rolfe answered evenly.

"I own some hotels here in California and thought you might be able to help me."

Interesting. "What hotels do you own, Mr. Westerman?"

"The Union Square in San Francisco, a small place called The Plaza in Santa Barbara, but the one I'd like to discuss with you is my 220-room hotel in Beverly Hills."

"Which hotel is that?"

"The Hills. Ever heard of it."

"Of course, sir!" The Hills was as famous in its way as the Audley.

"Good. Then let me get straight to the point. My general manager at The Hills has been trying to find a house manager for months. Interested?"

"Yes, sir." He stopped breathlessly.

"Good. The job's yours for six months, and if Bordoneros likes you after that, it's yours to keep. When can you start?"

* * * * *

"Remember," André Bouchard said when Rolfe handed him his resignation. "Icarus' wings melted when he got too close to the sun."

* * * * *

Murtoch wept when Rolfe left, although he'd promised not to. "You're going to go very far very fast," the older man said. "I'll miss you. Perhaps someday you'll be my boss. I hope you'll remember me."

Rolfe kissed him fondly, feeling embarrassed by his lover's weakness, but almost sorry for his pain. "The only way I'll be your boss is if I own the company."

Chapter 8

1969–1971

Dear Mummy,

   I'm sorry you had to find out about my move to California from Mike. I should have written—wanted to write—but in the hurry I simply didn't have a chance. The anger in your letter is entirely justified. I assure you, it is not that I wish to have nothing to do with you, as you claim. I've been under enormous pressure and simply haven't had time.

   Anyway, Southern California is just like the brochures describe it: golden sunlight; smell of hibiscus, oleander, and bougainvillea; shiny convertibles; miles of palm-lined freeways. And the women! A garden of blonds. One of them is sure to make me forget Chantal (much to your relief, I'm sure).

   The lobby and exterior entrance of The Hills is beautiful, but the rooms don't live up to the rest of the hotel. The décor hasn't been changed since the hotel opened. They've replaced things, but always in bits and pieces. One year it's bedspreads and drapes, the next headboards, and so on. They've never stood back and modernized the entire design.

   Nevertheless, the place is wildly popular. Beverly Hills is a glitzy part of Los Angeles, close to the movie studios with great shopping nearby. The Hills is where glitzy people like to stay. As one British guest told me, "I suppose nouveau riche is better than no riche at all."

   I'm not sure about Antonio Bordoneros, my boss. He is as in love with himself as Tristan was with Isolde. During our interview, he kept looking at himself in a mirror behind the couch where I was sitting and preening like a peacock. Anyway, he took me to his place on the hotel grounds for a drink. It's a palace. But it is Westerman's bucks (you see? I'm already speaking like an

American), not his. The man lives like a maharajah.

Until the moment I saw his digs, I thought I had big-time accommodations. A nice one-bedroom apartment a few minutes from the hotel is part of my employment package. Of course, the reason it's so conveniently located is because I'm the one on call twenty-four hours a day, not Bordoneros. He's far too important to be disturbed!

I hope to show it all off to you soon. Any chance of your getting away from 10?

Your loving son, Rolfe

He recognized hypocrisy in the letter, but so what? Obviously, he could have written his mother earlier, told her of his departure, but would she have tried to stop him? Would she have even cared? At least she pretended to now. Good. Serves her right.

* * * * *

Bordoneros thought of himself as a celebrity in a city full of celebrities. Mixing easily with studio heads, producers, directors, stars, and agents, he made his hotel their preferred place for a business meeting or a liaison. It was clear to Rolfe that the GM relished being part of show business. All the other guests were left to the new house manager.

"I don't want to deal with details anymore," Bordoneros explained. "I'm the face of this hotel; you're the intestines. When people think of the hotel, they think of me. I'll set the objectives; your job is to execute them. Do that, and we'll get on fine." He looked at Rolfe without warmth. "I've agreed with Mr. Westerman that you'll have freedom, within limits, to make the changes you want. Just don't try to compete with me. It's a fight I promise you'll lose."

Really? Rolfe thought. We'll see.

* * * * *

In penance, he called his mother. "Things are going well," he reported. "It was simple to motivate the team. All they want are clear goals and someone to lead them. I've instituted some of the techniques I put in at the Audley. Each day I can see the staff's attitude change for the better. Even the guests are noticing it."

"What about friends? Girlfriends?" she asked.

"I don't have time. I've had a few dates, but there's no one in particular. It's all very casual."

"When are you coming back to Holland?"

The question startled him. "What are you talking about? I've just got here. There's no accumulated vacation time."

"I don't mean a holiday. I mean permanently. There is as much opportunity here as in the States. It's time you took up a real career."

Didn't she realize he was never coming back, at least not for good? His exasperated sigh was her only answer.

"Don't take that attitude with me," she snapped. "Don't you ever worry about me, thousands of miles away? You haven't even asked how I am."

I can't win, Rolfe thought, feeling an all-too-familiar hollowness. "I'm sorry, Mother. How are you?"

* * * * *

The food and beverage department was losing money. Rolfe presented the problem to Bordoneros.

"What's the reason?" the GM asked.

"For one thing, the food and beverage manager is worthless. I know you worked with him in New York and that he's your friend, but his best days are long gone. For another, the bar manager is buying his own liquor and selling it instead of ours. Our chef's getting kickbacks from his suppliers. Our backdoor man is on the take, and the night shift's room-service people are telling some of the guests they can't sign the late-night checks and have to pay cash, which they then stuff in their own pockets. Our menus are labor-intensive and not well thought out. No one's bothered to ask the customers what they like. We throw out more food each day than we serve. Our wine prices are too high or too low, and we've got bottles in the cellar that have been here since Noah's Ark because no one wants them. Want me to go on?"

"You've convinced me," Bordoneros sighed. "Do what you have to do, and tell me when it's done."

* * * * *

The hotel's printed materials and advertising were old-fashioned. One of the hotel's guests, owner of a large California retail chain, recommended a new advertising agency when Rolfe asked him about it. "These guys have just left a big firm; they used to work on our account. They're bright and creative, passionate about consumer research, and best of all, they're hungry. The Hills will be important to them."

Rolfe met the team and liked their style. They presented him with a plan.

"I want to know only two more things," he told them. "The cost and the timetable."

Soon the hotel had a new slogan: "The Hills—Simply the Best."

"It's not just a marketing gimmick," Rolfe explained to his department heads. "It's what we are. No excuses, no false promises. We say we're the best, and we'd damn well better be. If we deliver, our guests will come back. If we don't, we 'simply' won't have a job."

* * * * *

Within a month, he had moved all of the management teams' offices, except for Bordoneros's and his two personal secretaries', to a little used storage area and created four boardrooms, replete with burled wood tables to match the newly installed paneling, high-backed leather chairs, and built-in wet bar. Each room had its own adjoining marble bathroom. Soon, corporations from all over Southern California were vying to hold their meetings in these new rooms. Bordoneros never said a word about them.

"I'm not sure he's even seen them," Rolfe wrote to Riverstone. "Nonetheless, he's in his element. I make sure his picture is taken and published every time a reporter and camera show up. His fame is growing as fast as his ego. Right now, he's dependent on me, and I'm going to make sure it stays that way."

* * * * *

In mid-January, Westerman received the year-end financial statements for The Hills. The improvement must be young Ritter's doing, he thought. Nothing else had changed. He arranged to meet Rolfe.

Their breakfast started at a quarter to eight. At half past eleven, Rolfe shook the Californian's hand and apologized for taking up so much of his time. "I hope I didn't bore you too much. I'm passionate about the hotel and didn't realize how much I was babbling on," Rolfe lied, knowing exactly what he was doing.

* * * * *

October 9, 1969:

Marla Danion, who's been in the movies forever, has been our guest for the five weeks she's been filming. Last night she ordered more liquor than usual. The service waiter went to her room and found not only empty bottles but also Ms. Danion with two young men. The waiter alerted security, who called me.

I arrived at her suite at 11:45, and let myself in. Ms. Danion was dressed in a flimsy negligee. She looked ridiculous, saggy breasts almost down to her navel, her arms and thighs flabby and wrinkled. She was screaming obscenities at the young men. One of them called her "you old slut." He was naked, had the longest cock I've ever seen. The other man was wearing a gold lamé jockstrap concealing an enormous bulge. I wondered if he'd stuck an orange down there. He had a bodybuilder's chest and shoulders but a tiny head. What a moron.

He told me Ms. Danion often paid them to have sex, but this night was so drunk she couldn't come, so held back their fee. His friend had gone through her purse and taken all the cash he could find. It wasn't enough. They wouldn't leave until they'd been fully paid. That's why she was screaming at him.

Ms. Danion had dug ugly scratches on his cheek with her fingernails.

I called Adam Collins, the public relations manager at her studio, and told him I thought Ms. Danion should leave. He gave me the impression this wasn't the first time she'd done this. Anyway, he promised me she'd behave if I let her stay. The studio didn't want a scandal. I said I'd have to add 50% to our bill for our trouble. He didn't seem to care. I should have made it 100%.

* * * * *

Late one evening in April 1971, Bill Brady, The Hills' chief of security, called Rolfe at his apartment. Bill was a former captain in the L.A. Police Department, and if he thought it was an emergency, it was.

Rolfe rushed to his office.

"Lew Levenson—you know, the guy who runs Enderton Studios—has taken a two-bedroom suite, number three-thirty-three," Brady told him. "Mark Walters, head of Talent Pool International, is with him. Tonight they apparently gave a party for a few special friends. The party got out of hand. I was called in when a guest in the adjoining room heard a woman scream."

"What did you find?"

"When I got to the door, Walters told me to mind my own fucking business. Given who these guys are, I called you first thing."

Within minutes, Rolfe and Brady were knocking on the double

door to suite 333. No answer. Rolfe knocked again.

The door opened partway. A towel-clad man, his chest and back covered in black hair, peered out.

"Walters," Brady whispered.

"I told you once to fuck off," the agent snarled then, but seeing Rolfe, adopted a more conciliatory tone. "Everything's all right in here. We don't need any assistance."

He tried to shut the door. Rolfe jammed his foot in the opening and shoved. Walters stumbled back into the suite. No one else was in the room.

"See, there's nothing wrong."

"If you don't mind, sir. I'll check the bedrooms." He started toward the one on the left.

"Don't you dare go in there."

Rolfe ignored him.

"I'll have your job."

"You wouldn't want it," Rolfe said. "You've got to deal with too much slime."

He strode into the bedroom. A short, pear-shaped, naked man disappeared into the bathroom. The famous Lew Levenson's backside, Rolfe thought, his attention drawn to whimpering sounds coming from the bed.

Handcuffed to the four-poster was a teen-age girl. Red welts covered her face, vivid bruises inflamed her neck. A tall, even younger girl with long auburn hair, bruises in her arms, and tears coursing down her face, huddled in the far corner, half hidden by the window drapes. A small mirror, lines of cocaine, a razor blade, and a tightly rolled hundred-dollar bill lay on the bedside table.

"Go and look in the other bedroom, Bill," Rolfe said, struggling to keep his voice calm. "Make sure no one leaves.

"Mr. Levenson," he called into the bathroom through the locked door, "Please get dressed immediately and come out."

"It's the same deal, Mr. Ritter," Brady reported from Walters' room. "Two more girls, both naked, huddled together on the bed, frightened out of their minds. Cocaine on the bedside table."

"He wanted us to perform together." One of the girls followed Brady into the master bedroom. "When we wouldn't, he started hitting us."

"Put on your clothes ," Rolfe barked. "Bill, get these ladies dressed, keep them in the bedroom, and take their statements. I'm going to have a talk with our guests."

Moments later he faced Levenson and Walters in the living

room. The men stared at him, Levenson ashen-faced, Walters wearing a surly expression revealing nothing but contempt.

"Gentlemen, we have a problem," Rolfe said, improvising. "As I see it, we have possession and use of illegal drugs, sex with a minor, assault and battery, unlawful detention, and judging by appearances, statutory rape. I have an obligation to report this to the police."

"Nonsense," Walters said. "This was a private party; the girls were here of their own volition, and they brought the drugs. So get the fuck out of here. Antonio Bordoneros understands. I want to speak with him. Now!"

He's right, Rolfe thought, knowing that if his boss were here, the business would be hushed up, the girls would be paid off, and the general manager would be having a celebratory drink with these two pieces of shit as though nothing had happened. But Bordoneros isn't here, and he's not coming. This is my time.

"Shut up, Mr. Walters. You're in enough trouble already."

Walters glared. Rolfe felt the hairs on the back of his neck bristle.

"I need a drink," Levenson said and headed for the bar.

"Sit down. Now!" Rolfe's audacity astonished even him. When did I suddenly grow balls? he wondered.

Levenson stopped and turned back. "Going to the police would ruin us both. It was only a bit of harmless fun that got a little out of control. Surely you understand."

I've caught you with your peckers out, beating up young girls, drugs everywhere, Rolfe thought. What's not to understand?

"I'd like to avoid a scandal for the hotel," Rolfe said carefully. "We don't want the *Times* to get hold of this. The Hills would survive, and it might even be good publicity for us." He chuckled humorlessly. "But not so for you, your families, and your business."

"All right," Walters said. "How much?"

"He means we'll make it worth your while," Levenson added.

Rolfe looked at the two men. "Okay. For the hotel's sake, I'll save your skins."

Levenson took out his wallet.

"No money," Rolfe said. "But the women will need something, say ten-thousand each to keep quiet. Checks made out to cash will be fine. I'm sure they won't bounce."

"Usury!" Walters was red-faced.

Rolfe went on implacably. "From now on, you'll make The Hills the center for all of your business and social activities—yours and your stars'. I'll have a standard business agreement drawn up stating appropriate rates and conditions, and will have it to your offices by noon tomorrow. I expect it signed and on my desk by four o'clock tomorrow afternoon." He exhaled with a confidence he didn't feel. "Agreed?"

Levenson grunted. "Sure. Why not? It's ice to a fucking Eskimo."

"You both realize I'm breaking the law and, as such, at the very least risking my career. I don't want anything from you right now, but one day I might need a favor—and if that day comes, I expect you to do it unhesitatingly."

"Ridiculous," Walters said. "That's an open-ended blank check."

Rolfe shrugged and picked up the phone. "Charlene, get me the police."

"He's got us, Mark," Levenson said. "Put down the phone, Mr. Ritter. We agree."

Two hours later, Rolfe sealed a box containing the rolls of film he'd taken in the room; the girls' statements obtained by Brady along with the numbers of the two men's checks; a plastic bag with the mirror, razor blade, and cocaine; and another bag containing the glasses Levenson and Walters had been drinking from. Tomorrow, I'll put it in my safe deposit box, he told himself as he went to bed.

Information is key. Knowledge is power. He wondered what the favor might be.

* * * * *

"Do you like your job?" Westerman asked.

Rolfe, seated in his boss's suite at The Hills, wondered what was coming. Had Bordoneros exerted enough influence on Westerman to get him fired?

"Yes, sir!"

"Too bad."

"Why, sir?"

"Because it's about to change."

If he were fired, there'd be no place to go. He hadn't been in America long enough to create a saleable resume. England was out of the question. And Holland? Never!

"—Union Square Hotel."

He hadn't heard the start of Westerman's sentence. "I'm sorry, sir?"

"I asked if you'd heard of the Union Square Hotel."

"In San Francisco?" A monolith; Rolfe thought of it as a woolly mammal.

"That's the one. As you know, it's one of our holdings."

"Indeed. You told me that when we first talked."

"Well, it's a mess. I spent all morning fighting with its general manager, Tom Gantry. It's performing so badly you'd think it was infected by the plague. When I pointed that out to Gantry, he accused me of milking the hotel rather than fixing it up. I told him to stop being impertinent. He told me to—and I quote—"Take the fucking hotel and shove it up your ass.""

Rolfe had met Gantry once and liked him. He wondered what Westerman had really done to provoke the outrage. "I'm sorry, sir. That was unfortunate."

"For him, not for you. As of tomorrow, I'm appointing you as acting general manager until I decide what to do."

CHAPTER 9

1971–1972

Rolfe read Riverstone's notes on Steve Westerman during the flight to San Francisco. He'd started small, inheriting two run-down apartment buildings in San Francisco from his father and later selling them at a profit. With the proceeds, he bought an office building at the edge of the financial district, and then, as it prospered, another. Somehow, he had also acquired the three hotels.

Now, he was developing a major office complex on Geary Street. But he had run into serious financial trouble. It wasn't only the slowing economy that was hurting him; Westerman had also used nonunion labor on one of his buildings and now the unions were getting back at him. Everything was slower and more expensive than he'd anticipated. Beyond all that, he had a new, young, free-spending wife, paid serious alimony to his first wife, and subsidized three ne'er-do-well children.

Now Rolfe understood why Westerman was so delighted with the increased profits of The Hills and why he wouldn't, or couldn't, put more money into the Union Square. No wonder Gantry had been so upset.

* * * * *

He strode into the hotel's executive offices at 8:00 A.M. sharp. A middle-aged woman in a black dress sat in front of Tom Gantry's office.

"You must be Mr. Ritter." She and extended her hand. Her eyes were red and puffy. "I'm Dorothy Felton, Mr. Gantry's secretary. He told me you were a good man and to be nice to you."

"Sit down, please," he said kindly.

She glanced at him gratefully. "I don't know what happened. Mr. Westerman phoned and told me Tom wouldn't be returning and that you'd be taking over."

"For a while, anyway. How long did you work for Tom?"

"Twelve good years."

Rolfe wondered what had kept them together. The outer office was in need of paint, and her job must have been dull. He doubted it was sex. Loyalty, he decided.

"Your job is safe. I'm going to need your help."

* * * * *

"I've never paid much attention to this hotel," Westerman said as they lunched in the nearly empty restaurant.

It looks it, Rolfe thought. Same goes for the food. His grilled halibut was dry as cardboard.

"Have you had a chance to look over the hotel yet?"

"This morning."

"And?"

"It's too early to tell." He didn't know what else to say. Maybe Gantry was right.

He'd walked through the hotel with the various department heads. The place had become nothing more than an old bed factory. The guest rooms were shabby. The front desk, the lobby, and the restaurant were outdated and very loud. The back of the house was filthy and disorganized. The kitchen was a disgrace; Rolfe guessed the chef hadn't seen the interior of the mold-ridden cold room in years. Tom Gantry had failed to make even the most elementary changes. Clearly, no funds had gone to improvements and the only money spent on maintenance had gone to bare-bones emergency upkeep. And Rolfe hadn't seen a single smiling, welcoming face anywhere in the building. I don't belong in this place, he concluded.

Keeping these thoughts to himself, Rolfe said simply, "I've never worked in a unionized hotel. It'll take time for me to get used to it."

Rolfe thought he saw disappointment on Westerman's face. What does he want? he wondered. Revelations? Instant wisdom?

"Watch out for a union man named McCory, Bud McCory," Westerman said. "He's young, but he's a pisser—out to make a big name for himself."

"Thanks for the warning, sir. I'll keep it in mind."

After a short pause, Westerman added, "I don't know what your role here will be in the long run, but I'm pleased to have a fresh set of eyes and a strong pair of hands on board."

"What do you want me to do?"

"Keep things going as they are. I want you to understand every inch of this place. Then, give me a business plan—what you'd do if you were running the place." He winked at the young man. "Who knows? Maybe someday you will be."

* * * * *

Dear Uncle Mike,

It's worse than I'd initially thought. Built in the 1930s, it looks it. Two restaurants and 800 rooms of equal mediocrity. Run-down coffee shop, cocktail bar, and enormous convention and exhibition space, all usually empty. The Grand Ballroom once housed every major social event in San Francisco. In its time, it must have been really something; now it's just an old dowager gone to seed.

I might be able to do something, except that the union contract is the worst in the city. There's no way to motivate anyone; they have full job security and no productivity incentives. Without the union's help, I'm lost.

How's Mum? I haven't heard from her in weeks. I know she's mad at me, but if you speak to her tell her I love her. Try explaining that I'm trying to be like Dad in my own way. Maybe that'll soften her up.

Rolfe

P.S. No, I haven't heard from David. Just thinking about him makes me cringe. But I still wonder if I'd have been here without his help.

* * * * *

A week later, Rolfe entered the chrome, leather, and glass reception area of the Westerman Group. A woman in her early thirties came out to meet him. Wearing a dark blue suit and a matching Chanel scarf, she had chestnut hair, hazel eyes, rounded cheeks, a compact body—the look of a milkmaid, save for her graceful hands.

"Shall I compare thee to a summer's day?" he quoted his parents' beloved Browning. "Thou art more lovely and more temperate."

She looked at him as she would a lunatic. "I'm Susan Lockyer, Mr. Westerman's assistant," she said, leading him back to the anteroom. A red light was flashing on her phone. "He's just finishing a conference call, and then he'll be with you."

"Rough winds do shake the darling buds of May...."

She wasn't listening. He leaned against her desk and picked up a framed photo of a man in his thirties astride a horse in a field of long grass. He watched her face flush. "How long have you been with him?"

"I'm not with him anymore." She took the photo from his hands.

"I didn't mean him," Rolfe said, coming to his senses. "I certainly didn't mean to pry. I meant Mr. Westerman."

"Oh." She recovered her composure. "I'm sorry. I thought you meant—. I've been with Mr. Westerman just over three years."

The red light went out. She looked up at Rolfe. "He's free now," she said.

Extraordinary eyes, he thought.

* * * * *

"Your honest assessment," the real estate magnate said, sitting behind his art deco desk, silhouetted against the picture window, flanked by dozens of Lucite "tombstones," each symbolizing the fruition of a deal.

Rolfe had thought through his answer long before their meeting. He summarized.

"It's worse than I expected," Westerman sighed. "I knew it was bad. But this . . . Fuck Gantry! What are your ideas?"

If there was anyone to blame, Rolfe was fairly certain it was Westerman himself. Still, some things are better left unsaid, and what he said next would be important.

"First, I suggest making some quick fixes to get us moving in the right direction. I'd start with cleaning out as many of the deadbeat staff as the union will let us. Get some paint on the kitchen walls. Re-carpet the ballroom. Sponsor a few of our own social events and hire a PR firm to promote them. Feature California food instead of faux-European."

He glanced at Westerman, who seemed to be taking his recommendations well. "I'll help in any way I can," Rolfe added. "I assume you'll want me to stay here until you appoint a new general manager."

A flash of irritation crossed Westerman's face. "I like you, Rolfe, but don't ever try to play me. You and I both know you're the new GM."

Rolfe kept his body taut, his expression nonchalant. But he wanted to hug every decrepit pillar in the hotel. Westerman watched him closely. His bankers had insisted on the immediate appointment of a general manager, and he'd pay Ritter half of what he paid Gantry. Of course, he didn't want this young up-start to know that.

"Thank you, sir. I won't let you down," Rolfe said. "I'm grateful to you and Sir Alan Germaine."

"Who the hell is Sir Alan Germaine?"

* * * * *

Rolfe closed the door of Westerman's office. Stopped at Susan Lockyer's desk and impulsively kissed her on the cheek.

She fumbled with the phone to put it on hold. By the time she looked up, all she could see was the back of his pearl-gray suit and the soles of his shoes as he danced his way to the reception area.

Good God, she thought. What happened in there?

* * * * *

The hotel union's leader, Bud McCory, was delighted by the news of Rolfe's appointment.

"This Dutch kid will be a pushover," he told the head of the Teamsters local. "I'm going to make him eat so much shit his eyes will turn brown." He licked his lips. "And the topper is, it'll add to the pressure you're putting on Westerman."

* * * * *

Rolfe organized lunch with his department heads. The chef was conspicuously absent.

"I'm young," he told them. "This is my first general manager's position. I've never dealt with unions before or directed so many people." He felt something in their attitude. ... Was it admiration or contempt? "But I'm neither stupid nor lazy, and since I have to prove myself, I'm going to be tougher on you than anyone you've ever worked for.

"This hotel's a shithouse. I've seen cleaner pigsties. It has no organization, no energy, no planning." He scanned the room, look-ing at each of them in turn. "Tomorrow morning at eight, you will each have on my desk a set of short-term objectives for your department. After that, if I accept them, you'll have thirty days to meet those objectives. If you don't, you will have failed to meet the basic requirements of your position and your employment here will be terminated, union or no union. It's as simple as that.

"So here's the deal: You can be part of an exciting future, or you can leave. By the time we're done here, working at Union Square will be a privilege. If you want to leave now, you'll be given a severance package. Make up your minds by Friday."

He walked out, went to the men's room, and threw up.

* * * * *

As first move, he fired the chef, the porcine Ulrich Gerhardt, and planned to replace him with a thirty-three-year-old French sous chef he'd seen at the Stanford Court.

"You and I both know it's time for you and this place to part company," he told the German. "I've made appropriate arrangements for you to take early retirement."

"What did you say?"

"You heard me. It's for the best."

The chef's face turned red. "How dare you talk to me that way? You're nothing! A snot-nosed kid who thinks he invented hotels."

Rolfe was unruffled. "Calm down. You'll have a stroke."

"Don't tell me to calm down," Gerhardt screamed. "I don't have to listen to you, you piece of Dutch shit."

Rolfe stared at him unblinkingly. "I want you out of the hotel after the dinner service tonight. If you're here one minute past eleven o'clock this evening, security will remove both you and your possessions."

* * * * *

An hour later, Susan Lockyer was on the phone. "I wanted to warn you. Your chef just barged into Mr. Westerman's office. I've never seen anyone in such a rage."

"Ask your boss to call me the minute Gerhardt leaves," Rolfe said evenly, picturing her red cheeks and green eyes.

"I'll do that."

"And I'd appreciate your advice on other matters. Will you have dinner with me tomorrow?"

There was a long silence, then, "Why not? I can't wait to hear how this all works out."

* * * * *

Twenty minutes later, Westerman called. "Why don't you reconsider? Gerhardt's been with the hotel a long time. He's catered for me here and in Lake Tahoe."

Aha, Rolfe thought. I heard rumors about the sex parties for lenders and investors. So Gerhardt knows dirt you don't want revealed.

"I'm afraid I can't. I won't have any authority if he stays." He could hear Westerman's anxious breathing. "Don't worry. I'll make sure he leaves without a fuss."

"I'm counting on you." The real estate man's voice was hoarse.

* * * * *

"You've received a call from Mr. Westerman," Gerhardt said, glaring at Rolfe an hour later. "So you know I'm staying."

Rolfe sat back, looking calmer than he felt, convinced he could smell brandy on the chef's breath, and put his feet on the desk. "On the contrary. Not only will you be leaving as planned, but the hotel will contact the police to bring criminal charges against you for theft. Beyond that, we've instructed our lawyers to file a civil suit for damages."

The chef sat down in front of Rolfe's desk, his hands trembling. "Go on, you young bastard. Tell me what you have."

Nothing, Rolfe thought. But there's obviously something, otherwise the man wouldn't be terrified. Bluffing, he ticked off a list of accusations: "Affidavits from suppliers detailing their kickbacks to you. Others say you had goods shipped to your home and charged to the hotel. You'll be facing jail, fines, bankruptcy, payment of damages to the hotel, an IRS investigation, and possible deportation."

He swung his feet from the desk, and handed Gerhardt the phone. "Personally, I don't give a damn what happens to you. You're just a cook gone rancid. Mr. Westerman supports me on this. Why don't you call him to verify it?"

The chef's eyes watered. Rolfe, repelled, knew at least some of his accusations had hit home. "Only because of your long service and Mr. Westerman's good will are we prepared to allow you to resign gracefully and to honor your pension. On top of that, we'll pay you a thousand dollars a month as a consultancy fee for one year. In exchange, you'll list all the suppliers you colluded with and agree to keep everything you learned about the hotel and Mr. Westerman confidential. If you hold anything back, or even think about breaking your word, this entire case goes to the DA. Do you accept these conditions?"

The chef's chest heaved.

"Yes or no?"

"I'll think about it overnight."

"You'll answer now."

Silence.

"Yes or no?"

"Yes," Gerhardt whispered.

"I didn't hear you."

"Yes, you little motherfucker. I accept your terms."

Rolfe pressed the intercom. "Dorothy, get me Josh Leonard at Chambers, Butler, Gibson, and Litteman immediately."

The law firm represented not only Westerman but also the hotel. Josh was the lawyer responsible for the hotel's business, and Rolfe had admired and trusted him from the start.

"Please get here as soon as you can," he said to Leonard after he'd explained the situation. "I won't let him leave the office until he's signed the documents."

* * * * *

"You had nothing on that fat bastard, did you?" Josh asked the next day. Rolfe had invited him for a thank-you drink before his eagerly anticipated dinner with Susan, and they were sitting in the hotel's bar.

Rolfe grinned. "How did you know?"

"You'd never have offered him the consultancy fee if you had."

"Touché."

Rolfe asked Josh about his background. The Stanford-educated lawyer was the son of Russian Jews who changed their name from Leibowitz when they came to America. "A good thing too," the lawyer admitted. "Chambers Butler isn't particularly kind toward 'others.'"

"Then why join? Why stay?"

"I joined because it was far and away the best opening available. And I stayed because I like my colleagues. Besides—"

"Go on."

"No. Someday I'll tell you my sordid story, but not now. I don't know you well enough yet."

The lawyer's cherubic face was without expression. He blinked at Rolfe behind round eyeglasses. To judge from appearances, Rolfe thought, the story couldn't be all that bad. The man was innocence incarnate.

"Have you sent Westerman a copy of the Gerhardt documents?" Josh asked.

"Walked them over this morning. He didn't seem ecstatic."

"He's got a lot on his mind. Between that self-centered wife number two, his worthless kids, his building problems at Geary Street, the union, tenants, and creditors, his balls are in a ringer.

98

Watch yourself with him. He thinks you're king shit now, thanks to what you did at The Hills. But if things get tighter for him— well, desperate people do desperate things."

"I'll remember," Rolfe said, once again appraising the little man. Josh is sincere, he decided. Honest. No hidden agenda. He decided this man could one day be his friend—his friend and confidant.

* * * * *

Dear Uncle Mike,

What a year! The hotel's performance is improving, and so is the cash flow. Westerman gives me a free hand, but he won't release any money for physical improvements. It's like arguing with a brick wall. I understand how the little Dutch boy felt with his finger in the dyke, trying to hold back the North Sea.

I'm working 12–16 hours a day. My social life revolves around an out-of-work actress and a doctor at Children's Hospital who specializes in gastrointestinal problems. I don't think either of them is long for my world.

Actually, I've had three dates with an interesting woman. She's Westerman's assistant. I like her, but I'm damned if I know whether she likes me. A wonderful laugh, smart as all get-out, apple-tree fresh, but when I approach her I feel like Joshua without a trumpet. There's no way I'm getting those walls down. Why do I bother? you ask. Well, if you don't know, I do! Because she's special.

By the way, Westerman looked blank when I mentioned Sir Alan Germaine. You didn't have anything to do with my getting that job at The Hills, did you?

* * * * *

Rolfe spent endless, sleepless hours working out his master plan for Westerman. He asked Josh Leonard to recommend a good designer who could refurbish the Union Square at low cost.

"Ted Pemberton," Josh said. "Young—about my age—and the best. And he's looking for a project that will make his name, rather than one that'll make him rich."

"I'll see him."

"Great. What are you going to do about systems—automation, computers?"

"Hadn't thought about them."

"Aha! I'm right: You're nothing but a Dutch peasant. Jesus, Rolfe, computers are the future. You're running a big business—you said it yourself, a rooms factory. How're you going to keep track of reservations, billing, supplies, personnel, guest histories?"

"The same way I always have."

"That's like driving a horse and buggy when your competitors are speeding past you in Ferarris. It's time to ride the wave of the future. I've got this friend, Ross Engleson, at IBM. He'll find the best person in their company to help you."

* * * * *

Two weeks later, Josh ushered Momo Takenaka into Rolfe's office.

She was dressed in a body-hugging black trouser suit that accentuated small breasts and hips, and small silver earrings in the shape of dragons dangled from her petite ears. Her black hair fell over her shoulders like spilled ink, framing her long face, unusual in an Asian. Her skin was smooth, tight, and lightly rouged, and thick lashes curtained her shiny black eyes. Her full lips, when they opened to smile in greeting, revealed perfect teeth.

Nature at its kindest had performed a miracle, Rolfe thought. He couldn't imagine what path had led such a creature to the computers at IBM.

Josh told him her colleagues called her "Momo the Merciless." He wondered why. She was not about to tell him. All business, she put a carousel of slides into a projector, darkened the room, and began her presentation. The brilliance of her demonstration, not the brilliance of the woman herself, won him over.

"You're saying you can develop a system that not only tells us which rooms are empty and which full, but also which guests have checked out and whether the rooms are cleaned and made up?"

"All linked to your front desk and reservations office," Momo answered. "And your reservations people can describe each room available to potential guests."

"But this has never been done before in the hotel business," Rolfe argued.

"There's no crime in being first, is there?"

Rolfe laughed, her conviction swaying him. "Explain your labor concept again, please. No slides this time. Only simple English. It's all I understand."

"I doubt that, Mr. Ritter." She met his gaze unflinchingly.

"We'll develop a system that will enable you to forecast your occupancy every day for a month in advance. Then, we'll feed in staffing guidelines so you'll know how many people you'll need for every day."

"If it works," Rolfe said, more to himself than Momo, "I'll know exactly how many part-time people I'll need to bring in; no more, no less."

"Precisely. And it'll work. I'm sure of it."

"But again, it's never been tried before."

"Computers don't make mistakes, Mr. Ritter. People do."

* * * * *

"What do you think of this place, Mr. Hotel Manager?" Susan asked as they were finishing cake and coffee at Etienne's. As always when they dated, she had insisted on something simple, impersonal. He had taken her to one elegant meal; she seemed uncomfortable. She'd declined when he invited her to his apartment and hadn't offered hers.

"It reminds me of a brasserie I used to go to in Paris, Lipp."

"And who was the young woman you squired there?"

How did she know? Was his expression so transparent? "Her name was Chantal."

"Pretty name."

"Pretty woman."

"Tell me about her."

Rolfe shook his head ruefully. "My first flame. Introduced me to the wonders of the flesh—and then betrayed me." He was suffused with the memory of Murtoch. Suddenly it was uncomfortably warm, and he swallowed quickly to stop the familiar bile rising in his throat. "She was a piece of work." And so am I.

She was staring at him as though she could see into his brain. Was she mocking him? If so, he didn't care. Her round, open face was endearing. There was nothing conniving about her; he felt he could tell her anything.

"And by betraying you, she broke your heart."

He took her hand. "Long ago mended."

"Well, mine hasn't," she said, surprising him. "Not quite yet."

He felt secretly pleased. It explained her effort to keep him at a distance. "Tell me," he said sincerely.

She waited a moment, as though deciding how much to say. "His name was Bob. Bob Easton. He was a jazz musician. You might not think of me going out with a musician, not demure little

Susan Lockyer, but I did. And I loved every second of it. He took me to all the clubs, to parties I can't even begin to describe, and he brought out a part of me I didn't know existed and was pleased to discover." A hint of a smile played on her lips as she spoke, giving him a glimpse of her sensuality.

"We were together for more than two years. I loved him deeply. I don't think I could ever love somebody as much again."

"And he broke your heart."

"Drugs. He started taking heroin, and he just—disappeared. At least, the Bob I loved did. The new Bob humiliated me. He was unfaithful. Sarcastic when I asked about it. Treated me like I had no feelings, no needs. Then one day, in between sets at the club, he collapsed and died. Just like that. I was there. I watched it. And God help me, I was glad."

Squeezing his hand, she bent her head to collect herself. Then she raised it to meet his eyes. "That's why we—you and I—why we've never made love."

"I'm not like that," he said.

"Shhh," she breathed, putting a finger to his lips. "You don't have to say that. I know what you're like. And when I'm ready I'll let you know. I hope you'll be patient, but if you can't wait—if you find a new Chantal—I'll understand."

* * * * *

On Christmas Eve he arrived at her apartment carrying an airlines bag. "Presto!" He took out a bottle of Dom Perignon and two flute glasses.

They toasted each other. "To us and to Christmas," he said.

"To us," she repeated. "And now, Mr. Ritter, it's time for you to prove you're the great chef you say you are. I've bought a porterhouse. Work your magic."

Several hours later, after they'd finished their meal and the champagne long gone, they were sharing a bottle of Pauillac.

"Time for your present," he said, going back to the carrier bag and handing her a small box wrapped in silver paper.

She opened it. Inside was a gold bracelet. "It's for charms," he said.

"But I haven't any."

He handed her a smaller box. "You do now."

She took out a miniature gold building and held it to the light. "It's a model of the Union Square," he said. "Our hotel. Without you, I couldn't have made it work."

"It's beautiful." There was a catch in her voice. "I didn't expect anything so grand. And all I got you were a couple of things to keep you warm over the winter." The same mysterious smile he had noticed when she spoke of Bob played on her lips.

"Oh?" he said. "What two things?"

She stood and pulled him toward the bedroom. "A sweater."

He turned her to him and kissed her, feeling her relax into the embrace as though they were the most intimate of lovers. "And?" he asked. "The other present?"

She lay on the bed and held out her arms to him. What the smile promised, she fulfilled.

* * * * *

By the end of the most profitable year the Union Square Hotel had known since Westerman bought it, the master plan was finished. Design by Ted Pemberton; capital costs, profit and loss accounts, return of investment calculations, and new system by Momo Takenaka; ingenuity by Rolfe Ritter. All were securely in place.

"Impressive," Westerman said. "Well done. Leave it with me to think about. But I see no reason it can't be implemented next year."

Rolfe walked back to his office elated. Tomorrow was New Year's Eve. He and Susan would celebrate. He sat at his desk and thumbed through the pile of pink message slips that had accumulated over the past days. One of them iced his spine: *Chantal Le Peron wants you to return her call.*

CHAPTER 10

1972–1973

Chantal! Why now?

He balled the message in his fist and heaved it into his waste-basket. Damn! He retrieved it, spread it out on the desk. There was a peculiar, not unpleasant sensation around his heart. It might be fun to see her, he thought. Let her see who she tossed away.

He dialed her number.

"Chantal Le Peron."

"It's Rolfe."

"Rolfe. Darling. I wasn't sure you'd call back." Her voice was breathy, eager. It excited him.

"I have an ironclad rule: When a Frenchwoman calls, return it."

She laughed. "It got you into trouble in the past."

"True. But I like risks."

"I'm glad you took this one. You've done well, I gather. General manager at the Union Square."

How had she found out?

"It's been eight years," he said.

"Have you forgotten me?"

"Hardly. But I've moved on. There's another woman—"

"Of course there is. I'd have expected nothing else." There was a momentary hesitation. Plotting strategy, he guessed. "I'm not here to seduce you. It's just that I'm in San Francisco and wanted to see you."

Her voice was too enticing, too familiar. "Why?"

"I need your help," she whispered. "Please. It's urgent."

* * * * *

He decided his office was safest, so asked her to meet him

there.

If anything, eight years had improved her looks, he thought, amazed at the acceleration of his heartbeat. She was dressed simply in a gray suit, Hermes scarf, a gold pin in the form of a rose on her lapel, and gold earrings. Her face had the same freshness and fullness as it had when they'd met, and her expression contained the mixture of naiveté and sexuality he remembered so well.

"Hello, Chantal," he said, kissing her on the cheek as he would a business acquaintance before taking his position back behind his desk.

She sat opposite him. "Shy? Or are you still angry with me?"

"Not angry. Just ... surprised to see you." He played with a pencil on his desk. "What's the problem?"

"No small talk? Not even a 'How are you'? Never mind. I know about you. David Murtoch told me all about you."

Murtoch! Did she know about him and David? No, that man wouldn't be that stupid.

"I didn't realize you were friends."

"Oh, yes. He's part of my history."

"Which is?"

She settled herself more comfortably. "Thank you for asking. I stayed at the Plaza for two years after you left. Georges and I were living together. Then he left, and I went to Cannes to get over him. I got a job in convention services at the Carlton. Eventually, they made me director of sales."

It was a big job at a great hotel, Rolfe knew. "I'm impressed. Good for you."

"It was, rather. Anyway, I got sick of all that provincial sunshine and went on to London. My old boss at the Plaza, Monsieur Bergeron—you remember him, I'm sure—got me a job at the Latimer working for Murtoch. Again, as director of sales. That's how I came to know your pal."

"So what's brought you here?"

"I was getting bored and was offered a job as director of convention sales at the St. Francis, so I resigned and came to San Francisco."

"It wasn't because I was here, was it?"

"Don't flatter yourself." Her laugh gave him the impression that was precisely why she'd come. "Still, it turned out that the person I was to replace decided to stay at her job. Now I'm high and dry. No job, no money, nothing. I can stay with a friend for a week or so while her husband's away, but then I'm on my own."

"You can always go back to Europe," he said, half hoping she would. "With your language skills and experience, you could well land a decent position at any of a dozen hotels."

"But I want to stay here, build a new life. Like you, I've always felt I belonged in the U.S." She stared at him with the intensity that had so captivated him so many years ago. "Help me, Rolfe. I've no one else to turn to."

He wanted to kiss her, comfort her, make love with her—push her away, ignore her, punish her. "What do you want me to do?"

"Give me a job at the Union Square."

What? Impossible!

"It would be just business," she said quickly. "Nothing more than that between us. I know that part's over, and I'm not asking that we start again."

"There's nothing available right now." He felt as awkward as his words. "Why don't I see if I can refer you to a different hotel."

"Here? In San Francisco?"

He could sense a noose around his neck and that his own hands were tightening it. "If I can."

She stood. Her eyes glistened. "Oh, would you?"

* * * * *

"Do you know *any*thing?" Susan asked. They were back at Etienne's.

The question startled him. "What do you mean?"

"About life." She touched his hand to show she wasn't being hostile—but then, she never was. "You know hotels and numbers, food and wine. You know how to make love. But I mean other things, other pleasures. Have you been to the opera? To a jazz concert? To the theater? You told me you liked to read. What's the last book you so much as glanced at? What's the last movie you saw? When did you last go walking in the country? Or bike riding?"

"I run every morning," he said.

"Compulsively. So you'll be at your sharpest during the day. 'Mens sana' and all that. That doesn't answer my questions.

Her moon face shone at him, her eyes bright with love and concern. She could save me, he thought.

"Teach me," he said.

* * * * *

"It's Rolfe."

He could hear Chantal's intake of breath over the phone. "Any news?"

"Call Mark Andrews at the Stanford Court. He needs someone in sales. I recommended you."

* * * * *

She called back three days later. "I got the job!"

"Congratulations."

"I start on Monday. It's because of you. I'm very grateful."

"You're welcome. Good luck."

"That's it? No, Rolfe. I'm going to buy you a bottle of champagne and some oysters. We're going to celebrate."

"That's not a good idea. There's a woman in my life, an important woman."

"As you already told me. For God's sake, I'm not going to rape you. One bottle, a dozen oysters. Then we go our separate ways."

He sighed, defeated. "Tonight at seven—at Sabella's on the wharf."

* * * * *

When he woke up the next morning, the smell of Chantal lingered on his sheets. You idiot, he thought. What have you gotten yourself in for?

Well, it was only one time. They both had sworn to that. And if Susan never found out, what was the harm?

CHAPTER 11

1973

Guilt and desire brought him to Susan almost every night he was free. He bought a subscription to the San Francisco symphony; they heard a young Placido Domingo as Otello. At her suggestion, he read *Middlemarch, Emma,* and *Anna Karenina.* He teased her at first, grumbling that she'd make a poof of him, but soon he began to respond and asked for more.

In her bed, he was the teacher. Bob, it turned out, had left ample room for discovery. She challenged his mind, he challenged her body, and they both flourished.

"I'm happy," he wrote his mother. "Happy, for the first time ever." But even as he mailed the letter, he wondered if happiness was what he sought. Often when they made love and she whispered her ecstasy as he pleasured her, it was a different voice he longed to hear, a different body he wanted beneath his.

* * * * *

One day in April, Susan asked that they not go out so they could talk in private. She seemed preoccupied, unhappy. He wondered whether she'd sense his feelings of discontent or had somehow found out about the Frenchwoman.

"What's wrong?" he asked. "Are you okay?"

She put her hand on his. "I'm going to do something I promised myself I'd never do when I started going out with you."

He sat ramrod straight, wild thoughts warring in his brain.

"It's unethical, but you're my friend—more than a friend—and I've got to talk to someone."

So it wasn't Chantal, then. He relaxed.

She drew in a breath. "Since the New Year, things have gotten increasingly difficult at Westerman's. The Geary Street project's turned into a nightmare. The unions are torturing Steve. There are massive cost overruns and fewer tenants than projected.

Lenders on his other deals see what's going on. They're putting immense pressure on him. He can't pay them back. He's desperate."

He had never seen her so tense. "Go on."

"He was thrilled when you sent him your accounts from last year. A real profit! He could satisfy some of his lenders. But I heard him tell his accountants that if you thought he was going to spend a nickel of the money he promised you for refurbishing, you were nuts."

Rolfe's head started to pound. All my work, all that effort, and the son of a bitch was just stringing me along, he thought.

"It gets worse. He told the accountants he only had a $13 million mortgage on the hotel, and if he found a buyer he might get as much as $30 million. He asked for optimistic projections from them he could show to 'a couple of people' to see whether there was interest. Three days later, I sent the projections to Metropolitan Hotels, who, according to Steve, badly need representation in the city."

Metropolitan were a standardized mid-market chain, without, in Rolfe's view, any particular distinction. If they bought the Union Square, they'd gut its remaining personality—and probably its general manager. "And?" he asked.

"Bruce Hunt, the CEO, showed up last week, and Steve showed him your master plan. Hunt's a bully and a pig. He started fighting with Steve almost immediately. 'This is a pipedream,' he said after he'd looked over your plan. 'It's junk. The kid who runs your hotel is wasting your time.'" Her eyes filled with tears. "I shouldn't have overheard all this, but Hunt was yelling and I couldn't help it."

Betraying Westerman must be killing her, Rolfe thought. She was building up to something.

"This morning Steve had an offer from Metropolitan Hotels."

It was all Rolfe could do to control his panic. "For how much?"

She removed three folded pieces of paper from her purse. "Before I showed it to Mr. Westerman, I copied it. I shouldn't have. But I had to tell you."

Rolfe took the papers and read quickly. Twenty-eight million. They were trying to steal it! One condition in particular leapt at him: Westerman would be responsible for terminating the general manager, the controller, and the director of sales. Metropolitan would bring in their own people.

"How did Westerman react?"

"He whooped with joy. Oh, Rolfe, darling, what are you going to do? I don't want you to leave San Francisco."

"I may not have to." He kissed her palm. "You're wonderful. This must have been incredibly hard for you."

"I did it for us," she whispered.

"No one will ever know, I promise. Don't worry, we'll be fine."

"But how?"

"Beats me." An idea was already taking shape. "But these things have a way of working out for the best."

She smiled trustingly at him, sharing his excitement. In that moment, he thought he could never love a woman as much as he loved her. And he said so.

* * * * *

The next morning he told Dorothy he didn't want to be disturbed and sat at his desk thinking. He needed an ally, someone he could trust. His godfather? No, he'd be too clinical, and besides, he didn't know the hotel business. Susan? No, she'd be too torn between him and Westerman. Chantal? She knew the business, but could he trust her? No way.

Josh Leonard? Rolfe liked him but barely knew him. Plus, he works for Westerman. Still, he was the best choice.

* * * * *

"My career's at stake," Rolfe said, studying the man sitting across from him in the living room. "What if, hypothetically, Westerman wanted to sell the Union Square ... and he had an offer? What if I wanted to buy the hotel myself. How would I go about it?"

Josh grinned. "I knew it. You've been schtupping Susan Lockyer, haven't you? That's why she looks so rosy-pink in the mornings."

Rolfe glowered at him. "Schtupping?"

"Sleeping with her. She told you about the offer, didn't she?"

"I refuse to answer on the grounds it might incriminate us." He passed Hunt's offer letter to Josh, watching intently as the lawyer scrutinized it.

"Westerman hasn't sent it on to us yet, but I heard it was coming," Josh said. "I'll bet Steve hasn't read it thoroughly."

"How do you know?"

"At the bottom of the second page, it says that if Westerman accepts the offer, all Metropolitan has to do is put up ten percent of the purchase price as a deposit."

"So?"

"They'll have sixty days to perform due diligence, which means they'll send an army of people to go through all the accounts, to inspect the building, the roof, the wiring, the elevators, the plumbing—shit, the laundry room. If they find anything abnormal, or don't like what they find, or simply change their minds, then they can walk away without forfeiting their deposit or the interest on it."

Rolfe waited. What Josh was saying conjured up all sorts of possibilities.

"What Metropolitan's doing is giving themselves leverage to negotiate downward. In this case, Westerman is in such a hole, he'll have to accept a lower offer."

"Why are you telling me this?" Rolfe asked. "Isn't it unethical?"

"Sure. I'd get fired and probably disbarred. But I like you, Rolfe. And I like Susan. Besides, Westerman has stopped listening to me. Maybe if it were to come roundabout, from you or Susan, he'd pay attention. Anyway, the information isn't going to do you any good."

"Don't be so sure."

"You're not yet twenty-five. No one is going to back you or lend you the money to buy the Union Square."

"Please look at this." Rolfe handed him a copy of his plan.

Josh took his time reading it. "Wow! Impressive. Is it doable?"

"Absolutely."

"I hope you haven't shown it to Steve yet. If you have, he'll give it to Metropolitan to raise the price."

"I'm afraid I have," Rolfe said, feeling stupid. "Worse, Westerman's already shown it to Hunt, who said it was junk."

"He might not really think so. It could've been a ploy to keep the price low." He looked at the plan again. "I can't believe you were dumb enough to show it to anybody."

"I thought Westerman would be impressed by the numbers. How was I to know he was broke?"

"As my father would say, you're a naive schmuck." Josh shook his head. "Sometimes you're so mature you scare me. Other times, not so wise. Let me get this straight: You need the price of the hotel, plus four or five million bucks to fix it up, plus another million, say, for working capital. That means you'll have to raise about $thirty-five million in a few weeks, before Hunt is through with his due diligence."

Stated like that, and with such skepticism, Rolfe could see how fantastic it sounded. Still, he pressed on. "Humor me. How much could I borrow?"

"Twenty million, max. But even if you qualified for the loan, you'd need about 15 million in equity before you got the financing. It's a vicious circle. I'd say it was impossible."

"And I say, there's got to be a way. Think of the hotel itself! It could certainly rival the Fairmont, even beat it. Yes, I know it will be difficult, but difficult is not impossible."

Rolfe stared at the young lawyer, trying to infuse his own belief. "I'll find the equity. I'm only going to tell you this one time: Never underestimate me. Ever."

Josh blinked. "I know you're a winner, but—" he stopped himself. "Shit, maybe you'll pull it off. But you can't do it without a lawyer, you stupid bastard. You're a lost lamb in this world, aren't you? Well, fuck it. I'll try to find a way to help you."

* * * * *

"Why aren't you asleep?" his mother asked when he called her. "It's past one o'clock in the morning there, isn't it? What's wrong?"

"Mummy, I need a loan."

"A loan? How much?"

"At least half a million dollars. For equity."

There was a stunned silence. "Equity in what?"

"Hear me out," he said, feeling her disapproval already. He outlined his plan, his conversation with Josh. "But I've got to put up some money of my own, or nobody will even consider backing me."

"It isn't precisely money of your own, though, is it?" His mother's voice was icy enough to freeze the transatlantic wires. "It's my money, and you're asking me to throw it away."

"I'll pay you back double," he pleaded. "Within five years."

"Who in heaven's name do you think you are?" she blasted him. "You're only in your twenties, you don't have an education. Who in their right mind would lend you money?"

I need support, not anger, he thought.

But she was relentless. "You're just like your father. He was a risk taker, and it got him killed. I'm saying no, because I know what's best for you. I don't want you to destroy yourself. For God's sake, Rolfe, let it go. Come back to Holland."

He shuddered at her words' impact, not knowing whether she was trying to protect him or didn't want him to succeed.

"Forget it," he said. "I'm staying here. I'll find the money someplace else."

"You're mad," she said. "Listen to me—."

He hung up before she could go on.

113

*****

"Steve, it's Bruce Hunt. I hope you don't mind my calling you at home."

"Of course not. I received your offer the other day."

"And looked it over?"

"Under a microscope."

"Well, what do you think?"

"Interesting, but you need to sharpen your pencil. Your bid's much too low. There's a lot of interest in the property."

"Come on, Steve, I know who's out there," Hunt sighed. "We both know it's a generous offer."

"If that's your idea of generous, I'd hate to be on your payroll."

Hunt ignored the jibe. "What say we start the due diligence process now, even without an agreement. It'll speed things up. I'm sure we'll come to terms eventually."

He's smart, thought Westerman. He wants to suck me in, and he knows he'll be so far ahead that if and when somebody else bids, he'll have an edge. But what do I have to lose? I've signed nothing. "Sure. Why not?"

*****

Rolfe couldn't sleep. Needing fresh air, he dressed and walked around the almost empty Union Square. Finally, he sat down on a bench and faced the hotel. Only a few lights shone through half-drawn curtains.

His mind went back to that time in 1964 when he told his family he was destined to be a hotel manager. He'd achieved that goal with ease. But now . . . owner?

If he could find the money, would the Union Square be able to compete with the chains? The chains were getting bigger and more powerful. But they were also becoming increasingly impersonal, passionless, cookie-cutter hotels with their standard coffee shop mentality and indifferent service. His mother had proved that care for each guest paid off. Maybe the Union Square would be the first in his own chain. One with high standards, one that combined the power of the chains with the niceties of 10.

He stood, inspired. "Fuck it," he said aloud. "I can always get a job." To hell with safety. He'd take the risk, try to buy the damned hotel. He'd make it great, the lynchpin of a great chain. It will be the first Kestrel Hotel, he thought. You'll see, Mum. You'll see, Josh. Just watch me, Susan. I'm going to soar.

CHAPTER 12

1973

Late that Monday afternoon he removed his diaries from his safe deposit box, went back to his apartment, and started to read. At 4:00 A.M., having not slept a wink but still wide awake, with adrenalin palpable in his fingers, he dialed a number. It was 10:00 A.M. in London. Time to start the game.

* * * * *

"May I speak to Mr. Longbury, please. It's Rolfe Ritter calling from San Francisco."

Rolfe looked at his notes: Edward Longbury, chairman and managing director of Davenport's, an old-line merchant bank specializing in aggressive, large-scale loans. Married. Two children. Likes men in their mid-twenties.

"Good morning, Mr. Ritter, this is Edward Longbury. How may I help you?"

"I hope you remember me. I was a good friend of David Murtoch."

"Yes, I remember."

Rolfe felt the coldness in Longbury's voice. His stomach tightened. "I have a banking proposition for you. I'm sure it will be of interest."

"I'm extremely busy right now. If you send the information, I'll see that it gets to the right people."

"But it's for your eyes only. You understand, I'm sure, how much I'd hate to see confidential information about the circumstances under which we met disseminated."

Silence.

"I could come to London tomorrow, if that's convenient," Rolfe said.

"Actually, I'll be in New York later this week. Let's meet for lunch at the Four Seasons, Wednesday, at one o'clock."

"I hear the food is excellent, Mr. Longbury. I look forward to our meeting."

* * * * *

"Murtoch!" Longbury screamed over the phone. "What have you got me into? That shit Ritter's trying to blackmail me. I promise you one thing: If I've got a problem, so will you."

"Calm down," Murtoch said, shaken. "The boy blackmailed me, too. Used me to get to America. But he's never said a word, and his success has made me look good. If I were you, I'd consider his proposition carefully." He chuckled. "Ritter might make you richer."

* * * * *

"I've arranged for people from the bank to go through the hotel," Westerman said. "A matter of refinancing. Please give them anything they need."

A lie, Rolfe knew. It was the Metropolitan people starting their due diligence.

* * * * *

"Susan?" Rolfe kissed her neck.

She rolled over to face him and sleepily snuggled into his chest. "Yes, darling."

"I want you to do something for me. It's important."

"What?" She reached for his penis.

"If Bruce Hunt calls over the next few days, tell him that Westerman's away, but you'll get a message to him."

She eased herself down on him. "I can't do that."

"Yes, you can. You really can. Ahhh."

* * * * *

"Ritter? This is Bruce Hunt."

"Yes, Mr. Hunt. It's an honor speaking with you. How can I help you?"

"Cut the crap, young man. I know what you're doing."

"What's that, Mr. Hunt?"

"You're deliberately preventing my team from getting the information they need."

"I don't know what you mean." Rolfe, all innocence, tried to keep the nervousness out of his voice.

"You won't let my people inspect the hotel. You promise financial information, but you don't deliver. You've refused to tell them what business is on the books for the next twelve months. You won't even let them see the original floor plans. Be careful, Mr. Ritter. Don't cross me."

"Perhaps you should discuss this with Mr. Westerman. I can't do anything without his authorization."

"He's away and won't return my calls." The line went silent for a moment. "If you're planning any future in the hotel business, you'd better cooperate. If you don't let my people begin their work this afternoon, I'll have Westerman send your ass straight back to Holland."

* * * * *

The British banker was ensconced in a booth in the Grill Room of the Four Seasons restaurant when Rolfe arrived. "Another large scotch, no ice, a splash of soda," Longbury said to the waiter, without acknowledging the younger man's entrance or his proffered hand. "I don't like being threatened. I won't have it," was all he said.

Rolfe sat across from the British banker. "I apologize if that was the impression I gave. I only wanted to let you in on an attractive deal—out of friendship for David." He handed the banker copies of the Union Square profit and loss statements.

Longbury scanned them quickly. "What do you want from me?"

"A loan." Rolfe explained the offer from Metropolitan and his own plan for revitalizing the hotel. "Time is running short," he concluded, "but I'm convinced Westerman will accept the same deal from me if I make it without the due diligence contingency requirement. After all, I already know every inch of the hotel."

Longbury sipped at his drink. "I know about Metropolitan. Bruce Hunt's a shrewd, tough buyer. If they're prepared to offer twenty-eight million, it's worth a lot more. So you're right. It's an attractive deal. If I were to lend you the money, where will the twelve to fifteen million in equity come from?"

Josh had briefed Rolfe on how to reply. "I'm ruled by a confidentiality agreement and can't reveal my partners' identities. I can, however, assure you that they're a powerful investment group. Anyway, you shouldn't worry. Your loan's contingent on satisfactory evidence of the availability of the money."

Details were discussed. No food was ordered, but Longbury had a third scotch and then a fourth.

"Your proposal is interesting," he said at last. "I'll think about it. You'll have my answer by the end of next week?"

By that time, Hunt's people would have finished their work.

Rolfe would have no competitive advantage. "I'm afraid that won't do. I need your answer now."

"Don't be ridiculous. These things take time."

"They don't need to, sir. Not for you," Rolfe said, counting on his intuition. "You have the authority to make the decision subject only to your bank's verification of the facts as I've presented them. It shouldn't take more than a day to finalize a loan commitment agreement."

"It's not possible. Be practical," Longbury snapped. The man was flustered, his temper on the edge of combusting.

Liquor and rage are a dangerous combination, Rolfe thought. "It's a good deal, and I'll deliver as promised. If you don't accept it, I'll be forced to think it was something personal and vindictive. Surely, you wouldn't want me to think that?"

Rolfe watched the banker's eyes narrow. He held his breath.

"All right. Tell your attorney to contact Ben Bridges in my New York office. He'll take care of things." He stood. "But let me tell you something, you disgusting little shit, you'd better not fail."

* * * * *

Rolfe called Susan as soon as he got off the plane in San Francisco. "I need to see Westerman straight away. Can you arrange it?"

"Certainly, Mr. Ritter," she said in her most formal tone. "I'm sure he'll be delighted to meet with you."

"I love you."

* * * * *

Rolfe's first words were unrevealing. "Mr. Westerman, I hope you're pleased with last year's performance."

"You know I am. My pleasure was reflected in your bonus."

"Yes, I'm grateful for the money, but more so for the opportunity."

Westerman looked at him impassively. "You didn't come here just to thank me."

"I know you have short-term cash problems and that any renovations are out of the question. I've also heard rumors you're considering an offer from a chain to buy the Union Square."

Westerman sat poker-faced, but a muscle under his left eye twitched.

"Naturally, you want me to cooperate fully with the buyer?"

Westerman nodded.

"Then, I'm duty-bound to share everything with them, warts and all. So I know they'll find all the problems in the hotel and give you a haircut on the price. Of course, I want to do whatever is in your best interest and would like you to get the best price for the hotel."

"So ... what?" the older man barked.

"Therefore," Rolfe continued, "I'm prepared to offer you twenty-six million for the property. With no contingency for due diligence."

"You're out of your mind!" Westerman's roar seemed all the louder given the previous calm. "You can't afford a tenth of that."

Rolfe took a document from his briefcase and passed it over. "A commitment letter, sir."

Westerman scanned the pages, eyes widening. "Even if I believed this twenty-two- million-dollar loan was real," he scoffed, "where's the equity going to come from?"

"Mr. Westerman, please take me seriously. Don't you think my lenders satisfied themselves that the equity is readily available?"

"Jesus! You're serious," Westerman said.

Rolfe leaned forward. "There is only one last thing I should point out. My offer is only valid until six tonight. After that, the bid is withdrawn."

Westerman gasped.

Rolfe forced himself to remain expressionless. It was 4:30 in San Francisco and 7:30 in New York. Susan had told him Hunt was in Europe for a week and there'd be no one in Metropolitan's offices to take the inevitable call from Westerman.

After a long pause, Westerman sighed. "Okay, I'll let you have the hotel if you pay the other purchaser's price."

"And that is?"

"Thirty million."

Rolfe jumped from his chair. "Don't take me for an idiot. I know I'm inexperienced, but I also know their offer is twenty-eight million, and that's before you take the haircut after the due diligence that we both know is forthcoming. In fact, my terms have just changed, and you now have five minutes to make up your mind and countersign my offer. After that, the price drops by a hundred thousand, and will continue to decrease by that same amount for every five minutes you delay."

Rolfe looked at his watch, as shocked as Westerman was by the words coming out of his mouth.

Four long minutes later, the older man picked up his pen and countersigned one of the two copies of the offer. "You'd better deliver, young man. If you fail, I'll make sure you can't get a job as a dishwasher at McDonald's."

* * * * *

The next morning, Rolfe placed a call to Lew Levenson at Enderton Studios. By late morning, he hadn't been called back.

He tried Mark Walters, and was told the agent was in an all-day meeting. "My name is Rolfe Ritter," he told Walters' secretary. "Two years ago I performed a personal service for Mr. Walters in my capacity as general manager of The Hills. I'm sure he'd like to talk to me. There are loose ends to tie up and time is of the essence."

Mark Walters called back immediately.

"I'd forgotten about you," Walters said. "What the fuck do you want?"

"You no doubt remember our arrangement. I'm equally sure Mr. Levenson does. I'll be at The Hills tomorrow afternoon at three, in room 333; I'm confident you remember how to get there." His tone turned frigid. "I expect you and Mr. Levenson to be there on time. I have a business proposition for you both. Good day."

* * * * *

Rolfe carried his bulging briefcase from San Francisco to room 333 at The Hills, and was now sitting opposite two scowling men.

"If you will recall from our meeting of nearly two years ago, I said to you then that at some point in the future I might call in a favor. Gentlemen, that time has come—although, once you've heard my proposition, I suspect you'll find it is I who am doing you the favor."

"Now, you listen to me—," Walters began.

Levenson tugged at his sleeve. "Just this once, Mark, shut the fuck up. Let him talk."

Ten minutes later, Rolfe summed up. "I have a signed commitment from the bank and a firm agreement with Westerman. I've brought a file for each of you with copies of all relevant documents, plus the financial projections, which are based on a term sheet that I trust you'll find reasonable."

"I remember the place from years ago. It was pretty good," Levenson said. "How bad is it today?"

"Lousy, but I can fix it."

"Have you got good people to work with?"

"Some. But I'll get an even better team when we buy it."

"How much equity are you talking about?"

"You'll put up ten million, and I'll put up two million in the form of a fee that's due to me for putting the deal together. The price for the hotel is twenty-six million. With refurbishing, other costs, and my fee, the total comes to thirty-four million, twenty-two of which will be the bank's loan. The way the math works out, you'll own just over eighty-three percent, and I'll own just under seventeen percent. You'll be passive partners; I'll be the general partner and make all decisions regarding the hotel. I'll manage the hotel and take five percent of all revenue as my fee."

"You're just a snot-nosed, blackmailing kid," Walters said, standing. "Why would anyone do a one-sided deal like this with you? Go fuck yourself. Come on, Lew, there's nothing for us here."

"Show me what you've put together," Levenson said.

Rolfe handed each of them a bound folder. In addition to the financial history, it contained projections, term sheets, and various agreements. Toward the end, there were photos of the hotel and the sketches that Ted Pemberton had put together, followed by a section of photographs.

Their attention was riveted on that final section. Rolfe had photographed everything in the box, including the girls' letters and the reports from both the security officer and himself.

"There are additional copies of the photos in two separate safety deposit boxes, plus, of course, a box with the originals. My lawyer has instructions that if anything should happen to me, he's to turn copies of everything over to the *L.A. Times* and the *New York Times* and the originals to the police. Gentlemen, it's in your own best interests to make sure I remain healthy."

Levenson said, "We need a few minutes to discuss this." The two men disappeared into the master bedroom to talk.

Fifteen minutes later, the men emerged, Levenson with a tight smile, Walters with slumped shoulders.

"We don't have a fucking choice, do we?" Levenson said. "Okay, we'll do what you want. When will you destroy that fucking box?"

"Five years from the date of the acquisition of the hotel. When we've done this deal, you'll have fulfilled your side of the bargain. I'm keeping the box only to protect myself against two very smart businessmen."

Rolfe smiled. "Two final things. One: you'll make a lot of money on your investment and I'll wager you'll want to do more deals with me."

"Fat fucking chance," muttered Walters.

Rolfe took out his Cross pen and offered it to them. "And two: please sign the term sheets."

* * * * *

"Yes, Mr. Hunt?" Rolfe said after Dorothy had told him the chairman of Metropolitan Hotels was on the phone.

"I suppose I should congratulate you," Hunt said. "Westerman just told me he'd made a great deal with you and you're closing at the end of the week."

Rolfe felt a tingle of satisfaction, remembering Susan's proud kiss that morning. "True."

"That's what I wanted to talk to you about. You're young, obviously an entrepreneur. I'm offering you a million dollars to assign your agreement to Metropolitan. You won't put up a dime or borrow a penny, and before you're twenty-five years old, you'll have a million bucks in the bank. What do you say to that?"

"I'm sorry, Mr. Hunt, but I'm going to keep the hotel and make it as great as it deserves to be. Thank you for your offer. If I do decide to sell at any time I'll call you."

"Don't be condescending, young man," Hunt answered. "I told you once before to be careful. The offer won't be available next week. Now, I'm warning you. Think about it and call me tomorrow."

"There's nothing to think about, Mr. Hunt. It's my hotel."

* * * * *

They finished at 11:30 at night. Josh turned over the last page of the purchase and sale agreement, and leaned back. "We'll sign this tomorrow, but there's something I've got to know. Who are your partners?"

"You keep asking, and I keep answering: I can't tell you."

"That won't hack it. Either you trust me or you don't. Christ, I've risked my career for you. I could get disbarred for what I've done."

"Josh—"

"I mean it. Tell me, or I'll fuck up this deal, and Westerman will have to go back to Hunt."

"Lew Levenson and Mark Walters."

"Jesus, how the hell did you get that pair? They're a goldmine, if you don't screw it up."

"They were impressed by my work at The Hills," Rolfe said

122

evenly. "Let's get on with this. I want to understand how it really works."

＊ ＊ ＊ ＊ ＊

Josh explained the deal. Rolfe would be set up as the head of a management company, which would receive a fee of five percent of all hotel revenues. The hotel would pay all of its costs, interest on the loan from Edward Longbury and a fixed return on the $12 million invested by Rolfe, Levinson, and Walters. From what remained, if anything, the management company would take 20%, and the rest would go to the three partners.

"You'll have two sources of income," Josh concluded. "If the hotel succeeds, you'll be rich."

Rich. Wonderful. Of course, it would succeed! He would use the money to start the finest hotel chain ever. It's my destiny, he thought. It's what I promised my mother, Mike, and myself.

"I'll use whatever I make to build a global hotel company with standards the rest of the industry will have to follow," he said.

"In other words," Josh said, caught up in the vision, "you're going to achieve the impossible."

"Precisely." He appraised his new friend so intently that Josh had to avert his eyes. "Want to come along?"

"Do I. But only if I'm your number-two man. Think of me not as your lawyer but as your *consigliere*. I'll quit my job. You'll match my salary and give me five percent of the management company. Together, we'll dominate the world—the world, shit, the universe! What do you say?"

Book Two

"We shape our dwellings; thereafter they shape us."

Winston Spencer Churchill

CHAPTER 13

1973

In September, the Yom Kippur War broke out in the Middle East. An oil embargo ensued; prices shot up; Western Europe and the United States teetered on recession. Businesses cut back on travel. People opted for stay-at-home vacations. Occupancies plummeted at the Kestrel Hotel in San Francisco.

Besides, it wasn't a pleasant place to visit. Signs saying Pardon Our Dust, We're Renovating to Make Things Better did little to salve the complaints of the few guests. Each time Rolfe saw the mess or looked at the reservations log, he felt worse. His cash reserves were rapidly depleting. Levinson's and Walters' hectoring phone calls increased his feelings of impending doom. He wondered how he could have so grossly underestimated the problems and costs of the renovation.

Looming behind the daily concerns was the need to improve the deal with Bud McCory's union, who, he'd been told, was planning to "crucify" him.

* * * * *

"Come on, my boy, we're going to get drunk." Josh grabbed Rolfe's arm and dragged him to a new bar just off Union Square. They ordered drinks. Ordered more. Rolfe unloaded a litany of his problems.

"So what you're saying is that the hotshot hotelier otherwise known as Rolfe Ritter isn't Superman," Josh said. "And this is news?"

"Hey! Watch your lip, you manipulative Jew. I'll have you disbarred for insulting behavior."

"Just try it, you Dutch tulip. In the meantime, you'd better quit whining and come up with a solution. My future's in your hands."

"If you're so smart, you come up with one."

"Okay. Let's torch the hotel, collect the insurance, and live off the proceeds."

Rolfe chuckled. "Tempting. Maybe we should just close the bloody place while we fix it up."

"That's not such a bad idea," Josh said. Suddenly sober, he started scribbling on the tablecloth. Minutes later he pointed to a spider's web of numbers. "If closing the hotel means we finish the renovation three months earlier, we're better off financially. As it is, we're pissing off every guest that walks in the door and pissing away so much money in operating costs and customer refunds, we might as well just flush thousand-dollar bills down the toilet. So what the hell. Let's close the fucker till we can reopen in style."

Rolfe examined the numbers. "It's worth thinking about. Meanwhile, let's have another drink."

Two drinks later, Rolfe clasped his friend's hand. "Are you sober enough to give advice on a personal problem?"

"Probably not," Josh answered. But I'm not too drunk to listen."

* * * * *

"Let me get this straight." Josh's words were slurred. "For the past month or so you've been two-timing Susan with a French broad who years ago shat on you from a great height."

"That sums it up."

"Now you're feeling guilty and want absolution."

"Advice, not absolution."

"Same thing. Listen carefully. You've got a good thing going with Susan. She's a classy lady, and God knows, you need one. What's more, she's content to share you with the hotel. But you're finished if she finds out about what's-her-name."

"Chantal."

"Chantal. And you know it. Why not walk away from Chantal once and for all?"

Because she's a drug, Rolfe thought. Because sex with her is like nothing else in the world. "You're right," he said resolutely. "I'll give her up."

* * * * *

The next afternoon Rolfe was sitting in Bud McCory's featureless office. A forty-five-year-old ex-barman from Sausalito who'd fought his way up the ranks to become head of Local 151 of the Hotel and Restaurant Workers' Union. McCory seemed as broad as he was tall, and had a face as hard as a block of granite, with dead gray eyes to match. His completely bald head added to his air of menace. The lamp above Rolfe had no shade, and the light from the bare bulb glowed in McCory's eyes.

He's more ominous when he's quiet than when he talks, Rolfe thought, remembering their casual meeting of a few months earlier.

"I've wondered when you'd get your bony ass up here," the union man said in a voice of false pleasantry. "You may have made yourself popular with some of my people at Union Square, but you ain't getting jack shit in the way of a break from me. I'm going to make an example of you, and then every fucking hotel in San Francisco will tremble, wondering whether they're next on my list. So if you came here looking to make a better deal for yourself, you're shit out of luck."

"That's very illuminating," Rolfe said, his tone as pleasant as his adversary's. "You've been more helpful than you realize. But I didn't come here about a better deal on the Union Square. I came to discuss something else. I plan to buy more hotels, and it'd be to our mutual advantage to discuss how we might work together in the future."

Ignoring his throbbing head, he continued. "Please understand. I didn't come here about the payments you made to Ulrich Gerhardt. Nor to make anything of the fact that he gave you confidential information about the hotel, copies of our employment files, and minutes of the management committee meetings. Nor that he used your money to 'persuade'—if that's the right term— other key members of the hotel staff to support your union." He took a breath, dimly aware he had said too much. "I'd never do that. I want us to be partners."

McCory's eyes glared diamond hard. "Listen to me carefully. You mean nothing here. You are nothing. This is my city, my union, and nothing you do can affect me in the least. Your threats are jack-offs. If any of that crap comes out, it'll be his word against mine, and whose do you think is louder? So don't threaten me with that bullshit again."

This man is terrifying, Rolfe thought. He's faced far tougher opponents than me.

"As I said, none of that will ever come up. Of course, Gerhardt depositing money, far more than his salary, into his bank account each time you gave him cash was sheer stupidity. That we have copies of the deposit slips—which, by the way, coincide with his diary entries of when and where he met you—would, naturally, be irrelevant. It's merely a coincidence that we have photographs of him entering and leaving this building on those dates. Of course, his signed affidavit would give the press plenty to gossip about, but that shouldn't worry you. As you say, it's your city."

Rolfe licked his lips; he was lying. McCory was unflinching. He impassiveness was unnerving. Nevertheless, Rolfe pressed on.

"I want to find a way of working with you. Our contract with your union is too harsh. We can't survive financially as it stands. I need your help to make it less onerous, and I assure you we'll be good employers for your members. We can make this a win-win situation."

At last, an expression on McCory's face: amusement. "I'm listening."

"We're in trouble. We can't keep our doors open. I'm in debt up to my eyeballs, and there's nowhere to turn. If things don't improve, I'll have to close the hotel and declare bankruptcy."

McCory stretched like a lion flexing its muscles. "You're fucked ... partner. Dead in the water. So get your pretty-boy Nazi ass out of here. I promise you'll sign any contract I put in front of you, even if it says you have to fuck your mother in the center of Union Square."

Rolfe stood. "So be it. Just remember I extended my hand in friendship, and you rejected it. Tomorrow, I'm closing the hotel. The first people I let go will be your members. I'll tell them you don't give a damn about them. You can't give them strike funds, because we'll be closed; you can't strike what's closed. You'll be vilified for putting so many union members out of work and hurting their families. The local merchants will hate you. You're up for reelection. This will kill you."

McCory stood too. Rolfe could see the working of his jaw; something had hit home.

"Fire them and be damned." McCory said. "Do you think I care about a few lousy families? When the other hotels see I've made you close down, they'll shit themselves. I'll get great fucking deals from them. So go fuck yourself."

Rolfe moved toward the door, stopped and turned. "By the way, I've been wearing a hidden wire and microphone. When the media air the tapes and the 'few lousy families' hear what you think of them, you'll have trouble being reelected dog catcher. Too bad. I'm glad I didn't make the large contribution to your reelection campaign that I'd intended. I'm sure your opponents will find good use for the money. Good afternoon, Bud. And fuck you!"

Rolfe walked out, adrenaline pumping. The folly of his brava-do welled up, and he shivered uncontrollably, his shirt soaked with sweat.

I've blown it, he thought. I'm going to lose everything. He knows I'm bluffing.

* * * * *

The next day, Rolfe called a meeting of the hotel staff. Builder's dust hung in the air. He could sense the anticipation.

"I've got to tell you the hard truth. The recession is draining us, and the union wants to take advantage of our misery; they're being completely unreasonable. They don't seem to care whether you have jobs. I can't keep things going the way they are." He paused, hating what he had to say next, the words turning to bile in his throat. "I have no choice but to shut down the hotel. I hope it's just temporary."

He looked around the room, registering the shock and bewil-derment of his staff, but he had to follow through with the threat he had made to McCory. He knew there was speculation whether the hotel would survive, and if it did, would it union or non-union. Pain and humiliation worked over him as he looked at the faces fixed intently on him. Even though this was hard for him, it would be a damned lot harder for them.

The first people he fired that afternoon were the union organ-izers.

"You're living dangerously, too dangerously," Josh warned.

Four days later, the hotel closed.

* * * * *

"The kid's fucking nuts. He's shooting himself in the head, but he could take me with him," McCory complained to Tom Sullivan, the union's lawyer.

The next day Sullivan contacted Josh Leonard. "This is ridicu-lous. There was no need to close the Union Square."

"Ritter's upset and offended. He's thinking about a lawsuit against McCory for colluding with the chef. Your client called him a Nazi, and he's real sensitive about that. His father nearly died fighting the Nazis. I'll try to stop him, but any influence over him I once had—"

"Well, what can we do?" Sullivan asked. "What does he really need?"

They discussed wage concessions, labor cuts over the long

term, productivity, the phasing out of jobs when the workers holding them retired. "If I can get McCory to agree, he'll insist the
organizers be rehired and all wages and benefits lost during this
closure restored."

Josh merely grunted.

Sullivan sighed. "All I can do is pass it on. I don't think there's
a chance in hell Bud will buy it."

* * * * *

"Do you think he'll cave?" Rolfe asked when Josh told him
about the meeting with Sullivan.

"Don't count on it. And for your own health, don't go anywhere
for the time being. I've got security boys watching your apartment
and office."

* * * * *

McCory's call came the next afternoon. "Look. Ritter. We got
off to a bad start. I'm sorry I called you a Nazi; I didn't realize who
your father was. My older brother died on Omaha Beach, and I
still get real upset."

You liar, Rolfe thought, knowing McCory never had a brother.
He said nothing.

McCory continued. "Let's have a drink tonight and see what
we can do about this fucking mess you got us into."

They agreed to meet at seven on the wharf.

"Hey, kid! Don't come wired this time. You may find it fucking
hard to walk if you do."

* * * * *

McCory hugged Ritter like an old friend—patting him down,
Rolfe knew. He walked the young man to a table on which sat a
half-empty glass of whiskey and a nearly empty bowl of popcorn.
McCory swallowed the rest of his drink and signaled the waiter for
another. "What'll you have?"

"A draught beer."

Five silent minutes later, McCory's glass was empty. Rolfe's
sat untouched.

"What you've done is fucking insane," McCory growled. "You're
making serious enemies, me among them."

Still silent, Rolfe focused on his glass.

"But maybe I was too harsh on you. I needed to see what you're
made of."

Bullshit.

"I'll give you the productivity agreement, and I'll even tell you which people you don't have to rehire or replace. But I'm not giving you any wage concessions—forget it."

"Thank you for the drink, Mr. McCory. We've nothing to discuss."

McCory grabbed his arm. "Hold on, kid. There's plenty to talk about."

The union man's face was inches away from Rolfe. There were red streaks in the corners of McCory's eyes, blood in the granite.

"You can have the concessions Sullivan and Leonard were negotiating. But once you start making a profit, I want my members to get an annual bonus. Agreed?"

Rolfe shrugged. "It's a start."

"I also want the tapes and affidavits destroyed, if they ever fucking existed."

"If we come to a deal, you have my word. What else?"

"Finally, you'll give me twenty-five thousand for each local campaign I run in. I'll figure out how to do it so there's no paper trail. When I go for national leadership, you'll help me big time."

The Dutchman held his hands together under the table to keep them from shaking. "And in exchange your union won't strike this or any other hotel I choose to buy for the next five years."

McCory signaled for another drink. "Agreed. But if one word of this gets out, I'll make sure all of your hotels are struck so bad you'll have to close them real fucking fast. And if you ever try to fuck with me again, I swear to God I'll have you killed."

It was not an idle threat, Rolfe knew. He had made a pact with the devil.

CHAPTER 14

1974

It was New Years night, and to compensate for staying in bed the evening before—as soft and warm and intimate a time as Rolfe could remember—they were drinking champagne cocktails at the Top of the Mark. The night was clear, but the sparkle lay beneath them, not in the stars: San Francisco in its glory.

Susan was dressed in a Halston dress Rolfe had bought her for the occasion. She looked, he thought, regal, a farm girl princess. For the first time, he told her about his encounter with Bud McCory.

The concern in her eyes struck at his core. He did not anticipate empathy; he had half expected her to berate him for being foolhardy, as his mother would have done.

"Weren't you scared?" she asked when he had finished.

"Terrified."

She stared at him, astonished. "Then why are you smiling?"

"Ah," he said, exaltation welling in him from the place she had pierced. "Don't you see? I loved every minute of it."

* * * * *

His mood was not as jubilant when the Kestrel Hotel reopened. Only a few people trickled in. Business was even slower than before the old hotel had closed. Rolfe paced impatiently up and down the lobby, trailed by Levenson and Walters. It was so quiet he could hear their footsteps on the marble. Susan joined them. He sent her away roughly; this was no time for her sympathy. Bud McCory showed up too.

"Fucking disaster," he said, and left without another word.

"There goes our investment," Levenson growled. "What's Plan B?"

Rolfe wheeled on his partners. "Damned if I know. Jesus," he said, desperate. "Do something."

That night he lay awake in the penthouse apartment, his

depression growing. Why weren't the guests coming? What had he done wrong? The hotel was beautiful, a masterpiece, his dream and his achievement. But nobody gave a shit, and nobody would. He'd bet everything, lost everything. He imagined the self-righteous look on his mother's face when he'd have to crawl back to The Netherlands.

At 2:00 A.M. he gave up trying to sleep and dialed a number.

"Chantal? I need you."

* * * * *

On the afternoon of the hotel's third day, Mark Walters called. "You owe me a big one. I've 'done something.' Get your ass down to the lobby."

Rolfe raced down. Mona Cameron from ABC's San Francisco affiliate stood in the center of the floor, interviewing Natalie Wood and Robert Wagner. The women carried calla lilies taken from the lobby vases. One camera crew roamed the restaurant and bar while another went in search of the modern bedrooms. The segment would air on the early evening news.

The next day, the restaurants started to fill at noon. By one o'clock, crowds were lining up to get tables.

By four o'clock that afternoon, the lobby was so crowded with sightseers that Rolfe felt the need to limit their numbers inside the building. A line of people waited eagerly outside, stretching from the porte cochere all the way around the block in both directions, as the hotel banquet staff served them complimentary beverages. The hotel's restaurants were fully booked until ten-thirty that night. The bar was crowded to capacity, with customers two and three deep.

Rolfe and Josh sat in the lobby at midnight, amazed by the day's events.

"What about the rooms?" Josh asked.

"Sixty percent booked," Rolfe answered. "And we're full to capacity Monday to Friday next week, and already at seventy percent for the next two weekends."

The lawyer grinned. "Tank Gott! I vas vorried dat maybe I vould need a real job."

* * * * *

Early the next morning, Rolfe referred once again to his diaries and made some calls.

"This is Rolfe Ritter. I don't know if you remember me?"

"I'm sorry I don't," replied Sir Robin Colloway from his chairman's office at Westerly Industries' London headquarters.

"I was a friend of David Murtoch's, and we dined with you at your house on February twenty-third, nineteen-sixty-six. Do you remember? Bishop Atherton was also there, and—"

"I remember."

"I've read that you're setting up an office and plant near San Francisco and, as the owner of the best hotel in the Bay Area, I want to make sure we get your business."

Rolfe could hear breathing, and finally a burst of laughter.

"That's the most blatant threat I've had in a long while! Murtoch taught you well. Write to me with all the details."

* * * * *

"Mr. Collins?"

"Yes. Who's speaking?"

"My name is Rolfe Ritter. I own the new Kestrel Hotel in San Francisco."

"And?"

"You may remember, I bailed your studio and Marla Danion out of a, shall I say, embarrassing situation at The Hills on October ninth, nineteen-sixty-nine." Rolfe could hear nervous breathing. "You do remember, don't you?"

"Yes."

"I need a favor in return."

"Go on."

"I'd like the studio and its stars to use this hotel anytime they're in San Francisco. It's a great hotel. Your people will be perfectly comfortable, and there will be no hardship."

"Meaning, you won't go to the media about that night?"

"The thought never crossed my mind."

* * * * *

Dearest Mother,

It's a triumph! What a great feeling! The hotel's exactly as I imagined. You must have felt just like this when 10 opened. You and Jan must come over as soon as possible. Name a date, and I'll reserve the bridal suite.

He received no reply.

* * * * *

Rolfe invited Momo Takenaka to his office. "I have a challenge for you," he said, as she settled into a chair and smoothed her short A-line skirt over her thin but shapely thighs.

She was as serene and remote as a queen sculpted in jade. "I'm listening."

"When I was at the Audley in London, I put in a manual system for compiling guest records. I noted everything—dates of arrival, departures, the room they stayed in, their preferences, quirks, peccadilloes, even their complaints—on cards, which were color coded. Blue one for an old guest, white for a new one, red for travel agents and people in the trade, yellow for VIPs, and green if the guest had ever complained."

"And you want me to automate this on the computer?"

"Yes. Can you do it?"

"When do you need it?"

"A week?"

"Are you in a hurry?"

"Yes."

"Then, I'll have it to you in five days."

* * * * *

"I hear the hotel's going well," Riverstone said over the phone. "Your mother boasts about it."

"I wish she'd tell me that herself. Sometimes I think she's proud of me, but then she seems to resent my being successful in spite of her. At times, I even think she wants me to fail."

His godfather ignored the comments. "I wanted to tell you—I'm retiring."

Something that shouldn't be changing was about to change. Jan, Margaret, Mike. Right or wrong, he wanted them immutable. "I don't believe you," he said. "You'll never stop."

Riverstone chuckled. "Just my day-to-day job. I'm staying on as chairman of the Prime Minister's Committee for Coordination of Intelligence Activities."

"Impressive."

"Only if you're in British intelligence. . . . Speaking of which, I need a favor—not so much for me as for my successor."

Rolfe recoiled. "Uncle Mike, I can't do it. The last time I almost got killed. I've lost my nerve. Anyway, I've got too much to lose."

"Aren't you curious?"

"No," he lied, trying hard to suppress the familiar feeling of excitement.

"I'm going to tell you anyway. Then, if your answer is still no, that's the end of it."

"I don't want to—"

"We think one of our own agents is doubling for the Chinese and spying on us. We want to send him to San Francisco to see if he'll get in contact with Chinese agents we know are over there."

"And you want him to stay at the Kestrel?"

"Precisely. You'd intercept his messages, telexes, and letters. Plant bugs in his room, his suitcase, even his shoes, if possible; we'll get them to you. And photograph everything you can find in his room, picking the locks of his briefcases, if necessary. You remember how, don't you?"

"Very funny. Can't somebody else do it?"

"Not on such short notice. You're the only one I trust."

"Tell me it's important," Rolfe said, feeling his resolve crumble.

"It's vital. If I'm right, it could be the worst betrayal of the British Foreign Service since Kim Philby."

He clenched his fists to control his adrenaline. "If you put it that way, I'll do it."

* * * * *

He planned it meticulously. This wasn't just some government employee. This was a professional spy who would be triply cautious and probably leave all sorts of anti-tampering tricks to protect himself from prying eyes.

Each time Rolfe let himself into David Yang's room, he took Polaroid shots of the layout and replaced everything he touched exactly as it was.

He found and bought replicas of the spy's briefcase and luggage, and spent hours practicing picking the locks until he could do it without leaving so much as a hairline scratch on the lock's surface.

Planting the new micro-bugs was easy. He'd dismantled one of the hotel clock-radios and the new touchtone telephone, inserted the listening devices so well that they looked like part of the devices' internal mechanisms, and reassembled both perfectly. Yang would have to take them completely apart to find them.

Rolfe had the spy's dry cleaning sent to his office. "I'll take it up there personally; I want to double-check the room," he explained to the baffled housekeeper. Carefully, he unstitched the lapel of the gray worsted suit, inserted a tiny microphone, and stitched it back meticulously.

The doormen were under instructions to offer Mr. Yang the

hotel's car and driver, which would enable Rolfe to keep track of his comings and goings. If he declined this service and took one of the regular cabs from the stand, the driver would be asked about his destination. If he were to be picked up by an unknown car, the head of hotel security could check the license plate number with the police records and get an address.

Rolfe told the few staff involved that the hotel had been asked by "the authorities" to cooperate in an ongoing investigation. He instructed them to be discreet, and to keep it confidential. Not one batted an eye.

* * * * *

"Uncle Mike?"

"Rolfe, my boy! Good to hear from you."

"You were right about our mutual friend."

Silence. Finally, softly, "When can I have the information."

"This afternoon. I'll drop off the package as instructed. I've done what you asked."

"I know you have. I'm grateful."

"How do you know? I only just told you."

"I have my ways. You didn't think we'd stop protecting you just because you were overseas, did you?"

* * * * *

The Kestrel soared like its namesake bird. Society groups and charitable organizations vied with each other to reserve the best weekends for their balls and events. Parents booked weddings, confirmations, and bar mitzvahs far in advance. Business executives flocked to the hotel.

Lew Levenson and Mark Walters visited "their" hotel. "We're staying the night," they announced.

"Every show biz big shot has to stay here," Rolfe said. He turned to Levenson. "It would bring a better return on your investment if the hotel were featured in some of your movies."

Lew grinned. "You're good, very good. You're still a blackmailing son of a bitch, but you're our blackmailer. How about giving us that box and the fucking photos."

"Time's not up. They're perfectly safe with me."

They clinked wine glasses. "Friends forever," Walters said.

* * * * *

Rolfe passed the *San Francisco Examiner* to Susan over breakfast in her apartment on a lazy Sunday morning. "How about, as you Americans say, them apples?"

She read aloud:

> Having established himself as one of San Francisco's premier hoteliers, Rolfe Ritter is earning a reputation as a world-class showman. At the annual ball for the Vienna Opera, this young Dutch transplant to San Francisco brought over fifty Viennese violinists to play Strauss waltzes.
>
> Guests at the Navy Ball were serenaded by the merry tones of Navy pipers, while at a party to welcome the Indian Trade Commission, diners hardly had time to recover from a single goldfish in every glass before they were comforted by the arrival of an elephant in full ceremonial regalia.
>
> One thing is for sure: Kestrel's competitors can't rest on their laurels.

* * * * *

Margaret called. Rolfe could tell something was wrong from the moment he heard his mother's voice. "I was going to accept your invitation—"

"Why that's great!"

"—and come without Jan. But now I'm not."

Riverstone had told Rolfe that Jan was running the entire Dutch intelligence operation, so his staying home was not a surprise. But his mother?

"Why not? Won't you change your mind? Susan's been looking forward to meeting you."

"Really?" Margaret asked, sarcasm dripping from her voice. "And Chantal as well, I suppose?"

Oh, God! Rolfe felt his face flush. "I don't understand."

"I know that Chantal Le Peron is in San Francisco and that you're seeing her."

"Did Mike tell you?"

"As a matter of fact, Jan did. But what difference does that make? If she's there, I've no interest in being with you."

"Mother—"

"Don't patronize me. You'll lose Susan and end up at least as hurt as you were that last time in Paris."

"Chantal came to me for a job. I found her one, not with me. That's all."

"Don't lie."

Maybe she's jealous, he thought. But it's none of her business. He said, "If you don't want to come, fine. But don't try to dictate my life to me."

There was a long silence. He decided to change the subject, an attempt to end their conversation gracefully. "I'm still sad about Grandpa. Have you sorted out his affairs yet?"

He could feel his mother trying to control her anger. "I've put his house on the market."

"What about the rest of his estate? Is it a mess? Do you need help?"

"Thank you, but Jan gave me all the help I need. Besides, it's not very complicated. In addition to the house, he left me two million pounds, and ..." Her voice trailed off.

"And?"

"And he left you one million pounds in a trust you can't touch until you're thirty-five. I don't understand why; you'll inherit everything I have anyway. It's baffling."

* * * * *

The morning edition of the *San Francisco Chronicle* lay, as always, at the door to Rolfe's apartment. He picked it up and turned to the Social and Arts section to see if the Kestrel had been mentioned. There was the headline, in bold large type: "San Francisco's Most Eligible Bachelor." Beneath it was a photo of Chantal draped all over him at the French consulate's ball.

Hot coffee from his nearly full cup spilled over the page.

* * * * *

Of course, Susan saw the *Chronicle* too. The caption under the photo read: "The glamorous Chantal Le Peron of the Stanford Court Hotel with Rolfe Ritter of the Kestrel." Is a merger in their future?

Her phone rang. Hesitantly, she picked it up.

"It's me," Rolfe said.

"You've got one hell of a nerve calling."

"Let me explain."

Her tears were of rage, he knew, not of sadness. "How long has it been going on?"

"There's nothing going on. I just helped her get started in San Francisco. It's true we were lovers in France—I told you about her—but here she means nothing."

"How could you be so—public?"

"I had to attend the event at the French Consulate. Chantal speaks French. That's the only reason I invited her."

"But couldn't tell me? Right," Susan spat sarcastically. "After all the horror stories you told me about her. How could you?"

"She means nothing to me. You're the only one I care about."

"Right. The nights you were 'too busy' to see me. Josh's embarrassment when he had to lie to me about you. It all makes sense now."

"Wait. Let me explain."

"There's nothing I want to hear from you. How can I ever trust you again? Jesus, Rolfe. You said you loved me! Yeah, sure. Because I told you about Westerman. That's the way to get your love: betray someone. Well, you're the betrayal expert. We're through. You just lost the best thing in your life."

* * * * *

"She trapped you, didn't she?" Josh asked as he walked into Rolfe's office brandishing the *Chronicle*. "What a dumb schmuck you are."

"I know. I hurt Susan terribly. She doesn't want to see me again."

"Serves you right, you moron. The only chance you have of getting Susan back is to dump that French bitch now."

* * * * *

Bruce Hunt sat on the Eames couch in his office in Metropolitan's Purchase, New York, campus. Opposite was a journalist from *International Investor*.

"I understand you recently tried to buy the Union Square Hotel in San Francisco," the young interviewer asked. "True?"

"We had a casual interest in it."

"Then, how does it feel to be beaten by a twenty-five year old?"

"If we'd wanted to buy it, we would have."

"Have you seen the hotel since it was reopened?"

"Yes. Nice. For an amateur."

"You're calling Rolfe Ritter an amateur?"

"I could call him other things, but that will do."

"I understand he wants to build a chain based on the success of the Kestrel. Have you any comments?"

Hunt had tried to check his anger. Now it exploded. "Listen to me carefully. This Ritter is a one-shot wonder, a kid who's been a general manager for fifteen minutes and thinks he knows hotels.

But if he tries to expand, he'll fall on his face. The Kestrel's not a chain concept. I pity the investors in his folly—if he ever finds them."

* * * * *

"Please listen to me," Chantal implored.

"I told you to stop calling. I don't want to speak to you, let alone see you, ever again."

"I just want to apologize for the photo. It was stupid. I should never have allowed it happen."

"Let it happen? You arranged for it."

"I would never do such a thing," she said indignantly.

"Bullshit. You'll do anything to get your way."

"And what is that?"

"To fuck me over."

"Au contraire, mon amour. 'My way' is to look after you so you don't get into trouble."

* * * * *

Rolfe stared out the window, fury rising, playing back his conversation with Chantal. She could have meant only one thing. He called his godfather.

"Well, what do you think is going on?" Mike asked, unfazed.

"There are two options. Either she's spying on me for someone else, or she's working for you."

Riverstone hesitated. "You're right. She's working for me."

"You bastard! Why?"

"Actually, she's not spying. I sent her to San Francisco to look after you. After the trouble you got into in London, the breakneck speed you're going over there, and knowing that I might need your help from time to time, I thought my godson needed a guardian angel."

"Jesus, Uncle Mike. I'm a big boy now. I can take care of myself."

Riverstone sighed. "I wish I could believe it. But to me and to Chantal, you're still a boy."

* * * * *

"Susan won't return my calls," Rolfe complained to Josh. "Have you talked with her?"

"Virtually every day. I'm her friend. You're wasting your time trying to contact her. You've reopened her scars, and she's bleeding. There's no way she'll come back."

"I miss her," Rolfe said plaintively.

"Well, I'll say what Susan is too refined to say: Tough shit."

"What do I do?"

"Count your losses and attend to our business," Josh said. "A lawyer friend of mine from Chicago who represents the Hirschberg family called me yesterday. The Hirschbergs own three hotels—L.A., New York, Chicago—that they don't know what to do with. They're badly run, in tatters, same situation as the Union Square. They're thinking of selling them rather than refinancing. The lawyer thinks there could be a bargain in this deal."

It was as though Josh had jumpstarted his heartbeat. "What's the angle?"

"I have the appraisals here. Look them over; they're really low. If we go in with an unsolicited offer just above their value, my friend thinks the Hirschbergs will sell."

"Isn't your friend being unethical? He's giving you inside information about his own clients so we can buy their properties cheap."

Josh grunted. "He'll get an enormous finder's fee in cash, which you'll pay him. Besides, since when do you care about ethics?"

* * * * *

"Lew, it's put-up time again."

"What are you talking about?"

Rolfe explained.

"Great, kid." Rolfe could almost see him puff out his chest. "We'll do the same deal as last time. Don't worry; we'll find the debt. And boy, after what was quoted in *International Investor*, Hunt's going to be really pissed at you."

Lew was right, and Hunt would be a formidable enemy. "Does that worry you?" Rolfe asked.

"Who gives a shit about Hunt?" Levenson said. "Go make us more money."

CHAPTER 15

1975

Bruce Hunt was livid. He snapped open the neck of his mono-grammed white shirt and yanked down his Dunhill tie. His pale, lightly freckled skin was beet red and his eyes blazing, he stormed into his regular Monday morning management meeting in the boardroom of Metropolitan's New York offices and flung the real estate section of the *New York Times* at the man sitting at the far end of the conference table.

"I suppose from now on I have to get my information on your fuck-ups from the newspapers!"

Ben Richardson, senior vice president of development, cringed. "I'm not sure I understand.".

"That's the damn problem. You don't understand!" He glared at Richardson. At five feet, eight inches Hunt's body was too small for the high-backed leather chair at the head of the table. "Why don't you read the article to us so we can all understand."

"'Kestrel to expand,'" Richardson read.

"What's that, Ben? Speak up!"

"'Kestrel to expand,'" Richardson repeated, the paper shaking in his hands. "'Rolfe Ritter, owner of the fashionable Kestrel Hotel on Union Square in San Francisco, is acquiring hotels in Los Angeles, Chicago, and New York from the Hirschberg family of Chicago for an undisclosed price, Mr. Ritter announced. Ted Pemberton, who designed the Kestrel San Francisco, will oversee their conversions.

"'With four Kestrel hotels in major markets, we're on our way to creating a new brand,' the twenty-eight-year-old, Dutch-born hotelier told the *Times*. 'It's time for our industry to give customers what they want, not what a bunch of staid hoteliers tell them they can have.'

"'Marty Benton, a senior consultant at Kirkbride and Connelly, which often advises the hotel industry, said, 'The

Kestrel in San Francisco has not only pioneered new design, but has set new standards for operations and service. I'm sure the new hotels will be equally forward-looking. Ritter's young, I know, but young ideas are what the industry needs. The worst mistake anyone could make is not to take him seriously.' The Hirschberg Hotels comprise . . ."

"Enough," Hunt snapped. He glared at the three men around the table. "Ben, were you oblivious to this too? Or did you simply forget to tell me? What about your talks with the Hirschbergs about converting their hotels to Metropolitans? What about Jack's plans for the upgrades? And you, Fred, weren't you setting up some sort of financing with Chase?"

He waited. Nobody spoke.

"Exactly. You didn't know. You weren't in discussions or doing a goddamned thing. You weren't setting up. In fact, you were all sitting at your desks with your thumbs up your asses while this kid from nowhere waltzed into our market."

"Bruce," Richardson said, "let me explain."

"What's to explain? You blew it. Each of you. By tomorrow morning I want plans from all of you on how we're going to stop the little shit dead in his tracks, or by Christ, I'll blow all of you into such little pieces, Ritter will be serving you as appetizers at his new hotels."

* * * * *

The ride to his home in Greenwich usually soothed Bruce Hunt, no matter the amount of traffic or hassles in his day. but tonight the luxury of the backseat and the smoky comfort of a single-malt from the limo's bar did nothing to relax him.

Ritter. They'd spoken before, argued before, and he was reluctantly impressed by the young man's energy and ambition. But as a direct competitor?

True, Metropolitan remained and would remain the largest hotel chain in the nation. The loss of three hotels did nothing to change that. He had other properties, plenty of them, in Los Angeles, New York, and Chicago. But the Hirschberg hotels would have been useful in his new upscale, full-service concept.

Having been an upstart in the industry himself, he knew the threat a smart newcomer represented. Knew that his three top lieutenants would come up with nothing practical in the way of stopping the Dutchman. Knew that if he wanted it done he would have to mastermind the strategy himself. And tonight, that realization gave him a headache. He didn't want another power struggle in business, not when everything at home was so difficult.

He thought of his wife, Carol, suddenly ambitious too, spending more and more time with charities and boards and now demanding a spacious apartment in New York so she could entertain her society friends, "and not be ashamed of the way we're living." Christ! They were already living so high it was like flying without a plane. Who the fuck needed a $4 million co-op at the Beresford when they had the mansion in Greenwich and the condo in Palm Desert?

Carol was getting out of control, and so was their fifteen-year-old daughter, Mary. Already, she was going out with high school seniors, and he was sure their pockets were filled with cash and God knows what drugs. Sure, they were polite enough to his face, but so cravenly horny he thought of them as goats. He could hear her come home after midnight, even on weekday nights, with some boy in tow—hear their laughter, followed by the more ominous silence. Carol and he were unable to stop her—this angel-faced, golden-haired child, once his princess, now somebody else's God–knows-what. Carol told him it wasn't as bad as he imagined, that Mary had sworn she was still a virgin and drug-free. But he didn't believe her anymore, didn't believe anybody or anything anymore.

The car phone rang. "It's me," Carol said when he picked up. "I'm frantic. The school phoned this afternoon. Mary's been cutting classes. If she doesn't pull herself together, they'll expel her."

His stomach lurched. "No way they'll do that, not with the money I've given them."

"That's not the point. Mary's in trouble, and you've got to do something about it."

"Damn it, Carol, you're her mother. You talk to her."

"I've tried," she said, her voice little-girlish in a way he still found irresistible. "Honey, I've tried and tried, but it doesn't do any good. I need you with me. She's our daughter. If we're not united in this, we'll lose her."

After nineteen years of marriage, he was still in love with his wife, and he knew Carol would never ask for his help unless it really was serious. He'd help her, of course; as both of them had acknowledged many times, they were a team. They'd talk to Mary tonight—or, better, after he'd settled this Ritter matter so his mind could be free.

"We'll talk to her this weekend," he promised. "She's a good girl. This is just an adolescent thing, all those teenage hormones raging."

Carol laughed. "Teenagers aren't the only ones with raging hormones, you know."

"Are talking about you or me?"

"I'm talking about we."

He grinned, knowing that tonight, given his present anger, he'd be able to take her with the savagery they both relished. "Hold the thought," he said, "till I get home."

When he hung up, he called Tricia, his secretary. As usual, she was still in the office. "Track down Rolfe Ritter at the Kestrel, San Francisco," he told her. "Make a phone appointment for tomorrow morning so he and I can chat.

$$* \ * \ * \ * \ *$$

The call came at eight o'clock. "It's a Mr. Bruce Hunt for you," the switchboard operator announced.

He's prompt, Rolfe thought. Since waking, he'd spent the morning anticipating what Hunt might say, but nevertheless, his heart was speeding. "Put him through," he said, more confidently than he felt.

"Ritter speaking."

"Rolfe, it's Bruce Hunt. Good morning. I hope I'm not disturbing you." Charm oozed through the receiver like hand lotion.

"Not at all. Your secretary said you'd call. What can I do for you?" He picked up a pen and pulled a yellow legal pad toward him.

"I read about your deal on those Hirschberg hotels."

I was right, Rolfe thought. He must be climbing the walls. He waited for Hunt to continue.

"The properties are in lousy shape."

"I agree that they haven't been looked after as well as they could have been."

"Nevertheless, they'll make great hotels once your man Pemberton has worked his magic."

"I hope so," Rolfe said, enjoying himself. "Otherwise I'm going to look like an idiot."

Hunt laughed, not a pleasant sound. "You'll do fine with them."

More silence. What was this all about? Rolfe wondered. Hunt wouldn't set up a phone meeting just to tell him he read the *Times*.

"Anyway, I just want to congratulate you on the deal. I'm astonished the Hirschbergs sold. From what I know, they're great buyers but lousy sellers. Some day you must tell me how you did it."

"Lucky timing, I guess," Rolfe said.

"There's no luck about it, and you know it. Look, I admit I underestimated you. You've done well with San Francisco, and now you'll do well with the Hirschberg hotels. They're good assets."

Rolfe tapped his pen against the pad. What was coming?

"I remember our first conversation wasn't that pleasant, but given that life is long and the industry small, our paths are bound to cross often, and I thought we should mend fences."

Rolfe kept quiet, the drumbeat of the tapping pen in his ears.

"We should meet," Hunt said. "Do you get to New York?"

"Not much, but it should be more often now that we've started work on the Manhattan property."

"Well, next time you're in town, let's have lunch. Just have your girl call mine so we can set it up."

A new man? Rolfe wondered, or the same old son of a bitch? Maybe he's accepted the fact that I'm here to stay and wants to become allies. And maybe not.

"Lunch would be delightful," he said. "Your hotel or mine?"

On the pad he wrote in capital letters: "BRUCE HUNT—NEW YORK???? BE CAREFUL!!!"

* * * * *

"Stratman? It's Bruce Hunt."

"Yes, sir," the suddenly alert private investigator from the Manhattan firm of Montgomery, Stratman and Kobler answered.

"I need a detailed and absolutely confidential investigation into someone, and I need it quickly. Can do?"

"Can do. Details and confidentiality are our stock in trade, but you know that already."

"Good. The party's name is Ritter, Rolfe Ritter. I'll need everything you can get, public and personal. Everything."

* * * * *

Dear Mike,

Week after next I'm flying to New York, where I'll have lunch with Bruce Hunt. Four months after I bought the San Francisco property, I had a visit with Ben Richardson, Hunt's point man from

149

Metropolitan. The pompous son of a bitch strolled in dressed like a Brooks Brothers mannequin and treated me like an ignorant peasant. He told me the day of the independent hotel was over and that I couldn't survive without an experienced management team, a national sales and marketing organization, a strong reservations system, and the corporate support "only a brand of the caliber of Metropolitan Hotels could offer." He told me they needed another location in San Francisco and hinted Metropolitan would give me a small loan if they would agree to manage the Kestrel for me.

Metropolitan would have to charge management fees, of course, and marketing fees, accounting service fees, technical service fees, purchasing fees, etc.—plus a management fee of 4% of revenues, which he claimed would merely go toward defraying their corporate expenses incurred in building up a great brand, and, in case that wasn't enough, 10% of the operating profits of the hotel.

"So you see," Richardson said, "our motives are truly aligned."

My money, their pockets. Some alignment! I should have told him to take a flying fuck, but instead I asked him to send over his standard management contract and the annual reports and so on for Metropolitan. I wanted to show them to Josh Leonard, so he could cut and paste the best bits for future use. When I saw it, I nearly threw up. It was a greedy, one-sided piece of crap. He must have thought I'd just stepped off the banana boat.

If that's typical of the kind of guy Hunt hires, I'll have to count my fingers after I lunch with the Great Man himself. We started off badly a few years back; now suddenly, he's smiles and snake oil. But maybe I can use him before he uses me. Who knows, something may even come of all this.

Love to Mother, if you speak to her.

Rolfe

* * * * *

"Watch out," Josh warned. He and Rolfe were sitting in Rolfe's office studying the information Richardson had sent over. "Even their sales pitch can't hide what a schemer Hunt is."

Rolfe peered at his second-in-command. Josh had the look of a commander before a battle when his troops are outnumbered. "Tell me."

Josh stood, stretched. "I'll keep it simple. Seems there was once a chain of inns called Metropolitan—you know, competitors to Holiday Inn, mostly franchised. Larry Lucas, its founder, took it public, made a fortune, and mostly got out before the stock fell from twenty-three to three bucks a share. The board eventually replaced him with one of the directors, a guy named Randall Baltringham III, head of a food chain company, but a know-nothing where hotels were concerned. He brought in a New York law firm to help him out. They sent over a thirty-four-year-old partner specializing in real estate financing to head up the team. And that man was—"

"—Bruce Hunt," Rolfe yelled. "Ta-da!"

Josh remained stony-faced. "Hunt must have been one ruthless bastard. He fired anyone associated with Lucas, slashed costs, sold any property that didn't fit his vision, got rid of franchisees left, right, and center, and brought in a team of MBAs, Richardson included, loyal to him alone.

"By 1974, Hunt was chairman and CEO. He split the company into two divisions, one for inns and one for hotels, and changed the name to Metropolitan Hotels. His plan was, and remains, to dominate every sector of the lodging business. So right now full-service hotels, like the Hirschbergs, are his focus."

Rolfe felt a flicker of fear, a flicker of excitement. "I'll sit with my back to the wall."

"One more thing," Josh said. "His team's known as 'Hunt's Panzers' for the way they execute his plans. 'Heil Hunt' seems to be their motto."

"Shit. What have I got myself into?" Rolfe asked rhetorically.

"Want me to go to the meeting with you?" Josh said. "I hate to think of you with that piranha without an ally."

A realization was forming in Rolfe's mind, which made the upcoming meeting with Hunt all the more enticing. If his life was going to be a battle against the best and if the best was already wary enough of him to want a meeting, then he knew which ally he wanted, and it wasn't Josh.

"No thanks. I'll go it alone."

* * * * *

"Cheers, Bud. Good luck on the election." Rolfe raised his glass of wine and clinked it against McCory's half-drunk glass of Jack Daniel's.

"Thanks." The union boss smiled, revealing gold fillings that gleamed in the diffused light of the Kestrel Los Angeles bar. "And thanks for your contribution. The twenty-five grand will come in handy."

"Glad to oblige." Rolfe finished his wine, signaled for another round. "I like how compatible we've become," he said. "After that rocky start, I'm glad we're friends."

McCory roared. "Friends! It's amazing how a little vigorish can make a friendship vigorous." He leaned closer; Rolfe could see the broken capillaries on his cheeks. "Remember, you wanted me to smooth out those union problems in Chicago and New York?"

"Sure."

"I can do it."

Surprise.

"But it'll be expensive," Rolfe said.

Another roar. "Took the words right out of my mouth. Twenty-five for each hotel."

More "contributions," Rolfe knew. Straight into McCory's wall safe. The union man already had the election sewn up. "Sure, Bud, if that's what it takes."

"Consider it done." He gulped the rest of his drink and stood.

Rolfe stood with him and put his arm around McCory's shoulders. "There's one other thing you can do for me."

"Name it, amigo."

Rolfe kept his tone neutral. "I need to find out everything I can about Bruce Hunt."

McCory stopped short and twisted from Rolfe's embrace. He whistled. "That cocksucker's so anti-union it makes me sick. Okay, I'll dig around. It'll be a fucking pleasure. But you sure you know what you're doing?"

"Doing?" Rolfe asked, bland as a headwaiter. "He and I are having lunch next week, and I thought it would be helpful to do a little research so I know what to expect."

* * * * *

"We need to talk," Josh said.

Rolfe glanced up from his desk. "Can't it wait? I'm on my way to the airport."

"I want to say it now. You're not going to like it, and I don't want to keep it bottled up until you get back."

What was that in Josh's expression? Concern? Fear? Suspicion?

"Shoot."

"You've changed, Rolfe. I don't like it. You've got no time for anyone; you don't want advice; you think you have all the answers. This meeting with Hunt is an example. How can I help you if I don't even know what it's about?"

What the hell is he talking about? Rolfe thought, struggling to control his rising anger. He knows I'm killing myself to build up something for us all. "I'll tell you about Hunt after I've had lunch with him. I don't know myself what he wants. Frankly, I resent your attitude. You wouldn't have a job without me."

"And you wouldn't have much without me. I'm the best friend you have, remember. Even God needs friends."

Rolfe stood, shoving papers into his briefcase. "That's all you wanted to talk about?"

Josh met his gaze. "That and the fact that your cockiness will get you in trouble, and I don't want you to drag me and everyone else down with you. Watch out, Rolfe. Hubris is a powerful force."

"Didn't Hubris play linebacker for the forty-niners?"

"It's not a joke," Josh said. "This is me talking."

Rolfe's rage exploded. "And this is me telling you to go fuck yourself!" Rolfe exploded.

Josh's face went red, but his tone remained mild. "That's just what I'm saying. Once upon a time, you'd listen to your friends."

"But today I've got to catch a plane." Rolfe strode outside, stifling an impulse to smash his friend in the mouth.

Arrogant prick, he thought. Even my friends are my enemies. He stood still for a moment, breathing deeply, trying to expunge his rage and disappointment. Remarkably, his hands were shaking.

Josh came out and headed down the corridor. "Have a good flight," he muttered to Rolfe's retreating back.

* * * * *

The meeting with Mary was a disaster. She was sullen, obstinate, and secretive about her nightly whereabouts. Worse, she spoke in a polite but flat voice, as though to guidance counselors or a prying priest. Her father's threats did not move her, nor did her mother's tears. Eventually, with elaborate courtesy, she asked to be excused, and they had no grounds for keeping her. Helpless,

Bruce and Carol Hunt simply stared at her retreating figure.

Hunt went to his study and closed the door. He opened Stratman's report quickly, hoping it would take his mind off his lack of influence over his daughter.

It did more than that. The investigation revealed that:

> Josh Leonard, Ritter's general counsel, was homosexual.
>
> Ritter was a womanizer whose slew of sexual partners included Susan Longbury, Westerman's ex-assistant, and a French woman named Chantal, for whom he'd arranged a hotel job in San Francisco.
>
> Ritter's widowed mother was having an open affair with the head of Dutch intelligence.
>
> Ritter's father was quite possibly a double agent during and after the war, who had been murdered under suspicious circumstances, run down by a car.

Juicy stuff, certainly, and immensely valuable if needed. Hunt put down the report, feeling better. Still, he thought, a little dirty laundry didn't explain how Ritter had progressed so fast at the Audley hotels, particularly with that staid, over-bred Brit, Sir Alan Germaine. Nor how he had shot up like a meteor in San Francisco. Good God! The kid was in his twenties.

There had to be more; Hunt knew it, smelled it. He'd keep Stratman on the case until he dug up what Hunt was looking for.

* * * * *

"Are you alone?" McCory asked when Rolfe picked up the phone in his New York hotel room.

"Yes."

"Good. Listen carefully." The union man spoke rapidly.

"Jesus!" Rolfe said. His stomach tightened as he thought of the meeting to come. "Tell me more."

* * * * *

Rolfe stood in the lobby of the Kestrel Hotel, New York, picturing it not as it was, but as Pemberton had envisioned it: Asian art, Persian carpets, modern Swedish cut-glass chandelier. In six months, it would be the greatest of all the Kestrels, equal to the Plaza and the Pierre—with the ever-present arrangements of calla lilies in the public areas, the smiling young staff, the best French and California wines, a kitchen bettered by none. Moments like these, when his vision was clear, brought him intense happiness.

What would my father think of all this, he wondered, of these magnificent hotels that bear his name.

Rolfe looked at his watch. Hunt was already twenty-five minutes late.

A Mercedes pulled up in front of the hotel, its chauffeur opened the back door, and Bruce Hunt emerged like royalty. He's shorter than I thought, Rolfe noted, meeting Metropolitan's chairman on the outside steps. He felt a chill.

Hunt appraised him with a tightlipped smile. "So, Rolfe, we meet at last. What a pleasure."

"The pleasure's mine."

They walked through the lobby, Rolfe acutely aware of how woebegone it looked. "After lunch, I'd like to show you some model rooms we've set up. I'd like your thoughts."

The short man shook his head. "I'm afraid I haven't got time to be involved in that sort of nonsense. I'm surprised you have. Besides, we have our standard rooms, and that's good enough for me."

Fine, Rolfe thought, he's not interested—or too interested. But why is he so rude? He's the one who asked for this meeting. "Then why don't we go straight into lunch? I've had the chef prepare a special menu for us."

But when Hunt glanced at the menu, he spurned it. "This is far too rich to eat at lunch. I'll have a Caesar salad and an iced tea."

Josh is wrong, he thought. There can't be two Gods, and Hunt's got me beat hands down.

"I asked for the meeting because I want to tell you about Metropolitan's plans," Hunt said without preamble. "We're going to have a Metropolitan economy, mid-scale, or upscale property on every street corner in this country that needs a hotel. After we've done that, we're going to do the same around the world. By the time I'm finished, Metropolitan will be as well-known a global brand as Coca Cola, and we'll have the biggest market share of any lodging brand ever. No one will ever touch us! The stock market will pay us handsomely for 'owning' the market. It's as simple as that!"

This is just a business to him, Rolfe realized with a shock. He's only interested in market share and stock price.

"I hope you understand, hotels are a commodity, a product like breakfast cereals on a supermarket shelf," Hunt said, as if reading his thoughts. "I intend Metropolitan to have most, if not all, of the products on that shelf."

"That's where we differ," Rolfe said. "The Kestrels are based on quality, service, and above all, people. I don't want to dominate the market, I want to lead it."

Hunt grimaced. "A noble ambition. But the game is not about quality, it's about quantity. Distribution. Scale. Market share. With your attitude, you'll never be able to grow a chain."

"I disagree," Rolfe said pleasantly. "What's more, my chain will be made of solid gold."

Fury blazed in Hunt's eyes. "Then you'll go bankrupt. I'm rolling out hotels without the 'quality, service, and people' claptrap. Our hotels are standardized operationally and physically. Every room is cleaned exactly the same way by following our seventy-seven-step standard operating procedure. Everything's run by the book, my book. Clean. Comfortable. Attractive. Whether you're in Atlanta or San Diego, you know what to expect. I don't need hoteliers; I need army sergeants."

The man's nuts, Rolfe thought. From a different planet. He felt suffused with power. If it came to a battle between them, no matter the numbers and the distribution, he knew he would win. "Then you might as well have robots running the hotels. There's no personality or individual flair involved. And first-class customers want just that—class, and they'll pay for it."

"That's your trouble," Hunt scoffed. "You're an idealist, not a businessman. But you'll find out you can't trust a multimillion-dollar business to a manager more interested in a special menu than a balance sheet." His voice was hoarse with intensity. "Don't fall in love with hotels. In the long run, love always kills."

"Wrong, Bruce. Love is what makes life worthwhile."

Bruce Hunt was not used to being contradicted, Rolfe knew, or to being addressed by his first name. He waited for the reaction.

What he got astonished him. "Look, Rolfe," the chairman said affably. "We got off on the wrong foot. This isn't about philosophy; it's about cooperation. We both know it's going to be hard for you to catch up with the big boys like Hilton, Sheraton, and us. It'll simply take too much time and money. You're smart, you've done very well, and I know you and I could work together."

My ass, we could work together, Rolfe thought. You hate my guts, and I'm quickly beginning to hate yours. "It's kind of you to suggest it," he said, "but I've already told Ben Richardson I don't want a management deal."

Hunt smiled. "So Richardson reported." His tone was maple sugar. "You're right, of course. That wouldn't suit your objectives.

No, what I'm suggesting is that we buy your four hotels. We need top-of-the-line hotels, a first-class chain, jewels in our crown. Sell them to us, and you'll make millions."

Stop now? Sell? Is he seriously proposing...

"Here's the exciting part," Hunt went on, a between-us-titans tone replacing the sugar. "I want you to be president of Metropolitan Hotels for Europe, the Middle East, and Africa. You'd be responsible for building a new chain for us, with new standards, concepts, style—just your thing. You'd have a free hand, within reason, and you'd never have to worry about raising capital again." He leaned forward and lowered his voice. "And once you've built the chain, you'd be the obvious man to be my successor."

Rolfe was staggered. In his scenarios, he had expected many things, but not this. It took him a moment to let the words sink in, another few to analyze them. If he sold the Kestrels at age twenty-seven, he'd have enough money to keep him comfortable for the rest of his life. He'd also have a chance to build a line of quality hotels without risk, and he'd be the successor to the most powerful man in the hotel business.

Why am I even considering this? he asked himself. "Within reason" means they'd have me by the balls. "Obvious man" means I'd be in direct line of fire. And I'd be working for a man I loathe. His successor? Horseshit! I'd be lucky to ever see the inside of his boardroom.

"I'm immensely flattered by your offer," he said. "It's very tempting."

Hunt beamed in anticipation, a stalker closing in on his prey.

"But I've got to say no. The timing's wrong, I've got too much left to do, too much left to prove."

Hunt put his glass of tea carefully down in its saucer. "If it's a question of price for the properties . . ."

"No, I'm simply not selling."

"You're making a big mistake. Surely you see that."

"I don't think so. For one thing, I think your strategy's absolutely wrong."

"We can work that out as we go along."

Was he pleading? "For another, you and I both know we couldn't work together for more than a week—"

"I'll give you a five-year contract."

The words came out before Rolfe could stop himself. "And finally, I believe this is all a ploy to get me to sell—and if I ever do sell, it would never be to you." He waited, breathless.

Hunt's face turned dark and in his eyes was a malevolence Rolfe associated with falcons. "You're nuts," Hunt said, the quiet of his voice as menacing as the deadly silence of an approaching hurricane. "You're arrogant, ungrateful, and rude. If you were my child, I'd beat the crap out of you. You think you're hot shit because you've done a couple of deals. But you're going to fall flat on your goddamned face, and it can't come too soon. When it does, and it will, I'll walk all over your back."

He got up, leaning on the table for support, the sinews in his arms trembling. "Somehow, you stole the Union Square when I had a deal with your boss. You've turned me down twice. There won't be a third time. As of here and now, I'll do everything I can to destroy you. And I never fail."

He walked out. Rolfe watched his receding back, noting red earlobes and clenched fists.

I've made an enemy, a vicious one.

* * * * *

On the return flight, he wrote a letter:

> *Dear Susan,*
>
> *My darling girl, I miss you. I just had a meeting with Bruce Hunt, exciting and terrifying, and now all I can do is wish we were together so I could tell you about it. But more, I want to tell you how sorry I am about us. I acted like a fool. Missing you the way I do—with such pain, such longing—makes me realize that no other woman means anything to me—certainly not Chantal. I don't blame you for being angry; I blame myself for provoking that anger. And now I ask forgiveness. Humbly. On my knees. Your ardent suitor.*
>
> *I'll call you. If you hang up on me, so be it. But I want you to know how much I love you and how much I want you back—us back. Oh, the fun we had. Remember? Oh, the fun we could have in the future. Imagine.*
>
> *Your adoring Rolfe*

He mailed it from the airport. He would wait till he was sure it had arrived and then call her.

CHAPTER 16

1975

"I was wrong. I'm sorry," Rolfe said. He and Josh were drinking Chablis in Josh's apartment. The lawyer had been reluctant to see him, and was still chilly. "You should have been at the meeting with Hunt. I behaved like a major league asshole, opened my big yap when I should have locked it tight, and pissed Hunt off to the point where we'll have to fight him for the rest of our lives. All I had to do was listen and flatter him. Instead, I had to prove my balls were as big as his."

Was that amusement in Josh's expression? It was difficult to tell.

"Apology accepted," Josh said. "He'll forget about it soon. We're irrelevant to him."

"You should have seen him. He's like Doctor No, a megalomaniac willing to do anything to destroy a competitor. And I had the audacity to be that competitor and to turn him down."

"So how can he hurt us?" Josh asked, his amusement vanished.

"I have no idea, but one thing's for sure: I'm high on his shit list."

Josh was unfazed. "Then let's go after him."

Rolfe looked at him in amazement. "Are you out of your mind?"

"The best defense is a strong offense. Right now, we have only four hotels, just fleas on the elephant's hide. But what if we actually had a chain? What if we had a brand name as important as Hilton or Sheraton?"

"Well, we don't."

"But we could, if you play it right. Listen, right now you're a one-man band. You make every decision yourself, big or small. That's why I'm so mad at you. But what if you had an organization? Accountants, a sales team, a personnel department, someone to look after the hotels on a daily basis, and most important—"

Rolfe sat forward.

"—a president. Someone to run things managerially, so you can do what you do best: make the deals, be the creative engine, set the standards, motivate people ... lead. Then, you'll see a business grow, and you'll have Hunt shitting in his pants." Josh was pacing now, his excitement infectious.

Fifty Kestrels, Rolfe thought. A hundred! Why not? "I don't need a president," he said.

"If you don't hire one, you'll destroy what you've built so far— or Hunt will. And I won't be around to watch it."

"Oh, yes, you will. I don't need a president, because I've already got one." He stood and put his arm on Josh's shoulder, knighting him. "Yes, you big schmuck—you. You're the only one I trust. You know what needs to be done, and you'll let me be the hotelier, and you'll only be too happy to tell me when you think I'm full of shit. That's what presidents—and true friends—do." He raised his glass. "Mr. Leonard, congratulations on your appointment as president of Kestrel Hotels, Inc."

Josh sat down. "That wine's made you nuts. Let's find a real president. We'll work on it tomorrow when you've sobered up."

Rolfe laughed. "Gotcha! It's easy to be wise when you don't have the responsibility, isn't it? Well, I'll make it easy. It's you or no one."

"You're serious, aren't you?" Rolfe had never seen his friend so dumbfounded.

"And not drunk. The first thing to do is hire top people in every position. If we're going to do this, we'll do it right. Hire that Momo woman, for example. She's crackerjack at operating systems and technology. And then get the others—only the best. Somehow, we'll get the money."

Josh poured more wine for them both. "If you're willing to accept the risk of me running your business, I accept."

"Great!"

"There's only one condition."

"What?"

"You're going to damn well let me be president. Give me the authority I need and don't undermine me, ever. Agreed?"

"Agreed!" Rolfe shouted. "God help us both! God help Kestrel Hotels, Inc."

* * * * *

By 1:00 A.M., the euphoria had disappeared. Unable to sleep,

Rolfe replayed the meeting with Bruce Hunt, and each time the Metropolitan CEO's threats seemed more ominous. It was madness to compete, madness to expand when he already had three hotels that needed refurbishing and repositioning. But Josh was right: It was suicide to stand still.

He thought of his mother, who would urge him to pull back, and his father, who would spur him on. He worried about money, about loyalty, about his own abilities, about how many Murtoch- and McCory-type deals he'd have to make, how many bribes he'd have to deliver, how much more blackmailing he'd be forced to do, how many gutters he'd have to crawl through. I'm alone, he thought. I need someone with me. He picked up the phone.

After seven rings, a "Hello?"

"Susan, it's Rolfe. I need to talk to you."

She hung up.

So be it.

* * * * *

He told Josh about it the next morning.

"You amaze me," Josh said. "Are you so egotistical that you think a woman as hurt by you as Susan will come back because you want her to? That French tail might. So might some of your other bimbos. But Susan, if you haven't noticed, is a lady. A real lady with real pride."

Rolfe hung his head. "Then I've lost her. Is there a chance she'll reconsider?"

"I'll be your Cyrano," Josh chuckled. "Let me try to win her for you."

"How?"

"If I'm president, I'll need someone to be our corporate secretary and take over a bunch of the stuff I used to do. Susan's ideal. You know she's trustworthy, and she handled all kinds of things like this for Westerman. I know she's bored stiff working for some buttoned-down senior executive vice president at Trans-America. How about it?"

* * * * *

"I've been working on Susan for a month," Josh said as they were walking to the bank to arrange a working capital loan. "I think she's ready to join us."

"Really?" Rolfe clutched the umbrella that was protecting them both from the drizzle. "Despite me?"

"She's fed up with her job. Anyway, she told me she felt as if she'd been part of Kestrel from the beginning."

They crossed the street silently. When they reached the bank, Josh stopped his boss with a gesture.

"You need to convince her that you'll treat her as a professional and not hit on her when you're lonely, horny, or drunk. I've promised her, but she wants to hear it from you."

* * * * *

They met for breakfast at the coffee shop in the Trans-America building. When she came in, he saw how drawn she looked, how tired. As usual, she wore a skirt and blouse, having made no effort to dress up for him, he realized. She sat wearily and kept her eyes locked on the coffee cup in front of her, even when a waitress came to fill it.

"Josh and I need you," he said. "He says you might work for us—for him—and I'd like that very much."

"Do you have any idea how much you hurt me?" she asked, her voice so low he had to learn forward to hear her. "Two men in my life, two betrayals. Yours was worse. But I don't hate you, I really don't. Otherwise, I wouldn't be here." She shivered, as though cold. "I hate myself for being an idiot."

"How could you not hate me? I was a shit."

At last she raised her head. "True. But you are who you are, obsessed, restless, unmanageable and self-destructive and, God pity me, exciting. There's no room for a woman in your life, not as a real partner. So in a strange way, I don't take your betrayal personally."

Was it true? he wondered. That he was incapable of a partnership with a woman? He had felt the pain of desertion when Chantal left, but if he'd suffered at all, it was an adolescent suffering, nothing like what Susan had experienced—because of him. "I'm sorry," he said. "For hurting you. For not loving you enough."

"An apology. Good." She brightened, and when she sipped her coffee, her hand was steady. "That's condition one."

"Condition for what?"

"For my taking the job. Isn't that why we're here?"

He had almost forgotten. "Of course. What's condition two?"

"I'll get to it. Shouldn't we have something to eat?"

She was toying with him. Well, let her. He signaled their waitress.

It wasn't until their eggs were placed in front of them that

Susan continued. Whatever playfulness there had been in her was gone. "I've had plenty of time to think," she said. "Night after sleepless night. And here's what I've decided. First, no more serious relationships. I'll go out, have fun, get laid, enjoy myself, but if I feel any emotion coming on, any love, poof, I'll blow him away." Her tone was light, but he could hear the determination behind it. "So what will I do with my life if that part's missing? Work. I'm good at what I do and can get much better. When I said you were exciting, I didn't mean as a lover, but as a visionary. I really do believe you think differently from anyone else in this industry— that you're unique, that Kestrel Hotels will dominate the industry, and they'll be great hotels. If I were an outsider, if I'd worked for Trans-America all my life and only read about you, I'd sense that. Knowing you, though, will make the workplace more dangerous, I'm doubly convinced. By working for Kestrel, I'll find out whether I can be great too."

There was fire in her, fire and ice. It was a mistake to lose her, perhaps the worst he would ever make, and he longed to tell her so, but all he said was, "Why dangerous?"

"Because you might really fall in love with me. But Rolfe, if you do, if you ever once don't treat me as a colleague, as a professional, as a member of Josh's team, then I'm off to Metropolitan, Hilton, or Sheridan." She laughed. "With all that experience working for you, I'd be irresistible." She took a deep breath. "Agreed?"

Tears visited his eyes. He blinked them away. "Agreed."

"Excellent. Your eggs are getting cold."

* * * * *

"One of my senior partners at my old firm told me about a supercharged real estate lawyer in New York. I want to find a way to get to him," Josh told Rolfe as they drove to the airport en route to Los Angeles.

Rolfe sighed. It was the day after his breakfast with Susan, and he felt listless, numb. "What do we need another lawyer for?"

"Because he undoubtedly has great connections in New York. Besides being a fixer, he's a Talmudic scholar, and a little Jewish class won't hurt."

They pulled into the airport's parking garage and found a space. "Why don't you just call him up and ask for an appointment?"

"Because Ron Falkman's so busy he won't take clients unless they come recommended." Josh turned off the ignition. "I wonder if

Lew Levenson knows him. If so, maybe you could call Lew and—"

"That's his name? Falkman?"

"Yup. Ron Falkman. People call him 'the rabbi.'"

"Nobody needs a rabbi more than Lew," Rolfe said. "I'll call as soon as we get to L.A."

Levenson knew Falkman; a meeting with Josh was arranged.

* * * * *

Mike Riverstone hung up the phone and made himself a pot of tea. His godson had surprised him with a call; he had never heard Rolfe so vulnerable. He dialed a number in San Francisco.

"Chantal, it's Mike. I have a job for you."

Her laugh was merry. "Good. I need the cash."

"It's Rolfe again, I'm afraid. I'm worried about him."

Her tone changed. "No. A thousand times no. Rolfe is still an adolescent. All he wants to do is fuck. He makes me feel like a whore."

"Look," Riverstone said sharply, "you've always been happy to take our money. What if I double the fee?"

"For double, I'd even think about fucking you. But you're forgetting one problem. He hates me and won't talk to me."

"Let me think about it."

At eight the next morning, he called back.

"I have a plan."

"Oooh," she said. "Wonderful!"

CHAPTER 17

1975

Dear Son,

How terrible about Susan. You were so high on her, so much in love. What happened? Jan says Chantal played a part in the breakup. You should have listened to me about her. But you don't respect my advice. You won't grow up. When you do, let's hope there's one good woman who'll have you.

Now, Jan tells me Susan's come to work for Kestrel. I don't understand. Please, if you can spare the time, explain to your loving Mother

The letter went unanswered.

* * * * *

"Summit meetings," as Susan called them, were held at 7:30 every Monday morning in Rolfe's office, with she, he, and Josh in attendance. No minutes were kept; no other staff members were present.

Not for the first or last time in the three months since Susan came to work at the Kestrel, "Where are we going to get the money?" topped the agenda for the meeting.

"That son-of-a-bitch Hunt was right," Rolfe complained. "Not only do we have to buy properties in major cities, but we need to set up a proper corporate office, reservations centers, a real infrastructure. To amortize that, we're going to need a lot of hotels."

"Then buy them," said Josh, laughing. "Solve the damn problem in one fell swoop."

"Buy them with what?"

Josh leaned back, his calmness an antidote to Rolfe's anxiety. "If you find the right deal, you know we'll find the capital. God knows what we'll have to give away to get it, but we'll get it."

"Maybe the best place to start is in Europe," Rolfe said. It was an idea he had pondered for some time. "I've done some preliminary investigation. There are good deals possible in Germany, France, maybe even London."

Susan held up a hand. "One step at a time. Right now, we can barely cover the cost of the people Josh is recruiting. Our new head of marketing—Andy McDonald—cost a fortune to lure away from American Airlines, and he's recruiting salespeople as fast as he can. Josh hasn't even hired that Momo woman yet. Who knows what toys and people she'll need."

Josh nodded. "Falkman won't be cheap, even if he agrees to help. He says he's got to meet you first before he takes us on as a client."

All of this meant debt, Rolfe knew. A huge staff and four hotels. It didn't add up. "And our money source?"

Josh grinned. "The bank, you moron, where they keep the money! We'll go to the bank, you'll sign a personal guarantee, and they'll lend us the dough."

Rolfe sat quietly as the implications of Josh's rejoinder sunk in. Never before had he put up his own money; a personal guarantee meant personal risk. A strange feeling fell over him. Suddenly, the atmosphere felt oppressive.

"What about Momo?" he asked. "What's taking so long to hire her?"

Josh leaned forward. "She wants to be sure you're not the cowboy you sometimes appear to be. If you want her, you're going to have to convince her you're serious. I'd bet the same goes for Falkman, too."

Serious. I've taken chances before, Rolfe thought. But nothing like this. Make the move, and I'll be up against the Hunts and the Hiltons, playing high-level poker against bettors with more experience—and infinitely greater cash reserves. Talk about dancing on the head of a pin! What's the worst that can happen? Bankruptcy. Humiliation. Disgrace.

He felt an electric charge travel up his spine, an exhilaration he expected mountain climbers might experience when they look up at the most formidable peaks. "First thing," he said, "is that we blow this town."

"Jesus!" Josh exploded. "What's wrong with San Francisco?"

"Nothing. It's a great city. But we're only here because it's the site of the first Kestrel. It's not a power center. Everyone we hire will have to be imported. And every New York, L.A., or Chicago firm will know we're still hicks."

Susan smiled. It was this kind of enthusiasm, Rolfe knew, that had convinced her to come back. "So . . . New York?" she asked.

"L.A. I like the weather, it's got great domestic and international airline connections, and it's more relaxed than New York. We'll move our headquarters to Century City."

Josh wasn't buying. "Priorities!" he shouted. "The move will cost a fortune, and we've got to concentrate on staff."

"It'll be more expensive to move later," Rolfe said quietly. "And easier to attract staff to L.A."

"You've made up your mind, haven't you?" Susan asked.

Rolfe nodded.

"Then don't fight him, Josh. After all, it's his money."

Josh shrugged. "When?"

"No later than six months from now. You and Susan find the offices."

"Shit!" Josh said.

The meeting was over. But "It's his money" reverberated in his thoughts.

* * * * *

The logs were turning to embers as Bruce Hunt put down the final draft of Metropolitan's annual report. My opening statement's good, he decided. And the picture's terrific. Carol was asleep by now, and the music from Mary's room had long since quieted. She had been staying home lately; perhaps their endless talks were working after all. Peace, he thought, knowing it was temporary and relishing it all the more.

The phone rang.

Please, God, for once let it not be about Mary. He picked up the receiver.

"Bruce Hunt here."

"Mr. Hunt, my name's Bud McCory. I run the Hotel and Restaurant Workers' Union in San Francisco.

Hunt went through his mental Rolodex. McCory. Yes. McCory. Tough. Wildly ambitious. A growing force, soon to be a real national power. I'd better show him where the real power lies.

"Mr. McCory, it's nearly midnight, this is my home, not my office. I suggest you call our general counsel or head of human resources tomorrow to discuss any issues with our San Francisco properties."

"I'm not calling about your business," McCory said coldly.

"Then what?"

"Ritter."

Hunt's brain ached. "Who did you say?"

"Ritter. Rolfe Ritter."

I should hang up now, Hunt thought. There's scum at the other end of the wire. And how did he get my private number?

"Interested?" McCory asked.

"Yes."

"We should talk about him face to face. And soon."

"Call me at work tomorrow, and we'll set up a time to meet at my office."

"No way." The voice was implacable.

"I don't understand."

"The conversation we'll have is not one that should take place in your office or mine. If you're interested, I'll call you on this line tomorrow night, and we'll pick a neutral place to meet. I understand you have a comfortable hotel in Memphis."

"Memphis! Hold on, Mr. McCory. I can't change my schedule to suit you. Who the fuck do you think you're talking to?"

But Bruce Hunt was speaking to a dial tone.

* * * * *

As Rolfe entered Ron Falkman's office on the fifth floor of the office building on 55th and Park Avenue, he thought of his recent conversation with Lew Levenson.

"It's easier to get to the Pope than Falkman," the producer had said. "But if he likes you, he'll open every door in America."

"Sit down," Falkman said now, waving to a chair opposite his paper-strewn desk. "Coffee?"

"No thanks." Rolfe looked around the office. Desk, shelves, floor and side table were all overflowing with books, papers, momentos and files. The walls were covered with photos of Falkman's family, in groups, individually, at bar mitzvahs, at his daughter's wedding. On a shelf were pictures of him with Adlai Stevenson, Dwight Eisenhower, Golda Meir.

"My life in pictures," Falkman said. "And only I can make sense of my private filing system." He indicated the papers.

Falkman was a small man, no more than five foot six, his unlined face belying shocks of wiry white hair. He was trim and wore hand-tailored suit trousers and a monogrammed shirt. Buy the best, Rolfe thought wryly. A wedding ring, no glasses (contacts?), professionally manicured nails, dazzling shoes. A lawyer, maybe. A businessman, definitely.

"Lew told me a bit about you," he said, "but I want your own take on your business and what you think I can do to help you."

It was an opportunity Rolfe relished. As he talked, Falkman took careful notes on his legal pad. When he finished, the lawyer simply stared at him, holding his head on his thumbs, two hands in front of his nose.

"Let me sum up." He fixed his brown eyes on Rolfe. "You're driven, ambitious, obsessed, compulsive, greedy—and that's coming from a man who lives in a city full of greed-driven, over-ambitious, obsessive-compulsive real estate mavens."

Rolfe looked at him curiously. "Mavens," Falkman repeated. "Experts. You're young, you've surprised yourself with your own success; you've taken some shortcuts you're ashamed of. Tough. Put them behind you.

"You're haunted by your own demons. So what? You want your mother to think you are as good as your father. It'll never happen, so move on.

"Finally, you're sure what you want your future to be. It's a big dream, and for the first time you're beginning to believe you can actually do it, but you're still not certain. You want to be admired, even loved, but you're eating yourself up because you've made an enemy of Bruce Hunt. You're frightened of him, and rightfully so. You need a big deal to get you into the big time, but you don't know really how to do it or who to trust, and you're counting on me for introductions and advice."

Rolfe sat transfixed.

"Have I got it?"

God knows how, Rolfe thought. Especially the part about his mother. "Bravo! I knew you were a lawyer, but Lew didn't tell me you're also a psychoanalyst."

"And soothsayer," Falkman said, obviously pleased. "Here's what's going to happen to you. Hunt's going to do everything he can to stop you. He'll badmouth you to everyone in the real estate business, tell your suppliers you're broke, tell your potential lenders you'll stiff them, outbid you on deals even if it means he loses money. It's going to hurt like hell, but you're going to have to suck it up and ignore it. If you make it a personal battle between you and Hunt, you'll lose."

"Jesus. You make the future sound horrible."

"Remember, you're playing in a pool with piranhas," Falkman said calmly. "And you've got two choices: eat or be eaten."

Could there be any question? "I'll need you with me. Will you help?"

Falkman shrugged. "I'd be honored. But I'll only be as loyal to you as you are to me. Never argue about my bills, never lie to me, never twist facts, never try to cheat or manipulate me. If you do, my young friend, you're on your own. You won't like that, I promise. Are we agreed?"

Rolfe felt the lawyer's eyes bore into his soul. "Agreed."

Falkman sighed, as though a great contract had just been signed. "Excellent. Now tell me what you know about the Ainsley Hotels."

The question was so unexpected Rolfe's mind went blank. Then he remembered. "Good locations. Tired, old fashioned. I really haven't given them much thought."

"Well, think about them now. They're clients of one of my partners. Sixteen hotels, five thousand rooms. They're in major markets: Washington, Miami, Boston. And secondary ones like Detroit, Philadelphia, and Minneapolis. Think you could handle them?"

"Convert them to Kestrels?" Rolfe was conscious of the pounding of his heart. "Hell, yes!"

"My partner and I have been discussing the possibility ever since I first heard you wanted to see me," Falkman continued smoothly. "Steve Ainsley, their founder, died last year, and his son, John, is making a real mess of things."

Rolfe moved to the edge of his chair.

"If you think it's a fit, we'll see if John has any interest in selling. He's got tax problems, and we may be able to structure something for them that works out for you as well."

Rolfe jumped up. "What do I have to do?"

Falkman smiled condescendingly. "Nothing, dear boy. Leave it to me. I'll be in touch."

* * * * *

Bud McCory was sitting in shadows at the back of the restaurant. He's obviously been watching me from the minute I walked in the door, Hunt thought, and sensed at once this would be a formidable adversary—or ally.

McCory waved him over, and the men shook hands. A glass of scotch sat at Hunt's place.

"McAllens," McCory said. "Your brand, I think. Me, I'm an Irish whiskey man myself. Could never cotton to the refined stuff.

170

I guess it's in my genes."

How did he find out my favorite drink? Hunt wondered. "What about Ritter?" he asked.

McCory chuckled, but said nothing.

Hunt's anger flared. "Mr. McCory, I've flown over a thousand miles at enormous inconvenience to see you. So please don't screw with me; just tell me what you want."

McCory downed his whiskey in a gulp. "Now, that's not the way to start a conversation with your new best friend," he said, his brogue exaggerated, like an Irish comedian's.

"I'm here for information, not friendship."

McCory was unfazed. "You can't have one without the other."

"Okay, okay. We're friends."

"That's better. Have your drink, and we'll talk."

Hunt sipped.

"I know you don't like unions," McCory said. "In your position, I wouldn't either. But I'm willing to bet you dislike that fucking punk Ritter more."

Was this some kind of set-up? Why was McCory so eager to communicate his dislike to a man he'd never met. "Let's assume that I don't like Ritter," Hunt said. "What's the point of this meeting?"

"Simple. I can help you get information on him that you can use whenever you want. Together, we can destroy him."

I shouldn't be here, Hunt thought. I'm not a conspirator; there's something fishy. "Why would you want to destroy Ritter?" he asked.

McCory signaled for another round of drinks. "Same reason I want to help you."

"And that is?"

"Money!" McCory roared. "Boatloads of fucking money." He lowered his voice. "Ritter thinks he's my friend. I do some small stuff for him. He thinks—and he's right—that I can fix things. So, with you, it's a simple proposition: The more money you give me, the more information on Ritter I'll get you, and the more I'll fix things."

"Fix things?"

"Don't pretend to be naïve. You know what I'm talking about; you just don't want to fucking well admit it."

Oh, dear God, Hunt thought. This lunatic is serious. "Even if I wanted to agree, how would I get the money to you? You know how tough it is to do that in a public company."

"Not so tough. There's a respectable law firm here in Memphis. You'll pay them a monthly retainer for 'advisory work.' The amount doesn't really matter to you, does it? We'll both get what we want."

Hunt could almost taste the pleasure of ruining the Dutchman's life. "All right. I want to know everything about Ritter's plans. What deals he's looking at, how much he's paying, who he's trying to hire—anything you can find."

"Simple enough." McCory's voice had dropped to a whisper, and the brogue was gone. "Do we have a deal?" He offered his hand.

Hunt shook it. "I've got to go," he said, feeling suddenly as if he was covered with vermin. "When will I hear from you?"

"When you've paid the first invoice."

"Fine," Hunt gasped, and fled from the restaurant.

* * * * *

McCory watched him go, smiling. He pulled a tiny cassette recorder from his pocket and pressed the stop button. "You're mine," he said to himself. "Now, I've got both of you."

CHAPTER 18

1975

Rolfe came back from New York, jetlagged but adrenaline-high, to find that his office had been trashed. His desk drawers lay empty on the floor; his filing cabinet's lock was broken, files strewn about haphazardly; a picture of his mother lay face-down, its glass frame smashed as though in fury. The couch's pillows were thrown about the room; the Jim Dyne lithographs were forcibly yanked off the walls; the carpet had been pulled up at the corners. There was, Rolfe knew, nothing valuable for the burglars to find—he kept his confidential files in his home safe—but the sight sent a shock through his body as though he had been physically assaulted.

"Mine's just as bad." Susan was standing in his doorway, her face grim. "And Josh's. He isn't in yet, but I looked." She came in unsteadily and sat on the chair facing his desk. "It doesn't look like they took anything. The important files are locked in the file room, but they didn't touch them. Weird."

"It's a warning." Rolfe was sure of it. "Whoever did this, and it's easy to guess who, was sending a message."

"Hunt?" Susan asked.

"Who else?"

"What are you going to do?"

"I don't know. But I do know he isn't going to scare us off. And if Hunt is behind this, it's only because we've scared him."

* * * * *

"Ted?" Josh called, walking down the hallway of his high-rise apartment.

"In the kitchen."

When Josh entered, he found the designer sitting at the kitchen table, head in hands, an almost empty vodka bottle in front of him.

"Ted! What's wrong?"

Pemberton looked up. His eyes were rimmed in red. "Forgive me. I've done something terrible. I should have told you earlier."

Alarm coursed through Josh's brain like mercury. "Told me what?"

Ted inhaled. "About three weeks ago I had a call in the office from someone who wouldn't give his name. It was a man with a deep voice. Chilling. 'Pemberton, we know all about you and Josh Leonard,' he said. 'We know you're lovers.' 'So what?' I said. The man seemed to spit the next words: 'We know your boyfriend hasn't told Rolfe Ritter, and he's the one giving you Kestrel business.'" He started to sob.

Josh put his arm around Ted's shoulders. "It'll be okay," he said, knowing it wouldn't. Bile ate into his stomach.

"No, it won't. It gets worse."

Josh paused for a second. "Go on."

"He said 'they' would keep our secret if I told them what projects I was working on for Kestrel. Deals, conversions of hotels, plans for new hotels. That kind of thing."

Josh's ears were filled with a pounding noise. "What did you do?"

"I wanted to protect us!"

"What did you do?"

A whisper, "I gave them what they asked for."

"Oh shit!"

"He said they'd ruin you. Make sure Ritter fired you and that neither of us would work again if I didn't do what they said."

Disgust and dread mingled in Josh's mind. "There's something else, isn't there?"

Ted nodded. "He said if I said one word to you or anyone, I'd have difficulty walking again, let alone hold a pencil."

Josh struggled to digest the news. "Why now?"

"What do you mean?"

"You said the man called three weeks ago. Why wait to tell me until now?"

"I had another call from him this afternoon. What I was feeding him wasn't enough—and really, I don't know more than the three new Kestrels. So they said I had to get you to give me information, look at the papers you bring home, make you talk about things over dinner and after, after—"

"After what?"

Ted choked. "He said, 'after you sucked your boyfriend's dick dry.'"

Josh took Ted's hand and kissed it. "What did you say?"

"I told him I'd do it, but he had to promise it'd be the last time."

"And did he?"

"He just laughed. 'We own you,' he said and hung up." Ted paused. "What's going to happen to us?"

"We'll be all right," Josh said, thinking of his trashed office. "I need to think about it, that's all."

"What do I do in the meantime?" He crossed his arms on the table and laid his head against them.

Josh stroked his hair. "Do nothing. If they call again, stall them. Meanwhile, know this in the depth of your heart: I love you."

* * * * *

Momo was already at the bar when Rolfe entered the Century Club, a long glass in her hand.

"Bloody Mary?" he asked.

"Virgin," she said. "Do I need alcohol for this lunch?"

Rolfe took in her black trouser suit and long black hair, its sheen reflected in the noontime sun seeping through floor-to-ceiling windows. No, but maybe I do, he thought. Her beauty was staggering.

"Let's go to the table," he said.

She ignored his outstretched hand and preceded him to a window table overlooking Sunset Boulevard. They both ordered the tiger prawn salad and iced tea. Rolfe watched her closely. There was a slight tremble in her lips, a demureness in her downcast eyes, and he wondered if she were nervous.

Hardly. "Is something wrong?" she asked. "Dirt on my nose?"

"No," he said, realizing he'd been staring. "It's just—"

"Realizing I was a woman, not just a computer geek?"

"Not at all," he said, though she had read his mind.

"You're not the first, if that's any consolation," she said seriously. "It's a problem for women like me. We can't be professional and feminine at the same time."

Now, she was deliberately appraising him.

"I can imagine. It must be a male-dominated world at IBM."

She smiled. "I don't know why they hired me. I suppose they saw how well I'd done at MIT and thought Momo was a man's name."

Her olive-skinned cheeks showed symmetrical dimples, and her large, black, almond-shaped eyes twinkled. "Imagine their surprise when I turned out to be a single, half-Japanese woman who towered over most of them."

"I was impressed by your work," he said. "You were a lifesaver when we were setting up."

"I'm glad."

"Josh Leonard was impressed too. He suggested I try to hire you."

"Yes. I gathered that was the purpose of the lunch."

"I'm planning to grow the company," Rolfe said. "We need a far more sophisticated communications system, inter- and intra-office, and I'll need a director of communications once we're running."

She shook her head. "'Once you're running?' I thought you wanted me for the one project. If it's full-time, I'll have to decline. I'm afraid I can't leave Los Angeles."

Why? Rolfe wondered. A man? "But you're willing to give up the IBM job."

She laughed. "I was going to anyway. They may have hired a woman, but there's no way they'll let her advance."

He looked at her steadily, relishing the thought of her presence in the office. "Then it's only that you wouldn't come to San Francisco?"

"Exactly."

"Well, what if we came to you? What if Kestrel moved to L.A.?"

She stared at him for a moment, obviously trying to see if he was joking. "You'd move your office just to hire me?"

"Absolutely." He grinned. "Though, actually, I'd planned to come here before I knew you were available."

Her laugh was full-throated; he saw the slight sway of her breasts under the suit. "You have a reputation as a good hotelier," she said, "and I've seen your openness to new systems. You're smart. But I have some questions about your business before I can give you an answer."

He was astonished how quickly she had taken over the conversation. Wasn't he supposed to be evaluating her? "Shoot."

"I'd like to understand your long-term vision and objectives, how you plan to execute the strategy, and your timetable for growth."

"That's all?" he asked facetiously. "What about the meaning of life."

"Only when we get to know each other better. Right now, I'm interested in how well you're capitalized, how you intend to pay for the organization you're building—to say nothing of the new offices—and where you're getting the money to buy new hotels."

Rolfe told her as much as he could and watched her absorb the information. Their salads came and were eaten; they had melon sorbet and coffee for desert. All the while, she asked and watched and processed, and he found himself talking more excitedly than he had since he'd described his dreams to his mother some ten years before.

"All right," she said. "I'll join you. Assuming we can work out salary and title."

He didn't know whether he liked her assertiveness or resented it. Both, probably. "Eighty-five thousand a year. Communications director," he said.

"One-twenty-five. Senior vice president." There was no hostility in her tone; she was stating facts. He watched her, considering.

"I want to sit on your executive committee be involved in all aspects of the company," she continued. "I think I'll have ideas and concepts not confined to communications systems, and I want to express them directly to those who count. When it comes to communications, I want the freedom, money, and authority to put in leading-edge technology everywhere it's needed."

She sat back, totally at ease, waiting.

"That's it?" Rolfe asked, stunned.

"For the time being. Please understand, I respect what you've accomplished so far. I like Josh Leonard and think I can work well with him. I know I'm good at what I do, but I'm equally convinced I can do more. If my move from IBM is to make sense, it's got to be upward. I want to grow as Kestrel grows; that's what makes the job attractive."

Attractive. The word stuck in his brain. She stood. "You don't have to make a decision now. Let's say you'll have an answer for me by Monday. Okay?"

He felt as if he had been hit by Mohammed Ali, but the blows hadn't hurt. "No need to wait," he said. "The job's yours."

She held out her hand. He rose to clasp it, realizing he was smiling idiotically. "Good," she said. "I'll fly to San Francisco tomorrow to talk to Josh and meet the rest of your people, then officially start when you move to L.A."

"I look forward to it," he said, and bent to kiss her cheek, but she was already walking toward the exit.

* * * * *

Josh came into his office two weeks later. "I need to talk to you."

Rolfe was putting papers into his briefcase. Boxes were stacked in his office in anticipation of the move. "Can't it wait? I've got a date tonight."

"It's urgent."

The dire tone of Josh's voice made Rolfe look up. His friend's face was ashen.

"I'm resigning," Josh said.

"What?"

"Effective immediately." It was obvious Josh was struggling not to break down.

"Your resignation is not accepted," Rolfe said sharply. "Now, for Christ's sake, tell me what this is about."

"Please don't push me," Josh pleaded. "Just let me go." He sat heavily on Rolfe's couch.

"Don't be ridiculous," Rolfe said. "I'm your best friend. Tell me. There's nothing so bad we can't handle it together."

Josh bowed his head. Rolfe made no effort to push him. Finally Josh said, "Metropolitan beat us out of two management contracts last week."

"True. And it's infuriating. But it's the luck of the draw."

"It wasn't luck," Josh mumbled.

Rolfe suddenly felt cold. "Go on."

Josh took a deep breath. "There's a lot you don't know about me. About my personal life."

"I don't pry. I know that you and I, together, are Kestrel, and that without you, Kestrel doesn't exist."

"I'm gay."

Relief flooded like a cooling breeze. "That's why you're leaving?"

"Yes."

"Susan was right!"

Josh winced. "How the hell did she know?"

"She didn't. She heard a rumor from someone at First National. You know how uptight those guys are."

"Why didn't you tell me?"

"Because I don't give a shit. If they're not going to lend us money because a member of our staff's homosexual, fuck 'em."

"Most banks feel that way."

"Then fuck 'em all. Besides, if the deal means money to them, they'll work with us no matter what. And as for me, this is 1975, not 1875. What possible difference does it make to me who you take to bed?" But he thought back to Murtoch. If homosexuality was so dangerous to him, maybe Josh felt the same way. He remembered, too, the sensation of making love to a man. Horrible. How could anyone voluntarily...?

"I only take one lover to bed," Josh said, grimacing.

Rolfe waited. Josh was silent. "Okay, I'll ask. Who?"

"Ted."

"Ted?" This was too much. He couldn't digest it. "Our Ted?"

Josh smiled wryly. "Our Ted. If I'd told you about us, would you have given Ted the work in the first place?"

"Probably not. I don't believe in nepotism. But I did, and he's done a great job, and if we get the Ainsleys, he'll design those, too." He felt a spasm of fear. "What does any of this have to do with your resignation?"

"Because Ted's being blackmailed, and I'm trying to protect us."

Rolfe felt as if he were swimming upstream. "Blackmailed?"

"I'll spell it out for you. I've told Ted about what's going on here—pillow talk. When the blackmailers couldn't get what they wanted from our files—surely you remember the break-in—they nailed Ted. And now they've told him to get more information from me, or else. They've threatened him physically."

"Fuck!" Rolfe tried to reconcile it. Fury turned to resolve. "You stupid schmuck," he said to Josh. "Next time, tell me about anything that affects our work. But you're not going anywhere. Tell Ted he's still the best designer in America, and we use only the best. And tell him that when the blackmailers call, give them my number. Don't worry. They won't touch Ted. There's no point."

Josh looked up. "Are you sure?"

"Absolutely," Rolfe answered, more confidently than he felt. "One last thing. We can't keep secrets from each other. For God's sake, trust me."

"Rolfe, I—"

He held up his hand. Josh's gratitude moved him and filled him with shame. Josh slept with a man out of love, while he...

Both men stood and embraced, and Josh silently left the room. Rolfe sat back at his desk, staring vacantly at the papers he had prepared to take home. He knew, of course, who the blackmailer was. Rage returned, with it an unslakable urge for revenge.

Hunt.

* * * * *

The limousine passed the United Nations building on its way

downtown, but Rolfe was too intent on what Ron Falkman was saying to concentrate on the usually inspiring sight.

"Let me get this straight," he said, still not believing. "You and your partners have persuaded John Ainsley to sell me the Ainsley hotels for one-hundred-fifty-six million?"

"It hasn't changed since I told you thirty seconds ago," Falkman said patiently. "Granted, we've got to play some tax deferral games in the deal's structure, but that's basically it."

Rolfe started to chuckle. "At $30,000 a room, it's an incredible deal. How'd you swing it?"

"Trust me, it's a good deal for John too. You both serve each other's purposes." Falkman clutched his battered briefcase on his lap.

"Still, where am I going to find that kind of money? I can't keep going back to Lew and Mark."

They passed the Fulton Street Market. "I keep telling you: trust me. We're going to meet Dan Davison at Waring, West and Golden. I sent him the numbers, and he'll find you the capital. He's expensive, but worth it."

"How expensive?"

Falkman sighed. "You'll find out soon enough."

* * * * *

The investment banker was resplendent in gleaming white shirt and red suspenders. His thirty-seventh-floor office over-looked the Statue of Liberty. But it was he who carried the flame, Rolfe thought. The red hot flame of money.

"To sum up," Davison said, "you need one-hundred-fifty-six million to buy the hotels, fifteen million to refurbish them and to pay closing costs, another five mil on top; that's a total of one-hun-dred-seventy-six million. I'll arrange mortgages for one-hundred-thirty-two million, which means, if my math's correct, you'll need forty-four million in equity."

Your math's been correct since you learned to talk, Rolfe thought, noting the look that passed between Falkman and the broker. He felt manipulated, rushed into something he didn't understand. "What was the extra five million for?"

Davison seemed offended. "My fees will be just over three mil-lion—about six percent of the equity. The balance, nearly two mil-lion, is pocket change; you'll need it sooner rather than later." He brushed his hand through his thick brown hair and glared at Rolfe through frameless glasses.

"The fees are fine, Rolfe," Falkman assured him, sensing Rolfe's shock. "Standard. Besides, Dan's going to find you all of that forty-four million."

Davison placed a spiral-bound green book in front of each of them. "The mortgages are easy, but in order to get the rest, you're going to have to put up everything you've earned from the existing Kestrels and personally guarantee it." He turned to the final page. "As you can see, it's expensive money, but if you're as good a hotel man as your reputation says you are and if the numbers Ron sent me are correct, you'll squeeze through."

"And if I don't 'squeeze through?'" Rolfe asked, the overload of adrenaline in his stomach making him ill.

Davison smoothed his hair where he had tousled it. "You lose everything. But I still get my three-point-one million. It's paid upfront."

* * * * *

On the flight home, Rolfe remembered Bouchard's warning about Icarus. If the hotels failed, his wings would melt and he would plummet back to earth, ruined. He remembered the smells and sounds of his life as a kitchen boy and suddenly felt immeasurably young, a boy. An imposter. Yet, to back out now would be to lose Davison's and Falkman's faith—and once lost, he knew, it would be irretrievable. The taxi taking him back to his apartment felt like a prison. He could barely breathe.

It was twilight when the taxi pulled up. He paid the driver, grabbed his overnight bag, and stepped out. A blow smashed his shoulder, and when he wheeled to see what had happened, another hit the side of his head. He reeled back, looking for purchase, desperate for help. A third blow sent him sprawling to the sidewalk, and he saw a man standing over him, features indistinguishable in the dusk, arm raised to strike again. In his agony, he could not tell whether the man was wearing a mask. He called out, but his throat had been hit and no sound came. When he tried to bring up his hand to shield his face, he knew his arm was broken, and all he could do was curl himself into a fetal position and wait for death.

A woman screamed, "Stop! Help! Police!" She flung herself at the attacker, pummeling her fists on his chest, still screaming.

"Fuck!" his attacker grunted.

Others had heard the woman, and now the street was filling with people.

"Get him!" a man cried.

The assailant shoved the woman off him, turned, and fled, but Rolfe could not take in whether he had gotten away. His brain was foggy; his eyes clouded, and he closed them against the meager light. He seemed made of pain.

"Call an ambulance," the woman yelled, and knelt beside him.

He knew the voice, but it came from another place, another time, another life, and he could not place it. The woman bent to kiss his forehead. He fought to open his eyes. A specter. Chantal.

CHAPTER 19

1975

Rolfe awoke in a hospital room, feeling drugged and disoriented. His wristwatch had broken in the attack—he remembered that detail, although little about the beating itself—and there was no clock in the room. To judge from the silence surrounding him, it was the middle of the night, but he couldn't be sure. He was, surprisingly, in little pain, though there was a cast on his left arm and his ribs were tightly bound in bandages. He was shot full of painkillers, he realized, his discomfort only a slight headache and fierce thirst.

The door opened. A nurse looked in on him.

"I'm awake," he called out. "What time is it?"

"Three-thirty." Her voice was low, muffled, heavily accented. Eastern European?

"Could you turn on the light?"

She did. He was in a single room. White walls. A landscape print in a thin aluminum frame. A door to the bathroom. A night table. Two hard, straight-backed chairs. A window with the shade drawn. On the ledge, a vase of flowers.

The nurse brought him water from the night table, and he sipped it insatiably. "How badly am I hurt?"

"Not bad." The same, husky voice. As though she had a cold. "Broken arms. Ribs. No concussion."

"When can I get out?"

"One day. Maybe two."

He breathed deeply in relief. The nurse switched off the light and sat by his side on the bed. What was this? She pulled down the sheet, drew aside his hospital pajamas, leaving him exposed.

"What the hell are you doing?"

She began to stroke him and with her other hand unbuttoned her uniform, and then brought his hand to her uncovered breast.

He began to laugh. "Chantal!"

"Hush," she said. "Just enjoy. I've read many times that this was a common American fantasy." She was using her real voice now.

"How did you get in here? How come you were at my house when I was attacked? Why was—?"

She took him in her mouth, exerting an on-and-off pressure no other woman in his experience had learned so well. His questions stopped, he closed his eyes while his ecstasy mounted, and he knew that he was addicted. She was his heroin, his Circe, his initiator, the ideal of his fantasies, the best, the perfect, the supreme...

Ahhhh.

* * * * *

Later she told him she had just returned to San Francisco and was coming to see him in hopes that he would take her back, when she happened on the attack and was able to intercede. Glorious coincidence. As for tonight, it was simple enough for her to buy a nurse's uniform and slip past a sleepy night watchman. He used to like it when she played nurse, and she thought this would amuse him.

Yes, he acknowledged, he was amused.

He would spend the rest of his hospital stay pondering how best to return the favor. But right now, could she—?

No, no. She had to go. Besides, he mustn't be greedy.

She left laughing, and soon he was asleep, to be awakened in the morning by a distinctly different nurse bearing breakfast. The effects of the painkillers had worn off; walking the few steps to the bathroom was an agonizing adventure, and he found going back to bed did little to relieve the ache in his sides and shoulder. His mind burned with rage at Hunt; he wanted his revenge. But his cast and bandages made him feel powerless.

A visit from Josh and Susan revived his spirits, and when they left and he could think less about Hunt and more about the future, he did so with an optimism that was a welcome change from his dark thoughts of the day before. He might have been flying close to the sun, but it exuded a welcome warmth.

* * * * *

Susan threw the first page of the *San Francisco Chronicle* on Josh's desk. "Shit!" she said.

"And good morning to you, Susan." Josh picked up the paper. "What's put you in such a good mood?"

"Bottom right-hand corner," she growled.

"'Hotel magnate in distress, saved by damsel,'" he read. "'Kestrel CEO Rolfe Ritter was attacked outside his apartment by an unknown assailant at ten forty-five last night. In a dramatic rescue, French hotel executive Chantal Le Peron...'"

He paused to look at the picture at the side of the article. Rolfe lay on the sidewalk, Chantal kneeling beside him like Florence Nightingale, an ambulance in the background, a police officer looking on.

"Shit!" he said.

They looked at each other.

"The bitch is back."

CHAPTER 20

1976

Rolfe wrote to his mother.

The good news is that we bought the Ainsleys.

The bad news is that they're eating us alive. Last week Ted Pemberton told me that the $15 million we budgeted is only half what we'll need to do the job right. There's no other way. I have a clear image of what a Kestrel should be, so there'll be no compromises on décor, quality, or service, not now or ever. If a Kestrel Hotel ever looks like a Metropolitan Hotel, it would mean someone else is running the company.

Then Susan waltzed in and told me she needed to hire three people to handle our internal audit function. I blew up, told her they were unnecessary. She said I was naïve. Me, naïve?

Andrew McDonald, our marketing director, laid out a convincing case for opening sales offices in New York, Washington, L.A., London, Frankfurt, and Tokyo. I said why not Ethiopia and the moon? He said they could wait.

I've had to crawl back to Davison for more increasingly expensive cash. Luckily, the new Kestrels are flourishing, and even the Ainsleys as they now stand are just about breaking even.

Momo Takenaka's been a godsend. She has the most amazingly logical mind! But like everyone else here, she wants the latest technology and only hires the best (viz, most expensive) people. And no, don't ask. She gets on better with Susan and Josh than with me.

The truth is, I'm seeing Chantal again. But before you take the cyanide, it's nothing serious. Just a salve for the libido. She has absolutely no interest in anything

other than a casual relationship. I promise.
Do let me know how you and Jan are. I miss you.
Your loving son

Rolfe put down his pen and reread the letter. Cool and dutiful, he thought, like a good newspaper. He wondered if his mother would ever let him close to her again, or if he would want that closeness if it were offered. Screw it. As with mother, so in life: go it alone.

He thought back to his phone conversation with McCory after the attack. "I've been asking around," the union chief said. "No one knows who the assailant was."

"Hunt," Rolfe said bitterly. "Someone hired by Hunt."

McCory hesitated. "I'm not sure. Why would he attack you?"

"He wanted to kill me."

"It's not his M.O. God knows he's competitive, but he'll try to beat you financially and logistically."

"Maybe. But it wasn't a coincidence that I was attacked. Someone was waiting outside my apartment and knew I was coming home that afternoon, and nobody hates me enough to do that except Hunt."

"Do you think he'll try again?" McCory asked.

"I don't know." Rolfe's hand holding the receiver was damp with sweat. "But it sure scares the shit out of me. Did you dig up anything more on him that I can use?"

"Not on him directly," McCory said. "This guy leads the life of a monk. But his daughter, Mary, the fifteen year old? Well, that's another story. Seems like she likes pills, weed, and sex, not necessarily in that order."

* * * * *

"Put Mr. Vermeij in the conference room," Hunt instructed his secretary. He scanned the confidential folder on his desk. Get the facts on Ritter, and you wind up finding out about someone else as well. I'll bet those two despise each other, he thought.

In Pieter Vermeij's rise at Amstelveen Bank, he'd made several deals for his clients with Hans Steinmann of Solveng Hotels, and at the moment Solveng Hotels were Hunt's main preoccupation. He waited long enough to let Vermeij sweat, and then strolled into the conference room, where the Dutch banker had set up charts for a presentation on Amstelveen Bank's qualifications to represent Metropolitan in Europe.

As the banker talked, Hunt studied him carefully. Not as tall as Ritter and stockier, but similar blond hair and blue eyes—typically Dutch. Vermeij was dressed conservatively in a custom-tailored suit, and his watch was solid gold with a crocodile skin band. He spoke fluent English, and his command of the figures was exemplary. A valuable ally, Hunt considered. Just the man I'm looking for.

"Very interesting, Pieter," he said when the banker finished. "I'm sure we'll be able to do business." He looked at his chief financial officer and treasurer, both signaling their agreement. But then, when did they not?

"For starters," he went on, "I'd like to retain you to represent Metropolitan in acquiring Solveng Hotels. Are you interested?"

The Dutchman's stoic features masked what must have been pleasure. Large fees would be involved. "Interested? Of course. I know Hans Steinmann well. He's getting older, and I hear his daughter, Dagmar, is pressing him to sell. Steinmann's headquarters are in Munich. If we set up a meeting for week after next, your timing might be perfect."

Hunt beamed. Perfect, he thought. For more reasons than you'll ever know.

* * * * *

"Hunt's excited about a deal in Europe," McCory said to Rolfe over the noise at a Lakers game. Rolfe was spending more and more time in Los Angeles as the day of the move approached, and he had made it a point to suck up to the union boss.

"What deal?"

"Don't know yet, but I'll find out." The game was tied, and the crowd was roaring. Basketball—all American sports—bored Rolfe, but McCory had insisted on this venue and supplied the tickets.

Some Laker named Kareem, who seemed to be a particular favorite, made a shot from a long distance and the roars increased. Rolfe put his hands over his ears. "I can't stand it here anymore," he said. "Just let me know what you find out as soon as possible."

"Lucky you put me on retainer," McCory shouted when Rolfe stood. "Otherwise, this stuff would cost you a fortune."

Rolfe shook his hand. "I'm grateful for everything, Bud. You know I am." It was difficult to tell if McCory heard him. The union man was engrossed in the game.

* * * * *

"A stroke of genius," Vermeij told Hunt as the chartered Gulfstream 2 took off from Munich for Amsterdam. "To have offered Steinmann the chairmanship of Metropolitan in Europe and invite him on your main board—brilliant. You probably brought the price down by a million dollars."

Hunt preened. "Do you think he liked the offer?"

"Liked it? It's perfect. He gets cash, stock in Metropolitan, respectability, publicity, and suddenly he's a transcontinental jet-setter."

"When do you think he'll give us an answer?"

"I'll invite him and his daughter to the bank's guest house on Lake Como for the weekend. I should be able to wrestle an answer from him there."

"Tell me about his daughter."

"A bit wild, I understand. Not particularly attractive, unless you like Amazons. Every time I've seen her, she's been with her father, but I hear she's got lots to say in the nightclubs when he's not around."

Hunt digested the news, thinking of Mary. Nothing unusual here. "The financing's arranged?"

Vermeij laughed. "I've told you a dozen times, don't worry about it. We'll sell the hotels to Dutch and German pension funds, and Metropolitan will lease them back."

The G-2 started its descent. Hunt fastened his seatbelt. Ritter will be sick when he finds out that his childhood friend helped make Metropolitan the market leader in Europe, he reflected. I'll have to spend a lot of time in Europe when that happens. Carol will like it, and it'll be good to get Mary away as often as we can. St. Moritz, Royal Ascot, the Aga Khan's place in Sardinia. Maybe I'll buy a place in Cap Ferrat or Antibes. It'll make up for not buying the new condo in Manhattan.

* * * * *

"So that's the plan," McCory summarized for Rolfe. "Metropolitan leases the Solveng hotels and suddenly has a real presence in Europe." The two men were in a limo crawling toward LAX, where McCory would catch his plane.

"You're positive?"

"Am I ever fucking wrong?"

"Sorry," said Rolfe distractedly. He stretched his shoulders, sometimes still sore from the attack of more than a year ago. The Ainsley hotels were running smoothly now; profits were higher now than even he had anticipated.

"Are you going after the deal?"

Am I? Rolfe wondered. Should I? Does it make business sense, or am I just trying to fuck Hunt. "What do you think?"

"I'd have thought you'd want a look in. What have you got to fucking lose?"

What indeed?

"By the way," McCory continued, "if you get this deal, it'll cost you. Informants in Europe are expensive going in, and I've promised my man a big fucking bonus."

* * * * *

"Anything the matter?" Chantal asked. They were sitting on the patio of the Bel Air Hotel, where Chantal had been hired as the new marketing director. "You seem distracted."

Rolfe didn't respond. He was thinking about Steinmann and the Solveng hotels.

"Don't worry," she said. "I have some new toys for us to play with. They'll take your mind off your troubles."

Ordinarily, the news would have excited him. "I'm sorry," he said. "Not tonight." He wondered how much he dared confide to her.

Hell, he thought. If I can get it off my chest, maybe I'll enjoy the toys. "Metropolitan's about to buy a company in Europe. If they do, they'll be so far ahead of Kestrel over there that I don't know whether we could ever catch up."

She put her hand on his thigh. "What company?"

"Solveng Hotels. Ever hear of them?"

"Of course. I even met Steinmann once years ago, and that awful daughter of his. He planning to sell?"

Ten minutes later, he'd told her all he'd learned from McCory. "What should I do?" he asked.

"Buy them yourself, naturally." She finished her drink. "But for tonight, you're coming with me."

He followed her eagerly.

* * * * *

"Thanks," Mike Riverstone said when Chantal had finished her report. "That young man's in too far over his head. He's about to drown, only he doesn't know it."

"Don't underestimate him," Chantal said. "He's got a good head on his shoulders." A great head, she thought, remembering last night. "By the way, I haven't received my November payment.

Isn't it due?"

Riverstone sighed, hating himself for spying on his godson but, as ever, obedient to Margaret's wishes. "The check's in the mail."

* * * * *

"I have a surprise for you," Chantal said, as Rolfe opened his apartment door.

"Good!" He reached for her.

"Not that kind of surprise." She handed him a silver wrapped package.

He ripped it open enthusiastically. A black notebook. He looked at it, disappointed.

"Go on, open it," she ordered.

He turned to the first page: *Solveng Hotels.*

"What's this?"

"Everything you wanted to know about Steinmann and Solveng."

"My God! Where did you get it?"

"From some German friends. You've been a good boy and deserved a reward."

"What German friends?"

Her hand went to his crotch. "Does it matter?" She unzipped him. "Why don't you read it in the morning?"

* * * * *

Rolfe waited until Chantal had left to read the information:

Solveng Hotels

Properties in Frankfurt, Munich, Hamburg, Dusseldorf, Cologne, Brussels, Vienna, Amsterdam, Nice, London, Budapest, Warsaw

Total number of rooms: 3,350

Standard: Five star

Quality: Good, but declining

Style: Dated

Management: Average age of managers, 55. Average length of employment, 17.5 years.

So what? Rolfe thought. I know this already. He kept reading.

Owner: Hans Steinmann (see biographical report)

Price: Unconfirmed rumors that Metropolitan Hotels has offered $168 million, cash and stock, plus a seat on Metropolitan's board of directors

Rolfe whistled and turned to the next page:

Strictly Confidential

The contents of this report have only recently been learned from impeccable sources, but have not yet been independently verified and are unknown to the German authorities.

The adrenaline rush was palpable. It was as though Chantal had deciphered a code and left him all-powerful.

Otto Mueller

Age: Born 1908, Stuttgart, Germany

Birth Home: Farm 18 miles outside Stuttgart

Siblings: 3 older brothers, 1 younger sister

Upbringing: 1917, father gassed at Verdun. Family moved to uncle's house in Munich.

Major Events:

1923: Started work as a bricklayer

1926: Eldest brother killed in an industrial accident

1928: Mother died, age 56, of no apparent cause

Nazi Affiliation: 1930, joins party. Active recruiter

Military Career:

1937: Joins Waffen SS

1939: Promoted to Sergeant. Served in France and Belgium in Jewish Resettlement Section

1942: Transferred to Dachau Concentration Camp. Mueller had a reputation for brutality. Eyewitness reports tell of whipping of women and children, torture of males. Specific reports of shooting randomly into line-ups and of beating two inmates to death with his bare hands. Disliked and feared by fellow soldiers as well as inmates.

Rolfe walked to the window and peered out. It was a brilliantly sunny day. The streets were crowded with people going to work. The report made him feel filthy, but he tore himself away from the sunlight and went back to his reading.

> 1945: Mueller told by his SS commander the end for Germany was near and to liquidate all evidence and escape. On a trip to Munich, he followed Corporal Hans Steinmann, 2nd Armed Division, a man with a similar height and build, to the toilets of the railway station bar, murdered him, changed uniforms, took his papers, switched identity tags, and disappeared.
>
> Marriage: 1946. As Hans Steinmann, marries Anneliese Brieman
>
> Postwar Career:
>
> 1948: Buys and sells burned out properties in Frankfurt, Dusseldorf, and Cologne. Rapidly becomes a millionaire. Daughter, Dagmar, born December 9.
>
> 1953: Acquires building near Frankfurt train station and converts to a hotel. Buys second hotel later that year; incorporates Solveng Hotels. Instrumental in development of Frankfurt Book Fair as means to attract foreign customers.
>
> 1959: Anneliese dies. No reports of subsequent love affairs; sex is evidently not Steinmann's preoccupation. Dagmar becomes his unofficial hostess. He dotes on the child.
>
> 1966: Dagmar, age 17, becomes salaried employee of Solveng Hotels. Steinmann now owns 15 hotels, some of them outside Germany. Father and daughter buy mansion on outskirts of Munich, where they presently reside. Rumors of "wild living" on Dagmar's part, but no scandal. Steinmann supports all major cultural institutions; on the board of the Oberammergau Passion Plays.
>
> 1975: Steinmann suffers heart attack, but recovers. His activities become more limited, but he is still active in management of hotel business. Dagmar seen as his likely successor.

Precisely the kind of man my father fought to eradicate—and died in the process, Rolfe reflected. And here I am trying to make him richer.

Should I drop out? he wondered. That would only mean Hunt will give him his profit, and leave me behind in Europe. His road became clear. Yes! He would buy the hotels, transform them into Kestrels, and in that way force Steinmann to pay recompense for his father's death, even if the German didn't know it. Steinmann would one day die, and in his place would be the son of The Kestrel.

* * * * *

Later that morning Momo came into his office with a spiral-bound book. "These are plans for our new reservations center in Omaha. Josh has reviewed them. All I need is your okay."

He glanced at the overview. "Expensive," he grumbled.

"At first," she acknowledged. "But by the end of the year, we'll save about a third on the cost of each reservation, plus we'll be able to handle a greater volume as we go. As things stand—"

"I'm convinced," he said. "Don't press it."

In the year she had been there, Momo had yet to make a major mistake. Rolfe trusted her with increasingly more management decisions.

"We've got something important to discuss," he told her. "Please ask Josh and Susan to come in."

Not for the first time, Rolfe understood the value of a team. These three people trusted him and trusted each other. Each had distinct individual skills: Josh, his intuitive ability to see into the heart of a project before it was fully formed; Susan, her clear-head-edness and fearlessness; Momo, her precision and organizational skills. Yet, working together they were able to hone those skills into something more. Thanks to the team, Kestrel Hotels, Inc. was already a powerful force in the hotel business. His job was to find the deals; theirs was to make them happen.

He told them about Steinmann, the Solveng Hotels, and Metropolitan's offer. Josh told him he was obsessed with Hunt and not to go near the hotels until they paid off Omaha. Susan said they couldn't possibly afford to buy anything new.

"I only fix computers," Momo said, shrugging.

"Then, it's two nays and one abstention," Rolfe said. "The ayes have it."

So much for teamwork, he thought.

* * * * *

"You're serious?" Riverstone asked. "He's going after Solveng?"

"He really is," Chantal confirmed. "Seems your report only whet his appetite, and did not put him off as you expected. He's obsessed with Bruce Hunt. Do you know he called Hunt's daugh-ter's school to warn them the girl was pushing drugs? Got her suspended, and now there's a court hearing. Rolfe told me as if he were proud of it. Now, Solveng's the new battlefield. How does it feel to be fallible?"

"I wish I'd never sent you that document," Riverstone grumbled. "God knows what he'll do with the information."

CHAPTER 21

1976

"Why don't you sell this place and marry Jan?" Rolfe waved his arms to indicate all of 10, not simply the empty lounge in which they sat.

Each time I come back, it seems smaller and more faded, he thought. Otherwise, it never changes. There are only a few guests here. Chains like mine are killing places like this.

He was in Holland on Margaret's invitation before a stop in Frankfurt for an anonymous inspection of the Solveng hotel there, followed by a trip to Munich. Usually, he did not visit 10 on his rare European trips, but this time, hurtling pell-mell into the future, he felt a yearning for his past.

His mother glowered. "This is our home. You were brought up here. It's where your father and I— where we were all so happy."

She still dressed formally for dinner and still wore her hair in a tight bun, but the lines around her eyes were deeply etched, and the backs of her hands were beginning to mottle.

She looks not old, Rolfe realized, but older. A dowager. He felt a jolt of sympathy.

"I worry about you," he said. "You could make a fortune selling this to a property developer. You've spent all your life working; isn't it time to live fully for yourself?"

"You've got nerve giving me advice!"

The explosion was astonishing and unexpected. He recoiled. "What did I say wrong?"

"Worry about me? How do you think I feel?" She shook her head. "Oh yes, I hear things. You're in debt, running around like a maniac trying to stay afloat. You're still with that French woman. You haven't taken time off for three years. And you have the gall to lecture me about my life."

Rolfe absorbed her tantrum. "I'm sorry for upsetting you," he said woodenly, vowing it would be the last time he came to

197

Holland. His mother was out of control.

"I have reason to be upset. If you'd taken me seriously, you'd have had a good career in the Foreign Service instead of spending your life running faster and faster to stay one step ahead of your creditors."

His mind flashed to a time in this very room when he had come upon his parents kissing, they unaware of his presence. He remembered the expression of joy on their faces, the pleasure they found in each other alone. His mother had often told him her marriage was magical. It was clear now that the magic had not disappeared, that Margaret longed for Wim as she had when she was a young woman, and he felt as he had then: shut out, humiliated, a lesser being. No wonder she didn't want to sell the hotel—or marry Jan.

"I know you wanted me to work in government," he said. "I chose business. But I'm trying to be like my father in my own way."

"Like Wim?" The sarcasm in her voice pierced him like needles. "Hah!"

What does she know? his mind screamed.

"How can I be?" he shouted, rage burning through his self-control. "You supported him, but never me. You've always tried to hold me back. When that didn't work, you pushed me away. You told me to have big dreams just like him, but when I did, you didn't understand, and when I fulfilled them, you didn't care." He glared at her. "And where did his dreams get him? Murdered!"

Her hands shook so violently she had to grip the side of her chair for support. "Yes, he died trying to save his country, leaving me to bring you up alone. Now you've left me all alone. My God, Rolfe, I miss him!"

There were tears in her eyes. Unmoved, Rolfe watched them fall.

* * * * *

"By the way, Rolfe's in town," Jan told his son during a phone conversation.

"Visiting his mother?"

"For a day or two, but he's in Europe on business. Margaret tells me he's leaving for Germany tomorrow."

Pieter's interest level rose. "Where in Germany?"

"Munich, I think. His mother wasn't sure."

* * * * *

Munich! Pieter hung up the phone in the study of his converted farmhouse in Boenebroek. It had to be a coincidence, surely. There was no way Rolfe could know anything about the Solveng deal, let alone be involved. Steinmann had been adamant that the negotiations with Metropolitan be kept confidential. Yet, Pieter didn't like coincidences, and this one made him uneasy.

Thinking it was better safe than sorry, he dialed Hunt's number in New York.

* * * * *

"You're sure you have no idea what Ritter's up to in Munich?" Hunt asked.

McCory sighed. "I've already told you, I haven't heard a fucking word about it."

"Why not?" Hunt challenged. "I'm paying you to know these things."

"You've gotten good value," McCory said, unconcerned. "Ritter's trip probably has nothing to do with Solveng."

"Right. And Richard Burton's affair with Elizabeth Taylor was strictly platonic."

* * * * *

"It's Bruce Hunt for you, Mr. Steinmann."

"Thank you, Gertie. Put him through."

The Metropolitan CEO's voice was sickeningly cordial. "Just wanted to tell you how excited I am about our deal. Can't wait to get you on our board."

"I look forward to it too," Steinmann said flatly.

"Any chance of getting contracts signed this week?"

"I'm afraid not. As I told you, I need to talk to my tax advisors. You'll hear from me at the beginning of next week."

A slight pause. Then: "No one else is talking to you, are they?"

Steinmann was outraged. "Of course not! I gave you my word. What do you take me for?"

"Sorry, Hans. Just getting antsy."

"You'll hear from me next week," Steinmann said, wondering what "antsy" meant. He hung up and opened the file his lawyers had given him: *Kestrel Hotels / Rolfe Ritter.*

* * * * *

The Solveng-Munich's dining room was empty at dinnertime, save for the small army of black-tailed waiters hovering around the maitre d's hotel stand at the restaurant's entrance. Rolfe, seated at the best table by the window, had come purposely early so he could look around before Steinmann arrived. High ceilings, marble columns, a huge hunting scene tapestry, its age simply highlighting its mediocrity. He had noticed as he entered that the bowl of fruit kept on the overcrowded desert trolley had been sloppily erected; not all the poached pears were placed stem-up. The flowers on each table could have been arranged by a child. Rolfe thought of the waste of labor, energy, and money the restaurant represented. If he bought it, there would be seismic changes. As it stood, it would be cheaper to give each patron ten dollars and tell him to eat somewhere else.

A bull of a man, with a young woman in tow, entered, spotted Rolfe, and approached, hand extended. Rolfe stood. It was not fat but muscle that made Steinmann so imposing, he realized, registering wide, ruddy Slavic features, tightly cropped silver hair, seemingly painted on the massive head, an Armani suit and Valentino tie. Rolfe could well believe this man had murdered women and children.

"Let me introduce my daughter," the German said. "Mr. Ritter, Dagmar Steinmann."

She's certainly no beauty, Rolfe thought, taking in a chunky, heavy-featured, dark-haired woman. A Givenchy black dress adorned with a single strand of pearls set off her pale skin, and rose lipstick highlighted voluptuous lips. She knows her good features and makes the most of them, he realized.

Steinmann ordered for the three of them, overly rich food that father and daughter both consumed with gusto. The German's eyes never left Rolfe as he talked; hers were always demurely cast down at her plate. There was, Rolfe considered, something obscene about the atmosphere, as though the dining room itself had been built out of a depraved past. Steinmann's anecdotes—he did not let Dagmar speak even when Rolfe asked her a direct question—were long-winded, and he dropped so many names that the floor was littered with them. The man was obviously accustomed to holding forth without interruption.

"You must try some of the Grand Armagnac from my private cellar," Steinmann offered over coffee. "Baron Edmund de Rothschild allowed me to buy several cases from his personal stock."

Feeling somehow cheapened for accepting, Rolfe let the golden liquor warm his throat. "I'd like to thank you both for a wonderful evening. Your history is fascinating, and your theories of hotel management match mine," he lied. "Clearly it would be inappropriate to discuss business this evening, but I have some thoughts I'd like to discuss with you. Can we meet tomorrow?"

Steinmann pulled a date book from his inside pocket. "Nine o'clock?" Clearly, he had no need to check his calendar; he had planned the meeting in advance.

"As you wish."

"I shall ask Dagmar to join us."

Rolfe bowed. "She will grace the meeting as she has this dinner."

They shook hands amid more bows and courtesies. Rolfe saw them out, went up to his suite, and flopped face down on the bed's heavy duvet. He thought he could smell dust. It was two o'clock in Los Angeles, but he had no desire to speak to anyone. He felt as if he were about to sell his soul. Again.

* * * * *

The conference room was airless, all mahogany panels and subdued light. The only decoration was an oil painting of hunting dogs ravaging a wild boar in a forest. Gone was the bonhomie of the previous evening. Steinmann stared at Rolfe unsmiling. Dagmar, still demure, looked at her fingernails.

"Mr. Steinmann, Miss Steinmann, I'm grateful for your time. So I won't waste it. I've heard rumors that you may—I stress may—be giving some thought to selling your company."

Not a muscle twitched in the Steinmann family.

"If that's the case," Rolfe went on, "please know how honored I'd be to buy your hotels and build on the fine legacy you've created."

He could barely get out the words. Only the thought of Hunt's attack kept him at the table.

"I guessed that was why you wanted to see us," Steinmann said at last, "and I agreed to do so only as a courtesy to my bankers. In fact, I am looking to sell, but I'm close to a firm deal with another party, so I won't waste your time or mine."

Hunt. "I have to believe that two competitors make for a better horse race. Either my offer will be better than my rival's, or it won't. If it's better, I can't see that it's a waste of your time."

Steinmann chuckled. "You're smooth, I'll grant you that. But I've made up my mind."

Dagmar put her hand on top of her father's. "Papa, what do

you have to lose? At least listen to him."

He took his hand away quickly. "I've made a verbal agreement with the other party. It would be unethical to undercut him in this manner."

"Don't be so stubborn," she pleaded.

"Don't interfere."

"It's my business too. Let's hear his offer."

"I told you to leave it alone!"

Rolfe watched, astonished. Dagmar was obviously not the subservient daughter he had imagined. Her face was flushed, her eyes animated. Win or lose, he was enjoying himself.

"What will you need?" Steinmann asked him abruptly.

Dagmar sat back, smiling.

Just like that! Rolfe thought. I wonder where the real power lies. "Information on each of your hotels, financial statements for the past five years, how much capital you've put into upgrades, projections for the coming years. A list of employees and their compensation packages. A list of all major contracts—you know, the normal sort of thing you'd look for if you were buying. Then it won't take me more than a week to come up with an offer."

Steinmann snorted derisively. "You've got forty-eight hours. Dagmar will clear her schedule and go over everything with you on a property-by-property basis. You'll do it here, in these offices, and you're to discuss this with no one but her."

Rolfe hesitated. Risky. He wished Josh were with him. But what did he have to lose? "If it's all right with Miss Steinmann..."

Dagmar appraised him unblinkingly. All she said was, "As you wish, Papa."

Steinmann got up. "Then it's settled." He left after a curt handshake. The office seemed less forbidding with his absence.

"I seem to have imposed myself on you," Rolfe said. "I thought I'd be passed on to an accountant."

"As he told you, Father doesn't want anyone to know he's interested in selling. Besides, I know the figures better than anyone else in the organization."

"But surely you don't want to sell. Aren't you your father's successor?"

"I wanted to go to university. Papa wanted me to join him. The business consumes me. I have no social life. I was the one who persuaded him to sell."

"You astonish me!"

She laughed for the first time since he had met her, and her face showed delight. "Mr. Ritter, there are many things about me that would astonish you. As we work together, maybe you'll find out what they are."

* * * * *

"She's amazing," Rolfe told Josh that night. "Organized, knowledgeable, open, honest."

Josh sighed at the other end of the phone. "You're not falling for her?"

"God, no! If you met her, you'd understand."

* * * * *

They went to dinner the next night to celebrate that their work was finished. Rolfe had called to L.A. to ask Josh to compose an offer, which they'd discuss the following morning. He had looked forward to seeing Dagmar in a non-business role. The girl was twenty-seven. He wondered if she were a virgin.

They went to a rival hotel, the Vier Jahreszeiten—it would be the competition for the as-yet mythical Kestrel-Munich, Rolfe thought—and dined on schnitzel and potato pancakes, accompanied by a superb Batard-Montrachet. They talked of rival hotels, schooldays, country versus city life, London and Paris, the particular perils of growing up poor and growing up rich. Dagmar was a vivacious guest; her low-cut Chanel dress allowed him generous glimpses of bosom. She ate robustly, and enthusiastically seconded his proposal of a second bottle of wine.

"I've read Papa's dossier on you," she said. "It says you've had many affairs. Tell me the truth: Why aren't you married?"

He was stunned as much by the knowledge that Steinmann had a file on him as by the question—far too intimate, far too early—but took it seriously and wondered how to respond. It was certainly a question he had asked himself. The truth was, he didn't think himself capable of love, at least not the kind he'd seen between his parents, not the kind Susan had offered.

"I suppose I've been too busy building a career," he said, noting the intensity with which she heard his answer. "You, I suppose, are too young even to have thought of it."

"Oh, no," she said, speaking as though to reveal an important secret, "I think of it all the time. But you've met my father. He never likes anyone who takes an interest in me, and even those who don't take an interest, like you. He mistrusts everyone I spend time with. For instance, I have to report every detail about us;

what I showed you, what you said, what I thought. Even though it's only business." She took a defiant gulp of wine. "It's infuriating. Especially…"

"Especially what?"

"Especially because he doesn't like you."

She blushed furiously; this was something he was obviously not supposed to know. Shit, he thought despondently, Steinmann's humoring me just to appease his daughter. "Why doesn't he like me?"

She put her hand on his, something she had done with her father, he remembered. He wondered how much significance it carried. "He says you're too young, too cocky, too much of a risk-taker, too unreliable. I think he's jealous. I saw the same report he did, and I read it differently. You're successful, bright, ambitious— and, I might add, quite handsome, though that's not in the report. Worse, because I stood up to him in our meeting, he thinks I like you. That's poison."

Was it? he wondered. Maybe the way to the father's hotels was through his daughter's heart. The idea appalled him and excited him simultaneously. It wouldn't hurt, he told himself, to play it out. And if it didn't work, he had his own report on Otto Mueller to fall back on.

"And do you?" he asked.

"Do I what?"

"Do you like me?"

He watched her face go red in the light of the half-spent candle. "I told you I did," she said, measuring her words. "I've enjoyed working with you."

"You know what I mean," he persisted.

She increased the pressure on his hand. The candlelight shone in her eyes. "I like you a lot," she whispered.

"Good," he said. "I like you too."

* * * * *

"What do I look like?" he asked the mirror as he shaved the next morning. The white lather accentuated the red lines in the corners of his eyes and the dark bags under them.

He reflected on their night of rough passion. She had been insatiable, her pent-up energy unstoppable. Gingerly, he inspected his body: scratch marks on his chest and back, bite marks on his shoulders, his penis raw. My God, he wondered, how long since she'd had a man? It had been blessed relief when she'd let herself out of his suite at 6:00 A.M.

Josh's phone call woke him twenty minutes later.

* * * * *

This time, Rolfe and Steinmann were alone in the conference room. Rolfe wondered where Dagmar was, but was glad of her absence. This could be an unpleasant negotiation, and he didn't want her to witness it.

"You have an offer?" Steinmann asked.

"I do, sir."

"I'm listening."

Rolfe took a deep breath. "I'll buy you out completely for all cash, or buy a majority interest in the company and you can stay on as a partner in the hotels. In the latter case, Kestrel Hotels would control operations and take a management fee for its services."

White spots of rage blossomed on the German's cheeks. "I'm no one's minority partner. What I own, I control!"

"Then I offer one-hundred-fifty million, all cash."

A pause. Steinmann stood. "Thank you, Mr. Ritter. The meeting is over."

Why? It was surely an aggressive opening offer. Under Hunt's price, but a good starting point for negotiations. "Please realize I'm talking about all cash," Rolfe said somewhat desperately. "There's not stock at stake; there's no gamble with my offer."

Steinmann sat down. His voice was calm. "Perhaps you didn't hear me. The meeting is over. Either you're a complete idiot or you take me for one. There's no deal."

The man's attitude put steel in Rolfe's resolve. "I don't think you're an idiot—far from it. I'm simply trying hard to make a deal"—he enunciated each word, syllable by syllable—"with Sergeant Otto Mueller."

The German's face went wholly white. Without warning, he sprang from his chair, grabbed Rolfe by the shirt collar, and slammed him hard against the wall. "Listen, you stupid, fucking blackmailing shit. Never repeat that name. Never even think it. If you do, I swear to God I'll kill you."

Steinmann's grip intensified, ice and no mercy in his eyes, nothing but hate. Rolfe, gasping for breath, knew he was dealing with Mueller himself now, all pretense gone, and knew the threat he faced was real. He held up his hands, palms up in surrender. The German's hold slowly, almost imperceptibly, relaxed.

When he spoke again, Steinmann's mask was back in place. "Sit down," he said. Stunned, Rolfe did as commanded.

"You've got balls, I'll say that." Steinmann, also seated, was now all affability. "I like a man with balls. I'll sell you all the hotels."

Rolfe was speechless. Was this some sick game? Steinmann was watching him calmly, obviously enjoying what he saw. "I want one-hundred-seventy-five million, all cash," he said.

Expensive, but at the top end of fair, Rolfe knew. He had a sudden vision of Hunt's face when he found out about the deal. Kestrel would choke Metropolitan; he would be revenged. In his mind, Rolfe could hear Josh's howl of protest.

"I accept your price," he said, his voice strong.

The German showed no elation. On the contrary, he moved his chair so close Rolfe could feel the heat of his breath. "There's one other condition."

Rolfe braced himself. "What's that?"

"The day before we close on this deal, you will marry Dagmar. This city will have the biggest reception it has ever held, co-funded by Kestrel and Solveng. You will sign a prenuptial agreement so that if you divorce her within five years or you give her a reason to divorce you, you will give her twenty million in cash and an additional twenty million to any children you might have together. And you will give her children."

Rolfe found it impossible to breathe; the room, Steinmann's face, the painting of the hunting dogs whirled before his eyes. The man was mad!

"She doesn't love me," he said at last. "How can you force her—?"

"But you're wrong! She loves you very much. She spent last night with you." Steinmann put up his hand to silence Rolfe. "I know what goes on in my hotel. So I challenged her this morning, and she announced you were the most wonderful man in the world. I told her she was naïve. She answered she had fallen in love the moment she met you at dinner and that last night confirmed it. I said she was being stupid, that she'd been taken in by a pretty boy opportunist with a silver tongue—which is, Mr. Den Ritter, just what you are. She said I was being jealous, that I didn't understand her feelings, that all my life I had stood in her way and that now at last she was breaking free."

He stopped, but only to gather strength. Rolfe could see his pain; it repelled him.

"We had the most terrible fight. I swear to you, I came close to striking her. But then, just as I raised my fist, I realized that I was destroying the one person in the world I loved. The one person who means anything to me, who has given whatever beauty there has been in my life.

"Yes, I was Otto Mueller, and in that name did things that haunt me still. But I did them in a different time, in different circumstances, and I am not ashamed of them." He glared at Rolfe.

"My daughter's happiness is all that has ever mattered to me, and if you are the instrument of that happiness, then so be it. You will marry my daughter, Mr. Ritter. You will make her happy."

It was as though steel bands had been placed around Rolfe's chest. He was being crushed by an avalanche, in total darkness. "No." It was all he could say.

"Yes!" Steinmann loomed over him, his face as grotesque as in a funhouse mirror. "If you reject this offer, I don't think you should count on a long life. If you go back home and change your mind, you're a dead man. And I'll warn you only once: If this information ever comes out, whether from you or anyone else, or if you ever hurt her in any way, I promise I'll kill you without a second's hesitation, no matter the effect on Dagmar."

He retreated, giving Rolfe a chance to gulp in air. "By the way," Steinmann said, his voice more normal now, "Dagmar has known the truth about me from the day her mother died. You and she alone will be the truth's custodians." His mouth twitched.

"One last thing. That information could hurt me, but it certainly wouldn't ruin me. I'll have your money, after all. There are many people like me. In Bavaria, particularly, my past would be viewed as a badge of honor."

Nausea filled Rolfe's body, its taste rising in his throat as he struggled to absorb Steinmann's ultimatum. How much do I really want Solveng? he wondered. Enough to throw away five years of my life on a woman I barely know? The daughter of a—he could not deny the word—murderer. He had to take Steinmann's threat seriously. If he simply went home, called off all negotiations, Steinmann might very well hunt him down, if only to avenge his daughter's humiliation.

He had no option. He would dumbfound his mother, shock Chantal—who would rather enjoy the irony—flabbergast Josh and Susan. But he'd have beaten Hunt! Kestrel would have an international identity. He would be the most powerful hotelier under thirty in the entire world. He would be on his way to his goal, if not quite in the way he had imagined. His skin crawled at the thought of yet another shortcut, yet another deal with the devil. Images of Murtoch, of Walters and Levenson, of his father's body and his mother's witch-face flashed in his brain.

"I'll marry your daughter," he said, watching Steinmann's satisfaction spread. "But I can only pay you one-hundred-sixty-two million dollars. And you'll make Kestrel International a fifteen million dollar loan for ten years at the German banks' lowest corporate rate. You want your daughter to be secure; I want my company to be secure."

The German looked at him without a flicker of emotion. "Done."

CHAPTER 22

1976

Susan and Josh were still reeling from the news. Their boss had done many harebrained things since they'd known him, but this was the most foolhardy of them all.

"I can't believe it," Susan kept repeating like a mantra.

Josh passed her his handkerchief to stem her tears. "I thought you'd gotten over him."

She smiled wanly. "Yes, our affair ended years ago. But I still care for him, and so do you. It's unbearable watching this obsession. What good does it do him to beat Hunt if he winds up destroying himself?"

"And us in the process," Josh added. "We can't afford to buy the Solvengs. But when I told him that, he told me we'd find the money someplace." His tone turned bitter. "Where? At the end of the rainbow?"

Momo joined them. "Trouble?"

They told her. There was silence as she digested it, then, "Why, that sly bastard. Good for him!"

* * * * *

"Royalty has used marriage for political gain for thousands of years," Ron Falkman said when Rolfe called him with the news.

"Does that mean I'm a king," Rolfe asked, "or just a prince?"

"It means you're a royal pain in the ass. Where in God's name do you expect to find the money?"

Rolfe could hear the concern in the lawyer's voice. It sobered him. "That's just what Josh asked. I figured Davison could swing it."

"I'll ask, but I doubt it. He doesn't do much overseas. I suggest you dig around Europe for an insurance company or pension fund that'll do a sale and leaseback."

A surge of hope. "Meaning what?"

"They'll buy the hotels and lease them back to you cheaply, taking some of the long-term upside as extra rent. It's been common practice in Europe for years."

"Sounds like a good idea," Rolfe said, relieved. "Where do I start?"

"How about asking your mother's boyfriend's son for advice? What's his name?"

"Pieter Vermeij. I'll call him."

* * * * *

"Rolfe can marry the Queen of Sheba for all I care," Pieter said. "But Dad, he asked me for advice on whom to contact for a deal on Solveng. That's the damned deal I've been brokering for Hunt! I had to choke down my surprise—God knows, I didn't want him to hear about my relationship with Hunt—and said I'd think about it. Now I'm thinking about killing him. He fucked me! No wonder I haven't been able to get Steinmann to return my calls. Do you know how long I've worked on this? How important it is to me. How much money I would have made?"

Jan listened in amazement. He had been with Margaret when her son called to tell her about the marriage, heard her gasp out congratulations in a voice usually reserved for funerals, saw her grief and her rage. "A German? A bloody German? At least he isn't marrying Chantal," was all she said when Rolfe hung up.

Now, here was Pieter spewing venom.

"Rolfe's always been a conniving bastard," Pieter went on. "You forced him on me when we were kids, but I hated him then and I hate him a hundred times more now. I don't give a shit that he's Margaret's son. If it were up to me, I'd ruin him!"

"Take it easy," Jan said slowly. "I told you long ago that when you take business personally, win or lose, you lose your greatest weapon: objectivity. And if you so much as hint at any of this to Margaret, I swear to God I'll disavow you as my son."

Pieter barely heard him. His mind was already focused on the call he now had to make.

* * * * *

"What are you going to do about it?" Hunt screamed into the phone. "Have you spoken to Steinmann?"

"Steinmann won't take my calls."

"Then what am I paying you for? Find out what's going on and where that son of a bitch Ritter's getting his money from. You'd better fix this, or I'll find another European investment banker, one who can get results!"

* * * * *

"How are you, Hans?" Hunt asked, as if he'd just left him the day before.

"Fine." The German was breathing heavily.

"Glad to hear it. I'm just checking on our deal. I'm ready to sign when you are."

No answer came from the Munich end of the line.

"No problems, I hope? Any details you want to change?"

More silence.

"Jesus Christ!" Hunt exploded. "It's true. You're selling to Ritter."

A gasp. "How did you find out?"

"What's the difference? I want to know about our deal. The chairmanship of Metropolitan-Europe. The directorship on the main board? The stock? Your word as a gentleman."

"We never had a written agreement," Steinmann said in a monotone, "and I've never pretended to be a gentleman. Kestrel offered a better deal."

"I'll match it. Increase it by five percent."

"You're too late," the German said. "I have a signed agreement with Kestrel. What's more, Dagmar Steinmann and Rolfe Ritter are getting married the week after next."

"What?"

"They'd be honored, I'm sure, if you could come to the ceremony."

So that's how he did it, Hunt thought, even in his fury wishing he'd come up with something equally clever. "I'm too busy to attend," he said, "and I'm sure the bride and bridegroom will forgive me if I don't send a present. But I'd like to give you a present. Now, in fact. Before the wedding. It's a dossier I've developed on Ritter. Read it, and if you change your mind about your arrangement with Kestrel, give me a call."

* * * * *

"I need to know how Ritter found out about Solveng," Hunt said. "Someone leaked it to him. Who?"

Bud McCory puffed contentedly on a cigar. "It won't be easy, Bruce. The answer's probably in Europe, and that's a problem."

"I don't care how much it costs. Find out."

Hunt slammed down the phone. McCory leaned back and watched cigar smoke cloud his office. "Perfect," he said out loud. "Fucking perfect."

* * * * *

"It's only a marriage of convenience," Rolfe told Chantal, having finally mustered up the courage to call. "Really. Nothing will change between us."

He could almost feel her shock. "You know that's a lie," she said, composing herself. "Marriage will change everything. We can't be seen together in public. We'll have to sneak off for quickies when you can get away." She snorted. "I'm not going to be your whore. We're finished."

His silence inflamed her. "Why didn't you call me immediately? Were you ashamed? Embarrassed? Frightened?" She paused. "Yes, that's it. Frightened, just like you were when we met. You're the same little boy with your same, pathetic little prick. It might be good enough for your new wife, but it sure isn't enough for me."

"Please listen..."

"I shouldn't have given you the Solveng file in the first place. Should have known your ego wouldn't let you leave it alone. My mistake. Now, you get out of it."

The phone slammed down on him. The prospect of his life ahead—his marriage, the ubiquitous Steinmann, his ever-increasing entanglements, the endless fight for money, the battles with his enemies, and the unexpressed scorn of people like Susan and Josh—for he was sure that was what they felt—overtook him, and a wave of fear hurled him downward. But the lights above still dazzled.

* * * * *

"I'm as upset as you are," Riverstone told Chantal when she reported in. "I was right: I never should have let you talk me into giving you that file."

She laughed. "Don't blame me. I've done everything you asked just to keep close to your beloved godson. It's not my fault if he's made a muck of things. But I'll tell you one thing: I'm not going back to him, no matter how much you're willing to pay. It was a cute trick you thought up, staging that attack and letting me 'save' him. You're smart, and I'll gladly go on working for you. But not with your godson, not even for more money. He's too much of a handful, that one is. With him, I've outlived my usefulness."

True, Riverstone thought. And now that Rolfe's bought those European hotels, maybe now's the time to begin using him directly.

CHAPTER 23

1976

"I've asked my father to join us," Pieter Vermeij said, shaking Rolfe's hand with as much cordiality as he could feign. "I hope you don't mind." Pieter had not figured out what he would say when the hotelier asked him, as he surely would, to put together a sale and leaseback of the Solvengs. Maybe he could persuade Rolfe to give up the deal altogether and so rescue himself with Hunt; maybe his father would help him talk Rolfe out of his plans. And maybe the moon was really made of cheese.

"Mind? I'm delighted," Rolfe said as he hugged his mother's lover with true affection and smiled at Pieter.

They ate lunch overlooking the river in Amstel Hotel's dining room, reminiscing about the times Pieter and Rolfe had played together as children. Rolfe remembered that in 1942 the hotel had become headquarters to the German high command. Fitting, given his terrifying session with his prospective father-in-law, he thought.

He knew there would be no talk of business until the meal was finished. Still, he sensed Pieter's nervousness. The banker's smiles seemed strained, his eyes rarely met Rolfe's, and he only took a few bites of his lifeless salade nicoise before pushing it aside.

The waiter finished serving coffee. "Congratulations on both the Solveng deal and your engagement," Pieter said. "You must be excited."

"Actually, more scared than excited," Rolfe acknowledged.

"About which? The sale or the engagement?"

"Both." The three men laughed.

"What a coup," Pieter said. "I hear you stole the Solvengs from under Metropolitan's nose. How did you manage it?"

Rolfe preened. He told his childhood rival carefully edited details of the back-and-forth with Steinmann, too involved in his story to notice Jan's disapproving glance at his son.

"Amazing," Pieter said when Rolfe paused. "And one thing more: How did you find out about the deal in the first place?"

"You're driving Rolfe mad," Jan interrupted.

Rolfe's antenna went up. "Not at all. But I'm afraid my sources are confidential." Indeed, what difference would it make to Pieter?

Jan excused himself to settle the check. "Have you any idea where I might find the financing?" Rolfe asked Pieter.

"You'll have a devil of a time with any bank. No one wants to lend to an unproven American, especially with so much money is involved." For the first time, he looked at Rolfe directly. "I do have one crazy idea, but it just might work."

Precisely the ally I need, Rolfe thought. "Let's hear it."

"Come at it another way. Sign the deal and then immediately resell for an immense profit. Then you can take your time to buy a different chain altogether."

"But I'd still need to find the money to buy."

"Not necessarily."

Rolfe looked at him, suspicion rising like a tide. "I don't understand."

"I hear Metropolitan was making a play for Solveng the same time you did."

"Where is this going?"

"Rumor has it that Hunt keeps calling Steinmann, trying to get him to change his mind. Metropolitan needs to be in Europe far more than you do."

How does he know how badly I need Europe? "What's that to me?"

Pieter leaned forward. "I bet I could broker a deal where you sign the contract to buy Solveng, but at the same time you close, Metropolitan buys you. That way, you never put up a dime, and you'd have so much money you can make a serious play for any hotel or group of hotels in the world."

The proposal hit Rolfe like a fist to the brain. Sell Kestrel? Now? I'm just beginning! The tide overflowed. Pieter was working for Hunt! It was the only possible explanation. The room whirled around him as if he'd had too much to drink, and he was only peripherally aware of Jan's return. He fought for self-control.

"So all I'd have to do is give up Kestrel?"

"Yes. For a profit of anywhere between fifty and one hundred million."

It was only Jan's presence that kept him from losing his temper. Calm settled on him like a drug. "Sorry," he said quietly.

"Sorry?" Pieter repeated the word as though he had never heard it before. "You're turning down a profit of one-hundred million?"

"Triple it, and I'd still turn it down. There's not enough money for Bruce Hunt to ever buy Kestrel."

Pieter sat immobile, the only sign of emotion a pulse beating in his forehead. "Then let me tell you this: I'll see to it that no banker in Europe will ever lend you a penny—for the Solveng deal or any other."

"What's this?" Jan cried, looking back and forth between the two enemies.

Pieter ignored him. "You've been lucky so far, but it's bound to run out some day. All that horseshit about being the world's best hotelier and living out your dream—it's a fantasy.

"Stop this now!" Jan said. "It's gone too far."

"What has? I've given him good advice, and what does he do? What he always does: ignore everyone and everything, and to hell with the consequences." He looked at his father. "Tell him to do the right thing for once. Go on, tell him!"

"It's you and Hunt, isn't it," Rolfe said. "Jesus Christ. You two-faced bastard. It's hard to believe. Well, you were always jealous of me. It's clear that hasn't changed." He stood abruptly. "I'm sorry, Uncle, but I should leave before I do something we'll all regret."

"Sit down, Rolfe. Pieter, shut up!" Jan's vehemence was so astonishing, his command so absolute, that both men obeyed. "I can't have you fighting. I won't tolerate it," he said. "There's to be no hatred between you. You must be friends and allies in all things from this day forward."

Impossible, Rolfe thought, and started to say so, but Jan stopped him with a glare. "I'm not insisting for me or for Margaret, but because it's what must be." He pitched his voice low. "I'm going to tell you something no other living person knows. Don't interrupt; this is difficult for me. When I've finished, you'll understand what I mean."

He took a breath. "As you know, Wim and I met at university and became inseparable friends. There, Wim met a young woman, Beatrice Hellerman—yes, Pieter, your mother—and because he was dating someone else at the time, he introduced Beatrice to me, thinking we'd like each other. He was more than right. Beatrice and I fell in love and soon married.

"The war came. Wim and I enlisted, went to Officers' Training Course. Eventually, Wim became commander of a covert intelligence team. I was made an officer in Military Intelligence and, when Holland fell, I was sent to London. Beatrice refused to come with me. Her mother was still in Amsterdam, too sick to be moved, and Beatrice wouldn't leave her behind.

"By 1940, Wim was spending much of his time behind enemy lines. The only way he could keep in touch with me was through messages to Beatrice. I visited Holland as often as I could, partly on intelligence business, but mostly to see Beatrice. As the Nazis tightened their grip, my visits became less frequent."

A chill ran through Rolfe's body. He guessed what was to come.

"In the spring of 1942, she wrote with the news that she was pregnant," the old man continued. "The baby was due in the winter. But I hadn't been in Holland since late December." For the first time, his voice caught. "Two months later, I went back to Holland. It was then Beatrice told me Wim was the father."

Rolfe looked at Pieter, who sat with his eyes closed, hands gripping the side of the table, his shock and pain so intense that, despite himself, Rolfe felt sorry for him. Jan was right: They shared this.

"Wim had barely escaped detection in Berlin and had fled to Holland. He was half dead with pneumonia. His nerves were shattered. Pieter, your mother nursed him back to health, helped him regain his confidence. In the loneliness of those days, neither knowing how much longer they would live—well, you were conceived."

He struggled for air, but when he spoke again his voice was strong. "At first, I wanted to kill him—my best friend had betrayed me in the worst possible way—but I couldn't stop loving Beatrice, couldn't stand the thought of losing her. So I forgave him as well as her and resolved to love the baby with all my heart and soul. Beatrice and I vowed that Wim would never learn the truth. Mike Riverstone may have known, but if he did, nothing ever showed on Wim's record. In London, of course, Wim met Margaret." He managed a smile. "Kind of ironic, isn't it, that Wim was my wife's lover and now I'm in love with his.

"In the final days of the war, Beatrice left you with a neighbor just before she and her mother were rounded up by the Germans." He looked at Pieter. "They were herded into a railroad yard; suddenly, soldiers opened the flaps at the rear of their truck, and mowed down ninety-five people, including your mother and grandmother, as a reprisal for a resistance attack. I heard about it a few days later from Mike," he said bitterly. "I dropped everything, rushed here, and found you, still with the same neighbor."

Pieter sat rigidly, his face white as chalk.

My God, Rolfe thought. If I'm having trouble accepting this, what must he be feeling? He felt his anger dissipate. Did Mother know? he wondered. Her brave hero, his role model, the father of the child who had hated Rolfe since the instant they met? No, he decided, she's no actress, she couldn't know. He reeled, struggling with the complexities of Jan and Margaret's relationship, as well as Margaret and Wim's.

"Now you understand why I wanted you boys to be together," Jan went on. "You're brothers, both my foster children, and nothing can change that." He fixed his gaze on Pieter. "From the second you were born, I loved you. It wasn't easy bringing you up alone, but it was a privilege that gave me the chance to know you inside out. You were a wonderful child then, and you're a wonderful man now. I'm as proud of you as any father could be, and I bless your mother for giving you to me."

Rolfe spoke, close to tears. "For God's sake, Uncle Jan and Pieter, whatever your feelings are, please keep this from my mother. It would destroy her."

"I swear it," Jan said.

"I won't tell," Pieter concurred. He kept his head down, evidently trying to untangle his feelings. Finally he said, "You're right, Father. Everything's changed. But in another way, nothing's changed. You were my father, and you still are." He spoke without animation.

This is a recorded announcement, Rolfe thought, and wished Pieter could show the old man some compassion.

Jan, however, seemed relieved by Pieter's words. "I should have told you when you were young," he said gently, "but I was a coward; I didn't want to lose your love." He looked at both men. "The reason I've spoken now is that I couldn't stand to see you tearing at each other. My God! You share the same blood, the same father. Yet, each of you wants to destroy the other. You, Pieter, faking friendship to get your own way. And you, Rolfe, wanting to use Pieter not out of loyalty but out of ambition; from him, you thought, you could get the best 'deal.' Of course I want you to work together, but you must work as brothers. If you can't—"

"Go on," Pieter said.

"If you can't, then I'll have failed as a father and as a man."

Rolfe's glance went again to Pieter. The banker had raised his head and was looking at his father with the seriousness of

Solomon.

At last he said, simply, "Thank you." Then he stood and offered his hand to Rolfe who clasped it warmly. "We must talk."

* * * * *

"No, Bruce, there's no doubt whatsoever," Pieter told Hunt the following week when he called the Metropolitan CEO at his home. "Ritter has all the money he needs to buy Solveng Hotels."

Hunt's growl was ominous. "Where did he get it?"

"I don't know," Pieter said flatly. "I tried all my sources, but I simply couldn't find out."

Chapter 24

1976

"**B**ring her in," Hunt told Barbara, his latest secretary. As he waited, he reflected on the call that had led to the meeting.

"Mr. Hunt," a woman with a delightful French accent had said, "my name is Chantal Le Peron, I think I can help you."

He'd recognized the name immediately from his investigator's reports. Of course, he reasoned, it makes sense. Ritter married that double-crosser's daughter and dumped this one as part of the deal.

What an elegant woman, he thought as he greeted her, admiring her tailored suit and cloche hat.

"How can you help me, Miss Le Peron?" he asked, shooing Barbara away and uncharacteristically pouring coffee himself from the porcelain pot she'd brought in.

"I'm sure you know I was once Rolfe Ritter's 'special friend,'" her eyes dropped demurely, "but I'm not sure you know that I'm an excellent hotel marketing executive."

"In fact, I did know," he murmured, fascinated. "Your reputation precedes you."

"I want to work for Metropolitan. With my expertise in hotels and my intimate knowledge of that man, I can help you make sure Kestrel's minor competition, at best."

"Why would you want to do that?"

"Because you're the only one who can outdistance him. I want to see that happen."

A woman scorned, Hunt thought, increasingly intrigued. This could be very useful. He smiled. "Tell me more..."

* * * * *

"She's a gem," Hunt excitedly told the shocked Henry Monroe, Metropolitan's senior vice president of marketing. "I hired her for your department on the spot. She won't come cheap, but I'm sure she'll be worth every penny. What a coup!"

* * * * *

"How's Chantal doing?" Hunt asked Monroe a month later.

"She's the best," he answered. "Every project I give her gets done without discussion or delay. She knows what she's doing."

"I want to spend some time with her to get insights into Ritter. Can you spare her for a day or two?"

* * * * *

He's spending far too much time with me. It's more than business, Chantal laughed to herself as she lay back on the chaise lounge in her Greenwich townhouse. He's got a crush on me. She poured herself a glass of red wine.

I'm going to seduce him, she suddenly decided, and make him think he seduced me. *"Non, je ne regrette rien,"* sang Piaf from the cassette player.

* * * * *

Susan picked up *Lodging Business Magazine* and flipped it open. Her eyes widened.

Chantal Le Peron Named Vice President Marketing for Metropolitan Hotels

Today Metropolitan Hotels named their first female vice president . . .

Amazed, she carefully read the article, looked up a number in her Rolodex, and dialed.

"Longstreet Investigations. How may I help you?"

"I'd like to speak to Stanley Longstreet please."

* * * * *

"Read this," Susan told Josh, tossing a dark blue folder onto his desk.

"I'm busy, can't it wait?"

"No," she insisted, "read it now."

He read quickly, then said. "Longstreet's good. Our Chantal's a piece of work, isn't she?"

"She's more than that. She's dangerous. I'm going to show this to Rolfe. He ought to know what she's like."

"Wait a minute," Josh said. "Let's think this through. You and I know that anytime she wants, she can lure Rolfe back. I bet she hasn't finished with him yet. Let's keep tabs on her and Hunt. We'll use it if Rolfe and the Witch Bitch look like they're getting together again."

* * * * *

"What a hell of a day," Rolfe told Josh and Susan as they sat at a pool-side table at the newly opened Kestrel Resort in Acapulco.

"The mayor wouldn't shut up, would he?" Josh asked. "I thought you'd have apoplexy waiting to cut that ribbon."

Rolfe and Susan laughed at the memory of the four-foot-eleven mayor with his enormous black silk top hat, standing on the tips of his toes trying to reach the microphone.

"What about the bishop?" she said. "He sprayed so much holy water around I thought I'd need an umbrella!"

Lulled by the backdrop of the fountains, their jets synchronized to soft music and the tinkling of the streams finding their way through the lava rock into the two infinity pools, they felt the tension of the day ooze away. Inevitably the conversation turned to work.

"We're growing too fast," Josh worried. "Our organization will never catch up with this rate of expansion. More countries plus more properties equal more overhead. Even Momo thinks we should slow down. She's having difficulty keeping our systems efficient."

"I agree with Josh," Susan said. "Not only do we need money for corporate infrastructure, but when you're running around like a one-armed paperhanger, trying to set ever-higher operating standards, designing the hotels with the latest bells and whistles, and coming up with potential new deals in places we've never heard of, you can't spend enough time raising money. Let's take a break and get ourselves straight for once, shall we?"

Rolfe smiled at them. "Look at the stars," he said. "It's so clear; we never get nights like this in L.A."

"What's that got to do with our conversation?" Josh asked.

"It's as clear as the night sky: We need a chief financial officer to handle our money raising."

"At last!" Susan said. "You look like you have an idea who you want to hire."

"I do," Rolfe answered. "Indeed I do. That's why I brought you down here with me. To celebrate Susan's promotion."

* * * * *

Hunt put down the *Wall Street Journal*. So Ritter's appointed his ex-secretary—make that ex-lover—as CFO. I've read about her for years in the reports. What a loser. They're all a bunch of losers. Chantal will love it.

* * * * *

"I'm going to need some fucking serious money for the national election," McCory told Rolfe when they met for a drink at the new Long Bar in the Kestrel in San Francisco.

"How serious?" Rolfe asked.

"From you, one-hundred-thousand."

"Jesus, Bud, that's a fortune."

"Yeah, but if I win, look at the power I'll have. It'll be worth your fucking while."

What choice do I have? Rolfe thought. And if he wins, I'll get my money's worth. "Sure, Bud. Do I deliver the cash the usual way?"

"No need to change." McCory didn't say that two days earlier he'd had the same conversation with Bruce Hunt and come away with the identical amount.

* * * * *

"If McCory wins, it'll help us enormously," Rolfe told Falkman as they walked along Manhattan's Fifth Avenue to a meeting with Davison at the Essex House Hotel on Central Park South.

"Be careful, dear boy. I know you like him, but the only person that man's loyal to is himself."

"He's always been a straight shooter with me. We're friends."

"I mean it, be careful. Remember, Joseph thought his brothers were his friends, and look what happened to him. They dumped him in a pit."

CHAPTER 25

1976

Jan and Margaret were married on the twelfth of December at Amsterdam's main registry office. Rolfe didn't find out about it until he called his mother on the twenty-fourth to wish her a merry Christmas.

"You got married?" he bellowed. "When?"

"Week before last. Jan and I decided to postpone the honeymoon. We're going to Positano the middle of January."

He was happy for her, he supposed—happy for Jan, too, who had wanted the marriage more than she. But to be left out! Why? Because he had always been left out. It was always Margaret and Wim or Rolfe and Wim, never the three of them, even when he was a young boy. When he had decided on a different career from his father's, it was Margaret who had tried to stop him, tried to make him a replica of her husband (sure to be the lesser man, sure to fail), told him, in effect, that she could never love him until he became Wim. That's why he had gone to America without telling her. Well, he supposed, tit for tat.

"Congratulations," he said automatically. "It's about time."

"I'm so happy, I feel like a teenager."

"Why did you wait to tell me?"

"Actually, Jan wanted to invite you and Pieter to the wedding." He knew it. "So why didn't you?"

She sighed. "I wanted a quiet ceremony. If you both came, then Christina and Dagmar would have had to be there too, and I'd have had to entertain you."

"That's crazy. Even if you didn't want us there you could have said something—told me, anyway."

"Ridiculous," Margaret said, her voice harsh. "You've got no right being upset. After all, you don't tell me what you're doing."

"Not true. I write to you all the time. I told you I was going to

223

marry Dagmar. You could have come to the wedding. I can't help it if you don't like what I did."

As he spoke, he knew how defensive he sounded, how like a little boy. For a moment he was tempted to tell her whose child Pieter really was, but he held back, not wanting to ruin her marriage forever.

I wanted her to marry Jan, he considered. She didn't want me to marry Dagmar. And he knew that both he and his mother had been right in their decisions.

* * * * *

"Dagmar's eating me alive," Rolfe confided.

Josh chuckled. "Is that a good thing or a bad thing?" The two of them were walking, shoes and socks in hand, along the surf near Santa Monica Pier.

"Not funny. You know what I'm talking about, you've seen the bills. She's spending money faster than I can make it."

"Joining the boards of the museum and the opera isn't cheap," Josh agreed, ignoring his soaked trousers and trying not to sound judgmental. "Those were steep donations you had to make. But you told me Dagmar's doing it for you because she thinks it's her duty to make the community aware of your importance."

"I hate that crap, and you know it!"

"Well, don't snap at me. I'm not the social lion, you are."

"Have you been to the mansion in Bel Air?" Rolfe grumbled. "What a money pit. I'm dreading moving in."

"Ted took me there," Josh admitted. "It's not a mansion; it's a palace. You know, he's working with Dagmar to decorate it."

"What does he think about the bloody place?"

"He says Dagmar's taste is German bankers' gothic."

Rolfe laughed. "What else?"

"He told me Dagmar's the only person he's ever met who can outspend an unlimited budget."

"It's not only that, it's her father. Every time I turn around, she's on the phone with him or he's staying with us. The evening before last, I came back to the apartment and he was sitting at my desk reading my papers."

"Jesus! What'd you do?"

"I screamed at him. Dagmar heard and started crying. Do you know what that bastard told me?"

"Go on."

"He said, 'I'm your lender, she's my daughter, and I'm entitled to know everything about you.'" He picked up a pebble and hurled it into the ocean. "Even my sex life, I suppose."

"Meaning?"

"Oh, I suppose it's all right. God knows I can't complain about frequency; she certainly never gets headaches. But Dagmar's so crude and aggressive compared with—"

"Chantal?" Josh finished the sentence.

"Yes, damn it, Chantal."

They walked in silence until they came to a bench by the bike path on Venice Beach and sat down to rest. "Now, listen to me," Josh said. "You're a dumb schmuck, so I'm going to give you some advice that, for once, you're going to damn well follow."

Rolfe bowed. "Yessir."

"I'm serious. You've still got four years or so before you can get divorced. We can't afford to pay the twenty million to her if you do it beforehand."

Rolfe grunted. "I know. I'm an idiot. Another pact with the devil."

"So don't play around, and if that's impossible, go as far away from her as you can and for God's sake don't get caught. Cause if you do, they'll own you."

"I'll be good," Rolfe said, trying to figure how long four years really was. "Come on, let's go back to the car."

* * * * *

It was Susan who broke the news that Steve Westerman had been hospitalized with a massive stroke. Inexplicably, Rolfe felt a twinge of guilt. He had done nothing illegal to buy the San Francisco hotel from his former boss, yet Westerman had never really found out how he'd done it, and as Kestrel San Francisco flourished, he felt that somehow Rolfe had cheated him. Susan, Rolfe knew, had always been fond of him.

He called Adele, Steve's wife. "How is he?"

"Terrible. The doctors say that even if he does recover, there'll be massive brain damage."

"Is there anything I can do?"

She suppressed a sob. "No. I've got the very best specialists. But thank you for asking."

Hypocrite, Rolfe thought. If Susan's right about Adele's character, the specialists aren't doctors, they're lawyers. Adele was adept at spending Steve's money, Susan had said, theorizing that her extravagance was one of the factors leading to his illness. Rolfe did not miss the parallels to Dagmar.

"Call me if you need any help with the hotels," he offered, remembering gratefully his first visit with Westerman. "I owe him so much. He gave me my start. Without him, there'd be no Kestrel Hotels."

"You're right you owe him!" Adele flared. "You stole the San Francisco hotel and ran it into the ground so you could buy it cheaply."

The accusation was as unjust as it was surprising. "That's unfair, Adele, and you know it."

"All I know is that Steve never forgave you, and neither will I," she said. "It's your fault he's dying. You broke his heart."

* * * * *

He hadn't been in The Hills for a couple of years, but when he walked into the lobby to the cheery greetings of the staff who remembered him, he could feel it had gone downhill fast. Buttons missing on uniforms, cigarette butts in ashtrays, the flowers at least three days old, paintings slightly askew, their frames dusty. Although he was due for a meeting with Levenson and Walters, he took a few minutes to continue his inspection.

In the garden, there were weeds in the flowerbeds, dead branches on the trees, the famed yellow and white umbrellas splotchy with dirt. The lifeguard reading a newspaper!

At least one of his innovations was still in use. The maids' carts were hidden in recesses, and the maids took a basket into each guest room with only the immediate cleaning materials they needed. No unsightly carts littered the corridors at any time.

He asked a maid to open a vacant room. The carpet had stains, as did the credenza. The drapes were an inch too short—one too many cleanings. In the bathroom, the soap was standard, the lotions cheap. There was nothing that would make a guest feel special.

What a goddamn shame! What a goddamn waste!

* * * * *

Lew Levenson poured himself a scotch from a crystal decanter on the sideboard set underneath a Chagall oil painting in his studio office. It was three days after Westerman's funeral.

"Do you think she'll sell?" he asked Rolfe.

"I'm positive. She'll want to turn all his assets into cash. According to Susan, Adele begged Steve to sell, but he was in love with The Hills and said it'd be the last thing he'd do."

"So now you think it's the first thing she'll do?" Walters asked. Rolfe nodded.

Levenson tossed down his scotch. "Then how can we help?"

"Find a way to buy The Hills for us. There's nothing but upside. But if she finds out I'm involved, it'll be the kiss of death. If she doesn't, The Hills will be Steve's memorial. I can't wait to restore it."

* * * * *

"You look happy," Dagmar said, as Rolfe tossed his jacket and tie onto their bed.

"I am. Let's celebrate." He led her to the living room where he opened a bottle of Dom Perignon kept chilled in the wet bar, poured the champagne into two Baccarat crystal flutes, and kissed her when she'd taken a sip.

"Celebrate what?" she asked, flushing with pleasure.

He lifted his glass. "Our newest hotel."

She laughed. "What's so special about another hotel?"

"It's not about 'another hotel.' It's The Hills. Our first luxury property."

"Doesn't it belong to Adele Westerman? She'd never sell it to you."

"She doesn't know it's me. Lew Levenson brokered the deal. After he offered her a part in his next movie, she didn't care who was behind it."

She shared his happiness. "Adele's an actress?"

"She thinks she is. Lew told me her screen test was so awful that when the picture's edited, she'll be lucky to end up as an extra." He kissed her again, enjoying the feel of her for the first time in weeks. "But the best part's this. At today's closing, Mark Walters told her she'd be the next Sophia Loren."

* * * * *

"Do we have a deal?" Chantal asked brusquely.

"Yes. You persuade Hunt to let me represent him, and I'll pay you forty percent of my fees." Pieter Vermeij's chuckle resonated through the phone's receiver.

* * * * *

"Rolfe's bought The Hills," Chantal announced, sprawled on a chaise in the presidential suite of the Boston Metropolitan.

"Old news," Hunt grumbled. "I hired you to be ahead of the game, not behind it. Anyway, I gather the price was outrageous."

"But it's more up-market than anything we own."

"True. Another Ritter ego trip."

She looked at him coyly. "And what about your ego? What if Metropolitan could acquire a luxury chain?"

"A chain?" She had his attention.

"The Audleys. Granted, they're a step below the very best right now, but with some cash and your know-how—"

"We'd be the leader instantly. Shove luxury up Ritter's ass." He paused. "But the Audleys aren't for sale."

She stretched seductively. "Sometimes, I'm ahead of the game after all."

* * * * *

"Do you really think it's possible to buy the Audley hotels?" Hunt asked Pieter Vermeij the next morning via transatlantic phone.

"I do. I know Sir Alan Germaine reasonably well. He told me last week that if the right buyer came along, one with buckets of money, he might be about to persuade the terrible twins to sell."

"The terrible twins?" Hunt asked.

"His younger siblings. If she says 'black,' her brother says 'white'—and if Sir Alan says anything, they tell him he's a horse's ass. But money's more important than family antagonisms, so Sir Alan can probably talk them into it."

"And Sir Alan's a seller?"

"Absolutely. He's in his seventies, his wife's been sick, his son was crippled in a skiing accident—all the signs are auspicious. But under the terms of the inheritance, he has to run the business unless the terrible twins agree to a sale."

Hunt could feel a rush of adrenaline. Things were bad at home—they'd had to put Mary in rehab and Carol was distraught, blaming him for their daughter's troubles—but this was compensation. If I'm no longer excited by the chase, he thought, I might as well be dead.

"I want you to represent me and buy the group."

Pieter hesitated. "I'll do it, Bruce, but it's going to take a while, so be patient. Even then it's such a long shot, I'll need a retainer."

"How much?"

"Twenty-thousand per month plus expenses."

"It's yours." He thought. "There's one other thing I'd like you to include in your services."

"Name it."

"I understand your father recently married Rolfe Ritter's mother."

"A few months ago. But that has nothing to do with my professional life."

"It does now. I want you to keep tabs on Ritter. Tell me everything you can find out about what he's doing and especially if he's nosing around Sir Alan."

"But that's unethical!"

"I don't see how."

You wouldn't, Pieter thought. But the idea intrigued him. By monitoring Rolfe for Hunt, he could monitor Hunt for Rolfe. "Your wish," he told Hunt, "is my command."

CHAPTER 26

1978

In April, Bud McCory was elected by a landslide as head of the 225,000-member National Hotel and Restaurant Workers' Union. Rolfe and Dagmar hosted a party to celebrate his victory in the main ballroom of Kestrel San Francisco, which had been decorated as an Irish village, complete with bars, shops, and a union meeting hall. McCory left on the arm of a blond actress, provided by Lew Levenson, and Rolfe knew he had more fodder for his safe deposit box, since McCory's wife had not been invited to the party.

* * * * *

"Daddy!"

Dagmar threw herself into her father's arms. This was the longest time they had ever been apart, but now Steinmann was in Los Angeles, for the first time visiting the mansion she had built and decorated in a style Rolfe loathed, all brocades, silks, tassels, and heavy furniture. Steinmann was suitably impressed.

Rolfe was in Hong Kong structuring the financing of a new Kestrel Hotel, so father and daughter were alone. The Ritters' cook had made them an Dagmar's favorite meal, schnitzel and potato pancakes, and both were flushed with Rhine wine from Rolfe's cellar. They talked of homeland, of her childhood, and, finally, of her marriage.

"You are happy?" he asked.

"I love him," she sighed.

"That is not an answer."

"Well, then, yes, very happy. Only—"

He waited. She hesitated. "Go on."

"Only, he doesn't want children. The first time I brought it up, he told me he didn't want any part of a Steinmann child and that he would leave me if I ever got pregnant. From then on, he has refused to even discuss it."

Steinmann's expression grew dark. "He 'doesn't want a Steinmann child.' How dare he say that! How dare he think that. It was part of the deal. *Gott in Himmel*, Dagmar, it would mean the end of my line."

"I know. But what can I do?"

"Get pregnant. You're on the pill?"

She nodded, embarrassed.

He didn't notice. "Then forget to take it."

She looked at him with wild eyes. "I did."

"And?"

"I got pregnant."

"You see! Splendid! When is the baby due?"

She bowed her head. "I aborted it."

"You what?" He stood over her, his face livid with fury.

"Had an abortion. The day I found out, he came home in a good mood. Better than good. *The New York Times* gave him a four-star award for the Kestrel Central Park South restaurant, and he's always thrilled at any prestige. We made love that night, more passionate and beautiful than ever before. I loved him so deeply and so tenderly that I knew I could not bear to risk losing him. Oh, Father, if I had a baby, he would leave, and this life, this glorious time with Rolfe, would end."

Steinmann looked at her with contempt.

"But he doesn't love you. You know he married you only to get the Solvengs."

"Maybe then. But he loves me now. I'm sure of it."

"Fool." He slapped her, the sound of the blow as shocking as the pain. She covered her face with her hands and leaned her head against the table, her body heaving with sobs.

"I'm sorry," he said. "I didn't mean—" He stood next to her and stroked her hair. "My darling girl, I would never hurt you."

Her sobs increased. The red welts on her left cheek blazed like a neon sign. He remained immobile, powerless, realizing that he, not Rolfe, had lost her love. He, who had given her everything, including this scoundrel who was about to cheat him out of his grandchildren. The irony of it twisted in his brain until he saw serpents.

But it was not too late. He waited until his daughter had cried herself to sleep, and then used the phone in Rolfe's study to dial a number in Greenwich, Connecticut.

"Bruce, this is Hans Steinmann. We need to talk."

* * * * *

"If you'd consulted me before you sold the Solvengs out from under me, I'd have warned you about Ritter," Hunt said, unable to stop his recriminations and not entirely displeased by the German's anguish. "The man has the morals of an alley cat."

The two men were sitting in Hunt's office. "I did it for Dagmar," Steinmann repeated. "You'd have done the same for your Mary."

The fuck I would, Hunt thought. His seventeen-year-old was now in at Silver Hill, a white-collar residential treatment center for addicts, sent there by a bitch of a judge who had lectured him on parents who think success is more important than family. He had bought the co-op to appease a devastated Carol. Steinmann was still talking. He forced himself to concentrate.

"Dagmar still claims to love Ritter, but I hate him. You want to destroy him and his company, and I'm here to volunteer my help."

Thoughts of Mary vanished. "How?"

"Through Dagmar, I can find out everything about his business. And I'll buy fifty million of your stock now and another fifty million the day he's destroyed. Anonymously, of course. I wouldn't want Ritter to know about it—that is, until he goes under and I can shove it in his face."

Hunt beamed. "After that, of course, you'll join the Metropolitan board of directors, just as we'd planned before you screwed me out of the Solvengs."

* * * * *

"You won't believe this!" Josh barged into Rolfe's office shouting. "They've just launched their own scheme."

"What are you talking about? And who's 'they'?"

"Metropolitan, of course. The same folks who lower their room rates every time we open a competitive Kestrel, who buy convention business away with money-losing deals, who spread rumors about our financial troubles to anyone who listens."

Rolfe excused himself to the man he had been talking to on the phone and replaced the receiver. "You told me not to worry about all that. 'If Hunt wants to lose money, let him,' you said."

"Right. But this time he's done something we can't ignore." He took a breath. "Metropolitan's just announced the industry's first frequent guest plan."

Pain sprang up behind Rolfe's eyes. "Like our Guest Bonus program Momo came up with."

"Not 'like.' It's identical. The only difference is they call theirs 'Metropolitan Merits.'"

"Shit! It's not possible. Unless—"

"That's right," Josh interrupted. "Unless someone gave the details of our scheme to Metropolitan." He sat down heavily in an armchair. "Six months work, down the goddamned toilet!"

"We can still launch, can't we?" Rolfe asked.

"Sure, but we'll look like copycats."

"Jesus Christ," Rolfe said as the implications drew clearer. "Who could have leaked it?"

"I don't have a clue. We kept this quiet, worked on a need-to-know basis only. Only a few people saw the whole program."

"Who?"

"The executive committee—you, me, Susan, Momo."

"It couldn't have been any of us. Are you sure it's not a coincidence?" Even as he asked, he knew the answer.

"Coincidence my ass," Josh said. "We've got a mole."

CHAPTER 27

1979–1980

Rolfe walked into the head of security's office at Heathrow Airport, feeling apprehensive. Mike Riverstone's message was, "See me ASAP." It was no problem for Rolfe to stop in London on his way back from Budapest, Prague, and Warsaw, where he had negotiated deals for new Kestrels, taking advantage of the cheap construction costs and Warsaw Pact government subsidies in Eastern Europe. Nevertheless, he wished he knew Uncle Mike's purpose. The venue was not arbitrary—there was some kind of mission involved. It was right here in London where he'd almost been killed for helping Riverstone, and he wondered what the intelligence chief had in mind for him this time.

Mike was not alone. Standing in a corner of the office, looking as searchingly at Rolfe as Rolfe looked at him, was a tall, wire-thin man of about forty, dressed in an impeccably cut blue suit, mirror-polished shoes, and a tightly knotted maroon tie. Large black-rimmed glasses covered watery eyes and rested on a nose obviously broken so many times Rolfe wondered whether the man was a former boxer.

"I'd like to introduce you to Kenneth Palmer," Mike said after he and Rolfe embraced. "Ken took over from me when I retired. I decided it's time you met."

Palmer strode over to Rolfe, hand extended like a maitre d' approaching his most important customer. Rolfe shook it warily.

"We want your help again," Palmer said.

Rolfe turned away, trying to suppress the familiar nervous thrill. "Thank you, no. I did what you wanted in San Francisco, and that's it. I prefer to live."

Riverstone chuckled. "If you hadn't disobeyed my instructions in the first place, nothing would have happened to you."

"What happens if I don't agree?" Rolfe directed the question at Palmer.

"Nothing at all."

"You'll have let us down, of course," Mike said. "And apart from missing the excitement I know you like, you might feel you let your father down."

"My father's dead," Rolfe snapped. His godfather's comment cut deep, and the words were out before he could censor them. "He got 'let down' doing precisely the kind of work you're asking me to do."

"There'll be no risk this time," Palmer said smoothly. "Besides, if you agree, you'll find it helps your business immeasurably. As the saying goes, 'You scratch my back, I'll scratch yours.'" The two intelligence men stared at him, waiting.

"I'm listening."

"We want to put our people in your new hotels in Eastern Europe," Palmer said.

"And if you arrange it," Mike answered, "we'll help as best we can to find opportunities for you in the Soviet Union."

Russia! From the moment he had bought the Solvengs and established a European base, Rolfe had longed to establish a presence in the heart of the Soviet bloc. Even in this era of belligerence, he could foresee the Cold War ending, and he knew the first Western hotelier in the Soviet Union would have unlimited prospects.

"Now, I'm listening hard," he said. "What sort of people?"

"Just a few here and there," Palmer drawled.

"Be specific."

Palmer glanced at Riverstone, who almost imperceptibly nodded. "We'd like our people in your management teams, in accounting, among the concierge and bell captain staffs, and in bar management."

"Bar management!" Rolfe couldn't repress a laugh. "In God's name, why?"

"Eastern Europeans like to drink. Big shots boast when they're drunk. We want you to replicate the Long Bar in the Kestrel San Francisco in your Eastern European properties."

Rolfe was enjoying himself. "First, tell me what your plan is, and then I'll tell you why it's impossible."

"Simple," Riverstone explained. "We want to make Kestrel bars the social places in each city. With our people running them, they'll get enough information to keep MI5 up to date on who's in and who's out, who's coming to what city when, who's sleeping with who, whose business is a cover for something else—everything they might want to keep their eager little brains churning."

"Then you'll have every table bugged, I suppose?"

Palmer folded his arms contentedly. "You suppose correctly."

"Jesus!" Rolfe shook his head, already caught up again in Riverstone's alluring web. "You guys would bug your grandmothers."

"If it would give us an advantage over a formidable enemy," Riverstone said gravely. "For all their seeming willingness to open up, the Soviets are still deadly and dangerous."

"And they wanted to kill me, or had you forgotten?" My father? The black cars? The night outside the Audley? "I think you're nuts," Rolfe said, "but if that's the way you want to play, so be it. But get another hotel-builder. I'm not your man."

"You're our only man, and you know it," Riverstone said. "The only person we can trust."

"Then let me tell you why it's impossible." He felt suddenly angry, manipulated. These men might be expert spies—though this discussion made him doubt it—but they weren't businessmen, and they certainly knew nothing about hotels. "If the bars are going to be social centers, they'll have to be tarted up. Made irresistibly seductive. Do you have any idea how much such gin palaces cost to build? Where am I going to find the money?"

"That's just it," Palmer said, his voice a hum of self-satisfaction. "Our Prime Minister Margaret Hilda Thatcher is going into the bar business."

* * * * *

Rolfe arrived back exhausted. Yet, the more he thought about his godfather's proposition, the more he relished being in collusion with British Intelligence. Riverstone's mention of Wim and his own Pavlovian responses to invocations of his father—guilt, competitiveness, unworthiness—had once more set his adrenaline going.

Still thinking about Palmer and Riverstone, he was less enthusiastic than he might have been about Andrew McDonald's report that Kestrel guests gave them much higher scores than for any other chain in the areas of service, décor, product quality, and value for the money. He almost unthinkingly approved Andy's suggestion that they use Carly Simon's "Nobody Does It Better" as the keystone of a new marketing campaign with the sole admonition that We've got to stay better, and we need a plan to make sure we do.

"Who should develop such a plan?" he asked Josh Leonard. "I don't want to use outside consultants; we'd have to teach them too much about our business before they began."

"There's only one person who's got all the skills we need," Josh told him.

"Who?"

"Momo." He laughed. "Da-dum! She's just been made head of strategic planning."

* * * * *

"You challenged me to figure out how we can make sure to replicate our service at every hotel, no matter how fast we grow," Momo said a few weeks later. "Well, I think I've come up with an answer."

"Tell me tomorrow, when I'm fresher," he said. "It's been a long day, and I'm due home in an hour."

"Having a home-cooked dinner in front of the TV is more important than the future of your company?"

"Very funny," he grumbled. "In fact, Dagmar's dragging me to the opening of a gallery in Westwood. Besides, it's the cook's night out, and my wife doesn't know where the kitchen is."

"Then spare me a few minutes to tell you what I think we should do." Her excitement was obvious. He wondered how she managed to look as fresh at the end of the day as she did at the beginning.

He smiled at her. "They're yours."

"It's so easy, I don't know how the head of strategic planning missed it."

"Before you, there was no head of strategic planning."

"Sure there was. You. Only you didn't have the title." She put her hand on his shoulder to show she was kidding. The touch startled him, and he looked at her quickly to see if she meant anything more by it, but she was staring at the flipchart she had brought with her.

"There are two stages. What we have to do first is take the things we do best and know our guests appreciate the most, write them down and quantify them. For example, we get the best guest satisfaction rating when we make sure a guest never has to wait more than three minutes to check in or out; our switchboard always answers after three rings; if room service promises delivery in twenty minutes and the food is in the room in twenty minutes; and when each time a guest orders a particular dish, it looks and tastes the same." She paused.

"Easier said than done."

"Not really. The first part is mechanized; we forecast our occupancy, figure out which hours are busiest for every service, and then staff accordingly for those hours. It's all about planning.

"The second part is harder, but it's what will keep us ahead of everyone else." She turned the page of the flipchart. *Attitude*, she had written. "That's the key," she said, responding to his quizzical expression. Everyone who comes into contact with a guest has to have a smiling, can-do, how-can-I-help-you attitude, and mean it."

He sighed. "Again, easier said than—"

"Not if we recruit the right people and train them to the very specific standards I've just written down. We give them bonuses when they succeed and fire them if they don't." She looked at him accusingly. "And that includes you, Mr. Ritter. When I came in this afternoon, you scowled at me like a lion defending his dinner. But if you're smiling and friendly and optimistic, the organization will follow."

He knew he was blushing. "Sorry," he said. "Get it down in writing so you can present it to the executive committee. And from now on, I'll be good." He picked up his briefcase. "That is, if Dagmar doesn't kill me for being late."

She didn't kill him. She just watched without recrimination as he showered and got into his evening clothes.

She rarely talks to me, he thought. I'm her ornament. And is that whiskey I smell on her breath?

* * * * *

Two weeks before Christmas, Rolfe returned to his office after lunch to find a package on his desk wrapped in silver paper. An envelope was scotch-taped to its side. He ripped it open.

> *R:*
>
> *I found this on a recent trip to Asia. I hope it gives you peaceful thoughts and helps you through your hectic days. I think of you always.*
>
> *C*

He opened the box. Inside was an antique bronze of two hands, palms up as if in supplication, mounted on black metal rods set in a marble base. They must have been detached from a larger figure, probably a Buddha, he thought—peaceful thoughts through hectic days. Exactly.

Chantal was working for Bruce Hunt, he knew, and the announcement had hit him hard. But his reaction wasn't fair. She had expertise in the hotel business and public relations; he, Rolfe, was married and had told her their relationship was over. Why shouldn't she work for Hunt? Still, when he saw her name in the paper as the hostess of a Metropolitan event, it rankled. So the present pleased him. At least she wasn't angry anymore.

He buzzed Miranda, his new assistant. "Get me Chantal Le Peron," he said. "She's at Metropolitan's corporate office in New York."

"It's beautiful," he said as soon as Chantal was put through. "Thank you. It'll adorn my desk forever. And thanks, too, for the note, though when I think of you my thoughts can't be described as peaceful."

She laughed. "When I saw it, I knew it was perfect for you. You were always good with your hands."

"I miss you," he said.

"And I you. New York's boring. And Bruce—well, he's a dear man, but he's not—"

"Not what?"

"Not you. In any way."

So she wasn't having an affair with him, he decided. He had wondered about that. The thought pleased him.

"How's married life?" she asked.

I get the message, he thought, but answered seriously. "Different."

"That good?" she said, obviously amused. "I hear you have the biggest house in Bel Air."

He grunted. "Dagmar has the biggest house. I just share a room."

"The bedroom?"

"From time to time." Her talk was exciting him. He thought of her instead of Dagmar in his spectacular bed.

"It's good to hear your voice," she said gaily. "Next time you come to Manhattan, let me buy you a glass of champagne. You can tell me all about Dagmar and your bedroom."

* * * * *

He flew to New York right after New Year's. A glass of champagne at the Metropolitan turned into dinner at Lutece. She did most of the talking, chatting about her life in New York, the new friends she had made, a new marketing campaign she was considering for Metropolitan ("I shouldn't be telling you this," she giggled), and her immediate boss, Henry Monroe, Bruce Hunt's number two—"and number two's a good way to describe him."

He laughed. "And Bruce himself? How do you get on with him?"

"I don't see him much. His days are regimented. You have to make an appointment to see him way in advance, even though you work for him."

Rolfe thought of Momo, Susan, Andrew, and Josh, who could burst in on him at any time. A difference in style, he thought, preferring his own. "Tell me more."

"As you'd guess, he's methodical, organized, always in control, always calm. Except when it comes to Kestrel." She lifted her wineglass in salute. "He's obsessed with you. God knows what you did to him, but mention your name, and he goes into a rant. It makes me cringe."

"So why do you stay?" Rolfe asked. "I still can't believe you're there in the first place."

She shrugged. "It's a good job. Where else am I going to find a position like this? With Kestrel?" She stared at him.

"You're right. Only I wish—"

She silenced him with a kiss. And later that night, it seemed the most natural thing in the world when they made love in his hotel suite.

* * * * *

On the flight back, a question obsessed him: How could he ever get in bed again with his wife?

* * * * *

"Congratulations. It's a fine piece of work."

Momo had finished the presentation of her plan to him, prior to showing it to the others the following morning. "Do you think they'll like it?" she asked.

"They'll be as knocked out as I am."

"You don't count," she laughed. "You're only the boss. I have to work with Josh, Andrew, and Susan."

How radiant she looks, he thought. She's proud of herself, and she should be.

"Do I need to change the presentation at all?"

"It's perfect. Relax, for God's sake."

Momo unplugged the projector and put the carousel of slides

back into its yellow Kodak box.

"It's a quarter to eight," he said. "Have you plans?"

"Exciting ones. A shower, leftover lasagna, Dallas."

"Then try something less exciting. Have dinner with me."

She looked at him, startled. "Dagmar's with her father at the German consulate," he explained. "They're giving him an award. Nazi of the Year, I think. Anyway, I'm free. Let's go upstairs to the club, and I'll buy you a meal. Then we can both go home early."

They sat at a window table and watched the lights of the city. When Rolfe thought about it afterward, he couldn't remember what had been said, only that he hadn't enjoyed himself that much since before he'd gotten married.

Neither of them noticed the nondescript man at the bar watching them intensely.

* * * * *

Dagmar recognized her father's handwriting on the manila envelope sitting on her Louis Quinze desk the following afternoon.

"I'm sorry to have to show you this," he had written. "But I have no choice."

She opened the envelope and with growing dread pulled out five eight-by-ten photos of Rolfe and Momo, sitting in a restaurant, deep in conversation. There was no way to misinterpret the emotion in their expressions.

Numb, she sat staring out the window, seeing nothing, the photos lying forlornly on the floor.

CHAPTER 28

1980–1983

Rolfe listened as familiar footsteps made their way up the stairs.

Dagmar let herself into the dark bedroom and opened her dressing room door. He heard the sounds of her undressing, the flush of the toilet, the on-and-off of the faucet, the opening door, her feet padding across the Persian carpet. She lay down beside him.

"Where have you been?" he asked.

"Out."

Irritation rose in him unchecked. He switched on the light on his night table and turned to face her. "That's obvious. Out where? With whom?"

She yawned. "Let's discuss it in the morning. I'm going to sleep."

"I want to talk about it now. You left this morning before I did. It's three-thirty now. You didn't leave a message when you'd be home, and that's unlike you. I was worried."

"Worried? About me? That's unlike you."

There was a stridency in her voice he had never heard before. "All right. I was worried you were with someone else."

Her laugh was unpleasant. "You, accusing me? You ,of all people?"

Did she know about Chantal? Rolfe wondered. He softened his tone. "I'm not accusing you of anything. I just wanted to know where you were."

He could sense her deciding how to answer. Seconds on the bedside clock ticked by. "I was in Montecito. At Sanjay Advani's retreat."

He sat bolt upright. "You went back to that charlatan?"

"Yes. I've been seeing him for weeks. And he's not a charlatan."

"A fake, then." He remembered his one visit to Advani's compound. Dagmar had taken him there, convinced they could both find "peace and harmony" through his regimen: walks, meditation, spiritual studies. He had found the fiftyish Punjab native no more convincing than an infomercial pitchman. "I thought you agreed he was feeding us a load of bullshit."

"You were rude to him. And you never asked me how I felt about him."

"Rude? I simply asked him how he reconciled his preachings on simplicity with his book and TV contracts."

"They're not incompatible. He has a message of supreme importance. Books and television are the best ways to deliver it. Besides, he forgives you."

"I don't need his forgiveness."

"I think you do," Dagmar said quietly. "His and mine."

"Yours? For what?"

"For Momo."

"Momo!" The word exploded from him as if she had discovered his most hidden secret. His relationship with Momo was platonic, but in his fantasies. . . "Momo's a colleague, part of the executive committee. How can you possibly think she's anything more?"

"You had dinner with her two weeks ago."

How did Dagmar know that? "True. Where we discussed her plan for a new campaign called 'Attitude.'"

She stared at him, trying to assess his words. "That's all it was?"

"As God is my judge! You were at the consulate with your father. She had worked late on the campaign. I took her to dinner. Period."

"You're not sleeping with her?"

"I swear it."

"Oh, thank God," she whispered. "Thank God!" She took his hand and brought it to her breast. "Rolfe?"

The storm had passed, he knew; she had not found out about Chantal. "Yes?"

"Something wonderful happened today."

He kissed the top of her head and began to caress her breast. "What?"

"Sanjay's going to dedicate his next book to me."

He felt a wave of revulsion, as though he had bitten into rancid meat. "When will it be published?"

"Soon. And in return, you and I are going to donate one-hundred-thousand to his foundation."

* * * * *

Susan and Josh sat in front of Rolfe's desk. She handed him a report. "Here are the brutal facts," she said. "Prime rate just went up to twenty-point-five percent. Our interest rates are generally two-point-five percent above prime. That means we're paying up to twenty-three percent annual interest."

"Significance?" Rolfe asked, a hollow feeling in his stomach.

"We don't have the money to pay the interest on our debts." Susan paused a moment to let the message sink in. "We've run through all our lines of credit. We're out of cash."

I've heard this story before, Rolfe thought, though we've never faced rates like this. "What happens if we don't pay the interest?"

Josh answered, his voice somber. "Our lenders will default us and come after both the company and you personally for repayment. We'll be forced to put property after property into bankruptcy just to protect ourselves. On top of that, you'll have to declare bankruptcy yourself, because you've personally guaranteed most of the loans. The crazy part is that the properties, the management company, and the Kestrel brand are worth a hell of a lot more than our debts."

Rolfe saw Susan and Josh share a look and realized they had discussed this beforehand.

"I know you don't want to sell the company or any of the hotels, but maybe you should," Josh said.

"Never!"

They stared at each other, neither willing to back down. "What happens if we explain the situation to our lenders and simply ask for their patience?" Rolfe asked at last.

Josh took his time. "Two things. First, you'll have lost your credibility, and it'll be a long time before they lend you money again. Worse, they'll force you to dispose of assets on a fire-sale basis."

"And the other thing?"

"You're not going to like it," Susan said, her face ashen. "You, Josh, and I signed financial statements for our banks and lenders, showing Kestrel Hotels' net worth, the property company's net worth, and your own net worth. The three of us know we boosted the value of all of the assets, neglected to mention many of our debts, our equipment leases, and those tens of millions in personal guarantees you've signed."

He shrugged, trying to push away his feeling of impending doom. "So? Nobody has to know that."

"We lied!" she shouted, her face flushing. "Apart from whatever they can do to us in civil court, we've consciously perpetrated fraud, and that's criminal."

Rolfe felt his head balloon to near bursting. "I didn't realize—"

"Of course you goddamned realized!" Josh interjected. "You knew full well what we were doing from the day we took our first working capital loan from the Bank of San Francisco."

"But criminal?"

"Yes, Rolfe, criminal," Josh said quickly. "Go-to-jail stuff. And let me tell you something, neither Susan or I are about to go to jail for you."

"You'll have to sell," Susan said. "It's the only way out."

He looked at their pleading faces, thought of what Dagmar would say when he told her they'd have to give up the mansion, and of Steinmann's joy at his humiliation. "I can't do it," he said. "I'm not going to sell. Not yet." He tried to smile. "Come on, guys. There has to be a way. For Christ's sake, buy us some time."

"I can start contesting bills, deferring payments," Susan said tentatively after a seemingly endless silence.

"'Atta girl! Will that do it?"

"Not even close," Josh sneered.

"So, what else?"

"There's one last resort. It's risky, but it might work."

Rolfe practically leapt from his chair. "Let's hear it."

Josh spoke as if at a wake. "We borrow from the reserves we've set aside to refurbish hotels in the future, and we hide the fact with some fancy wordsmithing and bookkeeping and a whole lot of pressure on our auditors. We've got lots of money sitting there, but remember, it's not our money, it's our partners', it's the hotel owners'. And if the lenders find out it's there, they'll want to get their hands on it."

"Will it be enough?" Rolfe asked.

"We'll be breaking every agreement we've made if we touch it."

"Will it be enough?"

"It may be," Josh whispered.

Relief flooded him like a balm. "Then let's do it." He put up a hand as Josh started to protest. "No more talk. It's decided. Do it."

"Okay," Josh said. "But I've got one more thing to say: What you're doing is risky and probably criminal. My advice is to sell. It's Susan's advice too. Because I love you and because I've loved the ride, I'll go along with you this one last time. But 'last' means last, Rolfe. If we get caught, it's your neck, not ours. I'll claim we knew nothing about this, and if you deny it, I'll spill every secret you've ever kept."

Rolfe turned to Susan. "You too? If this doesn't work, you're gone?"

She looked at him levelly. "Fucking A."

* * * * *

"It's not going to happen," Pieter Vermeij told Bruce Hunt in Hunt's office. He had an idea he wanted to tempt Hunt with and had flown to New York to meet with Metropolitan's CEO.

"Why not?" Hunt asked. "Surely, there's a price Germaine will sell for. Find it."

"Sir Alan wouldn't give me a number. He told me his younger brother, Geoffrey, doesn't want to sell at any price."

"Did Germaine give you a reason?"

"Yes. Whether I believe it or not is another matter. Geoffrey wants to stand for parliament and thinks he'll have more credibility if he's part-owner of the Audley Hotels than if he's just a wealthy man."

The Audleys were Hunt's target after Ritter had cheated him out of the Solvengs and snatched The Hills from under his nose. More elegant, more prestigious, and more expensive than the Solvengs, their acquisition would fulfill Hunt's plans to extend into Europe and would fuck Rolfe Goddamned Ritter once and for all.

"Why don't you believe him?" he asked.

"Because Geoffrey's twin sister wants to sell, and that's the kiss of death as far as he's concerned."

"Family," Hunt said, thinking of Mary, who these days categorically vetoed any plans he and Carol had for her.

"A member of my family is in trouble, too," Pieter said, finally getting to the matter he had come for. "Steinmann told you Rolfe's up to his ears in debt, and with the prime rate at twenty-point-five percent, he's got serious cash flow problems."

Hunt grinned. "That's right, but how do you propose to make use of it?"

"He trusts me. He'll believe me if I tell him an anonymous foreign group's willing to put up seriously high numbers for a majority position in Kestrel." Pieter felt no guilt. Whatever pleasure he had felt at the bond they had pledged when Jan revealed their parentage had dissipated long ago before the memory of childhood wrongs.

"Which foreign group?" Chantal had coached Pieter well. He could practically see Hunt begin to salivate.

"Metropolitan."

"Oho!" Hunt roared. "Brilliant!"

"I'll tell him the buyers want him to stay as chief executive and to keep his entire team together. He'll tell his bankers and creditors what's going on, if only to buy some time. I'll even bring in a Lebanese I know who'll pretend he's heading up a Middle-Eastern investor syndicate. Ritter's desperate. He'll believe anything I serve up. They'll put more pressure on him, push him to sell. I'll negotiate severance packages 'just in case' by telling him I'm protecting him and his people. Eventually, he won't be able to hold out. And just as the papers are being signed—voila, you reveal yourself, fire the lot of them, and, sooner rather than later, you'll buy his minority interest at a deep discount."

Hunt stood and grasped Pieter's hand. "Jesus," he said, "you're so devious I'd almost think you were American."

* * * * *

When he calmed himself, Rolfe went back to the hotels. They were his roots. They were what excited him. His title might be chief executive but he was first and last a hotel manager.

By the time he'd ended his European tour, he was refreshed. He had persuaded the general manager at the Milan hotel to increase the room rates and go for a more up-market guest, even if occupancy suffered. He'd told his Frankfurt manager to convert his loss-making gourmet restaurant into a much-needed meeting room, modified the bedroom design for the not-yet-finished Zurich hotel, and started a weekly lunchtime chef's table in the kitchen of the Paris Kestrel to which guests would be invited.

As he drove to the dock on Pont D'Alma, thoughts of his balance sheet had faded from his mind.

* * * * *

"Happy birthday," Rolfe said, clinking his champagne glass against his mother's as the *bateau mouche* he'd chartered to celebrate her sixtieth birthday passed in front of Notre Dame cathedral.

"Don't you think this is too much?" she asked, indicating the platoon of tuxedoed waiters and the brigade of chefs from his Paris hotel serving them on the normally crowded boat.

"You're the only mother I've got, and you're only sixty once," he said, feeling a wave of melancholy. He had hoped his "surprise"—the trip to Paris as well as the night cruise—would bring them closer together, but Margaret had remained studiously remote. He knew expectations of warmth were unrealistic. Still, he was pleased with himself for trying, and he allowed himself to hope—until his mother made him feel like one of her hundred suitors, meaning, no more to her than the concierge at their hotel.

"Jan told me you were worried about money," his mother said, unconcerned.

"Worried isn't the word. I'm forever on the brink of catastrophe. It's an endless struggle."

"Well, if your company's in trouble, at least you'll be personally all right."

He glanced at her. Her face was marble in the reflecting lights off the river. "Do you remember the one million pounds your grandfather left you in trust?"

He had forgotten. "Vaguely," he answered, noticing the change in the engine's noise as it began its approach to the dock.

"It's been ten years now, and the trust is due. The money's yours."

"It can't be ten years already!"

She smiled grimly. "I've got the wrinkles to prove it. Anyway, I've invested it carefully; it's worth a lot more than a million now."

The boat bumped up against the dock. "How much?"

"Three and a half million pounds," she said quietly.

Over $5 million dollars! Not nearly enough, of course, to rescue Kestrel, but as personal income, plenty for "fuck-you money." As Ron Falkman once described it: "Money no one knows you have. If things really go bad, you take it, say 'fuck you' to everyone, and walk away."

Well, everything was bad. If his beloved company survived, it would be more by luck than by judgment. His allies, Josh and Susan, had been treating him warily, and he felt the diminution of their love. What little had remained of his ethics was now in tatters. His marriage was in chaos. Chantal was working for Bruce Hunt. And Momo, the star of his fantasies, was as remote as a lighthouse across a black sea.

He took his mother's arm and helped her up the steps to the landing. "I don't want it."

She stumbled, and he had to hold tight to keep her from falling. "But I thought—"

"Keep it for another ten years," he told her, feeling foolhardy and lightheaded. "Invest it if you want, or let me sign it over to you. But if you keep it for me, do not—under any circumstances, no matter if I get down on my knees and beg for it—give it to me." She's looking at me as if I'm crazy, he thought. "Promise."

They had reached the top of the stairs, and she disengaged his hand. "Of course, darling. Whatever you wish. You know all I want is what's best for you."

CHAPTER 29

1984

"Sure you won't have a drink?" McCory asked.

Chantal stared at him wide-eyed. They were sitting at a window table overlooking the ice rink at Rockefeller Center. "What's this about, Mr. McCory?"

"Ah, innocence," he said. "How very attractive in an attractive woman." He returned her stare. "Let me warn you, I know everything about you."

"I have no idea what you're talking about," she said, her emotions betrayed by her reddened cheekbones.

"I think you do. You're using Hunt and Ritter at the same time. Quite the little double agent, aren't you?"

"So what?" she blazed. "I know that Rolfe and Bruce backed your campaign. Extortion, I think it's called. They both told me."

McCory felt her fear and smiled. "And what are you going to do with that knowledge?" He signaled for another Bushmills. "I'll tell you what—nothing. You're fucking those guys for your reason and I'm fucking them for mine."

She stood; he could see her tremble. "I'm not listening to more," she said. "If you want to blackmail me, go ahead and try."

"Sit down," he spat. "Now!"

She obeyed automatically.

His tone softened. "Blackmail's hardly what I had in mind. We're going to be partners."

"What?"

"Partners," he continued smoothly. "You and me. You're going to resign from Metropolitan and start your own consulting business. I'll bankroll you, you'll give me half the profits, and I'll make sure Kestrel and Metropolitan are among your first clients." He sat back, watching her carefully. A cat licking up cream, he thought. "Sound good?"

"And what am I giving you?"

"Information. Each of them trusts us and thinks we hate the other. We'll manipulate them into making us a fortune."

"I could give you information if I still worked for Hunt. Why the move?"

"Because this way you'll be mine," he said, "and I can keep an eye on you."

✳ ✳ ✳ ✳ ✳

"This is all we need!" Josh said, passing Longstreet's report on Chantal and Rolfe to Susan. "She's back big time, and he's doing little to hide it."

"Then Steinmann's bound to know. I wonder if he's told Dagmar, and if so whether either of them wants to do anything about it. God, he's left himself open to—" Susan sighed. "That idiot. I feel sorry for him."

Josh glanced at her. "Do I detect an old flame still burning?"

"Not an ember. No, I just can't stand it when he puts us all in jeopardy. Do you think he knows his Mata Hari's sleeping with Hunt?"

"I doubt it."

"Then you don't think he ought to be told?"

"Probably." He paused. "Your job."

"Oh, no! You're the president of this company."

"He'll take my head off."

"I'll buy you a new one." She grew serious. "Tell him, Josh. You've got to."

✳ ✳ ✳ ✳ ✳

"So that's why you've been so standoffish," Chantal said after Rolfe had related Josh's accusations. They were in his suite at the Los Angeles Kestrel.

"Tell me they're not true."

"They're not true. I've never slept with Bruce Hunt, and I never will. In fact, I'm about to quit Metropolitan, and start my own marketing consulting firm."

The news astonished him, though he doubted she was telling the truth about Hunt. "Meaning what?"

"Meaning, I can do work for you as well as Hunt—and anybody else who can pay for my services."

Maybe meaning that she and Hunt had a fight, he thought. If

252

they were lovers, they weren't anymore. But did it matter? Was she an opportunist, a liar, a Circe? Of course. To hell with it. Right now, he'd rather be in bed with her than anyplace else in the world. How dare Josh criticize him for his personal life?

"What services did you have in mind?"

She reached for him. "Marketing services. These others are only for you."

* * * * *

Rolfe was happy to agree to Pieter's request for a meeting, surprised that his half-brother was in America. The banker sounded excited on the phone. In person, he was practically twitching.

"I've got an overseas investor for you," Pieter said. "Someone who's been watching you for years, thinks you're God's answer to the hotel business. He's convinced Kestrel can be the most successful chain ever, and is willing to bankroll the growth."

Rolfe was unimpressed. "So he wants to buy me out? I'm not interested."

"Not buy! That's what's so attractive. He's willing to let you retain forty-nine percent. And he's willing to put up over a half a billion dollars."

"Jesus!" The number was staggering. The handouts to McCory, the cost of maintaining Dagmar—both would mean nothing. He could finally start clean. And with that sort of money to invest, he could get going in Asia—Tokyo, Singapore, Djakarta, Taipei. Why, with Momo's help—

"You'd maintain effective control," Pieter was saying. "You and your people would run the business just as you have, only you'd have all the capital you need to finish what you've started. He'd be a passive investor."

Dare I trust this man? Rolfe thought. He's sworn friendship, even demonstrated it, but... "Tell me who the buyers are."

"Buyer," Pieter corrected. "He's asked for anonymity until you assure me of your genuine interest. Then, I'll arrange a meeting between the two of you."

Rolfe stood. "Too vague."

Pieter shrugged. "I'll tell him you're not interested. You know perfectly well that to betray his identity would be an abrogation of my ethical principles—and I'd lose a shitload of commission, as you Americans say."

"Then all I can say is, I'll think about it. But keep this fish on the line. I'd be a fool not to take him seriously."

* * * * *

Bruce Hunt listened in silence as Pieter reported to him from a steamy phone booth by the departure gate at LAX. As he put down the phone, even the thought of another confrontation with Carol and Mary couldn't suppress his pleasure. He wanted—no, needed—to have Chantal. Now!

* * * * *

"For $100,000 you get to be told the question and the answer." Bud McCory chuckled as he called Rolfe moments after he'd put the phone down with Chantal.

"What are you talking about?"

"You'll hate yourself for the rest of your life if you don't take my offer." Rolfe felt the steel in McCory's tone. He was serious.

"Okay, Okay. What's the question?"

"Should I believe Pieter Vermeij has a passive investor."

Rolfe recoiled in shock. How in God's name would McCory know about Pieter's visit? "And the answer?"

"No fucking way!"

* * * * *

"Sounds like manna from heaven," Ron Falkman said. "Why would you turn it down?"

"You've said it a thousand times, Ron: 'Manna comes from God; investors come from hell." He shot Falkman a smile. "It sounded great when Pieter explained it, but McCory gave me an informed warning and I'm uneasy about it. It's a week later, and I've still got qualms."

"Then don't do it. Personally, I'd like to see you get rid of some of your burdens, but if there's one thing I've learned it's that you've got great instincts."

"You're probably right," Rolfe said, relieved. "So it'll take a little longer growing the best. Damn it, Ron, everything takes so much money."

"Remember Joseph's dream," the lawyer said. "Seven years' feast followed by seven years famine. In the immediate future, raising capital is going to get easier. Within seven years, things will go bust."

"What's that got to do with my cash flow problems? All your 'help' consists of telling me about Joseph's dream. Anyway, as I remember it, Joseph was put in prison for not banging Potiphar's wife."

* * * * *

The light in the corner of the office highlighted the left side of Kenneth Palmer's face, but the reflection on his glasses made it impossible to see his eyes. Maybe, Rolfe thought, nobody's ever really seen his eyes. "I'm sure you didn't come to chat on your way through L.A.," he said. "If you're anything like my godfather, you never do anything without a motive."

"Quite correct." The intelligence man's expression was blank as a sheet of paper. "We've got a friend in Moscow who wants to build some hotels."

Moscow! Rolfe moved forward in his chair. "Interesting."

"More than that. A great opportunity for both of us. This friend's one of our, shall we say, partners, a KGB man in a senior position in the Soviet Ministry of Finance. Our man believes that within the next decade, the Soviet system will crumble, meaning political and economic chaos, so he's decided to protect himself by doing business with us."

"What's his name?"

"Yevgeny Popov."

"He sounds like a first-class whore. What's this got to do with hotels?"

"His ministry's decided to build an eight-hundred-room hotel in Moscow, and probably another, smaller one in Leningrad. There's nobody in Russia who knows enough to build an interna-tional-class hotel, so he's asked for advice. I mentioned you."

"Who'll put up the money?"

"The Soviet government, and you'll do the rest. In exchange, we want the usual: a full rundown on everything he wants and does. By the way, those Long Bars in Warsaw, Budapest, and Prague are working out just as we planned. You're making some money on them, so they're profitable for both of us."

"I'll do it," Rolfe responded, his heart pumping at the thrill of more of his dad's work. "What's the next step?"

"You and Popov meet. There'll be a private dinner at your house on Friday, just a social affair, so you and he can get to know each other."

"Does Dagmar know about this?"

"She's not to find out."

"What am I supposed to do, lock her in the bedroom?"

"She'll be in Montecito on Friday."

True. He had forgotten. But how the hell did Palmer know? "And the cook?"

"Give her the night off. We'll use our own people as caterers."

"You've thought it through. How did you know I was going to say yes?"

Palmer grinned. "You had no choice." He picked up his hat from the table where he'd tossed it. "One last thing. Be careful. Popov's canny. He's been stationed in London and in Washington, and although he presents himself as just a Russian country boy, don't be fooled. He's smart, ruthless, and extremely dangerous."

* * * * *

Yevgeny Popov was dressed in an Armani suit, sported gold cufflinks and a Dunhill watch.

He can't hide his Russian-thug background behind European accoutrements, Rolfe decided.

Popov was no more than ten years older than Rolfe, but looked sixty. His beak-like features and dark eyes made Rolfe think of a vulture, a Soviet vulture; Rolfe wondered what he had eaten last as carrion. Jan had said he thought the KGB was behind Wim's murder, and memories of that day, his father tossed like a broken clown against an Amsterdam wall, flashed across his mind. Popov even reminded Rolfe of the black car's driver grown up, and he felt a wave of loathing, like a sickness.

They were quickly on a first-name basis, but Rolfe felt no friendship. Indeed, this faux-charming man sitting across from him at the dinner table, partaking of his best wine with a sailor's thirst, seemed the essence of evil. No wonder Palmer wanted to keep track of him and thought him dangerous.

"As you know," Popov said, turning to business over cognac and a Cuban cigar, "our government is interested in opening new hotels in Moscow and Leningrad. They are meant to cater to foreign guests, Europeans and, more importantly, Americans. In these areas we have too little knowledge to rely on our own people to develop the properties." He puffed complacently on his cigar, a man unaccustomed to dissent. "You come highly recommended. I've done some research, of course—I would be a poor public servant if I did not—and what I've found pleases me. Your hotels are a success, you have great personal magnetism and, judging from your house, an ability to live on a grand scale—very Russian. When the job is finished, I'll want only two things from you: your black book with your ladies' phone numbers and your penis transplanted onto mine."

He roared at his own joke, but Rolfe instinctively reached for his genitals. If the job was finished unsatisfactorily, he thought, the transplant might, indeed, take place.

"I understand you have a pragmatic approach to business," the Russian continued. "If so, you're unlike those hypocritical countrymen of yours with their piousness and their ridiculous Foreign Corrupt Practices Act."

In other words, Rolfe understood, instead of preventing direct payments to foreign officials, the law encouraged under-the-table bribes.

"What I propose is this," Popov said, crushing out his cigar and looking unwaveringly at Rolfe. "You design, develop, and manage our two hotels, and I'll accept your standard contract and terms. But you will add one percentage point to your management fee, so instead of four percent, you'll charge five. It'll be a good incentive for you to do your very best."

Pay me more? Rolfe wondered. What's behind it?

"There's another stipulation. You will deposit three million in my bank account the day we sign the contract, and you'll instruct those humorless gnomes in Zurich that two million is to be paid to me when the Moscow hotel opens and the remainder at the completion of the hotel in Leningrad. If neither is open after five years, the money will be returned to you with interest. If I live up to my side of the deal, I keep the money. That's incentive for me." He guffawed. "Oh, and I want twenty percent of all your management fees paid into that same account for as long as you run the hotels. And when I travel, I want to stay free in the best suite if you own a hotel in that city, and naturally I'll want a woman anytime I click my fingers."

Rolfe looked at him blandly.

"Now you know what's in it for me," Popov continued. "But I must give my masters something. So when we build the hotel, the KGB will have every guest room wired for listening devices and some for hidden cameras as well. We'll staff the hotel with agents who will keep them informed about everything that goes on. I'll arrange special parties from time to time for government people, and I want these carefully monitored by you or our designate. Information flowing out of them should be delivered to me personally. Beyond that and a few special services, there will be no other demands."

"What special services?" Rolfe asked, wondering how he would staff a hotel with an equal contingent of Russian and British agents.

"We'll know only when the need arises," Popov said. "I won't ask for anything dangerous to you. And unless you tell Mr. Palmer and his friends what I'm doing, your health is assured. But you'd never do that, would you, Mr. Den Ritter, son of The Kestrel?"

* * * * *

"He scares the shit out of me," Rolfe told Mike Riverstone the next day, imagining his godfather in smug retirement in his London flat. "He knows about my father. What else does he know about me? He wants his spies in my hotels, you want yours. It's a recipe for disaster. Yes, I'd love hotels in Moscow and Leningrad, but this isn't worth it."

"Kenneth will be disappointed, but I'm afraid that can't be helped," Riverstone said too smoothly. "He had to work hard on your dinner guest to persuade him to give the hotels to you rather than your competition."

"What competition was that?" Rolfe asked, knowing the answer.

"Why, Metropolitan, of course. Sure you don't want to change your mind?"

* * * * *

Bruce Hunt swallowed his second McAllens of the afternoon. "Shit," he said. "I was sure Vermeij had him set up."

"He's a fucking cat," McCory said, ordering a third Bushmills. "Nine lives—and a sixth sense."

Hunt grimaced. "Every time I turn around, there's that fucking carpetbagger. He's just made a deal to run hotels in Russia. That is territory I covet. I want him out of my life."

McCory lit a cigarette. "It might be arranged. When you get serious, I have an idea that might seriously damage that kid. But it's going to be fucking expensive, and even so, given the animosity between the two of you, you might be suspected."

"Tell me," Hunt said.

"Not until you're absolutely sure." McCory noted with pleasure that the Metropolitan CEO didn't flinch at the word "expensive." "When you say yes, it's war!"

CHAPTER 30

1984

"Remember," Momo said, "the deeper they bow, the more senior they are. You give your business card to everyone in their party, offering it with both hands, writing facing toward them so they can see your name. They'll offer you their card in return, and you must appear to study them carefully, whether or not you know their name already, and leave them facing you on the table during the meeting."

They were sitting at the bar in the lobby of Tokyo's Imperial Hotel, surrounded by a virtually all-male crowd. Everything was sharp straight lines, Rolfe thought. The rooms, the columns, the barely comfortable furniture. Not his taste, but interesting. He felt jetlagged, having arrived only hours before. Momo was fresh and impeccably dressed in defiantly Western black velvet pants and cashmere sweater—he could see the men's eyes following her and knew he was the object of their envy. She had preceded him by two days and was giving him a lesson on Japanese business etiquette.

"Form is as important as function," she went on. "There is an unwritten script to follow. For instance, we must be exactly on time for every meeting, but not early."

"And if we're not?" Rolfe asked, amused.

"Then the Hong Kong group that's our competition wins the hotel."

This was a Momo he didn't know. No banter, no jokes, no laughter. He realized how nervous she was, how much this project meant to her.

"But in the end," he said, "isn't it money that counts?"

"Not necessarily, though the money's important. For the Japanese, form is a matter of self-protection. Once a person does something out of the norm, it's called 'crossing the red line,' and that can be good or bad. If my cousin Koji's bank arranges debt and equity for this hotel and then, say, for Kestrel hotels in the U.S. or Europe—in other words, if he does something Japanese banks haven't done before, thereby 'crossing the red line,' other banks will follow, insurance companies and leasing companies will be next, and finally the large corporations. A herd mentality."

"So you think there's more in this for us than just the management contract for one Kestrel in Tokyo."

He watched the bar's light play off her black hair, saw it dance in her eyes.

"We've got a chance to be the premier deluxe hotel chain in Asia."

"Ah so," he said, drawing out the words in Japanese fashion. "Then I'd better not embarrass you."

* * * * *

"Yes, Josh, we got the deal!"

Rolfe described the meeting with Hideo Takahashi, the president of Tokyo Power, and the men from the bank. All seemed as anxious as puppies to please him, and he marveled at the job Momo had done to get her cousin Koji, a vice president with Edo Bank and Trust, to bring his banker colleagues on to Rolfe's side.

"Lord knows how much work the pair of them must have done before I arrived to convince them that Kestrel was better than our Asian competitor," Rolfe said. They had brought elaborate mock-ups of the proposed mega-complex, Kestrel's name prominently displayed on the hotel component. "There are plans for an enormous project in Akasaka. One million square feet of offices, which will be Japanese headquarters to the main U.S. investment banks; an enormous high-end retail mall; three movie theaters, a hundred luxury apartments, which we'll service; an entertainment complex with restaurants, bars, nightclubs, and a theater—all linked directly to the subway system by a couple of entrances. And, thanks to Momo, a Kestrel. Just what we needed—a true Asian flagship.

"They wanted my approval," he told Josh. "It was more a question of them selling me than my selling them." The adrenaline rush he had felt through the meeting had dissipated, and now he lay stretched out on his bed, receiver cradled in his neck, exhausted. "It won't surprise you to know that the place is as corrupt as anywhere else. The banks have pieces of the companies they deal with. In this case, Edo has virtually forced Tokyo Power to do this deal; will lend them their money, taking markups and fees on top.

And if we do any deals through Edo or borrow from them, they'll expect the same deal, here or anywhere else. Momo assures me they're better than most banks. Their fees are just exorbitant, not outrageous. By the way, we have to pay the bank an 'introductory fee' for good measure. Everybody's got an angle, and behind all that bowing and scraping, everybody's a killer on the take."

"In short," Josh said, "your kind of place."

Rolfe laughed. "True. Still, it's taken its toll. I'm bushed. Tell Susan, will you, that I'm going to take a week off here to recover."

"And Momo?"

"That's up to her. She'll probably go back."

"Right. Sure." Josh paused. "Only when you hit on her, be gentle. We can't afford to lose her."

"Don't be such a putz," Rolfe laughed. When he'd offered the week to Momo, she'd said she'd stay for "a couple days or so," and he looked forward to his immediate future with an anticipation he hadn't felt in years.

* * * * *

Over the entrance hung a gigantic nose; throughout the restaurant enormous ears, eyes, hands, and feet were laser-lit. A single blaring song, incessant as the drone of flies, played endlessly in the background.

"Mike Oldfield's Tubular Bells," Momo explained. "It's also the name of this restaurant."

The Rappongi restaurant was packed, but Momo was obviously known here, for they had been led to a reserved table in the back, as far as possible from the speakers. "Do they ever play anything else?" Rolfe asked.

"When the dancing starts. Then, it's rock."

He winced. "Couldn't you have picked something quieter?"

"I thought it would be good to show you the young Tokyo. This is the most popular place in the city. You'll have to make something like it part of the hotel."

"Okay. It's fascinating. Now can we leave?"

"Wait for dinner. The food's fantastic."

Sashimi to start. Minced quail on lettuce leaves. Kobe beef. A bottle of fine Australian Chardonnay. The superb food made him comfortable and, now accustomed to the din, he gestured at the couples on the dance floor dressed very much like young Americans in their twenties, only more expensively.

"I'm the oldest person here!"

"No, I am."

She wore a short skirt, black stockings, silk blouse open at the neck, and looked as young—as succulent, he thought—as any of the dancers. "Impossible!"

"It's true," she said. "How does it feel to be escorting an older woman?"

"Not bad, considering she's the most beautiful female in Tokyo."

She blushed, started to say something, and then caught herself.

"Go on," he urged.

"You'll have to get Koji a present."

He knew that was not what she had planned to say, but decided not to press her further. Nevertheless, he noticed a quickening of his heart. When she was ready, she would let him know.

"In fact," she went on, "you've already bought him one."

"Really? What is it?"

"A gold Rolex watch. He probably already has one; they're a sign of great status."

He tried to catch her eye, but she had lowered her head. "Nice of me. Where did I get it?"

"Through the Imperial's general manager. It'll cost you nearly twenty thousand bucks. They'll deliver it to your room tomorrow morning. You can give it to Koji before we go back to the States."

"You amaze me!" he said, indeed amazed. "How did you know I'd say yes?"

"By now, I have an idea how your mind works. I didn't think you'd want to send flowers."

He didn't know how to react or where this was leading. "Am I that transparent?"

"Not unless someone has studied you."

She was looking at him now, her expression unfathomable. "What do you mean?" he asked, intoxicated by hope.

"You're my boss, so you're worth studying. More than that, you're the smartest man in the hotel business. You have incredible instincts—you've demonstrated that here—and an almost prescient feel for the future."

Her answer disappointed him; he had wanted to hear something more . . . personal.

The personal came next, but not the way he imagined. "Recently, you seem to be dragging around a lot of dead weight," she said. "I know you want to build 'the best hotel chain ever' and that everything has to be perfect, even down to the height of those damned calla lilies, and I'm with you every step of the way. But sometimes I wonder if the price is worth it."

"You're right," he answered carefully, his mind filling immediately with an uneasy blend of Hunt, Murtoch, Riverstone, Palmer, McCory, Steinmann, Dagmar, Chantal, and his mother. "It isn't easy. But it's not only financial problems that have got me down; it's also the endless times I've sold my soul to get ahead. That's an even greater burden than forever trying to find money to keep going."

Now her gaze was direct and sympathetic. "Personal problems?"

"I'm afraid so."

"Want to talk about them?"

He hesitated. "They'd bore you."

She took his hand. A jolt of electricity ran through him at the unexpectedness of the gesture. "I'm interested in everything about you," she said. "I get job offers all the time. Do you think I'd have stayed at Kestrel if I weren't?"

What was she saying? That there was something more to their relationship than pure business? That she had agreed to stay on with him in Tokyo not to please him but to please herself? He had become so accustomed to being on his own, to suffering romantic disappointments without confiding his need, that her concern seemed strange to him—and, strangely, he opened his heart.

* * * * *

"And that's the story of Chantal," he finished. "Mysterious, infuriating, seductive Chantal."

"You love her," Momo said flatly.

"Love her? No, not precisely. I did when I was seventeen, but not now."

Her expression was unreadable. "Then why not give her up?"

It was a question he had asked himself a thousand times. "I don't know," he admitted. "Maybe because I've never found anyone to replace her." He caught her quick glance. "I'm lonely. There's no one—"

She was measuring him, he realized, trying to read behind his words. "What about your wife? Rumor is Dagmar was part of the deal for Solveng Hotels."

He acknowledged it with a shrug. "Soon to be ex-wife," he muttered reflexively. "Not my proudest moment." Memories of that grim afternoon in Steinmann's office flooded him, and he hoped Momo did not see his embarrassment. "But in the end it was she who left me, pregnant with another man's child." His voice rose. "That bloody swami of hers, a complete charlatan called Sanjay Advani. It hurt, though I'm not exactly sure why. Pride, I guess. Right now, sitting here with you, I don't know why I stayed in the damned marriage. I should have found the twenty million and paid her off the day after I married her."

Her voice was soothing. "But if Metropolitan had gotten those hotels, we'd still be playing catch-up. You made an incredible sacrifice for Kestrel. Not only did you marry a woman you didn't want, build her a showpiece estate, and get forced into an expensive social life you couldn't stand, but you could see the mistress you 'no longer love' only an odd night here and there. I'm grateful, and I know Josh and Susan are too."

Again, lowered eyes. He felt a surge of pleasure at her teasing.

"Enough about me," he laughed. "Tell me about yourself, Momo the Merciless." He had startled her, he saw.

"Merciless?"

"Isn't that what they called you at IBM?"

"So I was told," she said seriously. "But there, I had to be tough. I've spent my working life trying to prove I can be as good as a man. At IBM that wasn't easy. You know our culture. Imagine how I felt growing up as a half-caste, ambitious woman. Well, at IBM I outworked the men, forced my team to outperform the others—was, in fact, merciless. And when a vice president came on to me at a Christmas party, I answered loudly enough for my colleagues to hear, 'That's very kind of you, but I hear you've got a dick the size of a peanut.'"

He roared. "And they left you alone after that?"

"Nobody came within a hundred yards. But I still didn't like it there, so when Kestrel's offer came up, I accepted. And you, thank God, are gender-blind at work. So is Josh. Don't think Susan and I don't speak about it. Even when we're mad at you, we keep it in mind."

They sat for a moment without speaking. She was looking at him with a half-smile, motionless, save for her fingers playing around her glass of wine. Is she feeling the same tension? he wondered. The same charge?

"You haven't mentioned your personal life," he said at last. Madness! His hands were shaking.

"Nice Japanese girls don't speak of that sort of thing."

"Then be American."

"I fuck like a bunny." Then, seeing his shock, burst out laughing. "Not really. I'm hardly a virgin, but I'm into serial monogamy. There have been a few men, but not many and none now."

He felt his heart lighten. "Why not?"

"Nobody's been the perfect fit. At my age, I should probably be willing to compromise, but in that arena, I'm too merciless."

"Then what are you looking for?" he asked, willing her to give the answer he wanted.

"A man I haven't found."

Perfect! He lifted his glass and gently clinked it against the side of hers. Their eyes focused on each other. "Kampai," he said. "To two jaded warriors in a strange land."

* * * * *

They traveled the next day to Kyoto, the only city the Allies hadn't bombed in World War II, where she showed him its magnificent gardens. Then on to Nara, where they slept on futons in separate rooms and ate a sumptuous feast sitting cross-legged, wearing kimonos supplied by the *ryokan* inn set in a temple's grounds, where they were staying.

She opened up more about herself, describing her Tokyo upbringing by an American Army officer father and a Japanese mother and their move to the United States when she was seven. She spoke of her continual feeling of displacement and alienation, especially when her mother died and she was forced to travel with her father, a career soldier, from city to city, school to school. She could have gone either of two ways: collapsed or become strong. She chose strength, always electing the most difficult path for a girl belonging to no culture, to no set of rules. At a time when American culture and American rules dominated her world and half-castes were outcasts, she got a scholarship to Duke University and, after graduating third in her class, a masters from MIT,

Rolfe listened in awe. Then, in exchange, he told her his own story, in its way one of comparable alienation and success. By their fourth day together, they were intimate with each other's lives, though not with each other. After dinner, they would kiss goodnight—chaste, unsatisfactory kisses that Rolfe refused to interpret or prolong. There will be a right time, he thought on their way back to Tokyo on the bullet train, knowing how difficult it was for an employee to give herself to her boss, wanting to wait until she was certain he was more and less than her employer, and that love was possible.

On their last night in Japan, Hideo Takahashi, Koji Takenaka, Momo, and Rolfe, the men dressed in Western tuxedos, she in a black silk kimono tied with a patterned red and yellow obi, dined in a geisha house, each attended by a *maiko*—an apprentice geisha—who served them courses of a variety of beans, seafood, meats, and sweet pastries. Takahashi was an expansive host, and the conversation was easy, as if they were conquering soldiers, reliving their triumphs, while maikos played samisens and sang traditional songs in high-pitched voices. A limousine ferried them back to the Imperial, and Rolfe and Momo, remarking on the elegance of the evening, went as usual to their rooms after a swift kiss goodnight. Rolfe settled onto his bed to read a report Josh had air-shipped him from Los Angeles, and soon fell asleep.

He was awakened by the feel of a body snuggled against his back. Momo! He could tell by her perfume. Feigning sleep, he felt her hand reach around him, undo his robe, and reach his core. Her hand was cool. Instantly, he hardened.

"My," she said. "It's bigger than a peanut."

CHAPTER 31

1984–1986

Ihope to God she'll like her, Rolfe thought, holding the receiver close to his perspiring face. It was not hard telling Josh about Momo—beyond a momentary qualm about what it would do to the company set-up. His second-in-command had taken the news with amused equanimity, even pleasure—but his mother would be more difficult. He'd been rehearsing his speech, and now, having just returned from his morning run, he put through the call and promptly announced he was in love.

"I'm thrilled for you, darling," his mother said after a moment's silence.

"You don't sound it."

"It's only that the last time you were so excited it was about the French girl."

"Chantal." Rolfe bit down anger. "You should know her name by now. Besides, I was only seventeen. Puppy love."

"I understand you're still seeing her. She must be a grown bitch by now."

Damn Riverstone! Mike must have told her; how else would she know? Rolfe ignored the cruelty of her remark. "I'm no longer interested," he said.

"Have you told her yet? It's been twenty years. Do you think she'll take her claws out of you that easily?"

"She'll have no choice," he said coldly. "Come on, Mum. Say you're pleased for me. Is it so awful that I'm happy?"

"I don't know the girl," Margaret said. "I've met her only once. Tall, I remember. And Chinese." Was that scorn in her tone?

"Japanese-American." He fought down bile. This was more unpleasant than he'd imagined.

"Are you going to marry her?"

"Don't be silly. We just started seeing each other. Anyway, I'm not divorced yet."

"Ah, yes, the Dagmar problem. The divorce will have to be speeded up, won't it? At considerable cost, I'd venture."

"I said we weren't getting married."

"But you're thinking of it, aren't you?"

"Well—"

"See!" Margaret interrupted. "You're acting just as you did in Paris."

"Damn it," he yelled. "I've known Momo a lot longer than you and Dad did when you got married."

He could hear her breathing grow rapid. "That was different, and you know it. It was wartime. There's no comparison."

True. "I'm sorry, Mum. Let's make peace."

"You haven't changed. You're still as headstrong and compulsive as you were when you decided to go into the hotel business."

"I'm my father's son," Rolfe said softly.

"But you're not your father! He knew what love was."

"Is that why you betrayed him with Jan?" he asked, and before she could answer, he hung up.

* * * * *

"Talk about pathetic," Chantal told Bud McCory. "He was apologetic, told me he loved me still and always would, but that he loves this Momo more and wants to make it work." She laughed. "He's confusing me with someone who gives a damn."

McCory glared at her. "I don't think it's so funny. And to judge from your expression, neither do you. You get great information from him when you fuck his brains out. How'll you get it now?"

* * * * *

The onion-shaped domes surrounding Moscow's Red Square gleamed in the soft rays of the late afternoon sun. Are we being watched? Rolfe asked himself. Every cleaning woman, businessman, shopkeeper, and tourist they passed seemed to be spying on them.

Collar up against the wind, hands dug deep into the pockets of his overcoat, he turned to his companion, whose full-length, navy blue Gucci raincoat screamed fashion in a drab, gray world. "This is getting out of hand," he said.

Yevgeny Popov clapped him on the shoulder. "You're being too sensitive, old friend."

Rolfe wondered if Popov was right. Nevertheless, each week the Russian wanted still more information about the guests in his hotels. Two weeks ago, it was their credit card numbers. Yesterday, he'd asked that the rooms' surveillance systems be upgraded. Today, he'd pressured Rolfe for the master key system, with which he could print duplicate keycards of every one issued to each guest. During the past three months, guests had simply disappeared—without checking out, leaving luggage in their rooms and their bills unpaid. The government, Rolfe knew, would cover the bills, and probably the guests too—in coffins. But there was no backing down now, it was just as easy to make managers disappear as guests.

"Too sensitive, maybe," he said, "but you don't have to explain to your staff why I let these things go on when I wouldn't tolerate them anywhere else."

And you don't have to worry about Kenneth Palmer pressing you for more information either, Rolfe thought ruefully. Every time I talk to him, it's "What's Popov up to?"

"You'll think of something," Popov said airily. His fine clothes couldn't disguise his thuggishness. "But that's not the reason I asked you to Russia. I want you to do something else for me."

His queasy feeling intensified. "What is it?"

"You're using my own suppliers for everything in the hotels, right?"

"As ordered. And their prices are too high and the quality's lousy, nowhere near Kestrel's standards."

"Details. Are the hotel's guests complaining?"

"Most of them don't know good from bad. But the management team does."

Popov shrugged. "Let them find better quality elsewhere. You come to Russia, you get Russian standards."

Rolfe's reluctant silence conceded the point.

"I want you to use my suppliers in your other hotels in Eastern Europe," Popov went on.

Rolfe stopped walking. "Impossible!"

"Imperative," Popov said calmly. "This isn't a request. I don't know how long our politburo can rule those countries, but as long as they do, you'll do as I say." He let the threat hang in the air for a second, and then went on. "If you're a good boy, I'll share the profits with you."

Blood money, Rolfe thought. He had played dirty too, used blackmail and treachery, although only when he had no choice and always in pursuit of his dream, but this left him feeling as defiled as he did when he thought about David Murtoch. "Can't you ease up and do things bit by bit?" he asked.

Popov grinned mirthlessly. "Don't you understand? This is my time. My time! It may not last long, and I want to get all I can before it's over." He stared at Rolfe; there was obsession in his eyes. He had dreams too. "You knew what you were signing when you made the deals, so don't act naïve. I know everything about you. Everything. And the amazing thing is, the two of us are alike. If our positions were reversed, you'd be making the same demands on me, and I'd agree to them, like it or not. Isn't that right, tovarich? "

* * * * *

"Don't run to me for absolution," Momo said. "You made a pact with the devil, but you did it knowingly."

Rolfe recoiled. In the years they'd been together, he'd never seen her so unsympathetic. "You don't understand. I'm playing spy games with experts. Popov could have me killed!"

"It's your own fault. You were out to beat Hunt, and this was the price of the ticket."

"Maybe he'd like to buy the hotels from me now."

"Popov would never let you make that deal," Momo said. "I don't get you. Sometimes you're willing to debase yourself to get ahead. Other times you have the conscience of an altar boy."

"What do you mean, 'debase myself'?" Rolfe asked, badly stung.

"You used the hotel owners' money to save Kestrel when you had no right to it. You used McCory to spy on Hunt—still do. You sold yourself to Steinmann like a whore. Is that debasing enough?"

"But—"

"Now you're scared, and you've suddenly got a fit of conscience because Popov wants to get a few kickbacks from our hotels in Eastern Europe. Big deal! I'll bet he's cutting you in."

Rolfe nodded. "Popov was right," he said. "He and I are twins."

"Not exactly." She cupped his face in her hands and kissed him softly on the lips. "You're torn between your ambition and the things you have to do to achieve it, that's all. You're not the first businessman, nor the last, to be faced with that dilemma. But Popov doesn't have a qualm or a scruple. You've never killed anyone or had anyone killed. And," she added, kissing him more passionately now, "you're capable of love."

* * * * *

"Damn Ritter," Hunt said, peering into the night from his bedroom window. Though Carol was with him, he knew he was mostly speaking to himself. Not only had Ritter pulled off that Tokyo deal in the first place, now he'd convinced Osaka Gas to erect a similar Kestrel in Osaka and Koizumi Construction to develop a Kestrel resort in Fukaoka. "Shit!" he muttered.

Granted, he'd beaten Kestrel out in Chicago and Dallas, fought him to a draw in San Diego, aced him in Minneapolis-St. Paul—though that might not have been so smart, given recent losses there—and annihilated him in Vail. It was in Europe that Metropolitan was getting their ass kicked. Europe—and now, worse, Asia.

"He's got to be stopped," he told Carol, and went to his study to make a call.

"Bud," he said, "it's time to move."

* * * * *

2 Dead, 67 Hospitalized in Salmonella Outbreak at Kestrel Hotel, Los Angeles

Rolfe threw the *Los Angeles Times* on the boardroom table. Josh, Susan, and Momo looked at him expectantly.

"Only the Kestrel L.A.?" he asked.

"So far," Josh said.

"You've checked?"

"Of course. But for the damage it's doing, it might as well be at all the properties."

"How come?" Susan asked.

"Because all the major papers have the news, and virtually every group we'd booked has canceled. The damn phones keep ringing; individual clients are canceling too. Metropolitan already has a letter in the hands of every meeting planner, corporate client, and travel agency, telling them their hotels are safe and in compliance with all health and safety laws. They're even offering "try us now" discounts. It's a nightmare. We're closing restaurants, shutting floors down as fast as we can, laying off staff, cutting services and amenities, doing everything we can to hold down costs, but we're still going to lose a goddamned fortune."

"Hi, guys," Falkman said as he barged in, having caught the first flight out of New York after he'd received Josh's panicked call. "Are we having fun yet?"

"Fuck you," Rolfe said.

"Seems to be you who's getting fucked."

"You're right," Rolfe groaned. "Between the police, the insurance companies, every health authority in California, my partners, the hotel owners, the lenders, and the general managers, we've been put under siege."

"What are the police saying?"

"They're working off the theory that the salmonella was in food coming from one of our suppliers. The only reason they're still interested is because none of the supplier's other customers had infected produce."

"That makes sense."

"I don't think it's a supplier," Rolfe said slowly.

"Who then?"

"Hunt." He was as sure of this as anything in his life. "We're being sabotaged."

* * * * *

"Time to turn the screws," Hunt said.

"I disagree." Bud could hear the venom in Hunt's voice and inwardly flinched. If ever there was a time to stay cool, this was it. "If there's an outbreak in New York or Chicago, it'll look too suspicious."

"But I don't mean another outbreak. There'll be time for that, or some new plan that I hope you're working on. No, I mean it's time for you to turn the screws."

"Oh, but I already have," Bud said. "This very afternoon. Maybe you haven't heard. I've instructed all my union people not to go back to work in any Kestrel hotel until Ritter proves that they're safe."

* * * * *

Chantal walked into McCory's San Francisco office unannounced. "I had to talk to you personally; the phone's too dangerous."

"Always time for you," Bud said, smiling at her.

She wasn't buying. "Bruce Hunt gave me the impression the salmonella outbreak wasn't an accident. True?"

"Of course not." Bud kept his voice level.

"In the same breath he said you were keeping your workers out of Kestrel hotels."

"That is true. Can't go around putting my people in danger. So fucking what?"

Chantal looked at him with sad eyes. "I can't get the conversation out of my head. The way Bruce talked, the things he said." She paused, took a deep breath. "You two were behind this, weren't you?"

A clenched jaw was his only visible response. Seconds went by, his cold, unblinking eyes not wavering from hers. "I'm only going to say this once, so listen carefully. Keep your fucking nose out of what I'm doing. It's none of your business."

"But people died," she whispered.

"You don't know what you're talking about, and I'm not going to waste my time explaining it." He stood. "We're done here."

She didn't flinch. "Hold on, Bud. I'm your partner. But I didn't sign on for murder. I need to know what's going on."

He raised a fist; let his hand fall to his side. "You stupid bitch. You don't need to know anything. You've been playing both sides so long you wouldn't know right from wrong if it hit you in the face." He took a step closer to her, but she continued to meet his gaze. "Don't fucking forget you're in this game up to your neck. So don't get an attack of morals because your fucking imagination's run amok. Remember, if it's murder, you're an accomplice."

CHAPTER 32

1988–1989

Rolfe and Mike Riverstone sat at a corner booth in the bar of the London Kestrel, enjoying Scottish smoked salmon so thinly cut you could read a newspaper through it. Mike had arranged the meeting, and Rolfe had taken the opportunity to ask Mike to find out what he could about Audley Hotels and its owners, the Germaine family. Mike had given his godson what he wanted, but with a warning.

"You're going too fast," he said. "Do you really need to buy more hotels?"

What business was it of Mike's? The Audleys were top of the line, a jewel for Kestrel's crown. He felt a flicker of irritation, but kept his tone light. "You know what they say: If you stay in place you fall behind."

"Isn't it more accurate to say, if you stay in place you can't catch up to your father?"

The words sent a shock through Rolfe. "What do you mean?"

"That's why I wanted to get together."

"I thought we'd talk about official business."

"Not at all," Riverstone said. "Palmer tells me you're being well behaved, and your information about Popov has been invaluable, although he suspects you're not telling him everything." He put his hand up to stop Rolfe's protest. "It's time we talked about you for once."

Rolfe lost interest in salmon and pushed his plate away. "What's there to say?"

Mike's expression hardened. "Since you first came to London, I've seen you do some pretty devious stuff. Granted, I'm a fine one to talk, but my business is deviousness. Yours isn't, but you've made it so. All in the name, I think, of living up to your fantasy of your father."

Rolfe felt his chest contract as it had when they'd sat on the bench in St. James Park. "I'm my own man," he said stubbornly. "Living up to what I want to do."

"Then why cheat? I haven't forgotten Murtoch. I know about your blackmailing Longbury, about your safe deposit boxes, about your dealings with McCory, and about bribing half the Japanese banking community. I know you've been fucking over that Hollywood producer and his slimy agent friend—I've forgotten their names. And I know why you married Dagmar Steinmann. Is that living up to anything?"

"If I didn't do those things, I'd have lost out to Hunt."

"And you'd be second best. Rich and powerful and renowned and admired—but second best. Big bloody deal!" Riverstone threw up his hands in exasperation. "Look inside yourself. Do you really think it's Hunt you're competing with? That's horse manure. You're competing with your father, and he's the wrong man to measure yourself against."

Rolfe closed his eyes, grimacing in pain. For an instant he was a child again, exploring Amsterdam hand-in-hand with his father. Then he saw the car, heard the screams, and remembered earth falling on his father's grave.

Mike pressed on relentlessly. "Your father used women, was a blackmailer, paid bribes, planted evidence, even murdered. He said it was for some higher purpose, and it was, but he was disobeying my orders and Jan's. He loved those tactics, used them on the Russians when the war ended, and in the process he got himself killed. He was proud of himself, and whether she'll admit it or not, your mother was proud of him too. You take the same risks he did, but Margaret still puts you down and always will."

"Why are you doing this?" Rolfe whispered, whiplashed. The revelations about his father came at him like bullets.

"Because I want you to face facts." Riverstone's tone was sympathetic. "You can't live up to someone who never existed, and you're never going to please your mother. She tried to make you in Wim's image, and you rejected her. But you're trying to do the same thing, only it's a false image and it'll destroy you."

Rolfe swayed as his world spun around him. "What do you want?"

"Let your father go. Stop trying to live up to him. Be yourself at last. Live for you, not your mother. Enjoy this Momo you keep talking about." Riverstone's voice was hoarse with intensity. "Get rid of the obsession."

Mike didn't understand. There was work to do in Asia, in South America, in the Caribbean. "I can't do that, Uncle. I'm too close."

"You've got to." There were tears in Riverstone's eyes. "Your father's obsession got him killed. Don't let yours kill you."

* * * * *

"Hey, you lousy Dutchman."

"Hi, Buddy. How's my favorite fake Irishman?"

"Wanting to see you. I'll be in Las Vegas for the weekend. How about lunch on Saturday? Give me a chance to show off the new house."

It was a command, not an invitation. "See you then," said Rolfe.

Although it was past midnight, Rolfe was suddenly wide-awake. This was not a casual call, nor would it be a friendly get-together. The more jovial Bud got, the more serious his motives were.

* * * * *

Bud McCory's house sat high in the foothills of Las Vegas. A model, Rolfe thought as Bud gave him a guided tour, of too much money and too little taste. Tapestries in the Renaissance style hung on the walls of the foyer. The furniture in the living room was faux Louis Quatorze. There was too much gold leaf, too much dark wood, too many chandeliers. Rolfe was grateful when McCory led him to a terrace overlooking the Las Vegas hotels and casinos in the shimmering distance, the sixteenth green of the Mt. Charleston Country Club's golf course close by.

"What's so urgent?" he asked when they'd finished their lunch of hamburgers and fries.

"A couple things. You asked me whether I thought your friend Hunt was behind the salmonella attack."

Rolfe's pulse quickened. "Well?"

"There's no hard evidence, but it sure looks that way."

"Shit!" The fury that seemed to well inside him more and more these days detonated in his brain. He imagined Hunt on his knees before him, groveling for mercy.

"It gets worse, kid," McCory said calmly. "Someone's paid off some of the construction workers building your new hotel in Chicago. They're going to pour concrete down the vertical shafts connecting the fucking toilets. If they get away with it, they'll hold you up for at least a year—to say nothing of the cost."

"Jesus!" The pain in Rolfe's chest was so severe he had to double over to catch his breath. "How do I stop it?"

"Donate fifty-thousand to the Hotel Workers' Benevolent Fund. I'll do the rest."

There was no choice. "Done."

"One more thing: word is that someone's hired a pair of thugs to beat the shit out of Momo."

Rolfe tried to stand, but the pain was so excruciating he could not rise and was forced to grip the arms of his chair for support.

"Twenty grand more, and I think I can persuade the hit men to choose a different target. But just in case, I can have a couple of my guys watch out for her." He grinned. "That part's on the house."

Rolfe sat numb and white-faced. "I'm grateful, Bud, I really am."

"That brings me to the other reason I've asked you here. There's something I've got hold of that we can do to help each other. You're going to develop a fifteen-hundred-room convention center hotel and casino here in Vegas. It'll be built and run with union labor."

"No way!" The idea was preposterous. "I don't have the capital."

"Not to worry. Me and my partners will put up the money. We've already acquired the land on the end of the strip. But you'll be the owner as far as the world's concerned. Besides, the question isn't where or who the money's coming from. But how."

Rolfe looked at him quizzically.

"You better learn the rules. The Nevada Gaming Commission won't allow unions to own casinos—too many memories of the mob. Besides, anyone with more than a five percent ownership has to go through a rigorous licensing process, so that rules out the unions." He smiled at Rolfe benevolently. "But you and your guys can pass. You already have casinos in your hotels in Aruba, Puerto Rico, and Cairo, so you're a logical candidate."

He's right, the Gaming Commission will approve me in a moment, Rolfe thought. But I don't want their scrutiny, and Falkman will have a fit. A coil of suspicion began to form in his gut.

"Here's how it'll work," McCory went on. "We'll sell you the land for virtually nothing. Then we'll personally lend you a bunch of dough at below-market interest rates to fund your equity in the casino—figure fifty million. We'll have a friendly banker make a hundred-million mortgage on the hotel and casino. Bingo! You've got one-hundred-fifty mil to pay for the whole fucking place."

Too simple. Too good to be true. "What's in it for you?" Rolfe asked.

"Your loan will have a little incentive figure attached. On top of the interest, you'll pay the equivalent of ninety percent of the profits from your ownership, so you'll get a big fat fucking management fee plus ten percent of the deal. Of course," he smirked, "it can't be seen as coming from the casino, so we'll have to make it appear to be coming from some of your hotels. It's just fancy bookkeeping. If you behave yourself, we'll all make fucking fortunes." He held up a hand to stifle Rolfe's response. "Before you ask, we don't want to own these joints forever, so we'll make the loan to you for ten years, but whenever we're ready to sell the casino, you'll do it without question, and then you'll pay back the loan." He stopped. "Fucking brilliant, no?"

Revulsion made him sick to his stomach. He had played with money himself, but nothing so blatant. "Brilliant maybe, but totally illegal."

"Call it good business practice. If you want to sell the casino before the loans are due, we'll let you do it, but you'll give us the profits we think we'd have realized under our own timetable, even if it means selling your own hotels. To protect us, you'll sign a letter detailing these arrangements, to a company that has no apparent connection to us. The letter will never see the light of day. It'll be hidden, of course, unless you try something cute."

McCory will have me by the balls, Rolfe knew. And all that talk about protecting Momo and the Kestrel Chicago were blackmail—no casino, no protection. The $70,000 was just vigorish. When he looked up, he saw McCory smiling at him.

"Yeah, it's fucking close to the edge," he said, as if reading Rolfe's mind, "but it's our money, and you'll run a clean joint, so no one's going to be fucking hurt."

"I want to know who your partners are."

The union leader put a finger to his lips. "Listen, kid. There are some questions you don't even want to think about. Take it from me that they're clean and leave it at that." He finished his iced coffee and led Rolfe to the edge of the terrace. "The only thing that could go wrong would be for you to try and screw me and my partners. I know you'd never think of it, but my partners worry. I told them you'd keep your promise to pay every fucking penny due us from the casino, but these bastards were born suspicious. So if you ever think of taking a dime that isn't yours, remember: the very least that would happen to you is that the letter would go to the authorities and you'd be in jail without passing go."

Despite the intense heat, Rolfe felt chilled. "I'm interested," he forced himself to say. "But I need a favor in return."

McCory looked at him suspiciously. "Shoot."

"I want revenge on that bastard Hunt."

The union leader put his arm around the shoulders of the hotelier. "Ah, Rolfe. Are you sure? Haven't you both had enough?"

"He killed innocent people!"

McCory shrugged. "It'll take a shitload of fucking planning and a boatload of fucking dough."

"Whatever it takes, whatever it costs—do it."

"You've got to wait until everything calms down," McCory said. "Otherwise, it would be too fucking obvious you were behind it."

"I can wait."

"And I can do it." He stepped back from the railing and stuck out his hand. "Do we have a deal?"

Rolfe took the hand. "Deal."

CHAPTER 33

1989

L ew Levenson's 105-foot Bertolini yacht, Silver Screen, mean-
dered off the coast of Cabo San Lucas in Baja California, Rolfe
and Momo its only passengers for the weekend. It was Kestrel's fif-
teenth anniversary, and Rolfe had just presided over the opening
of his resort on the Big Island of Hawaii. At forty-one, he sorely
needed the rest. This morning, as they lay sunning themselves on
thick yellow towels, he and Momo had time for business talk,
something they rarely allowed themselves outside the office.

"Do you think it's really going to happen?" she asked. "The
Audleys, I mean."

"Absolutely," Rolfe said.

"When?"

"Soon." He opened his eyes. She was on one elbow, leaning
toward him, her naked breasts tantalizingly close to his face.

"Don't be so vague." She poked him playfully in the ribs. "I
want details."

"I got laid last night," he said.

"Unless you tell me, you won't tonight."

He reached his head up to kiss her breasts; she pulled away.

"Sir Alan called Pieter yesterday to confirm that he and the
siblings have accepted our offer."

"Why use Pieter on this deal?" she asked, surprised. "First of
all, it's nepotism, and second, why did you need an investment
banker at all?"

"Pieter was so pissed off when I told him I wouldn't sell the
company, so I wanted to throw some business his way. He can
untangle the European tax structure better than anyone I know.
Besides, I was worried Sir Alan would still think of me as the front
office manager at the Audley. I wanted someone he respects to represent our interests."

"Who puts up the cash to pay for it?"

"After you finished molesting my frail body last night, I called Koji, who went bananas at the news. Apparently, the owner of a chemical company in Nagoya had been in love with the Audleys forever. He doesn't seem to care what the price is, so long as he can tell the world he's the owner and we can show some projections for him to give to his banks, one of which happens to be Koji's. He's the same guy who bought the Monet from Sotheby's last year for one-hundred million."

"Clever boy."

"Your cousin wants you to tell me to be nicer to him. Translated that means he wants his personal kickbacks to be bigger. He thinks I'm too tough."

She pulled him on top of her. "Too tough? Or too rough? Ooo, I like that."

* * * * *

"Steinmann's had a stroke," Susan told Rolfe as they left the Wells Fargo Bank in Marina Del Rey for the drive back to Kestrel headquarters.

"Really! Is it serious?"

"Very. He's still in the hospital. Word is he won't ever leave."

Rolfe wondered why he felt so little now that the man he despised was dying. Relief? Joy? Retribution? None of the above. "How did you find out?"

"I ran into Dagmar yesterday when I was in The Hills. We had a drink together, and she told me. Seemed terribly upset."

Dagmar. Their divorce had been a blessing that brought him Momo. "I hear Advani's dropped her," he said.

"Like a red-hot poker. Once Brita was born, that son of a bitch wouldn't talk to her, let alone acknowledge the baby was his."

He felt a stir of sympathy. Dagmar wasn't an evil person, just naïve. "At least the baby will have good care. Once Steinmann dies, Dagmar' will inherit a fortune."

Susan pulled into the Kestrel parking lot. "She said something strange."

"Strange?"

"Her father still hates you with a passion."

"That's not strange, it's old news."

"Apparently he blames you for all of Dagmar's problems. She doesn't; he does. He promised Dagmar he'd take care of you sooner or later."

He turned to face her. "Meaning?"

"Dagmar's worried her father has some plan for after he dies."

"What plan?"

"She didn't tell me. Didn't know. When I pressed her, she said she shouldn't have brought it up."

"I'm glad she did. Maybe I can find out about it before the old bastard kicks off."

* * * * *

Rolfe hated hospitals, but he was barely aware of the sounds and smells as he paused before Steinmann's door. He came with the need to find out what he could; still, he had to struggle before he entered.

Steinmann lay inert, an array of tubing running from his body to the heart machine, catheter, and feeding I.V. to which he was attached. Rolfe thought he was asleep, but as he approached the old man's eyes opened.

"Come to gloat?" The German's voice was hoarse.

"I need to talk to you."

"Get out!"

"Not until you tell me what mischief you've planned."

"Worried I'm up to something?"

"Dagmar said you were."

The mention of his daughter's name seemed to enrage the old man. His pale face turned red, and his eyes glittered. "You made a promise, and you broke it and made my daughter suffer. Now you must suffer in return."

There was no possible response, Rolfe knew. To say he had stayed with Dagmar even after the five years had passed or that it was she who had left him would be like arguing with a deaf man. "Let it go, for God's sake," he pleaded. "Why can't you and I make peace?"

"Let it go?" A wan smile crossed Steinmann's face. He pressed the nurse's call button. "Never. I keep my promises." He lay back and closed his eyes.

Rolfe shook him by the shoulders. This man was a murderer, a devil with infinite resources. There would be no rest after he died. "Tell me," Rolfe shouted. "Tell me now!"

He stayed until the nurse forced him to leave.

* * * * *

Jan Vermeij called Rolfe in early September. "Mike died this morning," he said without preamble. "Heart attack. There was no pain, he died instantly."

The news tore at Rolfe's soul. His friend, mentor, moral counselor, and sometime boss was gone, and it left a void in him that no one else could fill. As a friend, a father, a spur, and a conscience, he was irreplaceable. "Mike's dead," he whispered to Momo, who was lying beside him. Then to Jan, "How's Mum?"

"Distraught. We only got the news an hour ago, and she's been crying ever since. She's usually strong, you know, but—Hold on, she wants to talk to you."

His mother's voice was made of tears. "First your father, now Mike," she sobbed. "I can't bear it."

His own grief was so powerful, for a time he could not find words of comfort. Finally, "He led a good life. He was a great man. A hero. Where and when's the funeral?"

"Saturday, at St. Edward's in London. You'll be there?"

He resented the question, did not fully understand what lay behind it. "Of course."

"And you'll be able to come back with me and Jan to Holland? Spend a few days? Maybe just the rest of the weekend?"

No, he thought. This is emotional blackmail, and I won't pay it. She had Jan to help her through this time. If he went, his mother's grief would smother his own. He pictured recriminations, arguments, coldness, more rejection. "I can't. I've got to be back in Los Angeles first thing Monday morning." He tried a joke. "At my age, I can't take that much travel in so little time."

"Mike was eighty-six," she said, and hung up. A reprimand.

Momo put her arms around him. Still warm from sleep, she embodied comfort. "I'm sorry," she said. "I know how much you loved him. I'm here for you," she added.

"I know," he said, kissing her. But it wasn't the same.

* * * * *

When Rolfe got to the office, Josh was appropriately solicitous, but there was bad news and Rolfe had to hear it.

"Three of our European general managers were seriously beaten up last night."

"Good God! Who?"

"Yves Gak in Paris, Jock Greene in Dublin, Rudi Bauer in Switzerland. All three are in hospital. Jock's in intensive care, but is expected to make it. Obviously, the attacks were coordinated and premeditated."

"Hunt!" Rolfe shouted.

"I'm not so sure. There was a common link between them. All three were Jewish."

"And they're our only three Jewish general managers in Europe?"

Josh sighed. "Precisely." He held up three sheets of paper. "Diethe Enderle faxed me these." He tossed the first to Rolfe. "This piece of garbage went to our major European business partners— meeting planners, travel agents, tour wholesalers."

Zionest Conspiracy

Kestrel Hotels is a Zionist front intent on taking over the European hotel business. We urge you to have no further commerce with their hotels and to warn your colleagues and staff members of the threat inherent in Kestrel's ongoing operations. To ignore this message is to invite retribution.

The International Organization for the Protection of Europe

"Here's a second one," Josh said, handing it to his boss. "It went to Verde International, our linen supplier in Europe."

Dear Sirs:

Do not risk being an unwitting part of a secret Zionist conspiracy to take over the European hotel industry.

IOFTPE and its thousands of members throughout the world are devoted to stopping Kestrel and other likeminded organizations clandestinely working toward this end.

Do not do business with them. Boycott them immediately or be boycotted by our membership.

The International Organization for the Protection of Europe

"And a third. It was on the desk of every one of our European managers and their executive committee members when they got in this morning." The one Josh passed to Rolfe was addressed to Fiona at the London Kestrel.

Dear Ms. Metcalf:

By now you may have heard of the fate of three of your colleagues at Kestrel Hotels in Europe. They are

*part of a clandestine organization behind a Zionist move-
ment to take over our industry. The IOFTPE is dedicated
to stopping them. They are using you and your colleagues
as dupes. Leave now or suffer the same fate.*

*The International Organization for the Protection of
Europe*

Rolfe looked up angrily. "Surely nobody believes this shit."

Josh shook his head in bewilderment. "You'd think so. But
every goddamned media outlet in the world were leaked copies,
and they're playing it up big with that hypocrisy that surrounds
the story with an 'Isn't it awful,' when what they're really saying
is, 'Listen to this.' It's the lead on *Sky News* every half-hour.
Anyway, most of the GMs are loyal and true, but their families are
panicked, our suppliers are calling for their money, and we're getting a boatload of cancellations."

"What do the police say?"

"They haven't a clue. They're dealing with a dozen different
postmarks in half a dozen countries. Interpol's never heard of the
IOFTPE; they're worse than useless."

"What's more," Rolfe said, with a conviction as certain as day-
break, "I could tell them who's behind this and it still won't do any
good. Because Steinmann's dead. Even from his grave he's kept his
promise."

CHAPTER 34

1990

The management team at Kestrel watched as Bruce Hunt's face filled the TV screen. The program was *Moneyline*.

"Our acquisition of Opal Hotels represents a leap forward for the lodging industry," he said. "Simply stated, as we expand the number of hotels in the Opal chain, for the first time consumers will be able to stay in luxury hotels around the world—in large and small cities, towns and resorts—with a certainty of consistent standards, service and experience. No company has ever done this on the scale that Metropolitan intends."

"It's the wrong approach," Rolfe said, irritated despite his promise to Susan to stay calm. "He doesn't realize that five-hundred-dollars-a-night guests want to be treated individually, not processed like battery-bred chickens."

"So you've told us a thousand times," Susan said wearily. "Why not listen to what he has to say."

"It seems the hotel business is going through a consolidation," the interviewer said, "with bigger companies swallowing up the smaller ones. Surely your acquisition of the Opal chain mirrors last year's sale of the Audley chain to Kestrel."

Hunt leaned forward. "But there'll be an enormous difference. Kestrel will cut costs, raise prices to pay off the debt accrued when they overpaid for Audley, and then they'll add increasing numbers of lesser hotels to the brand in an attempt to feed off the luster of what was once a wonderful company." He lifted his arms as if to fend off the calamity. "The final result will be a hodgepodge of mixed assets. In a few years, Rolfe Ritter will have ruined a great chain that took generations to build." He looked into the camera. "It's a darned shame. That's what it is, a darned shame, especially since he's proved he can't control the health or safety of his staff. You surely remember the salmonella episode not too long ago. Who's to say another outbreak—"

Josh shut off the TV. "Why listen to this drivel? He had to bring up safety issues just as the European hotels are recovering and the Audleys are generating real momentum."

"We're not going to overreact," Rolfe said. "They asked me to be on the show, but I didn't want to get into a shouting match with Hunt. His voice is louder."

"But we have to do something. The press will be all over us," Andrew McDonald said.

Rolfe frowned. "No interviews."

* * * * *

"The Atlantic City casino's up and running," Rolfe told Bud McCory.

"I know."

"Making any money?"

"Fistfuls."

"Then it's your turn. You owe me a favor. You know what I want. Move!"

* * * * *

The mountain air cooled them. They had made love so feverishly, so without inhibition or restraint, that though the penthouse suite of the Kestrel Hotel in Aspen was high in the Rocky Mountains, he had opened the sliding door in the bedroom to let the frigid outside air cool their bodies. It was a clear night, and the mountains silhouetted by the moon looked like giant kings wearing stars for diadems.

"I love you," he said. "More and more each day. I wake up thinking of you, go to bed dreaming of you. Auden said it: You are 'my North, my South, my East, my West, / My day at work, / My Sunday rest.'" He smiled, feeling ridiculously awkward.

Momo shivered, and slid the door closed. "I love you too." She hugged him and slipped back under the covers.

He walked to the closet and from the inside pocket of his coat took out the present he had bought for her. Yet, when he handed her the small box, her expression was sad. "Open it," he said.

It was a six-caret yellow diamond, set in a simple platinum ring. She gasped. "It's stunning."

He knelt by the side of the bed and kissed her. "Marry me. Be my wife, my lover, my partner, and my friend forever."

She closed the box and passed it back to him. "I can't."

His world stopped. "Why? Don't you love me?"

"Of course I do. I've never felt like this for any man."

"Then why?"

"Because I can't compete with your demons." Her eyes filled with tears. "I know you love me, and I realize how hard you've tried to change, but you can't, no matter how willing."

He felt a wave of heat and stood, moved toward the door, stopped and turned to face her. "I don't understand."

"You're obsessed with Kestrel. Every crisis consumes you, and the only person whose approval you want can't give it to you."

"It's your approval I need. Only yours."

"Yet, you've not let me into your life. Whenever you have those conversations with McCory or Popov, you close the door so I can't hear. You and Ron Falkman speak in a kind of code I'll never understand."

"I'll teach you the code. I'll—" he stopped. He could never let her overhear his conversations with Bud or Popov, no more than he could ever tell her about Murtoch. No, he could never let her see what he really was.

"I've tried to change; I'll try harder. Give me a chance."

She smiled wanly. "The competition's too tough."

"What competition?"

"With your father. He's the one whose approval you need. Every time there's a success, you wonder whether you've measured up to him. I can't compete with a ghost. Don't ask me to try."

He thought of Mike Riverstone's warning—another ghost's.

"It's over, Rolfe. It's tearing me to pieces, but I have to do this. Otherwise you'll destroy us both."

"Momo . . ."

"I'm leaving you and leaving Kestrel. Andrew's good. He can take over most of my duties."

His pain was excruciating, his anger so fierce he was afraid he would kill her. Naked, she went to the closet, took out her suitcase, and began filling it with her clothes. "I'll sleep in the living room, though I doubt either of us will sleep. Please don't come out until you hear me leave."

She finished packing, carried her case to the living room, then came and stood by the door. She held out her hands, a weeping goddess. "One kiss goodbye?"

There could be nothing this cruel, he thought. He took a step back. "Fuck you," he said. "I'll live without it."

* * * * *

The empty days blended into emptier nights. His pain was overwhelming. Momo refused any communication.

In desperation, he fell back on his old remedy—visiting his hotels. This time there was no solace in his creations. He failed to notice the details, large or small, ignored the crumpled up paper in an elevator's corner or the light out in the letter "R in the hotel's sign, sins that once would have led to firings.

Even reviewing plans for the Audley hotel in Laguna failed to revive his interest. Disconsolate, he returned home each evening to his own lonely bed, dozing and waking, reaching for Momo and finding air.

* * * * *

Three weeks later, his ex-wife Dagmar, dressed in a dark red suit, her hair cut, as always, in the latest Beverly Hills fashion, a three-rowed black pearl choker around her neck, arrived unannounced at his office door. Somehow, her appearance didn't surprise him. His life was already full of nightmares, and another seemed appropriate. It was late, everyone had gone home, but work distracted him and he rarely left the office before midnight.

"Come to gloat?" he asked, echoing her father.

She came in and sat down. "Hardly. I heard that you and Momo broke up, and I'm truly sorry."

"Then what do you want?"

"To make peace."

"I thought our war was over long ago."

"I want you to come back to me."

The idea was so preposterous that he laughed aloud. My God! The baby. Their house with its poisonous memories. Suffocation. "Never!"

"Hear me out."

He saw her father dying in the hospital bed. "Actually, I'm glad you're here. I have to know something. Did your father plan that anti-Semitic viciousness against Kestrel in Europe?"

She sat silently, but her cheekbones colored. He knew the answer. "So he told you what he was up to."

"No. He only told me his plans were in place."

"Sure he did." His sarcasm was obvious.

"Really. He was always torn between hatred for you and love for me, and he knew that I loved you and always would. So he didn't tell me any of the specifics. Only this. He couldn't resist."

"And you expect me to 'come back' to his daughter?"

"Maybe I can entice you."

He looked at her coldly. "I'm afraid I'm off sex for the immediate future."

She laughed. "I didn't mean sex. If you come back, I'll sell the block of stock my father bought in Metropolitan. I know Kestrel, and they are rivals. It'll drive their stock way down."

"And how would that help Kestrel?"

"You didn't let me finish. I'd invest all of the proceeds in your business. Fifty million dollars."

A war chest for the future, he thought. I could clean up my debts and have plenty left over. Why not! He'd lost Momo. His only constant lovers were his hotels. This way they'd be protected. It would be just another variation on the theme of a long list of ugly things he'd done for the sake of his one true love. The idea of using Steinmann's money a second time intrigued him, but not Dagmar's attempt to buy a father for her baby—a Steinmann grandchild. The flicker of a smile that had briefly appeared vanished as the reality of her motive repulsed him.

"I can't do it," he said with a hint of sadness. "You'll just have to live with your fathers' ghost."

* * * * *

Chantal peered over her wineglass at him across a table at the bar in the Four Seasons Beverly Hills. "I wanted to see you outside your office to tell you how sorry I am—genuinely—that things between you and Momo didn't work out." She was dressed in an Armani suit with a diamond choker. Rolfe thought she seemed happy.

"Thanks," he said. "I'm sorry you and I had to—"

"It was your loss as well. Are you over her?"

"Not really. Anyway, you look great. Things going well in your personal life?"

"What personal life? I'm too busy. Are you proud of me? I've become a marketing guru in my old age, clients up the yin-yang, as you Americans say."

He looked at her fondly. She was over fifty, he realized. "What old age? You're as young as ever—not like me." He pointed to his graying temples.

"Fishing for compliments?" She handed him a gold-foil-covered box. "I've brought you a present."

For the first time in months, he felt his mood lighten. He lifted out a photograph in a sterling silver frame. It showed the two of them, arms around each other, in front of the Sacre Coeur in Paris. "It's to prove I'm not so young either."

"But look at me. I was barely shaving."

"Not too young for some things."

Memories of their early nights sprang into his head. "Mmmmm."

"There's more in the box," she told him. He saw a thin silver flask and an envelope addressed R.R. *Gift Certificate for a CLP Full Body Massage,* read the note inside.

He unscrewed the top of the flask and smelled vanilla.

"Massage oil," Chantal said.

"And CLP?"

"Chantal Le Peron, obviously."

"Cute. Thank you. The picture's wonderful."

She leaned toward him. "When do you want the massage?"

He squeezed her hand. "I'm sorry, Chantal, it's too soon."

"No problem," she said, her smile fading. "I'll wait."

CHAPTER 35

1991–1992

"It's Popov," Rolfe said to Kenneth Palmer over tea in the limestone-floored courtyard of the newly opened Audley Hotel in Georgetown. "He's gone bloody mad."

Palmer watched him, expressionless. "Explain."

"He's asked for installation of a bugging system in every room and he's put 'invisible' cameras in all the elevators and suites. Jesus, you couldn't blow your nose in any of the hotels without the entire Russian government knowing about it."

"I'm not sure it's the government," Palmer said.

"Who then?"

"Our Yevgeny's become a powerful man. He's in control of one of the biggest crime syndicates in Russia. Those bugging devices and cameras are to get information on the government, not give to them. And, I might add, not to give to us."

"Christ alive!"

"Since the Berlin Wall came down, we've lost any hold we thought we had over him. He's using his KGB files and his spying system to blackmail government officials, left, right, and center. That way he'll be in a position to take control of the businesses the government sells off to the private sector." The MI5 man lit a cigarette. "The more information we can get on him the better. We need you to tell us everything."

An invisible noose tightened around Rolfe's throat. When Palmer acted on the information, Popov would know who supplied it. But to hold it back was unthinkable for the son of The Kestrel. "You'll be sorry I'll be dead when he finds out."

Palmer chuckled. "It isn't that bad. Besides, he won't find out. He hasn't in the past."

"Yes, but with his new systems, how will I know if he's spying on me? Christ! Maybe this teapot is bugged." Both men stared at it. Ridiculous, Rolfe thought. We're fantasizing. "Did you know Popov's got me diverting money from the Moscow and Leningrad hotels?"

"Divert? You mean steal?" Palmer was clearly astonished.

Rolfe ignored the question. "Here's how it works. The bulk of revenues at the hotels come from Western or Asian businessmen who pay mostly in dollars. That money goes straight to a Swiss bank account."

"Popov's?" Palmer asked. Rolfe nodded. "How does the hotel pay its bills?"

"From local currency the Eastern bloc guests pay, but mostly from the fact that Popov's been cooking the books to show a loss, and the Russian government covers all the losses. It's straight fraud."

Palmer shrugged. "He's sharing the loot with the appropriate government officials, so no one cares. What else?"

"He wants me to sponsor and organize a conference at our Moscow hotel, which the hotel will underwrite. Five hundred people."

"On what topic?"

"Doing business in the post-communist era."

"Bizarre," Palmer snorted. "He wouldn't waste his time with such nonsense unless there was something in it for him."

Rolfe passed him some papers. "Here's a list of people he wants me to persuade to show up."

Palmer scanned the pages. "I recognize a few names, a couple of bad apples here and there, but—Pavel Banyeov!"

"Who's he?"

"A freelancer. Did some work for us in the eighties. A Czech with an appetite for Western toys and Western money. We're pretty sure he's selling Russian and Czech arms to Iraq, and we hear rumors he's trying to acquire the nuclear weapons scheduled for destruction by the Russian government so he can auction them off. I thought I'd heard he'd fallen out with Popov. But you'd better find out what's going on."

"Me? Now, just a minute, Ken. I didn't agree to—"

Palmer sighed. "You've got no choice."

Before Momo left, I'd have been scared, Rolfe thought. Now, I don't give a shit.

＊ ＊ ＊ ＊ ＊

Popov didn't show up at the conference, but Banyeov did, recognizable from a photo supplied by Palmer. Rolfe acted as official host, keeping himself busy by making sure that the meeting hall was properly set up, that the acoustics and audio visual system were working flawlessly, that the staging of the speakers and their presentations were carried out efficiently, that there were food and soft drinks available at the breaks, and that the seating arrangement at dinner went according to protocol. Otherwise, he had nothing to do but listen to the conference through simultaneous translation earphones. On the morning of the third day, during a numbingly dull discussion of the intricacies of importing software into Russia, a bellboy approached. "There's a call for you," the young man said. "Follow me."

Rolfe noticed that Banyeov, too, had risen and was exiting the hall. As he drew near the Czech, an unseen hand yanked him back so that he stumbled. Irritated, he looked around. No one was near him, and he hurried after Banyeov, now walking ahead of him toward the pre-function area.

A shot echoed through the afternoon. Banyeov was thrown backward and landed hard on his back, a crimson stain growing large on his chest. For an instant, no one moved. Then, chaos. People rushed out of the conference hall, screaming. Rolfe knelt by the fallen man, watching blood seep out of his body.

Ivan Denyenko, the hotel's security chief, pulled Rolfe to his feet. "Let's get you out of here."

"Just a moment." Rolfe's eyes were riveted on the body. The vision of his father in his mother's arms, her lips awash in his blood, superimposed itself on the Czech's inert frame. Dazed, he allowed Denyenko to lead him through the buzzing crowd to the elevator.

Somehow, he got to his suite, somehow unlocked the door. He staggered in, his brain blinded by horror, and vomited on the marble floor.

* * * * *

Fully clothed, wretched, he lay on his bed, replaying the morning's events. Was the whole conference a ruse to set up the Czech? he wondered. Had Popov planned it? Had the Czech double-crossed Yevgeny? Was it conceivable that the bullet was meant for me? The hotel's phones would be bugged, and so would his suite. There was no way to call Palmer from the room. Instead, he used his cell phone to call Popov, but he was away from the office; no one knew when he would be back. I'll leave tonight on the midnight plane, he decided, as fear, shock, and exhaustion overwhelmed him and he drifted into fretful sleep.

He was jolted awake by the ringing of the telephone. "It's me," Josh said urgently.

"What time is it?" Rolfe asked, trying to focus.

"Seven in the morning here. How come you're asleep so early?"

"Long story. Why are you calling?"

"I'm watching *The Today Show*," Josh said.

Rolfe's mind cleared. "So?"

"I'm watching pictures of it now. Jesus, what a mess."

Did they have a story on Banyeov's death? Rolfe wondered. Impossible. "What the hell are you talking about?"

"A pipe bomb exploded in the lobby of the Manhattan Metropolitan last night. They're suspecting a terrorist attack."

"What?"

"You heard me, a terrorist attack."

"Oh, God. No!"

A terrorist, Rolfe thought, but not the one the police were imagining. Every word of his conversation with McCory flashed through his memory.

"Are you still there?" Josh asked.

"Was anyone killed?" Rolfe shut his eyes and braced for the answer.

"No. The cleaning crew and the night staff were the only ones in the lobby. But thirteen people have been hospitalized, four in serious condition. All the guests have been evacuated, and the hotel's closed until structural engineers can assess the damage. What a goddamned disaster. Anyway, I've put extra security on all our U.S. hotels. It could have been us."

Guilt and self-loathing made him put down the phone. No, he thought, it couldn't.

* * * * *

"This is the fourth time I've called him," Rolfe said an hour later as he spoke to McCory's assistant from the limousine taking him to the airport.

"And it's the fourth time I'll give him your message."

"Why won't he talk to me?"

"That's not for me to say. I'm sure he will as soon as he can."

What have I done? he asked himself. What if one of those people dies? He poured vodka from the limo's bar into a glass and swallowed it in a gulp. Who was he more terrified of, Popov or

McCory? He couldn't decide.

And what if Hunt found out who was behind the bombing?

* * * * *

"A terrible thing," Popov said, sipping hot chocolate in the lounge of the Hotel Baur au Lac in Zurich. "Even I, with all my contacts, haven't been able to find out who killed the Czech."

Rolfe tried to discern if the Russian was lying, a futile task. Yevgeny had lied so often that fact and fiction produced the same affect. "You're doing well," he said. Popov was dressed in a Saville Row suit, Turnbull and Asser pinstriped shirt, and handmade shoes from Jermyn Street. How many murders, Rolfe wondered, had paid for the clothes? Still...

"Yevgeny, everyone knows the hotel business is in lousy shape. When the Iraqis invaded Kuwait, the bottom fell out. Oil prices went sky high, travelers started worrying about terrorism. Even American travel is off, and businesses aren't bankrolling the expense accounts of the eighties."

"And what does this have to do with me?" Popov asked, stretching his arms over his head, fingers interlaced, like an over-stuffed capitalist.

"It's the time to buy," Rolfe said. "We've just acquired two fore-closed hotels, but there are others anxious to sell. Pieter has a Dutch consortium putting up the money, but it's chump change. I want you to do the same thing in a big way." He thought back to a question Falkman had asked last month: "Who do you know with a big chunk of dough who wants to diversify into U.S. real estate?" Every time they'd spun the wheel, the same name popped up: Popov.

"After all," Falkman had gone on, "you don't know he was behind the Moscow murder. You're in bed with him anyway. You might as well enjoy the screwing."

"You think maybe there are deals in Europe too?" Popov asked.

"Particularly in France and the U.K."

The Russian lowered his arms, leaned forward. "How much are we talking about?"

"I can find you over a billion dollars worth of hotels in the next couple of years. With bank debt, you'd need to put up half of it." Rolfe's tone was more confident than he felt.

"That's a big number for a Russian."

"For most Russians."

"Half a billion dollars?"

"Twelve percent guarantee on the equity, profits above that, and we'll sell in seven years when the markets are booming."

"You're certain you can find the bargains?"

"Absolutely. It'll be like stealing."

"Stealing, I like." The Russian's triumphant laugh reminded Rolfe of a tsar about to execute a peasant. "You've come a long way since you worked at the Audley, haven't you?" He stood. "You promise your old friend, Yevgeny, you'll make me rich?"

"You're very rich already."

"But I want you to make me very much richer. Do you promise?"

"Yes," Rolfe laughed.

"Good. Richer is better. Very rich I like better than stealing."

* * * * *

Business was bad. By December 1991, Kestrel Hotels had run out of operating money, and the banks refused further credit. At a year-end review, Josh and Susan presented Rolfe with their cash flow forecasts.

"This has to be wrong," Rolfe said. "Otherwise, we couldn't be paying interest."

"We're not," Josh told him.

"Not paying interest? What are you talking about?"

"You told me the twelve percent returns that you promised Popov and the others were our priority." Susan spoke patiently, as if Rolfe were dyslexic. "So I've been paying them at the expense of the banks. Conversations with them are pretty ugly. They're in the same bind we are."

"Why didn't you tell me this before?"

"Because you were too busy running around the world making deals we can't pay for," Josh snapped. "I hope you're hearing us now."

He looks tired, Rolfe thought. His hair's thinning, there are bags under his eyes, and his face is wrinkled. But hell, this was no time to be dispirited. Fortunes had been made buying hotels during bad times—and times had never been more terrible. "There'll never be opportunities like this," he said. "We've got to go forward."

"Not if we go broke doing it." Josh's face was pale with anger. "We're cutting corners just to survive."

Rolfe ignored him and turned to Susan. He wished Momo were here; he could use her enthusiasm and support. "Time for more imagination," he said, winking. "A little financial inventiveness."

"We'll have to," Susan sighed. "Only this time, it'll be a lot harder. Right now the word 'hotel' is right up there with leprosy in the banks' vocabulary. If we get through this, it'll be a miracle."

Was his team going soft? Ultraconservative? As old as Josh's face indicated? He felt a surge of pleasure; the old magic flowed through his blood. He liked tightropes. "Come on, gang. Of course we'll get through this. Do anything it takes. Just keep us going while I make the deals."

CHAPTER 36

1993

Rolfe walked in the lobby of the L.A. Kestrel feeling invigorated by his run. Minutes later, he sat with his feet on the coffee table in the living room of the suite where he now resided, dressed in his sweat-sodden running clothes, clutching a glass of orange juice in his hand, and talking to his mother. For a change, she had called him.

"I'm worried about Jan," she was saying. "He's losing too much weight, and he's always exhausted." There was a vulnerability in her voice that was new to him.

"Cancer?"

"The doctors say no, but I don't know if they're telling the truth. I don't want to lose another husband. I'm worried sick. Who'll take care of me if he dies?"

Pieter can, Rolfe thought wryly. That is, if Jan deigns to tell her Pieter is Wim's son. She can't expect me to. Still, he could hear her anguish. She loves him! he thought with a mixture of surprise and envy.

"I want to give you the money your grandfather left you," she said, as if hoping for his support.

"How much has it grown to?"

"Just under seven million pounds."

Over $11 million bucks! Susan could clean up all kinds of debts with that money. But then it would be gone, disappeared down a black hole; there'd be no fuck-you money, just in case. "Keep holding on to it," he told her. "Ten more years."

She sighed. "I don't want the responsibility. In ten years, I'll be eighty-one."

"You're Peter Pan, forever young." He hoped his voice did not betray his insincerity. "Please do it for me."

"Oh, I'll invest it for ten years, then. But if I die, you'll have the money immediately."

"You'll never die. You're immortal." Yegh! Why was he so unfeeling? He was in trouble.

"I've made my will," she continued, "so if and when I do, it'll be as easy to probate as Mike Riverstone's. He lived simply, only owned that flat of his in Maspeth Gardens, had some stocks, a government pension, an insurance policy, and cash in the bank—I was surprised how much."

"Who were the beneficiaries?" Rolfe asked. Mike had never mentioned a family.

"I was the only one," his mother said. She started to cry. "Amazing, isn't it? He had no one else to love him."

* * * * *

"Nice digs," McCory said, admiring Rolfe's suite. He was dressed in Polo slacks, Gucci loafers, and a casual silk shirt—Rolfe couldn't guess the designer—that must have set him back $400. Quite a rise, the hotelier thought. For both of us.

"We ought to be thinking of selling the Nevada casino," Bud said.

Madness! "Why?"

"Because the economy's in the toilet."

"I don't see it getting worse. Besides, the casino's still making a fortune, and we'll do even better once the Vegas entertainment park's finished."

Bud studied him closely. "Just fooling," he said. "Needed to see your reaction. No, Rolfe, what I want to do is build another casino, this time in Lake Tahoe. Same deal. You as 'owner,' the union the power behind your throne."

Another casino? He was already overextended, as Josh reminded him daily—but even more serious would be having additional obligations to the union man. Thanks to McCory, Rolfe had sent his message to Hunt, and to his horror people almost got killed as a result. They were square now, even. To pay back his enemy he had wallowed in McCory's filth, and he didn't like the way it stuck to him. "I can't do it," he said.

"Can't or won't?" Bud asked, eyes narrowing.

"Can't. I'm up to my ears in new projects."

"You always are. I think the real answer's 'won't.'"

As usual, the union man was right. He wanted nothing more to do with McCory, did not want to sink more deeply into the swamp. Greed had made him say yes to the casinos in the first place, but it was all his risk; only his head was in the guillotine.

"No, really, Bud, I can't."

McCory's smile was as fake as patent medicine. "Sure you won't reconsider?"

I'm making another enemy, Rolfe thought. Just as dangerous as Popov or Hunt. Well, fuck it. Who cares? "No. I'm with you until we sell Las Vegas and Atlantic City, because we made a deal and you lived up to it. Then I'm out of the casino business, not only in Vegas and New Jersey but everywhere else too."

McCory's smile broadened. He stood. Rolfe stood also, and the union boss gave him a parting embrace as cold as February. "I understand," he said. "Perhaps it's a wise decision."

But Rolfe knew that the only wise decisions, as far as McCory was concerned, were to do his bidding.

* * * * *

Rolfe had fought against it for two months, but now, shaken by his encounter with McCory and desperately lonely, he drove to Momo's apartment building, determined to see her—only to be told by the doorman that she was out.

Awash in humiliation, he waited in his car, watching the entrance and compulsively checking his watch. Ten. Eleven. Jealousy supplanted all other emotions, and he pictured her with another, faceless man, laughing, flirting, enjoying herself. She would bring this man home, he was sure, invite him upstairs as she had many times before, and she would make love to him with as much passion, as much inventiveness, as she had given to him. He wondered who the man was, whether it was somebody he knew (intolerable!) or a stranger (also intolerable). Well, he would not let him have her without a fight.

Momo's car drew up to the building's parking garage. She was alone! The relief was overpowering. There was no other man. She would take him back! He swerved across the road and followed her car down the ramp.

She took some time getting out of her car, so when she opened the door he was in front of her.

"Rolfe!"

She dropped her purse, and in his confusion he bent to retrieve it. When he looked up, he saw her anger. "Leave me alone," she said. "You're stalking me."

"Not stalking. I'm desperate. Listen to me just this once."

She tried calmness, though her hands were shaking. "Please. We said goodbye in Colorado, and this is only painful. I'm leaving for London next week; I have a job there."

Her news was a body blow. "What kind of job?"

"It's none of your business!"

"With whom?"

She moved to get past him; he blocked her way. "If I tell you, you'll know how to find me, and I don't want that."

This would be the last time he saw her? "There's someone else, isn't there? I know there is. Who?"

"You're pathetic." Her scorn was worse than her anger.

His breath quickened, and he put a hand on her arm. "I can't live without you. Really. These weeks have been agony." Even as he spoke, he realized how ridiculous he sounded.

"They haven't been so hot for me, either," she reminded him.

His hope grew. He could see her anguish. "Then, let's end the agony. Come back to me."

She brushed past him, and this time he let her go. "You like deals," she said. "I'll make you one. Get out of the hotel business. Get out of Kestrel. Sell it, walk away, whatever. When I see the announcement, I'll contact you and we'll talk. Until then, please, please ... there's to be no repeat of what happened here tonight. I'm out of your life, Rolfe. Leave me alone."

Another blackmailer, he thought, and his chest almost burst with rage. How dare she issue ultimatums? But as he watched her walk up the ramp, he knew that anger was futile and the only way to win her back was to renounce everything he had built.

He turned back to his car. The garage seemed enormous. The harshness of the fluorescent lighting beat into his eyes even as his mind recoiled. Give up Kestrel? Never! It was his oxygen, part of his bloodstream. He would cut off a limb for her, risk any danger. But to drain himself of his own blood was asking too much. He would have to find a way to live without her.

Book Three

"There is a precipice either side of you—a precipice of caution and a precipice of over-daring."

Winston Spencer Churchill

CHAPTER 37

1994

In March 1994, Kestrel ran out of money. With over 65,000 rooms in its 163 hotels in 26 countries, the 42 properties in which Rolfe had ownership were worth over $4 billion. That was one side of the balance sheet. The other side showed that he had obligations to his partners and to lenders for at least a similar amount. Kestrel's cash reserves were empty.

Rolfe got the news from Josh and Susan in an hour-long presentation featuring charts and spreadsheets, during which Rolfe fantasized about running just one hotel, delivering excellence at all levels, and getting paid a salary for doing it.

"There's got to be a hiatus," Josh concluded. "No more buying. And we've got to sell off some of our older properties or some of our outside businesses. Or maybe take the company public."

Rolfe listened calmly. Nothing in his chief executive's presentation surprised him, though he was disturbed by the seriousness of the problem. "No sales," he said. "Not of properties or outside businesses. And no IPOs. This is my—our—company, and as long as I'm alive, it stays that way."

"Bravo!" Susan applauded. "You—we—own a company that can't pay back its debts and will very likely sink like the *Titanic*."

Rolfe did not find her sarcasm amusing. He gestured toward the charts. "I see our results. Business has never been better."

"So what?"

"So the banks should be falling over themselves to lend us money."

"Well, they won't. I've tried everywhere. There's no place left to look."

"Bullshit! There's always money sloshing around. Find it."

Josh and Susan exchanged glances. Rolfe caught it. "What aren't you telling me?"

"You remember what we did the last time we got a case of the severe cash-shorts."

"I'm afraid so."

"Well, that was chickenfeed compared to what we've done this time."

Rolfe sat motionless. "Go on."

"We've already refinanced every hotel we own, even those where we're only partners. What's worse, every cent we've borrowed has gone straight to Kestrel—without giving our partners their share."

The implications were terrifying. Rolfe stared at the spreadsheets before him, but they blurred in his brain. He waited, his heartbeat palpable in his chest.

Susan averted her eyes. "All of the monies that the hotels contractually must have on reserve for capital expenditures have been borrowed, and I've used those funds to keep us going."

"But that money's not ours!" Rolfe shouted. "It belongs to the owners, the banks. We can't touch it."

Susan shrugged.

"There's more to it than that," Josh said. "Susan's worked out a system to take money from our hotels' bank accounts and use it to keep us afloat. When she thinks the money will be missed, she pays it back by borrowing it from other hotels' accounts."

"But that breaks every contract we've signed. It's stealing!"

"Right," Josh said. "Plain, old-fashioned robbery."

Rolfe walked around his desk and stood directly over his friend. "How could you let this happen?"

Josh jumped up, his face choleric. Rolfe moved back a step, seared by his heat. "How could I let it happen? You're the one who put us in this position. You're the one steering this leaking ship, and Susan and I have been left to keep it afloat, by whatever means necessary. We did what we had to do—because of you . . . and for you.

"I never told you to steal," Rolfe insisted, realizing how lame he sounded.

"No, you didn't. But we warned you a thousand times how precarious our situation was, and you said, 'Do anything.' Well, 'anything' included borrowing from the hotels' accounts. And we had no choice—because all you cared about, all you wanted to do was buy. Buy, buy, buy! Just to prove your dick is bigger than Hunt's!"

Rolfe caught his breath, and choked back an angry reply. "If we get caught by the owners..."

"There's more," Susan said.

He lost all energy. "More?"

"This time, we've scraped the absolute bottom of the barrel." She paused.

"Tell me," his voice now a dull monotone.

"We've gone through every penny in the employee pension fund."

Rolfe slumped into the nearest chair. The room seemed charged with electricity, and he felt impaled by it. "Won't the auditors notice?" he asked through bloodless lips.

"I don't think so," Susan said. "We've made up a trail of back-dated loans with the borrowed monies being repaid in and out, so there's a history of us borrowing and paying back with high interest rates. They shouldn't look exceptional to any auditor."

Rolfe raised his head. "I don't remember us doing that."

"We didn't. The entries are fake."

Rolfe covered his face; the electricity was attacking his brain. "Let me get this right. You've refinanced the hotels, both ours and our partners', and instead of giving our partners their share of the refinancing proceeds, you've taken everything for Kestrel."

Josh and Susan sat silently, watching him. There was nothing to refute.

"You've raided the capital expenditure reserves, money not ours in the first place, and so we've got no money to upgrade the owners' hotels when it's needed."

Again, silence.

A thought struck him, and he felt chilled. "Including Popov's?"

"Yes," Susan whispered.

One of his two most dangerous enemies. "The casinos?"

"No, not yet."

Rolfe exhaled. Then McCory might remain an ally.

"You've stolen the working capital and the profits from the hotels, and repaid it only when you think we're about to get caught. And you've raided the pension fund and faked the records to cover it up."

"That about sums it up," Josh said. "But, hey, you've got a chain of great hotels that are better than Metropolitan's."

The enormity of what they'd done jolted him to life. "You're both fucking crazy!" he screamed. "Don't you realize this is big-time fraud? This is criminal stuff. If anybody finds out, we'll all go to jail!"

"It, therefore, seems to me that it is mandatory nobody finds out," Josh said calmly.

Popov had the means to find out anything. "But how do we keep this quiet?" What are we going to do?" For the first time in his life, Rolfe had no back-up plan, no escape hatch, no options, and he felt the walls closing in.

* * * * *

"I need you to tell our partners that they'll have to wait a bit for Kestrel's share of the money on the Boston hotel," Rolfe told Ron Falkman in the lawyer's office.

"How long is 'a bit'?"

"A while. Maybe a long while."

Falkman's voice was cold. "I worked my ass off getting this deal. Because you wanted it. You insisted. I put my reputation on the line, and now you stroll in here and tell me you can't pay?"

"But—"

"No excuses! How dare you initiate deals like this when you don't have the cash?"

"I didn't know—"

"Didn't know what?"

"That I didn't have enough money."

"You, Rolfe Ritter, chairman of Kestrel Hotels, don't know how much money you have? Horseshit! You just played the odds, as always, hoping you'd find the money in the end."

"That's insulting."

"What's insulting is your pretending you'd come up with the cash. Is your not telling me the truth. Is your flat-out lies." He spoke now with genuine sorrow. "After all these years, to come to this ... find yourself another lawyer, Rolfe. I can't take any more chances with you. You might be a brilliant hotelier, but you're the biggest schmuck I know."

He'll come back, Rolfe mused as he left. When I come up with a sure-fire deal, he'll ache to be part of it. The thought cheered him, and he decided to take a walk for a while before going back to the hotel. He stopped to admire a Chanel dress in the window of Bergdorf Goodman and, inspired, took out his cell phone. "I'm in New York. Are you free for dinner?"

"See you at the apartment at eight," Chantal said with a squeal of pleasure.

* * * * *

Their lovemaking had little of the ardor of the past. Worry

dulled his appetite, depression his performance, and as if to explain, he started to tell her of the precariousness of Kestrel's financial position, though not of the chicanery that surrounded it.

"What exactly have Josh and Susan done?" Chantal asked sympathetically.

An antenna went up. A sympathetic Chantal was not someone he was used to. "Let's talk in the morning," he said. "Right now, I'm exhausted."

She pressed him further, but he closed his eyes and turned away.

In the morning, she brought him coffee in bed and kissed him on the forehead. He looked at his watch. "I've got to move. I'm due downtown at ten."

"Don't rush," she said soothingly. "You've got plenty of time." She kissed the fingers of his left hand and brought it to her breast. "You started to tell me about Josh and Susan."

"It's nothing," he said, getting up and heading for the bathroom.

She blocked his way. "But you said you'd tell me in the morning."

"It can wait." He pushed past her.

"I think you should get it off your chest now. It's obviously troubling you."

"Later," he said irritably. "I've got to pee."

He remained reticent after he left the bathroom and put on his clothes.

"You don't trust me," Chantal said. "If you won't tell me your news, why should I tell you mine?"

It was typical of her to play this kind of game. It used to excite him; this morning it made him cross. "Fine," he said. "Don't tell me."

"I'm getting married."

She had meant it as a thunderbolt, he knew, but the announcement left him unmoved. "Who's good enough for you?"

She looked at him coquettishly. "You mean other than you?"

"Come on, Chantal. Who is he?"

She paused for effect. "Actually, you know him."

His interest quickened, along with a stab of fear.

"It's Bruce Hunt. He's divorcing Carol. The papers are already in the works."

* * * * *

"What do you mean, he wouldn't tell you what was going on?"

Chantal held the receiver away from her ear. "I'm sorry, Bud. I almost had him, but then he stopped."

"Losing your touch?"

"Maybe. At least you know he's got serious problems."

"Yeah, but I don't know what problems, or what that devious prick's likely to do to get out of them."

"As I say, I did my best."

"There's only one thing you do well," he snarled. "So as soon as you're married, get the son of a bitch back into bed, and this time get him to open up."

CHAPTER 38

1994–1996

Susan and Andrew were huddled over Rolfe's office table, discussing the embryonic Internet. Andrew was thrilled with it. "Finally, we'll be able to get close to our customers," he crowed, "communicate without using travel agents as middlemen. The savings will be huge."

"How long before it'll happen?" Rolfe asked.

"We'd better start working on it now."

Susan had been listening intently. "What do you recommend?"

"We'll need Internet applications for all our companies. And we'll have to develop the finest websites. Metropolitan's already got an army working on theirs. We'll have to hire some new people, use some hotels as test kitchens."

Rolfe groaned. "More goddamn money. Stop!"

"Listen," Susan said. "We ignore this at our own peril. The whole lodging industry will change sooner rather than later, and we've got to lead the way."

"How can Metropolitan afford it?" Rolfe asked wearily, sick of living the hand-to-mouth existence forced on him by Josh and Susan, and constantly worrying someone would discover what they'd done.

"Because they're a public company, and with their stock price so high, they can spend money like water," Andrew said.

"I wish we were public," Susan complained.

"We'd never survive the scrutiny," Rolfe pointed out. "But if we have to compete, then let's compete. Get Josh on it as soon as he comes back from New York. We'll find the money somewhere." It was becoming a stock phrase of his. And each time he said it, he wondered if it were true.

* * * * *

But Josh did not return. At 6:00 A.M. the next morning, just as

Rolfe finished showering, his phone rang.

"Rolfe!" Susan's hysterical voice screamed. "My God, Rolfe!"

He had never heard her so upset. "What is it?"

"Josh is dead."

All the air went out of him, and he sat heavily on his bed. The familiar objects surrounding him—the Jim Dine lithographs, the bronze Buddha he had picked up in Thailand, the silk Persian rug that covered the floor, the lamps and books, tables and chairs—all seemed alien, as though belonging to another life, and he had to blink rapidly to reorient himself. He heard Susan sobbing at the other end of the phone, and the sound of his own heart beating.

"How?" he managed.

"Murdered."

No! This was too much. His best friend, his partner, his mainstay murdered? He couldn't comprehend it, couldn't take it in. A vision of Josh laughing at him swam into his head, and he expected the familiar voice to say, "Just kidding"—but there was no such voice, only Susan's anguish to prove that what she said was true.

"Tell me," he said at last.

She struggled for composure. "Chuck Larraby called—Josh's new operational VP. He was with Josh in New York. Remember? They were there to work with the regional operations team. Anyway, Chuck called and—" she broke off, unable to go on.

"Take your time," he counseled, grateful for her hesitation. If he could calm her, he could calm himself. "Chuck called, and—?"

"I don't know why he called me instead of you. Maybe he's scared of you. Anyway, he called. They had a breakfast meeting at eight. Josh had left a seven o'clock wake-up call, but he didn't pick up. So the service called again at seven-fifteen, and again got no response. Chuck called him at seven-thirty, but when he didn't answer, Chuck figured he was in the shower. When he called again at quarter to eight and there was still no answer, he got worried." She paused. "I can't imagine why I'm telling you these ridiculous details."

"They help. You're doing a good job, Susan. Keep going."

"Anyway, Chuck got hold of the hotel manager, and the two of them went to Josh's room. The newspapers were still outside the door; the do-not-disturb sign was still hanging on the doorknob. When they knocked, no one answered—of course, no one answered—so the manager used the master key and they went in."

She broke down again. Rolfe let her cry it out, heard her start to speak but stop, overcome with emotion, several times. He was numb now. It was as though she was carrying his pain as well as her own. Finally, she was able to speak again.

"They found him on the floor. His hands and feet were tied with wire. He'd—" a choking sound, a deep breathe, and then in a strained, hoarse voice, "He'd been shot in the head, apparently while kneeling, and had pitched forward. Chuck said he—oh, God—"

There was a new spasm of sobs. Rolfe waited, trying unsuccessfully not to picture what Susan described. "He had bruises and cigarette burns on his face and hands. He'd been tortured before he was killed. His eyes were open, wide with terror. Chuck said he—he—"

"Did he call the police?" Rolfe asked sharply, hoping the authoritarian tone would help her.

"Immediately. Chuck said they turned the hotel into a zoo. The manager's trying to keep it quiet, but there'll be press there soon, and the other guests will know. Chuck says the cops are questioning last night's shift now, and of course they've talked to him. He says that's why it took him almost an hour to get to me."

A thought struck Rolfe with such force it made him gasp. "Has anybody told Ted?"

"No. Chuck didn't think he should be the one. He wants you—"

"Of course. That poor man. It'll destroy him."

"I don't envy you," Susan said.

"Let's meet in the office in two hours. I'm too dazed now to think any further than Ted, but we've got to plan how to let everyone at Kestrel know, and we'll need a statement for the press. Do you think you're up to it?"

"I think it'll be good for both of us. Besides, I need to be with you, Rolfe. Nobody, other than Ted, loved him the way you and I did."

"I need you too," he said. And Momo, who would not be there. He fought back tears.

Numb with shock and grief, he stared at the phone a long time before he dialed Josh's home number. "Ted, it's Rolfe. I have awful news. . . ."

* * * * *

A slender fifty-five-year-old man, dressed in a gray suit, button-down white shirt, and red tie introduced himself to Rolfe with a disingenuous smile. "I'm Agent Albert Merton from our Los Angeles bureau. And this—" he indicated a younger, similarly dressed man who stood subserviently behind him, "is Agent Frattini."

"Make yourselves comfortable," Rolfe said, indicating two chairs in his office. "I'm curious, why is the FBI involved in this case?"

"As I explained to Mr. Falkman," Merton answered, unruffled, "There is a possibility Mr. Leonard's death may be linked to organized crime, given the style of the execution."

Rolfe shuddered at the last phrase. "I want to help in any way I can."

Merton and Frattini questioned him for two hours: Could he imagine any motive for the murder? No. Did Mr. Leonard have any enemies in the business world? Some, but no one who might want to kill him. In his personal life? Not likely. Did Mr. Leonard have financial problems? Not to anyone's knowledge. Was he aware Josh was a homosexual? Yes; so what?

"Your competitors say you run everything close to the edge," Merton said. "They say you're always short of capital and that you take huge financial risks. Could these have any influence on Mr. Leonard's murder?"

Had he talked to Hunt? Rolfe wondered, glaring at Merton. "I make it a rule never to listen to or to be influenced by gossip, especially malicious gossip from my competitors. I hope you adopt the same rule. Kestrel's finances are in splendid shape, mostly thanks to Joshua Leonard. I run one of the most successful hotel chains in the world."

"Yet, you have enemies. Don't I remember a salmonella problem in this very hotel not long ago?"

"We still don't know whether 'enemies' were responsible for that, do we? If they were, those were my enemies, not Josh's. And as I'm sure you remember, the FBI certainly wasn't effectual in that instance." He stood. "This time, I hope you find the killer . . . and quickly."

"Thank you, Mr. Ritter," Merton said with obvious insincerity. "Here's my card. If you hear or think of anything at all that could have a connection to Mr. Leonard's death, please contact me or Agent Frattini." He shook Rolfe's hand. "By the way, could you explain your relationship with Bud McCory?"

"Bud McCory?" How did his name surface? What might he have to do with Josh's murder? What does the FBI know about our dealings? If they investigated too closely... Terror added to his grief.

"Yes. McCory. His name came up in connection with the salmonella attack, and I was wondering if it might not come up here again."

"I don't see how it could," Rolfe said quickly. "Mr. McCory's business is with me, not with Josh."

"Indeed." Merton watched Rolfe unblinkingly. "To hear you tell it, everything has to do with you and nothing with Mr. Leonard." He turned to go. "Doesn't that strike you as a little odd?"

"Not at all. I'm the boss. Josh worked for me."

And am I responsible for his death? he thought when the agent had left. What have I done? Remorse would color his days forever, he knew. He could not imagine how he would go on.

* * * * *

The group stood under a damp, gray sky around Josh's graveside in a Jewish cemetery on the outskirts of San Francisco. Josh's father led the Mourners' Kaddish, the Hebrew words reverberating in Rolfe's ears.

He stood with his arm around Susan, her tears falling unnoticed on his shoulders, her hand clutching Ted Pemberton's arm. Since Rolfe understood only the sentiments, not the words, his gaze scanned the crowd. There was Josh's mother, grief-ridden and bent, supported by her younger sister. There were several people from Kestrel; Rolfe had closed the corporate office for the funeral.

And there—Momo! Yes, standing at the back of the crowd, her back erect, her long hair flowing over the shoulders and back of her black dress. If she saw him, she gave no indication of it. He longed to go to her, if nothing else to receive her words of comfort. But that would have to wait until after the service.

"Yit-gadal v'yit-kadash..."

Rolfe was jolted back to the moment as the coffin was lowered into the earth. He could picture Josh vividly, pouring another glass of wine, mocking the solemnity.

"Y'hey sh'mey raba..."

Susan put her arm around his waist as if to give him strength.

"Y'hey sh'lama raba..."

Rolfe looked again for Momo, but found instead a thin, gray-coated man taking pictures of the mourners. Merton! McCory had called to tell Rolfe he wouldn't be at the funeral. "It would only raise questions," the union boss had said. Right.

"v'al kol yisrael, v'imru amen."

Following the example set by Josh's parents, Rolfe shoveled wet earth on Josh's coffin. He looked over to the spot where Merton had been standing, then searched frantically for Momo. Both had vanished.

* * * * *

"I told the FBI nothing!"

The windows of the Chevrolet Caprice wagon were so fogged by the heat Rolfe and McCory were generating in their anger that the lights in the garage of L.A.'s Hyatt barely provided enough illumination for Rolfe to see McCory's face.

"What did Susan tell them?"

"Nothing. For Christ's sake, Bud, do you think we'd betray you?"

"You would," McCory said, "if it meant saving your ass."

Rolfe didn't answer to the truth of this. Instead, he said, "Merton thinks I know more about Josh's murder than I actually do. He's convinced it's linked with the company's affairs. He threatened to subpoena me and put me in front of a grand jury if I didn't cooperate and tell him everything about the people with whom we do business."

"And?"

"And he warned me if I lied or withheld information, he'd have me prosecuted and personally throw away the key."

"Typical FBI bullshit."

"He offered me immunity if I told him everything I know."

"Ignore 'em."

"How can I? If he starts digging into Kestrel—"

"He digs into me." McCory shifted in his seat so he could look at Rolfe directly. "You can't let that happen. Stonewall 'em."

"The man scares the daylights out of me. Do you think they're following me, tapping my phones?"

"Maybe. In any case, it doesn't hurt to be careful. Just don't fucking panic and go anyplace you're not supposed to be or make any calls to anyone you shouldn't be talking to."

The union boss's demands were oppressive. Rolfe would handle this as he wanted, no matter what McCory said. "Like you? Seems to me I shouldn't be here, and I shouldn't be talking to you."

"Seems to me we took adequate precautions. Christ, I'm getting good at it. The Feeb's been after us forever. Those guys are fucking paranoid. They think every union is controlled by the mob and Jimmy fucking Hoffa's body is buried in my backyard."

Rolfe's anxiety grew stronger. "How do you live with them on your back?"

"You get used to it. Right now, they're only trying to scare you. They know you didn't kill Josh—why the fuck would you? Who they're really after is me, and they think the way to get me is through you. So be careful. Keep your fucking mouth closed, and this'll pass. I know what I'm talking about."

Did he? Maybe if they caught Josh's murderer, they'd lay off Kestrel. "Who did it, Bud? Who killed Josh?"

"I don't know," McCory said, perhaps too quickly. "Maybe your friend Hunt's still mad at you."

* * * * *

He sat alone in his suite, listening to Mahler's "Das Lied von der Erde" the music coinciding with his black mood. There was nobody he could talk to about Josh's death.

Susan was the only one who might understand. But after her interview with Merton and telling him nothing, she had come into his and witheringly asked, "How much more must I do for you?"

The implication, he realized, meant she believed that Josh's connection to Rolfe had led to his murder, and maybe she was right. If so, it would be his greatest crime among myriad crimes, and there could be no absolution.

As he often did, he thought of Momo. If she wouldn't talk to him at Josh's funeral, she certainly wouldn't now. And Ron—well, any conversation with his lawyer would mean bringing up what Susan and Josh had been forced to do, and no lawyer would continue with a client who had countenanced—encouraged—such criminality. If only Mike were alive, Rolfe thought. He'd help me find the path through this maze.

He thought of his father, and again heard the thud of the black car and the sounds of his mother's screams—his mother, whose coldness brought no comfort now, as then. He closed his eyes and concentrated on the music. "Where am I going?" Mahler's angst-ridden question permeated his brain until he dozed upright in his armchair.

He awoke to the ringing of his phone. No more, his brain screamed. Please, God. I beg you.

A man's voice, unknown to him, pitiless. "We know what you've been doing with our money. Leonard told us everything before he paid the price for your crimes. You have broken your promises. You will learn to keep them."

The anonymous voice paused, letting his chilling words resonate, then: "You will put the money back within ninety days, or you will end up like your late friend, but you will suffer far more greatly before you die. If you say one word about this call to the FBI, your mother, her husband, and his family will meet the same fate. Again, you have ninety days. Do you understand?"

The line went dead before Rolfe could answer.

Guilt, panic, and self-pity overwhelmed him. They killed him to get at me, Rolfe knew now with certainty. But who was after him? How had they found out about what Josh and Susan had done? Who had arranged Josh's murder? Was it McCory? Hunt? Popov? Or did Steinmann arrange all this before he died?

One thing he knew for certain: No matter who murdered Josh and who was threatening him now, he'd have to pay back all of the money, to the most dangerous ones first. If only he knew who they were.

Not bothering to undress, he lay on the bed, but it was a long time before sleep came. Two hours later, bathed in sweat, he awoke to the sound of his own screams, his nightmare having abruptly ended with his father's body slithering down the blood-stained wall, the word "promise" throbbing in his brain, the rat of fear gnawing at his stomach.

CHAPTER 39

1996

Since he couldn't go to the FBI, he finally decided to confess to Falkman. The lawyer had flown in for Josh's funeral, and Rolfe caught him just before he was to return to New York. Over Breakfast at The Hills, Rolfe told some of the financial story. If it meant losing Falkman, so be it. If it meant gaining an ally, at least he'd have one. He could not go on alone.

"This is worse than the other times, isn't it?" Falkman asked, obviously shocked.

"Far worse."

"Then you'd better not tell me much more."

Talking was a relief. At least it kept his mind off his nightmares. "I need your help. We've got to raise big money quickly—within ninety days. The only thing I can think of is to sell properties. The public real estate companies will want to buy them at lousy numbers, and then lease them back to me at fat rents. The chains will want me to sell them my best hotels, and then take off the Kestrel name. The first option would mean I wouldn't raise enough money, and the other would mean the end of what I've built."

"So what?" Falkman asked unemotionally. "That's to be expected."

Rolfe had a momentary vision of the grin on Hunt's face. "I couldn't stand it. What I need is someone who'll buy some of my big hotels for cash and still let me manage them as Kestrels. I won't be greedy on price; it's speed that matters. I haven't got the time to appoint a broker or go through an auction."

"Yeah, and I want to be Prime Minister of Israel. What about your friend Pieter?"

Rolfe had thought of calling Pieter, but had held back. "Not this time. I don't completely trust him." He shrugged. "I guess I don't trust anybody except you."

"When I get back to New York, I'll make a few calls. Maybe I'll come up with something," Falkman said without optimism. "Anyway, finding money isn't your only problem. You've also got to find a replacement for Josh."

"I know, I know. But with everything else, I don't want to think about it now."

"You've got no choice. You can't possibly handle everything alone."

"How can I bring anyone in under these circumstances? Anyone I can trust, that is."

Falkman smiled enigmatically. "There's only one possible person."

"Who?"

"Susan."

"Susan!" For the first time since the threatening call, Rolfe laughed. "You're out of your mind."

"On the contrary. She knows everything about the company, and everyone on the outside likes her."

"But she's a baby!"

"She was a baby when you started Kestrel. She's grown up now—in many ways she's older and smarter than you—and she's every bit as inventive as Josh was."

His mind flashed back to him and Susan in bed together, her tenderness and gentle touch, her little-girl cries as she climaxed. But Ron was right. That was a long time ago. "She has no top-level managerial experience," he argued. "Besides, there's no other woman at the top of a hotel chain. What would people think?"

"Since when have you cared about other people's opinions? Anyway, they'd think you promoted the best person for the job."

"What about the Asians, the people in the Middle East? They think women are useful only to make babies."

"Those people care about money more than gender. Besides, you'll still be her boss, and at last reports, you're still a man."

Yeah. A man and a coward, too frightened to think clearly, too cowed to fight back. Fuck it! Maybe Susan was the right choice. She was older, smarter, and had more balls than he did.

* * * * *

His mother wouldn't let him have his fuck-you money. Besides, it wasn't anywhere near enough. Desperate, he took out his safe deposit box and scoured it for salvation. Nothing!

* * * * *

"What's wrong, Chantal?" Rolfe asked. He was in his car; she had called him on his cell phone.

"The FBI just interviewed me. They insist on seeing me again."

His shoulders sagged. What was going on? Had Josh's murder triggered a full-scale investigation of Kestrel? Had Josh left any clue to his activities on Kestrel's behalf? Were his financial maneuvers about to be exposed? Was Kestrel in jeopardy? Was he? "What did they ask?"

"They want to know what work I did for you. When I last saw you. What you told me. What I know."

"And?"

"I told them nothing important." She laughed. "Just how small your dick was."

"Very funny."

"But it's not me you should worry about."

"Who then?"

"Bruce."

Rolfe felt hollow, numb. "What about him?"

"He's having a field day, feeding them the names of everyone who has a grudge against you."

"Shit. If that's all they want to know, I'll tell them myself."

"That's not the point. He has a safe full of private investigators' files on you, and he's turned them over."

"Christ! Files on what?"

"I don't know, but he's smug, like an adolescent who got laid for the first time."

What could he possibly know? Rolfe wondered. The answer came to him quickly: everything.

* * * * *

Rolfe called McCory's private line. "Get Hunt off my back!" he said without preamble.

"Nothing I can do," McCory drawled. "But I hear he's telling everyone who'll listen that Josh's death means Kestrel's going down big time."

"And you can't stop him? He'll destroy me!"

"Well"—the drawl got more pronounced—"I can try."

"Thank God. I need somebody on my side."

"Have you seen how casino stocks are falling?"

What did that have to do with Hunt? "So what? We're not public. And the casinos are minting money."

"You're missing the fucking point. I asked you to sell at the top of the market. You refused. So now maybe we should sell before the public market completely tanks."

"No way," Rolfe said, setting aside a spasm of doubt. "Don't let a market blip panic you. There's plenty of upside left."

"You promise you'll sell when the fucking time's right?" It was more of a statement than a question.

"I promise."

McCory sighed. "Good. Then I'll see what I can do about Hunt."

* * * * *

"We do some work for an Anglo-French conglomerate in the United States," Falkman told Rolfe as the two men conferred in Falkman's office. "EUF. Ever hear of it?"

"No."

"Or its chairman, Sir Martin Treadwell?"

"Vaguely. Wasn't he sniffing around the Audleys some time ago?"

"That's the man. Started as an accountant in EUF's predecessor firm, United Products. Worked his way up to control the company, merged it with a larger French company, Europe Fonciere—hence EUF. Now he controls the whole empire. He's one hard son of a bitch, so tough he managed to talk the British Government into giving him a knighthood. Anyway, right now he's on an acquisitions binge, buying as many luxury consumer brands as he can get his hands on."

"What's it to me?" Rolfe asked halfheartedly.

"If you listen, I'll explain. Treadwell's been keen on the hotel industry as far back as the Audley sale. As always, he wants to buy a luxury brand. He wants to buy a luxury brand. When he found out we represent Kestrel, he told one of my partners he wanted to meet 'the man who solved the Audley puzzle and seduced the Germaines.'"

"He's not touching the Audleys," Rolfe snapped. "They're the very last properties I'd sell."

"My partner told Treadwell that. But he also said you were creative and may find a way to do something together."

His lawyer's enthusiasm only added to Rolfe's dejection. "It's a bloody waste of time."

"At least meet the guy. He'll be in San Francisco next week."

"Okay, okay. But in the meantime, do me a favor. The FBI are centering their investigation around me, and I'm terrified. I'll need a lawyer who specializes in this type of thing—find me the best. Why the hell they're not concentrating on Josh's murder, and why they still haven't found out who's behind the salmonella poisoning's beyond me. Merton told me they were 'cases pending,' whatever the fuck that means. Now they're all over my ass, and Hunt's feeding the fire."

"Calm down," Falkman said. "I'll find you someone. Besides, you're reading too much into this. Have you promoted Susan yet?"

"No," Rolfe grumbled, unmollified. "I'm still thinking about it."

* * * * *

Margaret was in tears. "The FBI has been here," she sobbed. "They came early this morning, woke up Jan, even though he's sick. They asked me questions for half an hour before Jan made them leave. Questions about you."

Jesus! His mother! They were relentless. He felt splattered by mud. "What sort of questions?"

"Do you have enemies, business problems, that sort of thing."

"What did you tell them?"

"The truth!" Her voice turned cold. He could visualize his mother sitting bolt upright, her hair pulled tightly back in a bun, indignantly holding the phone as if it contained some repugnant disease. "I told them I didn't know anything about your business, that you never discuss it with me. That I didn't want to know about it." Her implicit admonition rankled him. "By the way, they interviewed Pieter too."

* * * * *

"Mr. Ritter." A tall, lean man stood before Rolfe, who did a quick appraisal. Sandy hair framing a clean-shaven face. Guileless eyes under round, wire-framed glasses. A ready smile. Innocence incarnate. Was this really the son of a bitch Falkman described?

Probably.

"It's nice to meet you, Sir Martin." He indicated an armchair facing his. The Englishman sat.

"You've turned around Audley brilliantly." Treadwell had a flat, middle-class London accent; no Oxford or Cambridge there. "Quite a coup, getting the Germaines to sell. We tried for years and couldn't get close."

"Just good timing," Rolfe said.

"I've always felt good sense leads to good timing. You had it, we didn't." He smiled ingratiatingly. "Mr. Falkman told you why I wanted this meeting?"

"Not precisely."

"Then let me. I like tourism, the business of tourism. And that means hotels. Quite simply, I wish to build our hotel business to cover as many price segments as possible, from the low to the highest end. Audley and Kestrel, both under your command, represent the highest of the highest end, and that's where I'd like to start. I'd like to acquire your company. Interested?"

"The company's not for sale," he said reflexively.

"At any price?"

Rolfe hesitated, providing just the queue the Brit was looking for.

"So you are interested."

"Sir Martin—"

"Just Martin, please. Our technology guru tells me that your business philosophy is in line with ours."

"Who's that?"

"One of your alumni, Momo Takenaka. That's why I was sure we'd be compatible."

There was a buzzing in his ears, and his hand shook so violently he had to put his coffee cup down to keep it from spilling. "I didn't know..."

"I hired Ms. Takenaka as soon as I heard she was coming to London. When she found out I was thinking of making you an offer, she was most encouraging. The idea is to link Audley and Kestrel with our own luxury and top-end brands in other businesses. They'd be a great combination."

True, Rolfe knew. And it might be a way of seeing Momo again, working with her again. Had she encouraged Treadwell because she felt the same way?

He drew in his breath slowly. "Martin, I'm genuinely flattered. There's no one in the luxury consumer business I admire more, and your strategy of branding combined with growth is spot-on. But I've got to tell you: for the past thirty years I've dreamed of building a truly great lodging brand, and I can feel it within my grasp. Only when I've reached my goal could I think of selling."

Treadwell took off his glasses and massaged his eyelids with his thumb and forefinger. When he opened his eyes, they seemed to burn across the desk. "I'm a great believer in farming, Rolfe. If you have fertile ground and the right seeds, and sow and water them, eventually they'll grow. I'm patient. I can wait."

Why don't I sell now? Rolfe wondered. Then the threats would disappear, the money worries would vanish, the ceaseless anxiety would dissipate. He tried to imagine how he'd feel the day after he'd sold. His father's name in someone else's hands? Having Treadwell as his boss? Having anyone as a boss? No! Not now—not yet. Not even to get Momo back.

Ron had advised him to be creative. Very well. A rush of adrenaline coursed through him. "You're a deal junkie," Susan had once told him. True. He felt high.

"I've got an idea how we can get closer," Rolfe began. "We can cross-market Kestrel and Audley with your top-end consumer brands."

The magnate put his glasses back on. "Do you mean have joint frequent-user rewards?"

"As a start, but we can do a lot more. We can feature your products in our hotels, and you can rent retail or showcase space. Our respective brochures and marketing programs could include our combined products. I'll bet Andrew McDonald and your marketing people will think of a thousand packages, combinations and other promotions. Momo can certainly develop the technology to handle them."

Rolfe saw he had struck a chord.

"Let's do it!" Treadwell said. "Why not?"

"Because there's a hitch," Rolfe said. "Money. I'm sure Ron told you—"

"Indeed. That's why I presumed to come."

"I have some pressing cash needs, and the capital markets are tight right now." Rolfe tried to read Treadwell's expression, but couldn't. Surely the Englishman knew precisely how big a hole Rolfe had dug. "If you're serious about joining forces, why not buy a few of our Kestrel hotels. We'll keep managing them, it'll give your team a chance to learn our way of doing business, and you can decide if you want to plunge deeper."

"In other words, dip our toe in for starters."

Rolfe sat back. "Exactly."

"It's not quite what I had in mind."

"But it could work. Who knows what it might lead to?"

To Rolfe's surprise, for there had been no sign of it coming, Treadwell burst out laughing. "Our mutual lawyers told me you were creative. I suppose the idea's not so stupid."

Hallelujah! Now, how do I get him to commit? Rolfe wondered, the old buzz coming back. "I have an idea. Let's make a five-year management deal for five of our hotels that you'll buy now. If you don't like us at the end of that time and want to manage the hotels yourselves, we'll pack our bags and the hotels are yours, free and clear of Kestrel."

"I don't know," Treadwell drawled. "How would the stock market react?"

Sensing salvation, Rolfe rushed on. "If I guarantee to buy back the hotels at a fair market value but no less than the price you paid after the five years are up, should you choose to sell them, it's a win-win situation for you. Your stock can only go up."

"And yours?"

"That's my problem."

Another laugh. "I suppose you're right. Are you saying you don't want to marry, but at least we'd be sleeping together?"

Rolfe chuckled. "I'm an easy lay."

"If that's so," the EUF chairman said, "we've got a deal."

* * * * *

"No, Mr. Merton, I haven't thought of a reason why Josh was murdered," Rolfe said to the man sitting exactly where Treadwell had sat only hours before. "I told you before, there were no special problems I know of."

"Then, you wouldn't mind if we audited your books."

Fear churned in Rolfe's stomach. "Of course I'd mind. We're a private company. We have our books audited by Erikson and Palmer, and our partners and my bankers are as satisfied with them as I am. Your people wouldn't find anything different."

"Then why would you mind us looking at them?"

"Because my staff has better things to do than prepare for an audit. Because if even a hint of your inquisition leaks, it'll hurt our relationships with everyone. As it is, you've already caused trouble at The Hills by marching up to the front desk, flashing your badge, and demanding to interview the general manager. Now, tell me, what in God's name could she have to do with Josh's death?"

Morton was unfazed. "The professional style of the killing makes us think someone was upset with you or your company and made an example out of Leonard. We've been finding out a lot about you and your interesting past."

The fear was acid to his gut. "What do you mean?"

"We know about your dealings with Yevgeny Popov, for example. Now, there's an unusual character. How did you ever find him in the first place?"

Was it a bluff? Had they already traced Popov to Mike Riverstone? Whatever, Rolfe sure as hell wasn't going to tell them anything. "It's none of your damn business!" he exploded.

"I think it is. But that's for a grand jury to decide."

"I've committed no crime."

"A jury might be interested in Pavel Banyeov, don't you think? Quite a coincidence you were there when he was murdered."

Rolfe clenched his fists. He would not let Merton provoke him!

"Popov and McCory. That's quite an exotic crowd you run with. And what about your partners, the lenders? You're selling five hotels in a hurry. Why?" He watched Rolfe intently. "Financial troubles?"

"Believe what you like," Rolfe said at last. "I'm not obligated to tell you anything." He and Merton stared at each other. "But I'll say one thing: Josh and I were together for over twenty-three years. He controlled our finances without telling me the specifics of what was going on. If he was dealing with special problems at the time of his death, I didn't know about them."

Merton's face wrinkled as though he'd smelled something foul. "I can smell a lie a block away. You're not telling me anywhere near the truth. And I'm going to find out what you're covering up, even if takes dragging your sorry ass through fifty grand jury investigations."

Merton's glance bore into him. Rolfe's lips were dry. He said nothing.

"This is your last chance," Merton said. "Are you frightened of something? Someone? Is that what's holding you back?" He leaned forward, his palms flat on Rolfe's desk. "Let me help you. Your staff calls you a deal junkie. Here's a deal for you: Tell me what you know about McCory and Popov, and we'll protect you from whatever or whomever you're frightened of."

Rolfe tried to swallow.

"Think about it, Ritter. You're way out of your league. We're your only chance."

* * * * *

The voice from Moscow bellowed with laughter. "Relax, Rolfe. Everybody wants to know about Popov, now that I'm a famous capitalist. They're just fishing."

"Merton keeps bringing you up. He's got me scared shitless."

The laughter died. "You're going to make sure they don't catch any fish."

"Of course. You know that."

"This is good, my friend. Saying nothing keeps us all healthy."

"But I've got to know something."

"Your silence buys anything you want."

"Who killed Josh?"

There was a pause. "That, I don't know. But there's a rumor Hunt was involved."

* * * * *

Susan and Rolfe sat silently on the deck of her Malibu house, looking out over the Pacific Ocean, a half empty bottle of Grgich chardonnay between them. The deal selling the five hotels to EUF had closed at 4:00 that morning. Susan had finished the day repaying their outstanding debt with only thirty hours left on the ninety-day deadline.

"It's like selling my children," Rolfe said. "I know we had to, and thank God for Treadwell, but I hated to do it. Never again."

Susan merely squinted at the sun.

"Are you all right?" he asked. "You're very quiet."

She sighed. "I'm plain beat. Completely drained. It's too much, Rolfe. You can't drive me this way. It's killing me."

"I promise I'll never let something like this happen again." Even as he said it, he knew how insincere it sounded.

Another sigh. "You may actually mean that, at least in this moment, though I doubt it. Even if you did, at the next opportunity, the next drama, you'd be off to the races again, dragging me with you. It's a wonder I don't already have cinder burns."

"I won't. Just say, 'Rolfe, too much,' and I'll ease off. It's killing me, too, you know." It was true. He'd never felt more tired in his life.

She filled his glass. "I need a break."

"Good idea. Why don't you go to the Bermuda Kestrel and veg out for a couple of weeks? Or Fiji."

"That's not what I'm thinking."

He looked at her sharply. "Oh-oh."

"I'm resigning at the end of the year."

He knocked the bottle off the table. Wine doused his feet. "You're not serious."

"I am. Very serious. You've wrung me dry. It's beyond time for me to leave."

"You can't. I need you, especially now. I can't manage alone."

"You need a new president anyway. He'll hire his own CFO, and it won't be a former secretary like me."

"That's just the point," he said. "I've just hired a new president."

"Who?"

He reached over to clasp her hand. "You."

CHAPTER 40

1996–1998

Bruce Hunt, the keynote speaker at New York University's annual hospitality conference, looked ... majestic, was the word that came to Susan's mind. He had lost weight, and his silver hair was sleek and coifed like a show dog's. He stood at the dais in the Waldorf Astoria's Grand Ballroom, waiting for the crowd of some two thousand lodging executives to quiet, and then he spoke:

"Before I begin my prepared remarks," he told the audience, "I am thrilled to announce an unprecedented achievement in our industry and to introduce an extraordinary woman: Susan Lockyer, the first female president of a major international lodging company. Six months ago, Ms. Lockyer was named president of Kestrel Hotels, and she joins us today, gracing our conference for the first time. I say, 'Welcome, colleague.' You have proved there is no glass ceiling in the hotel business, only glass elevators. Take a bow, Susan."

The four large screens placed around the room showed Susan forcing a smile as she stood. To say she was stunned to have received such an accolade, least of all from Hunt, was an understatement. The praise was suspect, and didn't last long.

"It's a shame the company she heads is so second-rate," Hunt continued, a wink and a smile meant to imply he was joking. "Maybe under her leadership, it can grow to be Metropolitan's worthy competitor."

Susan blushed and sat down, fuming. She hadn't expected, nor did she want, any attention drawn to her at the conference. She hadn't wanted to attend at all, but Rolfe had insisted. She half-listened to Hunt's predictable forecast of profits to come and innovations already underway, thinking that all she wanted to do was return to her room at the New York Kestrel to make some of the calls on her phone list before catching the late flight back to L.A.

But as the panel discussion finished and she prepared to leave, Hunt stopped her.

"I hoped we'd have a chance to chat," he said. "It's important. Can you spare a moment?"

So much for the calls; she knew the "moment" would take longer than that and would probably agitate her. "If we can keep it short," she said coldly.

* * * * *

They sat at a small booth tucked into the corner of the Waldorf's Peacock Alley. "I hope this will be off-the-record, just between the two of us," Hunt said.

Susan shrugged. "What record?"

"I've known of you for years, obviously, and watched your rise with growing admiration."

She gritted her teeth; he'd never before acknowledged her existence.

"Without you, Ritter would have gone under years ago."

Ridiculous, she thought. There were fifty people who could have done as well, certainly at the beginning. The only reason she was needed now was because she knew Rolfe's business inside and out—and would keep quiet about it. "Mr. Hunt, I appreciate your comments, but you and I both know they're untrue. What do you want to discuss?"

"I like that—straight to the point." He chuckled, a chilling sound. "The vultures are beginning to circle around Kestrel."

She glanced at him quickly. "What do you mean?"

"Anybody who can read a newspaper knows Ritter's in trouble. First, Josh Leonard's death, and then your abrupt appointment as president—not, of course, that you aren't the right person for the job."

She grimaced at his insincerity. "Why don't you get to the point?"

"Senior members of your staff and some of your hotel owners tell us that not only is there festering unhappiness among them, but they're also worried about your financial problems. Your recent sale of five hotels to EUF only reinforces that impression." He puffed up. "On the other hand, our business is good. Way above last year's. Stronger than anyone else's. Our stock is at an unprecedented high. We're outperforming everyone."

She picked up her purse and prepared to stand. "I'm happy for you."

"Wait. I've been chatting with our investment bankers. They all feel we can be helpful to Mr. Ritter."

"Helpful?" Her outrage strangled her voice. "You've been trying to destroy him ever since the inception of the San Francisco Kestrel."

"That was just smart business. Nothing personal. I like Rolfe, always have. Anyway, it's not too late to rescue him, if we buy Kestrel and his partners' hotels and casinos." He smiled. "Cash and stock."

Susan clutched her purse to stop herself from going at his eyes. "And you expect me to be the messenger? You know Rolfe's number. Call him yourself."

Her fury seemed to amuse him. "I don't think you understand. Rolfe's built some fairly decent properties, I'll grant you that, but in this era of scale and consolidation, you can't survive without adequate capital. If you're honest with yourself, you know I'm right. You, if anyone, might be able to convince him to consider our offer. It's the best thing you can do for him."

The best way to commit suicide. "You're the last person he'd sell to."

"I don't think so. He's desperate; he can't possibly survive. Treadwell's money is only a stopgap. The only person in the lodging industry who can't see that is Ritter himself. This is his best, maybe his only, way out. Naturally, if it happens, you'll have a critical role in the merged organization. A rewarding role." He patted the top of her hand. "You have a duty, a clear obligation to save him from himself."

Now, she did stand, shaking her hand as though bitten by a wasp. "Excuse me, Mr. Hunt. I have to go to the ladies' room."

His eyes narrowed. "Let me warn you. If he doesn't sell to Metropolitan, I'll make sure that every piece of muck I know about Ritter and his company will come out—making him, the Kestrel brand, and you, personally, Susan, smell so foul that your best friends will cross the street to avoid you." He bore in. "You see, Ms. Lockyer, I know everything."

* * * * *

"What did he mean by 'everything'?" Rolfe asked when Susan reported to him.

"I have no idea," she said, still shaken. "I just went to the ladies' room and cried for ten minutes."

"Don't worry about it."

Not that he had any solution in mind. He meant, Let me worry for you. Worrying was all he was equipped to do now. Optimism was no longer in his character.

* * * * *

"Bruce couldn't wait to tell me what he said to that bitch Susan," Chantal told McCory over the phone from her Park Avenue penthouse apartment the next morning.

"Is he fucking serious?"

"Serious as I've ever seen him. His stock price is so high he thinks he can buy the world."

"I'd like that. Just make sure he stays interested in Kestrel. If Ritter tells him to go fuck himself, make sure he ups the ante."

* * * * *

McCory shut the door of the small conference room at the Admiral's Club at LAX behind him.

"What's so urgent?" Rolfe asked.

"There's a rumor Hunt wants to buy you out. True?"

"True. But where did you hear—"

"Jesus, Rolfe, why the fuck don't you sell? You'll clear fifty million, everyone will be fucking happy. We'd take his stock for our casinos in a minute. If you don't sell, those last threats on you will look like kids' games. And you'd better have a twenty-four-hour guard set up, unless you want your family beaten as well."

Rolfe's stomach roiled. Was this a threat? Hunt via McCory? Was the union leader just as rotten as the rest of them? "I'm not a seller. Not now, and never to Hunt."

"What are you hanging on for? The second fucking coming? We'd make a fortune on the casinos!"

"Not to Hunt," Rolfe said. "Not him. Not ever."

* * * * *

Rolfe looked in the bathroom mirror, noting the dark circles under his eyes. For the third night in a row, he'd been unable to sleep.

How the hell did Popov know about Hunt's offer?

I get the message, Yevgeny, he thought, remembering every word of the previous middle-of-the-night's call. You want to cash out while the market's white-hot. You don't give a fuck about me. Well, to hell with you. I'm not selling now, even if someone else doubles Hunt's offer. Business is too good. Why would anyone want to get out now? There's too much upside.

He splashed his face with cold water. Sell? Ridiculous!

* * * * *

"What's so important that you dragged yourself here from the Big Apple?"

Falkman flung himself into the corner armchair in Rolfe's office. "I'm worried about you."

"So what else is new?"

The attorney didn't smile. "I got a call yesterday morning from Norm Anderson."

The name meant nothing. "Who's he?"

"Metropolitan's general counsel. Bruce Hunt's yes-man."

It meant something now. "Let me guess. He wanted to persuade you to persuade me to sell out. You didn't come here just to tell me that, did you?"

"Look, Rolfe, they're serious. Anderson put a big number on the table."

"How much?"

"They'll take over all your debt, and buy out you and your partnership obligations. That's about four billion, and they'll pay seven hundred mil for everything else. By the time you've paid everyone out, you'll have made over fifty million."

Rolfe whistled. "Generous. But you know I'm not going to give him the satisfaction."

"There's more. If you don't sell, Hunt's not only going to the media with everything he's got on you and Susan—but he'll smear Momo as well."

Rolfe recoiled. "Momo! She's clean, totally clean. She knew nothing about what Josh and Susan were trying to do."

"Nobody will believe that. Anderson said Hunt would ruin her reputation to the point where she'll never get a car loan again, let alone keep her job with Treadwell."

A vivid picture of Momo's sad face that awful night in Aspen flashed into Rolfe's mind. To be the cause of more pain left him breathless. "For God's sake, why her?"

"Hunt knows how you feel about her. He wants your balls, Rolfe. On top of it, Anderson threatened to tell all of your lenders, partners, and owners to do forensic audits on everything you're involved in."

Exhaustion overcame him. He closed his eyes against the words. "What's a forensic audit?"

"A team of accountants—independents, most likely one of the big firms—will scrutinize every penny you've spent on the hotels. They'll find any kickbacks, any loans you made to yourself, any under-the-table payments to the unions, any diversion of funds from one account to another, interest you've kept on the owners' funds you've been holding. Unless you're squeaky clean, they'll nab you." He sighed. "And squeaky clean is not a description I'd use for you."

"But surely Hunt can't do that?" Rolfe said, knowing it was bluster. "Surely there's a law preventing a competitor like Hunt from interfering in my internal affairs."

"Oh, the auditors won't know he's behind it. And any of your partners and clients have the right to such an audit. It's built into their contracts." Falkman walked to the window and gazed out.

Finally, he turned. "Listen to me carefully. This is for real. Right now, Hunt is Wall Street's darling, and he wants your company. Don't be a schmuck all your life. The boom can't last forever. You've done brilliantly, achieved more than you ever dreamt. But if they haven't done so already, Popov and McCory'll be all over you to sell. All they care about is money, not the properties and certainly not you."

Rolfe nodded dumbly. "Therefore?"

"It's time, my friend. I'm proud of you. I know Susan is. Even your mother is, or so Pieter tells me. If your father were alive, he'd be all over the moon with joy. Take Hunt's deal and bask in your success."

"The only thing you didn't mention was the American flag," Rolfe said. "I'll think about it."

He escorted Falkman to a waiting limousine and returned to his office. His assistant buzzed him. "It's Mrs. Hunt. Will you take her call?"

* * * * *

Chantal poured champagne in the parlor of her suite at the Beverly Hills Metropolitan. The room was, Rolfe thought, overdecorated, the "antiques" too obviously fake, the brocade too abundant, the colors too vivid. Hunt wouldn't understand good taste if it fell on his plate.

"Bruce has told me what's going on," his former mistress said. "I'm worried about you. He's obsessed with ruining you."

"Thank you, but I've already been warned. And it was hardly a revelation."

"About Pieter?"

His spine tingled. "Pieter? What about him?"

"Bruce wants to crush him. He's convinced Pieter double-crossed him."

"What, on Solveng? That was years ago."

"On Solveng, yes, but also on Audley."

Another shock. "What are you talking about?"

"Didn't you know? Bruce retained Pieter to buy Audley."

"Jesus! That son of a bitch didn't tell me." So he was right to mistrust his brother. Nothing was safe. Nobody could be trusted. And as for Chantal...

She put her arm around him and kissed him gently. "You poor thing. Now, look how upset I've made you."

Her touch consoled him, his groin stirred. He returned her kiss. She had betrayed him often, he knew, but she was as alluring as ever. "Why don't you sell to Bruce?" she asked, stroking him. "He'll leave you alone."

So that was it. Of course her loyalty lay with Hunt; that's why she had called him. Her hand worked its wonders. "What about your husband?" he asked, wondering whether Hunt had asked her to seduce him.

"Bruce? To hell with him," she said, lowering her head and unzipping him. For as long as it took, he allowed himself to believe she meant it.

* * * * *

As he left Chantal's apartment, he thought about what he could do with $50 million. Invest and be comfortable for the rest of his life. Buy a house in England and share it with Momo; after all, he'd have followed her wishes and quit. Live without fear of Hunt, of McCory. Become an expert on his idol, Winston Churchill. Write—God knows, the hotel business had fed him enough stories to fill a library. Work for Palmer. Work for world peace. Get over his obsession and lead the life of a rich man. He was still young. Even if he could think of nothing now and even if Momo refused him, there'd be other jobs, other women.

It would be good not to have to struggle to find money, not to work eighteen-hour days, to have no obligations except to himself. Bruce's offer was tempting. More than tempting. And Ron would squeeze the bastard for every penny he could. Why not let go of his one true love and start anew? The world was a continuous adventure. He suddenly felt relieved, buoyant, lighter than he had in years. Yes! He'd be Rolfe Ritter, his own man, no longer beholden to The Kestrel. He'd call Ron in the morning.

He entered his apartment and poured himself a snifter of cognac, the finest on the market. He would never have to choose a lesser brand, of cognac or anything.

He idly opened the *New York Times* and turned to the business section. He eye caught the headline: "Metropolitan Goes East: Moscow's Newest Hotel Opens." An accompanying photograph of the ribbon-cutting ceremony was captioned: "Mr. and Mrs. Bruce Hunt, flanking the new hotel's owner, industrialist Yevgeny Popov."

Falling unnoticed from Rolfe's hand, the crystal glass shattered on the floor.

CHAPTER 41

1998

Rolfe tossed the newspaper on Susan's desk. "Did you see this? That son of a bitch Popov. If he'd wanted another damned hotel in Moscow, we'd have built it. He knows I hate Hunt. How could he?" And how could Chantal not have told me? he thought.

"Who knows how much Hunt had to pay to get the deal," Susan said. "Maybe it was so rich Popov knew you'd never spring for it."

"Bullshit! Anyway, that's it."

"What's 'it'?"

"I'm not going to sell. I was about to until I saw that picture, but now—fuck him."

She looked at him in disbelief. "You changed your mind because of one lousy photo?"

"Not the photo. What it means, what it proves: Hunt and Popov are in bed together."

"Are you out of your mind? You're walking away from the best thing for all of us. You're letting your petty jealousy—"

His glare was laser-hot. "Enough! I'm not selling to Bruce Hunt. You can tell Ron and anyone else who asks that the subject's off limits permanently."

* * * * *

When Rolfe left, Susan called Stan Longstreet. "I want to know everything you can find out about Missus Bruce Hunt. . . . No, not mister—missus. ASAP!"

* * * * *

It was late in the morning when Chantal returned his call. "That was great fun last night," she said. "When can we do it again? I've got some new ideas."

He was in no mood for her seductiveness. "Why didn't you tell me about Moscow? The hotel? Manipulating me. You used your

339

confidential knowledge of my business to get to Popov and you damned well used me."

She was unfazed. "Because I was sure you'd found out about it. Don't tell me you didn't know, with your intelligence network. And if you'd used it, you'd have discovered I never manipulated you. If it makes you feel better, I met your buddy Yevgeny for the first time at the opening."

The truth? Had he misjudged her? He chafed at the thought that he'd never know for sure. But she was right in one respect. One of his geniuses should have told him. "I'm sorry," he muttered.

"Forget it. Bruce is still in Acapulco. How about a repeat for tonight. My turn to supply the toys."

He felt heavy in his chair. It was an effort even to get the words out. "Not tonight. I'll call you when I'm up to it."

* * * * *

"It's your mother," Rolfe's assistant said. "She's crying."

It took him a moment to pick up the phone. "What's wrong, Mum?"

"It's Jan. He died this morning."

A door slammed in Rolfe's face. He had expected the news for a while, but the realization was awful. First Mike, now Jan; the links to his father had all but gone. And he could not console the only one remaining. His words were empty, even to his own ears. "I'm sorry. Truly sorry. Are you going to be okay?"

Her voice was flat, ungiving. "I don't have a choice, do I?"

* * * * *

The bitter North Sea wind blew on the faces of the few mourners at Scheveningen Cemetery. Jan had wanted to be buried close to the seaside resort he'd enjoyed as a boy; his parents' headstones lay nearby.

Rolfe felt detached, alien, though he dutifully held his mother's hand as Pieter and his family stood nearby. Memories of the liturgy he'd heard at his father's funeral filled his mind. This man, his mother's husband, had been no substitute.

Margaret had been stalwart. If she had broken down, it was in private. To him, as to the several friends who came by to offer condolences, she was polite, cordial, but cold. If there was real emotion, it was not in evidence.

At last the pastor's dry dirge finished, and the coffin began its slow descent. Rolfe drew his coat firmly around himself to ward off the cold and then turned with his mother toward the limousine. He would stay the night, leave in the morning. He couldn't wait to get home.

Other mourners were still standing by the grave. One, a woman in black, seemed to be watching him, and when he realized it was true, that she was indeed looking at him, he gave a little cry, dropped his mother's hand, and ran toward her.

Momo!

She was walking toward him, and he stopped short, waiting to see what she would do. Disappointingly, she approached his mother. "I'm so sorry, Mrs. Vermeij. I wish I could do something to help."

Margaret looked at her uncomprehendingly. "It's Momo, Mother," Rolfe said. "She used to work with me. You've met her several times in Los Angeles. She and I—"

"Of course," his mother said. The two women brushed cheeks. "Thank you for coming."

For the first time, Momo acknowledged Rolfe's presence. "Susan called to tell me. You have my sympathy."

Jesus! She sounded like a funeral director. "When can we meet?" he asked. "Are you free for dinner?"

"I'm sorry, I can't. I've a car waiting to take me to the airport. My flight back to London leaves in two hours."

She wasn't that close to his mother, Rolfe realized. What other motive could she have for coming other than to see him? "Then I'll come to London. We'll have dinner tomorrow night. Or lunch. Or a drink." He smiled sheepishly and held his arms out wide. "You see. I'm easy."

She smiled; at least he thought she did. "Dinner, I suppose," she said warily, and hurried away like a small child caught in a guilty act before he could say anything more.

* * * * *

That night, Rolfe and Pieter sat together in the sitting room of Margaret's house. She'd gone to bed immediately after a tasteless, somber dinner.

"I can't believe he's gone," Pieter said.

"It must be very hard. If your feelings toward him were anything like mine for my father, it's the greatest loss a man can face."

"Thanks. I could use some empathy. Your mother's been getting it all."

Rolfe thought of all the intertwined threads that knit this family. "I need to tell you something."

"About my father?" Pieter asked.

"About business. I know you've dealt with Bruce Hunt in the past."

Pieter eyed him suspiciously. "Occasionally. As a banker, there's no way to avoid him."

Rolfe struggled to decide how to handle the conversation. Straightforwardly. "Before I rejected his offer for Kestrel, and several times before that, there had been some ugly threats."

The news did not seem to surprise Pieter. "What sort of threats?"

"Physical ones. Against me. Against Mother. Against your father, you, your family."

Again, no hint of surprise. "It's the wrong time for exaggeration."

"I'm not exaggerating. Merely reporting."

"And what am I supposed to do about these 'threats'? Hide in the cellar?"

"Listen to me, Pieter," Rolfe said urgently. "You've never liked me, I know that. From time to time, you've tried to fuck me—no, don't try to dispute it; I have proof. But now that your father's gone, there's a reason for us to look after each other, and that's blood. As far as I'm concerned, you and my mother are the only family I have. Bruce Hunt and others have threatened me, and you and yours have been threatened as well. Choose not to believe me if you want, but be forewarned that doing so is at your own peril."

* * * * *

Momo sat opposite Rolfe at a window table at Nobu on Hyde Park Corner, their platter of sushi and sashimi untouched. At long last, he was able to look at her again, study her again, inhale her poise and her grace. She was unmarried, he learned, and apparently unattached, devoting her time to work at EUF and deriving sufficient pleasure from it. She lived in a two-bedroom flat on Primrose Hill, overlooking Regents Park. Since her job involved a lot of travel, she was there infrequently. Susan had been lucky to catch her at home to deliver the news of Jan's death.

She talked for a long time, and he content to watch and listen, emotions roiling his brain like turbulent tides. When she at last asked him to tell her about himself, the tides of his soul overflowed, and he told her of Josh's murder, of his loneliness, of Hunt's threats and of threats more terrifying, of the FBI, of Popov, of his financial problems. With every word, he felt more relieved. As always, she was the only one who could understand.

"So that's why you gave Sir Martin such a sweetheart deal," she said when the torrent had dried up. "You always claimed that selling your hotels would be like selling your children. In the end, though, you'd never have sold to Hunt, whether or not he had joined forces with Popov."

"Do you think I'm right not to sell?"

"Right or wrong, what's the difference? You've always wanted authentication from me, and I still can't give it. Nor absolution. The fact is, you're still obsessed. You'll never give up Kestrel."

"I would for you," he said, meaning it.

She smiled ruefully. "And you'd be miserable."

"I don't think so. Not now, seeing you after all this time."

"But after a few months or a year. As it is, you're full of self-pity. I can't imagine how much more awful it would be if you didn't have Kestrel."

He grinned. "Let's give it a try. I'll sell tomorrow if you'll marry me."

Neither surprise nor appreciation showed on her face. "No."

The word was a hammer blow, the end of an auction. "Just like that?"

"I've told you once, and I'll say it again: You're poison to me, Rolfe. I couldn't keep up, wouldn't want to keep up. As much as I love you, the answer was, is, and forever will be no."

He felt as if he were falling in slow motion. It was hard to breathe. "Why did you agree to see me, if the answer's always to be no?"

"To ask you, once and for all, to let me go. It's my only chance at a new life. I want you to swear it."

"Even if I come to you, having sold Kestrel?"

"Even then."

Rage constricted his chest as he stood. She stood with him and raised her face so that he could kiss her goodbye. "Okay," he said. "I'm out of your life. And frankly, I hope you live to regret it."

Her face was pale in the dim light. "I regret it already. Don't think this is easy for me."

He turned from her. "Then make it easier on yourself. Don't come to any more funerals, not even mine."

He could hear her gasp, but refused to turn back.

CHAPTER 42

1999

"That was a waste of time," Rolfe said as Falkman's driver opened the door of the limousine outside Merrill Lynch's offices in lower Manhattan.

"I warned you it would be a long shot," the lawyer replied. "They know your back's up against the wall. Unless you're willing to take a huge loss, nobody'll buy the properties."

"I might be willing, but Popov wouldn't let me take the hit, and neither would McCory. I can't pay my investors except by selling properties, and I can't sell properties because no one wants to invest in them."

"So you should have taken Hunt's offer. Anyway, now it's too late."

Rolfe turned to look at him. The afternoon sun glittered off Falkman's glasses, giving him a diabolical air. "What do you mean?"

"Met's stock has taken a hammering along with the other chains. Right now, he couldn't invest in a hotdog stand."

Welcome as it once would have been, the news was no solace. Rolfe felt as if he'd lost something, and gained nothing.

"There's nothing you can do about it," Falkman continued blithely. "You've managed to dodge every bullet 'til now. Dodge another." The driver pulled up in front of Falkman's 55th Street office. "You've made your choice to stay in. Now, it's victory or death."

"Victory how?"

"Find the money somewhere."

"And death?"

Falkman laughed. "If you don't find the money." He told the driver to take Rolfe back to his hotel, and then opened the door. "Have you still got that fuck-you money?"

"Yes. Why?"

"If I were you, I'd make sure I could get hold of it quickly. You never know when it's time to make your escape."

*   *   *   *   *

"You need to read this," Susan said, handing him a transparent plastic folder.

Longstreet Investigations, read the letterhead. He looked at Susan, eyebrows raised.

"Go on," she said.

He read, and cringed. Longstreet had compiled irrefutable evidence of the longstanding relationship between Popov and Chantal: photos, letters, emails, wiretaps. Its conclusion was clear. Chantal, not Hunt, had put together the Moscow deal.

"Bullshit!" Rolfe exploded, throwing the papers on his desk. "This is crap, and you know it."

Susan was unfazed. "How can you ignore it? Face it, Rolfe. Facts are facts. She lied to you."

"You went behind my back to Longstreet to find this out?"

She bowed her head. "I had to. You wouldn't have investigated her yourself."

It was true. "Even now, I don't believe it," he said, believing it and hating himself for being such a fool—a lifelong idiot.

"I think you should follow up on it," Susan said coldly.

"I will. Don't you worry, I will."

*   *   *   *   *

Still in his tuxedo, Rolfe shut the door to his study, not wanting anyone to overhear. It didn't matter anyway—he was, as always now, alone. He had hosted a dinner at The Hills for the top Kestrel and Audley managers in California, but it was a lackluster affair in which he took little part, letting good food and ample wine replace his usual bonhomie. The wine was too good. Nobody wanted to leave.

He dialed and waited for Popov to pick up his private line.

"I'm glad you called," the Russian said. "When are you selling? I want my money back."

"It's a lousy year. Everybody's nervous about the Y2K bug. After New Year's, investors will come back to lodging stocks and I'll sell then."

"You should have sold to Hunt, and I should never have believed your optimistic fairy tales."

"We've been through that. For now, I need to know something. Who arranged the deal between you and Bruce Hunt?"

The force of laughter was loud in Rolfe's ear. "You want to know if the elegant Mrs. Hunt, whom you've been banging for over thirty years, two-timed you. Right?"

Rolfe swallowed humiliation. "Right."

"The answer is yes. How does it feel?"

"What do you mean?"

"To have someone you trust two-timing you."

"I don't know, what you're talking about."

"You must think I'm a fool. I know everything."

"Everything?" Rolfe's mouth was so dry he could barely choke the question out.

"I know you've been two-timing me from the beginning, telling Riverstone and Palmer everything I was doing."

He gripped the phone until his knuckles were white. "Why didn't you stop me?"

"Because I fed you information I wanted them to have. Do you think I was so stupid I didn't know every one of their people you put in my hotels? My God! Do you honestly think you're that clever?"

Rolfe had never heard Popov this angry, so out of control.

"Well, you're not! Do you think I don't know who set the fires in the Audley Hotel thirty years ago? And who stole information from the Syrians and gave it to his godfather?"

There could be no answer. Shame covered him like sweat. He wondered if the Russians knew everything his father had been doing and merely waited to kill him when they felt like it.

"How does it feel now?" Popov screamed. "Your naïveté makes me sick!"

* * * * *

His whole life seemed made of lies and betrayals—Popov, McCory, Hunt, Chantal—outright liars. His mother, Pieter, Riverstone, Josh, Susan; each of them, at one time or another, had betrayed him, if only by using him for their own ends. And Momo? The worst betrayal of all. She had hurt him forever.

He called Kenneth Palmer. "I need to know if Popov was behind the attempt on my life outside the Audley Hotel."

The British agent hesitated. "That was before my time. Decades ago."

"Can you find out?"

Palmer was clearly exasperated. "I can try. We have the files. I'll get them out of storage and look through them. It'll take some time, though."

"Do it, please," Rolfe urged.

"All right. Not for you, but for Mike."

* * * * *

He called Popov back. "One question."

The Russian seemed amused. "Of course, my dear friend."

"How did you know about the Audley business? Do you know that someone tried to kill me afterward?"

"That's two questions. And a third, the one you're really asking, is whether I was involved."

Rolfe's silence acknowledged truth.

"The answer is no, my paranoid friend. I was just an underling then and hadn't even heard about you. Later, if I had wanted to kill you, you'd be long dead. You were far more valuable to me alive. You made me rich."

"Then, one last question, Yevgeny. Who murdered my father? Was it the KGB?"

A pause. "Your father made many enemies. Anyone could have killed him. And I see you've inherited his fatal flaw: He also asked too many questions."

The threat was palpable.

"Are you finished?" Popov asked.

"Yes," Rolfe whispered.

"Then I have one question for you: When am I going to get back my half-billion dollars?"

CHAPTER 43

2000

New Year's day, 8:00 A.M. Rolfe, exhausted, stumbled home after a marathon of parties and glared at the ringing phone, wondering whether to pick it up. He answered.

"I thought New Year's Eve was supposed to be fucking spectacular. We were going to make a fortune over the millennium, you told me. But last night—New Year's fucking Eve—you could have shot a cannon through our casinos and not hit anyone."

"And Happy New Year to you, Bud," Rolfe said. "I'd hoped for a last-minute pickup when people realized they were going to miss the festivities. They must have been frightened by all the press about airplanes falling and elevators crashing at midnight."

"Well, they didn't show up, did they?" McCory snarled. "This time, you've screwed up big time. You sweet-talked me into not selling when the gaming markets were hotter than a forest fire. You're the dumb fuck who refused to take a fucking great offer from Hunt. 'It'll get even better,' you told me. And the market nose-dived. Well, now I want out. And I want exactly what my partners and I could have had when you told us not to sell. Give me my fucking dough!"

This was dangerous. Of all his creditors, McCory seemed the most lethal. "Be reasonable, for God's sake."

"I've been too fucking reasonable already."

Rolfe thought his head would split. He closed his eyes.

"I've looked after you pretty good all these years," the union boss went on. "Gave you what you wanted on Hunt. Set you up in the gambling business. And now it's over. Fucking finis. Sell the casinos before my partners come after me. 'Cause if I have a problem, I'm your worst fucking nightmare."

"Jesus, Bud. Be patient. The casino market will get back to normal now that the world hasn't come to an end."

"Listen carefully, you cocksucker. I want to know exactly when and how I'm getting out, and I want to know soon. Figure it out, fella. And let's make this our last conversation about how you're going to pay me back every cent you owe me."

He slammed down the phone.

* * * * *

By the end of February, Rolfe could no longer hang on to the hope of an immediate recovery. The Dow Jones rose steadily, dot-com stocks soared, but lodging and casino stocks, despite good business, remained in their malaise. "Banks are willing to lend us money," he complained to Susan over dinner at Crustacean in Beverly Hills, "but their interest rates are prohibitive."

Susan peered at him. "That's the good news," she said.

"Why?"

"There's no incentive to borrow. Our profits aren't as high as we projected, so even if we were to refinance, there still wouldn't be enough to pay off the debt."

"Wait a minute. I thought—"

"Remember the money you borrowed short-term for the new hotels, timesharing deals, golf courses, etcetera, over the past couple of years?"

"Of course. They're doing well."

"You managed to sweet-talk the banks into lending you so much because we gave them projections we never had a chance of meeting. On top of that, you promised we'd refinance after the millennium."

His eyes twinkled. "Did I really promise that? Gosh. Me, make a promise I knew I couldn't keep?"

She didn't think it was funny. "Well, it's now the new millennium, and we've got to pay off those loans. What should I tell them to do? Get in line?"

"Sell off some properties. They're more valuable now that business is better."

"But people have stopped paying crazy sums. We'd have to sell off a bunch of hotels quickly, at rock-bottom prices, which would be nuts. And you'd have to use the money to pay off Popov, McCory, and the other goddamned investors, leaving the banks still to be paid."

"Stall them. Get the banks to give us short-term extensions. Explain how business is great and we're working on something big that'll fix the problems, make us all a fortune."

Susan brightened momentarily. "You really have something cooking?"

He stared past her into the abyss. "I don't have a fucking clue." But even as he said it, an idea began to germinate.

* * * * *

"It's Rolfe. Don't hang up!"

Momo's answer was a wail. "Rolfe, you promised—"

"This isn't about us. It's a business call, only that. I swear to you." He swallowed. "I've made up my mind."

"To do what?"

"To sell."

"You? Sell? I don't believe it?" Momo's incredulity echoed in his ears. "This isn't just a ploy to get me back?"

"I've told you, no. It's the only way I can pay back my debts."

"Then why involve me?"

"Because it's to you I'm selling."

"Me?"

He smiled at her surprise. "Well, actually EUF."

She hesitated, obviously slow to take in the news.

"And Martin's agreed?"

"He doesn't know yet."

"Rolfe, I don't understand. If he doesn't know, how can you be sure—"

"I want you to tell him. So you get the credit. Get the bonus. Shit, get to be the next CEO of Kestrel. Just set up a meeting for me. Tell him I'm serious. Then I'm out of your life again, permanently." Again, a hesitation. "Just set up the meeting. Will you do it?"

Resigned. "Yes."

* * * * *

As his limousine stopped outside EUF's Knightsbridge offices, Rolfe felt like a condemned man on his way to the gallows. He'd failed. Kestrel was about to belong to someone else. Momo was gone. No amount of money could salve the losses. Heavyhearted, he rode the elevator to the fifth floor of Treadwell's office building, where, following the chairman's secretary, he waded through oriental carpets, seeking a consoling thought. At least it's not Hunt. Not much consolation.

Sir Martin Treadwell stood inside his private sitting room with outstretched hand. "Welcome to London. I trust your flight was good?"

"Excellent." He looked at two Chippendale chairs surrounding a high-backed sofa and at a Degas bronze of a young ballerina.

"I understand you're about to receive the International Tourism Bourse Hotelier of the Year Award. Congratulations."

Rolfe shrugged. "Yes. In Berlin tomorrow. But that and a pound will buy me a cup of coffee." They both understood the hollowness of such honors.

Rolfe came to the point. "I enjoyed our last meeting. I've been giving it serious consideration. In fact, it hasn't left my mind for a moment." Treadwell was watching him carefully. "I'm delighted our organizations are working productively and profitably together. You were right: Our corporate philosophies are compatible."

"We can thank Momo for that. It's her knowledge of the two companies that's made the partnership work so well."

Treadwell's use of her first name sent a tremor through him. Could it be that the old man—? Rolfe shook his head to clear it. "I've come to the conclusion—reluctantly, I'll admit—that both organizations would be better suited if I sold you Kestrel outright." There, I've said it. "Let me assure you that my future role is not a consideration of the deal."

"Timing is everything," Treadwell said softly, and Rolfe's hopes crashed. "And as much as I want to buy your company, your timing is lousy. Tomorrow, we'll announce our acquisition of Deutschefon."

Rolfe knew of the German giant multimedia and telecommunications company. It would be a mega-billion deal. "Their chairman, Bertie Brandt, will serve on our board. It's an enormous step for us. A real branching out."

Treadwell went on, but Rolfe heard nothing except the sound of his own ruin and the end of Kestrel. He forced himself to listen. "Right now, we can't possibly take on another major deal. It's not that we can't afford it or can't absorb it, but the public markets for lodging stocks are down both here and in the U.S., and I don't think our stock price would hold if we bought Kestrel today." He looked at his guest sympathetically. "Let's keep working together. Who knows what the future will bring."

Rolfe knew too well and wondered why Momo hadn't warned him of the deal, why she had taken him up on his wish to see Treadwell. No matter. At least Treadwell was gentlemanly about it.

"Congratulations," was all he could offer.

* * * * *

The next day, after a sleepless night's in the Berlin Audley and a numb day of introspection, Rolfe dutifully accepted his award and forced himself to deliver an amusing, self deprecating, states-manlike acceptance speech. Alone and dejected, he walked weari-ly back from dinner toward the hotel, detouring to avoid construc-tion projects, trying to think his way out of the disaster that con-fronted him.

His steps echoed in the empty streets, his shadow lengthening and disappearing beneath mist-shrouded streetlights. He neither heard nor saw the car cruising the street behind him. Its black shape suddenly appeared in his peripheral vision, like a living mechanical monster, and then stopped abruptly at the curb. The car's door opened, a dark figure leapt at him, and he felt himself being dragged violently along the pavement.

Rolfe jerked his arm away, breaking his assailant's grip. With a scream, he bolted toward the end of the street, turned into anoth-er, and ran for his life. He heard a second car door open and close, followed by pounding footsteps in his wake. Panting, he raced down yet another street, the only light coming from an orange-shaded second-floor window. He turned the handle of the door beneath it. Locked. He began to run again; the footsteps followed him relentlessly.

An alley! He swerved down the narrow cobblestone gap between tall buildings and crouched down, hugging the wall behind an overflowing garbage can. He heard his pursuers rush past the alley entrance, and soon the sound of footsteps disap-peared.

Clinging to the buildings, he crept forward, his breathing starting to slow. The alley curved right, and he followed it to its end and peered around the building's wall. No one. He ventured out and hurried down the street.

The roar of a car's engine filled the dark night. A Mercedes, black like the one that had killed his father, swerved onto the side-walk as both front doors flung open. He tried to run. Too late! Sets of unforgiving hands pulled him into the car.

The door slammed, and the car sped off into the gloom. He tried to pull free, but the hands were too strong and held him at an angle from which he could get no leverage. The grip tightened. His arms felt as though they were being pulled from his shoulders, and he suffered a blow from a fist on the side of his head. A cloth mask smelling of oil was pushed over his face; the fist struck him again, and his resistance vanished. His face was pushed down onto a seat that smelled of cigarettes and mildew; plastic ties cut into his wrists. "My money," he gasped. "In my back pocket. Let me go!"

Ignoring him, the other assailant shoved Rolfe's face deeper into the seat, and he felt he might suffocate. The car bounced along a rough street. Cobblestones. Rolfe vomited. Someone laughed. Rolfe could feel the stinking mess on his face and neck. He gagged again.

The car sped through Berlin's night. Rolfe's mind was filled with images of the mugging in San Francisco. He heard himself scream. More callous laughter. Finally, the Mercedes stopped. The back door opened, and Rolfe was thrown like a sack of flour onto a gravel path. The air felt good. He could smell wet grass. His head was jerked back by his hair, and the mask was ripped off. He rolled onto his back, gulping in air, his face covered in blood and vomit.

Slowly, he opened his eyes to a thin crescent moon above him, and he whimpered like a beaten dog for mercy. It did no good. Four shadowy figures carrying clubs approached him, silhouetted in the headlights' beams. The tallest one kicked him in the stomach, and then his balls. Gasping in agony, he curled into a fetal position. The four men coldly, methodically, and systematically took turns beating him. Urine seeped onto his stomach and legs as the blows continued their merciless rhythm. He was about to die, he knew, and welcomed it.

"Enough!" The single word pierced the night. Instantly, the blows stopped. Rolfe's body was on fire, and he opened his eyes to see four men hovering over him. He tried to speak but choked on his own blood.

A booted foot sank deep into his kidneys. "Never forget, promises made are promises kept," the same voice said emotionlessly.

Another kick. Rolfe's grunt echoed unnoticed amongst the headstones. He heard footsteps and the slamming of the Mercedes' doors. The engine powered up, and the car swept past him, showering gravel over him. He lay motionless, damp seeping into his clothes, conscious only of pain.

* * * * *

Scattered impressions: Two groundskeepers coming upon him in soft morning light. The wail of the ambulance's siren. A ride on a stretcher so painful he could do nothing but scream. The remote voices of doctors, assessing the chances he'd live. X-rays and more X-rays. A needle. The dark. Relief.

* * * * *

Though slits of eye sockets in his swollen face, covered with bruises, abrasions, stitches, and bandages, Rolfe could barely make out the stocky figure of the man before him.

"Detective Walter Gruber," the man said. "Chief of Detectives, Berlin Police."

A doctor's face came into view. "You're a lucky man, Mr. Ritter. You have multiple lacerations to your face and body; they'll heal, but there will be scars. You have three broken ribs, a cracked elbow, four broken fingers on your right hand and two on your left. Your kidneys are badly bruised, but there's no permanent damage to your vital organs. Whoever did this to you knew exactly when to stop before killing you."

"Professionals," Gruber said. "We want to find them. Please, Mr. Ritter, tell us everything you can remember."

Rolfe stared at the face above him; there was too much hair sprouting from its nostrils. If he found one of his employees looking like that—

"I'm sorry," he said. "I remember nothing."

CHAPTER 44

2000

The sights and sounds were fragmentary, coming in half-realized moments when the drugs began to wear off and it was not yet time for a new injection. The sound of a plane's jet engine. Takeoff. A woman sitting by his side. Momo? Yes, it must be Momo, for she was holding his hand and her touch was gentle. No, it was a nurse with another injection. But the nurse didn't hold his hand, not in that soothing way. Wait, there were two women. That was it. There was a nurse and another woman. Momo. Yes, it had to be Momo. Except that was impossible, because he would never see Momo again. Then who—?

When he opened his eyes, he saw his mother, and he was able to imagine he was a little boy and she was there to comfort him. But it couldn't be Margaret. She was a phantom, a witch, a golem there to haunt his dreams, and this woman wasn't frightening at all. Still, he could have sworn it was her voice. And the voice said, "I love you."

* * * * *

By the time the drugs wore off and he had fully regained his senses, Margaret was back in Europe, and only the testimony of the doctors, nurses, and visitors convinced him she had been there at all.

* * * * *

Two weeks later, Rolfe called Pieter from his Los Angeles hospital bed. "I think the beating was related to my money problems. It means you've got to be extra careful. They may come after you."

To Rolfe's surprise, Pieter called back every few days to check on his well-being.

Ted Pemberton became a regular visitor. "It's your boy cheerleader," he'd announce, bearing cookies, grapes, and flowers.

"Calla lilies to remind you of your hotels. I think your mother fell in love with me when she was here."

Then, she had traveled with him. How strange. What did it mean?

When he had regained enough strength, he called her. "Were you on the air ambulance with me?"

"I plead guilty."

"But why?"

"When I read about the attack in the newspapers, I went to Berlin and arranged your transportation home."

"No. I mean why?"

"You were badly hurt. My place was by your side."

Did he hear tears in her voice? Were they for him or for Wim or for both of them? His throat constricted. Over all these years, had he been more to her than an unworthy substitute for his father? He felt a wave of shame, of guilt, of contrition. "It's funny. Doped up as I was, I had the strong impression you said you loved me."

There was a pause, a silence. Then, "But my brave darling, I do."

He tried to say something. No words came.

* * * * *

Susan showed up daily, keeping Rolfe up to date on everything at work. Given the attack, the banks had allowed a sixty-day extension on the paying back of all loans.

She's the only one left, Rolfe thought ruefully. The only one who was with me from the start.

But a thought intruded. She and my mother.

* * * * *

Chantal called frequently. Each time he hung up on her without speaking. Finally, the calls stopped.

* * * * *

"I've no idea why I was attacked," Rolfe told the poker-faced FBI agent, Merton. "Maybe it was a case of mistaken identity, being in the wrong place at the wrong time."

"I find it hard to believe that there is no connection between Leonard's murder and your beating," Merton said. "Besides, there's still the fact of your unusual dealings—and I'm being charitable—with McCory and Popov, who at the least are suspected of all kinds of racketeering. Your competitor at Metropolitan, Bruce Hunt, tells anyone who'll listen that you're the lowest form of life, and we both know you've got a list of creditors and investors screaming for their money."

He slammed his fist on the chair's arm. "What the hell is Kestrel involved in? What are you involved in?"

"Just trying to run a business," Rolfe said, exhaustion washing over him.

His brain hurt as he struggled to figure out what was behind the assault. Steinmann, reaching out from the grave to attack him in Hitler's capital? Popov, whose stomping grounds were once Berlin? McCory, who would have no difficulty organizing the attack from the States? Hunt?—he had been warned about Hunt. But what did the name of his attacker matter? He still had to find more than a billion dollars somewhere. A billion dollars!

Terror engulfed him. He needed someone to help him, to share his problems, to be on his side. Merton? After all, the FBI had promised him immunity and protection.

Merton must have sensed the thought. "Look," he said, mustering what pleasantness he could find. "I know you're not fundamentally a crook, just ambitious, but one thing leads to another. Tell me now, and we can stop any more attacks."

Then no one would be safe, he realized. It was the reason he hadn't said anything to Gruber, either. He had too much to hide, not only for himself, but for Susan, his mother, Momo. "I'm sorry to disappoint you, but there's no connection between a minor mugging in Berlin and Josh's death."

The agent's mouth tightened. "You've given me no choice but to let the IRS investigate you until they can see the bones through your skin."

* * * * *

The orchid's purple petals had long ago fallen; still, its bare stem rested in a lacquered clay pot by Rolfe's bedside. The floral arrangement had been there to greet him when, after the long weeks in the hospital, he'd returned home.

The card had read: *I hope it's worth it. Get well soon—Momo.* Rolfe knew exactly what she meant.

* * * * *

By October, he was back at work, and work meant an unsuccessful scramble for money and a visit from Ron Falkman.

"Susan's convinced we're going to have a slowdown in 2001," Rolfe said. "Even this month's been lousy."

"I think she's right," Falkman replied. "You're not the only one not making any headway. The stock market analysts know it and are being super-cautious. How are Popov and McCory?"

"Don't ask. I rarely get through a week without a screaming match with one of them. They're ready to kill me"—he reflected—"but I don't think they're the ones who've tried.

"I've tried to sell properties," Rolfe went on. "No one's paying big numbers. I've talked to every major chain, except Hunt's, about a merger. They all think their stock is too low and won't offer me enough cash to get out whole. I don't understand. Are Kestrel and Audley hotels no longer the best in the world? Why isn't everyone competing for them, now that they're for sale?"

Falkman sipped his tea. "The hotels are fabulous. I, for one, wouldn't stay anywhere else. But the world is about to change, and you'd better get used to it."

He grimaced. "How so?"

"Investors are finally realizing that the dot-com craze is nonsense. The tech sector's going to crash, and with it, the economy. Mark my words, we're looking at an economic train wreck of global proportions."

Rolfe's hands began to shake. His own tea spilled over the lip of his cup. "Jesus Christ. If you're right, I'll never get out."

* * * * *

"The IRS is over me like white on rice, and now I've been subpoenaed to appear in front of another damned grand jury in two weeks," Rolfe told McCory. "I've got no choice, have I? I've got to show up. Merton warned me that if I don't, or if I perjure myself, he'll make sure I get heavy-duty jail time."

McCory shrugged. "I've been in front of those goons a half-dozen times. It's a fucking kangaroo court. Tell them you know nothing and can't remember anything." He sat forward on Rolfe's office chair. "But if you tell them a fucking word about our dealings—"

"I know, I know. You don't have to threaten me."

"Right. We're allies. By the way, I've heard Hunt was behind your Berlin adventure..."

Confirmation! "Hunt's wife—" Rolfe began.

"The lovely Chantal," McCory broke in.

"—She's built a hotel with Yevgeny Popov in Moscow. Can the

three of them be after me?"

Another shrug. "Anything's possible."

The smug bastard, Rolfe thought. I wonder how he'd feel if he'd been attacked. But was it possible? No, not Chantal. Betrayal, yes. Greed, yes. But go after him? No.

"What can I do to stop them?" he asked, wincing with remembered pain.

"Fucked if I know," McCory said. "Why don't you ask Chantal?"

* * * * *

Chantal agreed to meet him at the Audley Boston.

"You didn't answer my calls," she pouted.

"Because you built a hotel behind my back." He was careful to keep anger out of his voice.

"It was a birthday present from Bruce. And Popov is a delightful man."

"He's a snake. Watch out for him."

She accepted a glass of champagne and smiled. "What do you think?"

"About what?"

"My new face. I've had the best nip and tuck Bruce's money can buy."

He scrutinized her. She did look younger. "Actually, it's Bruce I want to talk to you about."

"You mean you don't want my body?" She thrust her breasts toward Rolfe. "I've had these done, too."

"I think Bruce arranged the attack in Berlin," he said, vaguely repelled. He had once adored those breasts, loved to . . . "Was Popov in it with him?"

She backed away, hurt. "Impossible. Popov likes you. If you paid him back, you could be friends again. You see, I'm the one, not Bruce, who deals with Yevgeny. He doesn't like Bruce."

"What?" Rolfe exploded. "I thought the hotel was a 'present.' Didn't you tell me you met him for the first time at the opening?"

"Popov made me say that. You know I hate lying to you, but I had no choice—he terrifies me."

Turns within turns within turns. There was no one he could trust, no statement that might not be a lie. "He scares the shit out of me, too," he acknowledged. "Still, you could have given me a clue."

"You know I couldn't." She put her hand on his cheek, leaned in to kiss him. Suddenly, it was thirty-five years ago and Murtoch was leaning toward him to kiss him for the first time. Horrible! She was horrible! He pulled away. "One more thing: is your husband planning anything else for me?"

She threw her champagne in his face. "He hates you so much, anything's possible. But if he doesn't want to, I do!"

* * * * *

He was wakened by the phone. "It's your mother."

"What's wrong?"

"The kids."

She's crying, he realized. "What kids?"

"Pieter and Christina's. They're missing."

The words knifed into him. Was this his fault? Could he have prevented it by selling to Hunt? Was this what McCory had warned him about? "Tell me."

"Anouk's at university in The Hague, and Hank's finishing boarding school in Amsterdam."

"Sure." He pictured his niece and nephew—their ash-blond hair and high spirits.

"The police told Pieter they were picked up by similar black cars late yesterday afternoon. When they weren't in their rooms this morning, their friends called Christina. She called Pieter, and he called the police."

Kidnapped! Black cars! "Have they heard from whoever abducted them?"

"Not a word. It's awful. Pieter and Christina—"

"I'll call them," Rolfe said. "See if there's any way I can help."

* * * * *

"You warned me something could happen," Pieter said, his voice full of pain and frustration. "This has nothing to do with the kids, nothing to do with Christina, nothing to do with me. It's all and only about you. If so much as a hair on either of their heads is hurt, I will kill you. That's a promise. Whatever it takes, whatever it costs, get them back!"

Feeling as though he were being beaten once more in the Berlin graveyard, Rolfe dialed a long-remembered number.

"Palmer here."

* * * * *

"I've looked behind every tree in the forest," Palmer said eight hours later. "Damned if I can find anything. I've talked to Jan's successor. He's just as stymied. They've vanished."

"Keep trying."

"Of course. By the way, I got those files out of storage. Your friend Popov was a junior attaché in London at the time."

Rolfe wasn't shocked. Somehow, he'd known it all along.

"By the way, old boy," Palmer drawled. "I wonder if you'd do something for me."

"What?" Rolfe asked suspiciously.

"I need you to put one of my people on your senior team in your new Shanghai Audley. It's important."

Rolfe was silent.

"Well?"

"Not now," Rolfe pleaded. "Please, not now."

* * * * *

He spent the day in guilty agony, eagerly picking up the phone when it rang, slamming it down when there was no news.

Pieter was right. It was about him. But if so, what could the kidnappers hope to achieve? By dusk, he was praying to a God he did not believe in, promising anything if the children were returned unharmed.

Later, he sat unmoving in the darkness, dread gnawing at his soul.

* * * * *

The phone rang at 1:20 in the morning. "They're safe!" his mother yelled. "They just called from the railway station in Amsterdam."

Relief made his skin prickle. "What happened?"

"They were tied up, blindfolded, taken to a barn somewhere, and kept there for hours. At least they were together, but it must have been awful," Her breathing was rapid. "According to the children, they were well treated, but still—"

"How did they get away?"

"They didn't. They were simply taken by car to the station's side entrance, left there, and told to deliver a message."

Rolfe's jaw clenched. "What message?"

"'Promises made are promises kept.'"

His stomach heaved. After somehow finishing the call, he rushed to the bathroom and vomited until he thought his guts would explode.

* * * * *

"The grand jury was a bloody inquisition," Rolfe told Falkman a month later. "I was there under the pretense of an investigation into organized crime. What a crock of shit. The state's attorney kept me on the stand for five hours. Even then they kept the right to recall me. Between that and Merton threatening and cajoling every time I took a leak, I felt like I'd been through the wringer. As I left, Merton reminded me that the IRS was finding 'all kinds of interesting things.' He's a relentless prick! I don't know what they'd indict me on, but the strain of it has finished me off. You've got to sell. Hunt wins. I surrender."

"Give it a few more months; The market's lousy," Falkman urged.

"Damn it, I've given it a lifetime. Sell, and take me to dinner on your legal fees. There'll still be millions left over."

"I wouldn't want it. It's blood money."

"Yeah. My blood. Sell."

$$* * * * *$$

Two days later, Falkman called at eight in the morning. "You awake?"

"I haven't slept."

"I had dinner last night with Hunt's general counsel, Norm Anderson."

He forced himself to keep calm. "And?"

"I told him I'd been thinking about how well Metropolitan and Kestrel would fit, how one head office could be eliminated. I explained it wasn't only about economies of scale but more importantly how a combined entity would have such market domination that no one could catch it in a decade of trying."

Rolfe's mouth went dry. "How he must have loved this," he murmured.

"The son of a bitch said I was merely stating the obvious. I told him I hadn't discussed it with you, but wanted to float the concept to him."

"What did he say?"

"He didn't believe me for a minute. He knew you'd put me up to it."

"Okay. Of course he'd know that. Then what?"

"We talked about it for a while. He's amazed you've held on as long as you have, and he's convinced you have no one else to go to but him."

Hunt was right, of course. Still, it hurt like hell to have it rubbed in his face. "How did it end?"

"He said that even though their stock price is low, Kestrel, as the inferior company, would trade at an even lower multiple. If they bought you, it would be at rock bottom."

"Nevertheless, he managed to make you an offer. Which was what?"

Falkman told him.

The breath was sucked from his body, and he collapsed onto his bed. "Not enough to pay off the debts."

"Not nearly."

His next words were whispered. "What am I going to do?"

"You have three choices."

"Which are?"

"Keep dancing," Falkman said humorlessly.

"Or?"

"Take that fuck-you money and hide."

"Or?"

"Shoot yourself. Because as things stand now, there's no way out."

CHAPTER 45

2001

The grim expression on Susan's face presaged calamity, Rolfe thought. And her opening words verified his feeling.

"I'm going to tell you something you don't want to hear."

"Don't say you're leaving."

She glanced at him, surprised. "Actually, I'm thinking about it. Next year I'll be sixty, and that may be a good time to stop. But this is about Chantal."

"Not interested," Rolfe said hoarsely. "We're finished."

"You remember Stan Longstreet? The investigator who found out about Popov, Chantal, and the hotel in Moscow?"

"Old news."

"He's dug deeper. Stan got hold of her phone records—home and cellular—and came up with an unlisted number she's been calling three or four times a week for years."

He shifted uneasily. She was right: He didn't want to hear it.

"It's Bud. Bud McCory."

Chantal and McCory! Impossible.

"That precious marketing business of hers," she went on implacably, "the one we've given all that business to over the years, has always been funded by McCory. He's her partner."

He closed his eyes in humiliation. "That fucking bitch!"

"We've got to assume that she repeated everything you told her to McCory."

He thought back desperately. How much had he revealed? What did she know? How had Bud used the information?

"There's more," Susan said.

"What now?"

"Longstreet tapped Chantal's phone. He has a record of Chantal and McCory talking." She took out a small cassette player and pressed the button.

Laughter. Then, Chantal, unmistakably Chantal: "Rolfe still thinks you're his best ally against Bruce."

"The fool."

"And Bruce still thinks you're his best ally against Rolfe."

"And meanwhile, we get richer. Keep it up, Chantal. Which one of them are you fucking tonight?"

"Switch it off," Rolfe said. "I get the message."

* * * * *

The stillness in his apartment was oppressive. Rolfe paced its rooms, trying to think clearly. He needed to talk to someone, confess his stupidity, get some sympathy. Who? Susan had seemed to derive some peculiar satisfaction from breaking the news. Pieter had refused to speak to him since his children were kidnapped. His mother—no, he couldn't risk asking her. The "I love you" was to soothe physical pain, not psychological anguish. Despite himself, desperate, he dialed Momo.

"Rolfe! You promised never to—"

"Please don't hang up. I need to talk."

A long silence. Then, "What's happened?" No passion, not even curiosity, barely tolerance. Surely, when she heard his predicament, her heart would soften.

He told her in a rush, leaving out nothing, except Murtoch: his lifelong affair with Chantal, how business was getting worse each day as the recession was creeping in, his trusting of McCory, the casino deal, the plots against Hunt. He was winded when he finished, as though he had run the toughest race of his life.

"McCory's one smart cookie," she said without inflection. "He's bled you dry over the years, probably did the same to Hunt. He's screwed you both."

"You don't sound particularly sympathetic."

"I'm not. You brought it on yourself. You put him up to that bombing in New York, and I'll bet Hunt used him for the salmonella attacks on you. The three of you deserve each other."

"What should I do?" he asked. Pathetic. He was groveling to her.

"Do? Nothing. They don't know you're on to them. Keep it that way. Facts are friendly if you make them work for you."

His almost-forgotten mantra crept back into his mind: *Information is key. Knowledge is power.* He had long ago stopped writing in his diary, but he could reconstruct everything if necessary. "Bless you," he said.

"Happy to advise. But from now on, rely on Falkman. I'm moving on."

"What does that mean?"

"That I'm in a relationship, one that's working."

Rolfe recoiled. "Who is he?"

"None of your business. Goodbye."

By the time he regained enough breath to talk, she'd disconnected.

* * * * *

He awoke late the next day, eventually shuffling to the shower in his suite at the Kestrel in San Francisco—his first hotel, the one that had launched him on this nightmarish path. He'd flown in late the previous evening when his apartment had started closing in on him in the aftermath of Susan's revelation. Then, he started making calls.

By midmorning, he'd put a line through every name on his yellow pad: the chief executive of every publicly quoted hotel company, every venture capital firm, every private real estate conglomerate. Everyone, anyone he knew. Useless. He kept coming back to the awful letdown of his London meeting with Sir Martin Treadwell. Damn it, he thought, maybe he's changed his mind, and he dialed the EUF chairman's home number.

"I'm trying to decide on a strategic decision," he said after apologizing for disturbing Treadwell at dinnertime. "I really need your advice."

"In other words," the friendly voice replied, "you want to know if I'm going to exercise our contractual rights and force you to buy back the hotels."

Rolfe had forgotten that part of the deal he'd made when Treadwell had saved him after Josh's murder and bought the five hotels. The thought of having to find more capital made his palms sweat. It was tough enough dodging his creditors; a demand from Treadwell's public company would ruin him.

"Actually, I was discussing the matter with my board just last week," Treadwell continued. "We decided there's no point in owning them if we don't build or buy our own lodging brand, but couldn't decide if now is the time to make any sort of move. What do you think?"

Where's he going? Rolfe wondered. "Not now," he answered honestly. "At this moment, things aren't looking good for the industry. We're in a moderate recession. But lodging will bounce back. It always has. With both business and stock prices down, this might be a great time to buy a chain."

"And to build?"

"Riskier."

"And I presume the chain you refer to is Kestrel."

Rolfe took deep, silent breaths to slow his heart. "I'm still looking. Nothing's changed from the last time we met."

"Interesting."

Rolfe held his breath.

"I suppose one hardly ever has perfect timing," Treadwell muttered. "But yours are the brands we've always wanted."

Unable to sit sill, he paced the floor, receiver held tightly under his chin. "Would you like me to come to London to discuss it?"

A pause. Ominous, Rolfe thought.

"Probably. Let me sleep on it, and I'll get back to you tomorrow. I think there's something here that could work.

Hope, like a Lorelei, danced just out of reach before his eyes.

CHAPTER 46

2001

Treadwell's going to buy! Rolfe paced his suite, delirious. He could rid himself of debt, pay Susan what she deserved and let her retire as she wished and with honor. As for himself—well, he'd have to think of something to do. There was no way he'd manage the hotels under Treadwell, and Treadwell, if he was smart, would make sure he was completely out of the business when EUF took over. Maybe I'll write my memoirs, Rolfe thought. Train for the Boston Marathon. Join the boards of a few prestigious companies. Buy a couple of boutique hotels and go back to my operating roots. Whatever. At least he'd be free from fear, and Margaret and Pieter and his family would be safe. There would be peace, if not enough excitement, in his future. Hell, he'd had enough excitement for ten lifetimes! He'd miss Kestrel, but he'd get over it.

The phone rang. "Good morning, Mr. Ritter. It's your six o'clock call."

"Thanks." He'd been awake for an hour, luxuriating on minutes without worry, prospects without clouds.

This afternoon he would fly to London, negotiate a simple deal, and tomorrow sign a letter of intent with Treadwell. He'd visit his mother over the weekend. She had seemed pleased he wanted to see her; he would break the news to her in person. Maybe they would fully reconcile; maybe he could learn to tell her he loved her as she had told him. Last night he'd been able to tell those cheating bastards, Popov and McCory, that at last they'd get their money, and they could get the fuck out of his life.

He took a shower and then flipped on the television to catch the *Today Show*, more to break the silence than with any prospect of entertainment or information. But instead of the *Today Show*, the news anchorman, with a catch in his voice, was describing a catastrophic event that was taking place at that very moment in

New York City. A plane had crashed into the World Trade Center, and then another plane had crashed into the other tower of the trade center. Terrorists were suspected, but where they'd come from and what their intent was, no one knew. Another plane had plunged into the Pentagon; a fourth was heading for Washington—no, it had crashed in a field near Pittsburgh. There were rumors of a fifth. Air force interceptors were scrambling to head it off.

The anchorman's face was replaced by footage of the terrorist strikes, of the flames and smoke and devastation, of people running away from the sites, some screaming, some wounded, some in stunned bewilderment. Dressed only in a towel, Rolfe watched, transfixed. There would be no flight to London today. It would be hours before the implications of what the assault meant to him and to Kestrel began to grow clear.

He called Susan. "For Christ sake, wake up!" he yelled. "Turn on the TV."

He heard her television come to life, and her cry of surprise. "Go straight to the office," he ordered. "There's no way there'll be flights today, so I'll be by the phone. If anyone comes in, send them home. I'll try to get through to New York and Washington to make sure our properties are secure. As soon as you get in, send an email to all our hotels telling them to implement the full-scale disaster safety and security contingency plans. Then call me, and we'll decide what to do."

* * * * *

As the day sped by, Rolfe and Susan worked the phones , reassuring staff, arranging extra security, dealing with the chaos of stranded guests. All the while, the TV droned on, and they tried to comprehend the incomprehensible.

At 6:30 P.M., an exhausted Susan called Rolfe. "I've spoken to all the general managers. I've got emergency teams manning the phones in our offices here in L.A. and in London, Frankfurt, Hong Kong, and Tokyo."

"Our New York and Washington hotels are battened down so tightly a flea couldn't get in or out," Rolfe said. "I imagine it's the same for Metropolitan."

"It's the same for everybody. We've got guests sleeping on cots in ballrooms until the planes start flying again and they can get home. I have human resources people on hand as counselors to our staff. We've got plenty of supplies and provisions, and I've made sure there's cash in the hotels for emergencies. My throat's so sore from talking I'm going to dine on lozenges. If you want me, I'm at home the rest of the evening, and I'll be in the office early tomorrow. What about you?"

"I'll stay here overnight. If there's any communication possible, it'll be easier to reach me here than while I'm driving down to L.A." He smiled wryly. "That's what you get for building a global empire. When it's night somewhere, it's day somewhere else."

The real reason, he admitted to himself, was that he didn't want to go home. Not to that too-familiar silence, not to a bed with too many memories.

His eyes filled with tears. "Susan, I don't know how to begin to tell you how much I admire you. You were magnificent today; you've always been magnificent. You are Kestrel as much as I am."

He heard a sob in her throat and knew her composure was beginning to crumble. "My God," she said. "Those poor people. This poor country. What's it going to do to business?"

He had been wondering the same thing. "Damned if I know. Whatever it is, it won't be good."

* * * * *

"I've been thinking about you," Sir Martin Treadwell said. His call had come through early the next morning. Rolfe tried to read the chairman's voice; it had its usual hail-fellow quality. "When I couldn't get you at your apartment, I was worried."

"I was stranded here yesterday," Rolfe said. He wondered what yesterday's tragedy would mean to tomorrow's deal. "Everything's chaotic; everybody's afraid."

"Are all your New York and Washington people all right?"

"Yes, thank God. Nice of you to ask."

"What a disaster. God knows what it'll do to the economy. To travel."

"Once the planes start flying, everything will get back to normal. We'll have to postpone our meeting, of course, but I'd guess for no more than a week."

"I'm not so sure you're right about 'normalcy.' I think there could be a longer-lasting effect."

No follow-up on the postponement of the meeting. A hollow feeling permeated Rolfe's chest. He tried to put himself in Treadwell's place, and did not like what he found.

"Tourism is in for a terrible time," the Englishman continued. "The airlines will be particularly hard hit. And the hotels. I can't begin to guess when they'll recover."

Rolfe shuddered. "Six months maximum," he said with an assurance he did not feel.

"At the very earliest, given no more calamities."

There could be no response. Rolfe waited for the guillotine. Still, it was excruciating when it fell.

"Life is strange," Martin said quietly. "Yesterday, I woke up excited about our deal. Today, we both know a deal is impossible. Just mentioning it would make my stock fall like the Twin Towers."

An insistent thundering in Rolfe's head nearly drowned out the Englishman's final words.

"What a shame. Once again, lousy timing. "

* * * * *

Union Square was deserted, save for an occasional homeless person asleep in the shadows. Rolfe walked through it unseeing, his weariness unparalleled. I'm finished, he told himself. There's no way out. I'm a dead man.

He slumped onto a bench facing the hotel. The Kestrel, my first, he thought morosely, staring at the floodlit logo on the building's roof.

Josh, what shall I do? Help me.

Silence filled the square.

Who killed you, Josh? Who had me beaten in Berlin? Who took Pieter's kids?

How was Chantal involved? With Hunt? With McCory? With Popov?

Chantal! When did her betrayals start? As long ago as Paris, when she and I—no. It started here, in America. Is greed a virus that grows more deadly the deeper it infects?

His mind filled with a phantasmagoria of faces, of remembered lies, of his own sins. Shame and humiliation frolicked in his desolation. Everything he'd done and every corner he'd cut in the name of his dream was worthless. The kestrel on top of the hotel seemed to fly directly at him, to pluck at the demons in his brain.

He had to face Popov and McCory, he knew. One or the other would kill him for sure, and then they'd tear each other's hearts out fighting over the Kestrel's remains. A wry smile flickered across his face at the thought.

Will my death save my mother? he wondered. Save Pieter and his family? Whoever they were, they didn't mind kidnapping children or killing Josh to send a message. But if I were dead, what good would more violence get them? What would be the point? There would be nothing more to get.

What had Falkman said? "Take the fuck-you money and hide. Or shoot yourself."

Thoughts of death filled his head. Stop! his mind screamed. Find a way out!

He looked at lit windows in the hotel. Guests were showering, phoning, watching TV, making love—alive. His imagination flashed back to that night in 1973 when he'd walked around the square, wondering if he should buy the very hotel he now was looking at. He laughed at the irony. I'm sitting on the same bench as on that momentous night.

The same bench in Union Square.

The same damned bench . . .

Book Four

"You have to run risks.
There are no certainties in war."

Winston Spencer Churchill

CHAPTER 47

2001

A moment before he pulled the trigger, Rolfe jerked the gun from his mouth. Gagging, ears ringing, he felt the bullet's heat singe his cheek. An idea—intangible, unstructured, but briefly illuminated—flashed through his mind. Fuck it, he thought. I can kill myself another time. He heaved the pistol into the bay, inhaled deeply, and started running.

With each stride, the seeds of his salvation—a way out—grew.

"I'm not beaten yet," he shouted.

No one heard.

The faster he ran, the more his brain churned and the more his hopes rose. Each step had more spring than the last, each yard he covered added more form to his embryonic plan. He crossed the street, leaving the wharves behind, and climbed the hill toward Union Square, hardly noticing the incline.

At the Kestrel's front doors, Lennie asked, "Good run, Mr. Ritter?" and handed Rolfe a cool damp towel and a bottle of mineral water.

"The best," Rolfe said. "It's a great morning."

Lennie would have talked further, but Rolfe moved past him toward the elevators. He was in a hurry to get back. There was work to be done.

* * * * *

Ron Falkman picked up the phone in his New York apartment on the first ring. "The city's a war zone. Everything's shut down; everyone's in shock," he responded to Rolfe's question. "How about you? You coping?"

"Barely. Susan's pretty well the only one in the office; The airlines are grounded, and I'm stuck in our hotel in San Francisco, manning the phones, not that anyone has made a reservation at any Kestrel since the attack. I have no idea if we have enough money to pay our staff, and everyone's scared shitless. Apart from that, I'm doing fine."

"You sound like you're in a good mood. How come? Gallows humor? Have you any idea how bad things are going to be in the hotel business? A disaster is putting it mildly."

"So you think my values will drop?"

"So low a gopher couldn't find it."

"And Metropolitan's?"

Falkman chuckled. "At long last, you'll be in bed together." There was a roar of glee from San Francisco. "Okay, smart ass, what's going on?"

"Hear me out," Rolfe said. "I'm about to blow your mind."

The attorney listened intently as Rolfe laid out his plan.

"Let me get this straight." Ron's tone was incredulous. "You've run out of options to sell your company. Popov and McCory won't wait another month and are about to do Lord-knows-what to you. Susan wants to resign. The country, hell, the world, is topsy-turvy. The travel and lodging industry is tanking and can only get worse. And now you're going to launch a hostile bid for Metropolitan, backed by investors you haven't talked to."

"That about sums it up," Rolfe said mildly. "Only, it'll be a fake bid. Obviously, if Hunt takes me up on it, I'll have to find some cockamamie reason to back out."

"You know it'll cause chaos. Hunt will go nuts."

"That's the idea."

"And after all these years of Hunt hating your guts, you think he'll react by buying you out, not for cash but for Metropolitan's stock? Anything to keep you from buying him out?"

"Precisely."

"You'll give the stock to your creditors, who'll figure out that eventually it'll grow in price and they'll be able to sell it without depending on you to cash them out of the properties."

Rolfe grinned. "Brilliant, isn't it?"

"I don't know from brilliant, but I do know from outrageous. You've just redefined the word 'chutzpah.' What if he doesn't buy your business? What happens if he sells to someone else?"

"He won't. His ego won't let him. He won't give in, and he'll never retire. Don't forget, he's got complete control over his board; they'll do anything he wants. There's no way he'll sell his company to me or anyone else. When we bid, he'll counter-offer, buy me at any price to prove not only that he's outmaneuvered me, but that he's beaten me into submission."

"You're out of your mind!" Falkman exploded. "Do you know how farfetched this is?"

"I'm not looking for your approval. Just tell me what my chances of pulling it off are."

Falkman deliberated. He's taking me seriously, Rolfe thought.

"Five to ten percent. If you're lucky."

"That's better than anything else I've got going for me. But to do it I need an investment banker to represent me and launch the bid."

"No one in his right mind will take on you and your pipedream."

"Come on, you know everyone. The investment banking business is going to be lousy for months. Who's really hungry?"

Falkman sighed. "I'll find someone. Whoever it is will want cash up front, and you'll have to show up with real investors who'll at least say they're backing you."

Rolfe's excitement grew. He felt like he had that night he'd bid on the Audleys. "I'm going to try, Ron. What have I got to lose?"

* * * * *

"Are you serious, or are you trying to sell me an idea for a fucking movie?" Levenson bellowed. In his late eighties, his mind as sharp as ever, he'd long since retired from the studio, having sold it to a Japanese communications company. Still an active investor, Lew ran his business from his Beverly Hills mansion, where he, Mark Walters, and Rolfe were now sitting poolside in the warmth of the late afternoon sun.

Rolfe was caught up in Levenson's laughter. "Maybe I'd make money if I did sell it as a movie script."

Walters took a sip of Levenson's single malt. "So you want us to say we'll back your bid to buy Metropolitan, only you don't really want to buy Metropolitan at all—you want that son of a bitch Hunt to buy Kestrel?"

"You've got it."

Walters' demeanor changed. "What's in it for us?"

"Hold it, Mark," Levenson interceded. "We owe the kid. Think how much he's made us in the last thirty years."

"Granted. But we'll be taking a big fucking risk. Screwing around with securities laws . . ."

"That's why we pay our lawyers," Levenson said calmly. "If we want to do it, they'll find a way."

Walters' face brightened. "I know what we'll do! We'll fuck Metropolitan."

Rolfe stretched. The sun felt good. "Nothing I'd like better. How?"

"We'll buy options on their stock before you launch the bid. Then, we'll sell them for a fat fucking profit." Seeing the bewilderment in Rolfe's face, he continued. "When Hunt decides to reject the offer and go after Rolfe, we'll short the fucking stuff."

"I don't get it," Rolfe admitted.

"It's simple, you dumb schmuck," Levenson said. "We buy options on a ton of Metropolitan's stock before you bid. When you announce, Hunt's stock price will go through the roof, and we'll cash in our options and make a bundle. Then, we'll short his stock we just bought. Basically, we place a bet that when he rejects our offer and decides to buy you out, people will realize he's not selling no matter what, and his stock will plummet. As soon as it does, we collect on our bet, and presto, a second killing. We'll make out like bandits! It's just like gambling, only instead of a bookie, we play the stock market."

"Isn't trading on insider information illegal?" Rolfe asked.

"Who's going to tell them where we got it?" Walters said without a hint of a smile. "If I remember, you're the fucking person who blackmailed us in the first place."

* * * * *

"Got a pen?"

Rolfe had been waiting for Falkman's call.

"Bob Chapman at Hartman Corey. He needs the business, and he's expecting your call."

* * * * *

"Mr. Ritter," Chapman said too cheerfully. "Ron said you wanted to mount a bid for Metropolitan. Couldn't be a better time, in my opinion. He tells me he's supporting you and that you've some heavy hitters on your side. If the deal's good enough for Falkman, it's good enough for me."

"Glad to welcome you aboard," Rolfe said, feet on his desk, cradling the phone beneath his chin.

"We're at our best when the management and the board of a company don't want to sell and get in a fight with the potential purchaser."

"Which side do you specialize in?" Rolfe asked, seeing snakes either way.

"Either one. Provided they do what we say and pay us our fees. If Bruce Hunt had come to me first, I'd be doing everything in my power to fight you off."

"Then I'm glad he didn't. This time, you'll represent the potential purchaser."

"Agreed. But because this deal's so speculative, I want five million up front."

* * * * *

Rolfe and Susan watched from Susan's porch as the sun dropped toward the Pacific Ocean, a pink glow diffusing the sky.

"I didn't know things were that bad," she said.

He nodded gravely, shocked at how tired she seemed. How old.

"You actually thought about suicide?"

"Had the gun to my head."

She clasped his hand. "You poor, poor man. Why didn't you tell me?"

He sat silently, not knowing the answer.

"Well, Rolfe Michael Den Ritter, this is one hell of a mess, isn't it?"

"The worst."

"And the only way out is this lunatic scheme you've conned Mark and Lew into."

"Plus Bob Chapman, don't forget."

She snorted. "Bob Chapman, the investment banker who wants five million before he so much as sneezes. Sure, he's really committed."

Rolfe winced. "You make it sound so ridiculous," he said despondently. "I agree. This probably doesn't have a chance in hell. So quit. Resign now. Get out of town while I play this out. If it doesn't work, whoever's after me won't find you."

Only the luminescence of the sea provided enough light for Rolfe to see Susan's face. She was crying. "You'd lose from the get-go if your president walked away, and you know it. Besides, how do you think I'd feel after all these years if I left as soon as things got really tough. Some friend I'd be."

Tears came to his own eyes, and he thought how much more solid friendship is than romance, how much more he loved her now than when they were lovers.

"Where in God's heaven are we going to raise the five million?" he asked.

She stopped crying. "Five mil is only the beginning. If we're going to look serious, we'll need another five, maybe ten."

"That only makes it worse."

"Yup. You'd better find another piggybank."

* * * * *

Margaret met him with a little cry of joy. "I'm glad you're here," she said. "Really glad. I've been thinking about you every day. With Wim gone and then Jan, you're the only one left in my life."

He appraised her. Was she telling the truth, or was this some kind of irony? Now that the "real" men in her life had died, was he the best she could do? Did it matter? She had come to him when he was attacked and said she loved him. Had she meant it? He hoped so. And in her presence, for the moment, at least, he felt... safe.

Her apartment was tired-looking, he thought, promising himself he'd have it fixed up for her when this was all over. Margaret seemed tired, too, though, as always, she was immaculately dressed, her hair in a bun as tight as when he was a child. It was the look in her eyes that had changed; it shone with a warmth for him that he hadn't seen since his father had died. This must have been what had attracted his father and Jan too, this look of devotion. He wanted to embrace her, let her embrace him. Her need was palpable, but so was his, and maybe... He broke off the thought as he saw her expression change from love to sorrow.

He understood why. The scars from the Berlin beating were still vivid, he knew. His hair was gray, quickly turning white. Stress and exhaustion were mapped across his face.

"You need help," she said, "and you've come to me?"

He bowed his head. "Yes."

"Thank God! Just let me know how."

He wanted to fall on his knees before her. Finally, finally, she would make him well, and he loved her as he did when he was a child.

* * * * *

He told her everything, again with the exception of Murtoch. She listened attentively, punctuating his narrative with questions that told him she understood.

"I don't know how much I can do," she said when he'd finished.

"Beyond moral support and my love."

"How much are you looking after for me?"

"It's grown substantially," she said with a touch of pride. "I invested it conservatively for the most part, but I bought some technology stocks on Jan's advice—I think he got the tip from Pieter—and they did well." She paused, seeming to search for the names, but he was sure she knew them and was just playing with him, delighting in what she had done. "One was Microsoft, the other AOL. I don't have them any more. Sold them a couple of years ago and put the money into bonds and blue chips."

He laughed, once more amazed at her shrewdness. "You outsmarted the entire market! What sum does it come to?"

"About twelve million pounds. Maybe more."

He stared at her. "That's nearly twenty million dollars. A fortune!"

She smiled. "I'm happy you're pleased."

"Pleased? It's a lifesaver. Mummy, I need the money now. Tomorrow, I'll give you wiring instructions, and you can transfer it."

She sighed. "You know I can't do that. You told me to look after it for ten years and that under no circumstances should I give it to you before then."

"Yes, but things have changed. It's absolutely imperative that I get the money now."

"I'm sorry, darling," she said, smiling benignly. "It's nonnegotiable. A promise made is a promise kept."

The color drained from Rolfe's face as the words, those words, sank in. Rage flared. Damn it, this was his money. His fortune. He was nearly fifty years old, and she was keeping money that was rightfully his from him, as though he were a child who couldn't look after himself.

He saw her soften, watching him. "I'm afraid for you," she said. You've told me the trouble you're in and how slight your chances are. If I give you the money and you lose it, I'll have failed you as your mother and as what I hope I'll be from now on, your friend."

He heard Susan in her words and Momo. This time, he listened. "Thank you," he said at last. "You did exactly right." He took her hand and kissed it.

* * * * *

The second Rolfe woke up, he knew what to do. He waited impatiently for Susan to get to the office.

"I know where to get the ten million," he told her.

"Your mother said yes?"

"No. She saved me from myself, something rather more impor-tant. We'll get the money from McCory. Raid the casino's bank accounts. Steal the money from that sack of shit. He deserves it."

CHAPTER 48

2001

"You've caused me real fucking embarrassment," McCory said, sitting at the bar in his Las Vegas house. "I can't guarantee you'll come out unscathed."

Rolfe kept his tone casual. "Bud, I'm working on something big that'll fix everything. Just give me time."

"Time." McCory's disbelief was evident. "No way. Not unless I buy that you can pull a big fucking rabbit out of a big fucking hat. You're finished. Bad things happen in jail, if you even get that far."

Rolfe chuckled.

"What's so fucking funny?"

"I can't tell you what I'm doing, but you're too smart not to give me time."

"Bullshit!"

"You're not listening. Do yourself a favor. You and your investors should buy stock in Metropolitan. Now. Trust me. You'll understand why soon enough."

McCory stared at him over the glass of amber liquid he held in his huge hands. "Since you first bluffed me twenty-eight years ago with that wire shit, I've known you play a good hand of poker. Maybe I should give you time just to watch the game." Rolfe saw his eyes narrow. "I'll give you more time on one condition."

"What's that?"

"Let the union organize half a dozen of your hotels that we're not in today."

"Three," Rolfe said quickly.

"Who do you think you are, trying to negotiate?"

"Three," Rolfe repeated.

"Okay, four. Now get the fuck out of my house."

* * * * *

"So, my old friend, you've called to tell me you've paid back all my money."

"Not quite. But—"

"But nothing," the Russian snarled. "Time's up. You promised something, and you didn't deliver. The consequences, unfortunately—"

"Hold on one minute," Rolfe said sharply. "I've come up with an idea that'll clean up this mess once and for all."

"Another idea." Popov sighed. "Why should I waste a minute on it?"

"Because I'm still your best, maybe your only, way of getting your money back. Which do you prefer, that or a dead Ritter?"

There was an ominous silence.

"Don't you think I know you can kill me."

"All right, I'm listening. But be careful. If this is another of your schemes—"

"I can't tell you what it is. All I need is a little more time."

"No! What do you take me for, an ignorant peasant? Unless you tell me, we're through."

"Do yourself a favor. Buy or option Metropolitan stock. The reason will be clear soon enough."

Rolfe waited for the silence in Moscow to end.

"I'll think about it."

Thank God!

* * * * *

Susan entered the office carrying folders.

"You wanted me to come up with a way to justify merging Kestrel and Metropolitan."

Rolfe took the folders. "Actually, Chapman did. He insists we need it to demonstrate to Metropolitan's shareholders that we're serious."

"I wish we were," she said excitedly. "It's the ideal fit. The damn thing works like a dream!"

* * * * *

The corner table in the oak-paneled Journey's Bar in New York's Essex House was dark. The sound of the piano deadened their conversation to the nearby tables. A single candle illuminated McCory's intense face.

"I want you to find what Ritter's up to."

Chantal shook her head. "He hasn't talked to me in weeks.

He's furious about Moscow."

McCory gripped her upper arm. "I don't give a fuck how mad he is. Get me the fucking information! Do what you normally do. Use your twat instead of your brains."

She sighed. "I don't think he cares about me in that way any more."

"Just do it! And when you get the information, don't tell your husband. Do you understand? Don't tell Bruce."

* * * * *

The phone began to ring just as Rolfe opened his door. He picked it up in the study.

"I must see you," Chantal said.

Who sent her? Rolfe wondered. Hunt? McCory? Popov? There was only one way to find out.

Twenty-four hours later, Chantal sat next to Rolfe on his sofa holding a glass of Stolichnaya Crystal.

"Pick up the taste for vodka in Moscow?" he asked.

"Please don't start again," she said. "I made a mistake, and I'm sorry. If I'd known it would mean never seeing you again—"

"What brings you from New York?" he interrupted, his voice impersonal. This woman who used to excite him more than anyone he knew now seemed plain.

"I can't take it any longer."

"Take what?"

"Bruce. I hate him."

"Why tell me?"

"I can't stand to be in the same room with him."

"Then divorce him."

She didn't seem to hear. "When he touches me—" she shuddered. "It's you I want, have always wanted. I know you're upset about Popov—I wish to hell I'd never met him. But I'll never let you down again, I promise."

Tears fell on her cheeks, and she buried her head on his chest. "Please," she said, letting her hand fall to his crotch.

He watched with complete detachment. Why not play this out? he thought. See what she really wants. All these years she's used me. It's my turn now.

* * * * *

Satiated, Rolfe lay in Chantal's arms, his eyes closed.

"Rolfe?" She moved his hand to her breast in the familiar way.

"Mmmm?"

"That was wonderful. The best ever."

"Mmmm."

"Do it again!"

"Tomorrow morning. Let me sleep."

"Only if you promise we can go away together. Just you and me. Bruce won't care. And anyway, who cares about Bruce?"

"Sounds nice," he said. "But I've got to stay in Los Angeles."

She raised herself on an elbow and looked down at him. "Why?"

"Because I've got a plan, and I want to see it fulfilled."

She could hardly contain her excitement. "Tell me."

"You'll tell Bruce." More likely Popov and McCory, he thought.

"I swear I won't. I've told you I hate him."

Piece by piece he let Chantal draw out the information: his plan to merge Kestrel and Metropolitan, the backing he had from Chapman, the equity he was promised from Walters and Levenson.

"Brilliant!" she said when he was finished.

He squeezed her breast gently. Her heart was tripwire-fast. "I can't wait to walk into Metropolitan's boardroom and fire your husband's ass!"

"When?" It was as though he were making love to her again.

"No more than two weeks. Now, let me sleep."

He turned away from her and closed his eyes. His breathing grew heavy. Soon, Chantal eased herself from bed and left the room. He watched the red light on his bedside phone come on and stretched luxuriantly. Perfect! Absolutely perfect!

Within twelve hours, Bud McCory, Yevgeny Popov, and Chantal Le Peron had bought over ten million dollars worth of Metropolitan stock combined—each unaware of the others' actions.

CHAPTER 49

2001

Half-empty containers of Chinese food littered the Kestrel boardroom. It smells fetid, Rolfe thought, watching Susan and Bob Chapman pore over the papers between them. They'd been working non-stop for thirty-six hours. "Nearly through?" he asked.

Chapman looked at him with weary eyes. "The question is, Are you ready?"

Anger and exhaustion got the better of him. "I was ready two days ago."

Susan stretched. "Then we are, too."

"That's not what I meant," Chapman said. "Listen, Rolfe, and think this through. You'll be fighting Hunt in public. Like all cornered tigers, he'll try to rip out your throat. And the media will gnaw on the bones."

Rolfe swallowed hard. Lord only knows what Hunt had on him in those files of his. "I assume we'll do the same to him."

"Of course. And our teeth are as sharp as his. Nevertheless, it'll be painful. He'll hire the cleverest fighters on Wall Street. He'll put up every roadblock he's ever dreamed of, and then invent some more. There'll be full-page ads appealing to his stockholders. CNN and CNBC will have a field day."

Rolfe grunted. "I've been savaged before."

"Nothing like this, I promise you. Here's what I predict will happen: Their stock is at sixteen dollars. Tomorrow we make a bid at twenty dollars a share. They won't respond at first, or rather they'll issue a statement saying your offer's a joke. They'll bring up your grand jury appearances and the IRS audit, and say they're not considering it. At the same time, they'll authorize a poison-pill defense and a golden parachute for Hunt and his team, so if anyone gets control of Metropolitan and fires them, they'll make a fortune. It's an added deterrent to a purchaser."

"What's a poison pill?" Susan asked for Rolfe's benefit.

"A damned stupid law to defend management. I'll try and make it simple. If fifteen to twenty percent of Metropolitan's stockholders accept your offer, then every stockholder except you, the hostile bidder, gets to buy shares in Metropolitan at half the fair market value."

"You mean Joe Public can buy Hunt's stock at half price, but I have to pay full price?" Rolfe asked incredulously.

"You got it." Chapman shrugged. "That's why they call it a poison pill—it's meant to stop corporate raiders, not protect lazy CEOs."

"Ridiculous!" Rolfe exploded. "Inept management gets to sit tight? And in the meantime, no one will finance the deal if they have to pay twice as much as anyone else."

Chapman was unruffled. "That's why, when we go back with a second bid, say twenty-two-fifty a share, we'll make it contingent on their board removing the poison pill provision."

"And if they won't?"

"That's where the independent directors are meant to do their job. They should act in the best interests of the shareholders, not management. If they think that selling the company to Kestrel is the best way to realize shareholder value, then it's their duty to overrule management and accept your offer."

"But they're Hunt's cronies," Susan said. "We all know that."

"Don't worry. We'll remind them of directors' responsibilities and make sure they're so scared of getting personally sued they'll rethink their loyalties." He paused. "So have you got the testosterone for this? Do we bid tomorrow or not?"

Rolfe didn't answer him immediately. "I want a minute alone with Susan," he said. Chapman left.

"Do we go ahead?" Rolfe said, his heart loud in his chest.

"I know exactly how you feel. You're risking everything you've got."

"We've got," he corrected her. "And I don't want to do it unless you're with me—not out of loyalty, or an old love, but because, inside, you believe it's the best thing to do."

"You can't deny me loyalty or love," she said. "I'm with you."

He opened the boardroom door.

"We bid."

CHAPTER 50

2001

"Mr. Hunt, this is Steve Himmel. I follow lodging for the *Wall Street Journal*. Do you have any comment on Kestrel's bid?"

Bruce Hunt, alone in his office, felt his pulse accelerate. "Bid for what, Mr. Himmel?"

"Don't you know? Kestrel's launched a bid for Metropolitan. It's just come in over the wire."

The room went dark. He was afraid he was having a heart attack. "No comment."

Five minutes later, Hunt's general counsel, Norm Anderson, was in Hunt's office holding a copy of the letter Rolfe had sent to each member of the Metropolitan Board of Directors, detailing terms and conditions of the bid:

> With the current price of Metropolitan's stock at $15 a share, this $5 premium represents value to Metropolitan's shareholders that current management is not capable of harvesting. Their slow and limited reaction to the devastating impact on the lodging industry in the wake of the tragic events of September 11, is clear evidence that they are not maximizing shareholder value. Metropolitan's shareholders deserve a change. It is our belief that Kestrel's proven expertise at developing world-class lodging brands will quickly unlock hidden value in Metropolitan Hotels' existing businesses. . . .

Color spread across Hunt's face like an infection. He managed a laugh. "No one in his right mind will take him seriously. He's broke, and everyone knows that."

"He may be a derelict," Anderson said calmly, "but he's made a genuine offer backed by a respectable investment bank, which is,

I quote, 'highly confident that all the needed capital is in place to complete Kestrel's bid as presented.'"

He waited for a response, but got none. "Please listen, Bruce. He's released the offer verbatim to the press and the SEC. Legally, we have no choice but to take this seriously."

Hunt ripped Rolfe's letter in half and flung the pieces to the floor. "It's not my fault terrorists flew fucking airplanes into the World Trade Center during the middle of a recession. How dare Ritter say we can't harvest our value? What the hell else have we been doing? That mother fucker. I'll tear his fucking heart out."

Anderson had heard such tirades before. He waited quietly.

"All right, Norm," Hunt said. "What do we have to do to be 'legal'?"

"We issue a press release saying we received an unsolicited bid and are in the process of giving it appropriate consideration." He looked at his boss sternly. "Nothing more. Later today, we'll hold a board meeting by conference call. We'll use Mel Bernstein at Richter and Pearlman as our lawyer." Anderson smiled for the first time. "He's the most vicious son of a bitch I've ever met."

✳ ✳ ✳ ✳ ✳

When Hunt reached Chantal, she broke his heart.

"Take the deal," she said.

"What?"

"You've done brilliantly. Time to retire."

"That's ridiculous. I've got years left. Besides, sell to Ritter? I'd rather sacrifice Mary to the gods than do that."

His daughter had been in and out of rehab centers for fifteen years. Now clean, she was managing a Metropolitan in Indianapolis. Father and daughter spoke once a week, and Chantal knew he adored her.

"Don't be too hasty," she cooed. "This might turn out to be a blessing. You could spend more time with Mary, and when you're not with her, I've bought some special toys for us to play with."

Toys were not on Hunt's mind. "I hear Ritter's deal is real," McCory had said when he'd picked up the phone.

"Who from?" Hunt challenged.

"My banking friends, among others."

"How long have you known about it? Why didn't you warn me? For the money I pay you, I deserve better."

McCory's voice was cold, menacing. "First, I only found out about it when it hit the wire. Second, there are a bunch of smart financial people out there who think it's a good deal and want you to take it. And third—" he paused, "remember who you're talking to. If I were you I'd be fucking careful."

* * * * *

Rolfe put down the pen and reread the letter to his half-brother.

> *Dear Pieter,*
>
> *I'm writing you an hour before New Year's. I'm feeling lonely and think you deserve an update on my activities.*
>
> *I hope, by now, you've found it in your heart to forgive me for the kids' abduction. God knows, I'd never do anything to harm them. I don't know for sure who's behind the kidnapping, but I have a few ideas. I'm convinced your children were taken to threaten me and that they were never in any real danger. Small solace to you and Christine, I know. I am so very sorry, and one day I will somehow make up for all of the pain I've caused.*
>
> *What good the threats do, I don't know. I've tried to sell the properties, sell Kestrel—anything to raise enough money to pay everyone back. I should have taken the offer you brought me and sold way back then. I was even ready to sell to Hunt, but his stock was so low and his hatred of me so high that he told me, in effect, to go screw myself.*
>
> *So now I'm trying to buy him out. Our bankers think I've gone raving mad, but I promise I know what I'm doing. When it's all over, I'll tell you everything, but for the moment I ask you to trust me.*
>
> *In the meantime, I'm going crazy. I know you've done mergers and acquisitions all your life, but something this big is new territory for me, and every decision is on my shoulders. I'm exhausted before I even get out of bed.*
>
> *Metropolitan's hired a pit bull Wall Street lawyer named Bernstein, who told Chapman they were going to "grind me into dust." Why does this sound good to me?*
>
> *The Metropolitan board rejected my bid and adopted a "poison pill" policy. I expected that. They said they'd give Hunt a golden parachute in the event he loses control in a hostile takeover. I expected that too, but it still makes me want to puke. Now, we go to Phase II. Sometimes, I think it will work, but more often than not, I go to bed thinking it won't and wake up with the heebie-jeebies (an American term—means the runs).*
>
> *I get calls from my investors every day, wanting details, threatening, and cajoling. I'm in danger of my*

life, I know, if this doesn't work out. I keep promising that when I buy Metropolitan, I'll pay them back as well, but if things go sour for me, I want you to promise you'll go to Kenneth Palmer for help and protection. And if I die, I've left everything to you and your family. Ron Falkman has my will. Kestrel may be worthless, but my mother has money invested for me that will go straight to you.

Anyway, thanks for letting me get this off my chest. I think often of Mother and her offer of help. She's too weak to come here, and I'm too busy to go there, so when you see her give her a hug from me and tell her I love her.

Rolfe

Just writing the last three words offered him a moment of calm in a turbulent world.

CHAPTER 51

2002

Chapman was discussing the intricacies of their next bid, but Rolfe wasn't listening. His secretary had handed him a message: Call Momo Takenaka on her cell phone.

It had been almost a year since he had spoken to her, though he thought about her every day. Excusing himself, he went from the boardroom to his office and called.

Her voice was merry. "I've been reading about you in the papers."

How good she sounded. How he missed her! "They make me sound like a predator."

"Aren't you?"

"Only when I go after the things I covet."

"I want to see you."

His heart jumped. What happened to the other man? he wondered. "Where are you? I'll be there."

"Actually," she said languidly, "I'm in L.A."

She was here! He would see her at last! He was beyond joy. If he had killed himself, he would have missed this moment. And this moment was everything. "When?"

"This evening?"

He looked at his watch: 4:00 P.M. "Can't we make it sooner?"

She laughed. "I'm at the Peninsula. The bar at seven?"

"I'll try to make it," he said, and, hanging up, danced back to the boardroom.

*   *   *   *   *

He was early, and he was able to study himself in the bar's mirror. I look like shit, he thought. Haunted, scarred, old, and tired. Beaten.

"Rolfe."

He jumped, not having seen her approach. She was wearing a

beige Chanel trouser suit and alligator shoes. Two alabaster pearls served as earrings. "What happened to the black?" he asked.

She slid beside him into the booth. "I've changed. It's a different Momo."

"Is that good or bad?"

"That's for you to say."

He inhaled, the hint of her perfume making him giddy. "Good, then. It's brought you back."

She was silent for a moment. Then: "And you? Have you changed?" Her eyes were troubled.

He took her hands. She did not pull away. "How changed?"

"Is it a different Rolfe?" she asked. "To judge from the papers, you're up to your old ways."

He could not look in her eyes. There was no sense lying to her. "I'm still in this thing up to my neck, dancing on the ever-diminishing head of a pin. Submerged in debt. Dodging dangerous enemies."

"How dangerous?" she asked.

"You know, McCory and Popov. I'm way behind on repayments to them—to say nothing of the other investors. They've got me by the balls. What they'll do if I can't pay them back—"

"What about Hunt?"

"Believe it or not, he's my one chance. All that stuff you've read in the papers, it's a wild-assed gamble. Ron Falkman tells me I have, at best, a five to ten percent chance of pulling it off. If I do, I'm home free. If not, I'm a dead man."

"Don't talk like that," she said angrily.

"It's true, literally."

"Oh, my God!"

"There've been threats. Pieter's kids were kidnapped. It's why I was beaten up in Berlin. Why Josh was killed. I don't know if it's Hunt, McCory, or Popov, but I do know someone's been sending me crystal clear messages. 'Pay or die.'"

She started to cry. He took a handkerchief to stem the tears, and she held his hand to her face, clutching it with the passion he remembered.

"I should never have left you," she sobbed. "It was a stupid mistake. The man I loved was what you were, what you are, and it was ridiculous to want you to be someone else. I was jealous of Kestrel. I wanted to have all of you, but if I'd succeeded, part of you would have been lost. I've tried other relationships, one was serious. But I compared each one to you. Finally I had to decide: Do I take you for who you are or live forever without? And the answer is simple: I want you, need you. And if I've judged right, you need me."

After all these years, the words he'd waited for. Now, the saddest words he knew. If she returned to him, they'd kill her as surely as they'd kill him. First, probably. To let him have the full pain of it.

"I can't let you come back," he said. "As much as I want you, my darling Momo, no."

His own tears started, blinding him to her beauty and her plea, and he stood and walked away.

* * * * *

In all the years Susan had known Momo, she'd never heard panic in her voice, but after tonight's call, she'd driven wildly to the Peninsula. She now sat on Momo's bed, watching the Japanese-American woman fight to keep self-control.

"Tell me everything," Momo begged. "How bad is it?"

Susan explained, omitting nothing.

"Christ," she said when Susan finished. "He actually had a gun to his head? I mean, he's gotten out of scrapes before, always has. But this—" She shuddered. "I should have put it together after the Berlin mess. How stupid am I?"

"No more than the rest of us," Susan said. "All he ever wanted was to be the perfect hotel manager, but to do that he's spent his life in chaos. Now it looks as if it's caught up with him."

"Then he needs me now, more than ever."

"He can't take the risk of having you involved. I don't have a choice; I am involved. And his advice to me was to pack a bag and get out if things turn ugly. Nevertheless, I don't think they'll kill me; I hope it's only my career, and not my life, that's in jeopardy. But you—"

"You don't understand! I love him!"

Susan sighed. "I do understand. I love him too."

CHAPTER 52

2002

"So far," Chapman said, "Hunt's acted according to script. Offer rejected. Poison pill planted. It's time to ratchet up the pressure."

"I'm surprised no other bidders have appeared," Ron Falkman said, sitting by Rolfe's side in the conference room.

Chapman frowned. "I am too. They've probably figured Rolfe's got enormous private capital behind him and reckon they can't compete." He hesitated. "Or, more likely, they believe Hunt will never sell."

"Will he?" Rolfe asked.

"If I do my job properly, he'll have little choice. Anyway, it's time for phase two: We increase our offer."

"How high now?" Falkman asked.

"As planned, twenty-two-fifty a share, conditional on the removal of the poison pill."

Chapman is too sure of himself, Rolfe thought, a pang of dread in his stomach.

"In our letter to the board," the banker continued, "we'll cite examples in which the courts have found independent directors individually liable for wrong decisions they've made on shareholders' behalf. Now we'll find out what Hunt's board is made of. Sooner or later, there will be a price they'll have to accept."

"What happens after our revised bid goes in?"

"It'll get uglier and more personal. Be prepared to duck."

* * * * *

"What happens if they accept the offer? Then what'll I do?" Rolfe asked Falkman after they'd excused themselves to talk privately.

"Don't panic. You know they won't. What's changed?"

"It's Chapman. He's too damn convincing."

"That's why I chose him. Relax. Take it one step at a time. If you blink now, it's over."

* * * * *

"What are you going to do about Ritter's latest bid?" Bud McCory asked.

"Watch him rot in hell. The cocksucker's never getting hold of my company."

"Still, you have to do something to satisfy your stockholders?"

"Nothing—they think I walk on water anyway."

"What about your independent directors?"

"They'll do what I tell them."

"Get real. Their asses are personally on the line."

"You got any suggestions?"

McCory considered. He could hear Hunt's raspy breath on the other end of the phone. "I do," he said at last. "Turn the tables. You buy him out and get rid of that son of a bitch once and for all."

Hunt snorted. Chantal had recommended the same course the night before, "It's an option, I suppose," he said.

* * * * *

That afternoon, Susan signed the refinancing papers on her Malibu house, moved the proceeds into her bank account, and withdrew $50,000 in cash. With tears in her eyes, she packed a suitcase, put her passport and the cash on top, and left it in her hall closet. I hope I can stay, she thought. But if not...

* * * * *

"They're playing it just as we predicted," Norm Anderson announced. He and Hunt were surrounded by the high-priced group of investment bankers and lawyers who were advising them on their defense to Kestrel's bid. "What next?"

Mel Bernstein looked around the table. "Now, we get serious. We'd better think through every word we say and every move we make." He pointed a finger at Hunt. "The question is, Bruce, what do you really want? The market likes Ritter's bid. Your stock price is twenty-one-fifty. Do you want to make a fortune by selling, or do you want to fight? The decision is yours."

Hunt slammed his fist on the table. "What I really want is to crush that miserable, lying, cheating sack of shit once and for all."

"Fine," Bernstein said evenly. "But it's not going to be easy. Ritter's got legitimate backers, and he's made a good argument for combining the companies. You've got to have a viable explanation for your stockholders, and you'd better have an alternate plan if you turn this down."

"Oh, but I do," Hunt said, a smug leer spreading across his face. "We're going to make Metropolitan untouchable."

Bernstein sat forward. "How?"

"By buying Kestrel," he announced triumphantly.

Metropolitan's boardroom went silent. "But he's a buyer not a seller," Anderson finally blurted.

"He's got debts up the ass. Believe me, I know him. If the price is high enough, he'll take it."

* * * * *

Ron Falkman walked into Rolfe's office. "News," he said somberly.

Rolfe's heart plummeted. "Jesus! What's wrong? What news?"

"Chapman just had a call from Mel Bernstein. Hunt's rejecting the new offer."

"So why the gloom?"

"Gloom?" Falkman's face lit like a skyrocket. "Hardly. Just wanted to give you a little scare."

"Then—"

"They want to buy Kestrel!"

Rolfe leapt from his chair. His old friend hugged him. "You heard me," Ron gasped. "Bernstein says they've got to do something, otherwise their stock will drop like a brick. They're buyers!"

* * * * *

"It's beginning to look a lot like Christmas," Rolfe sang as he dashed into Susan's office, pulled her from her chair, and danced her around the room. "The plan worked!"

* * * * *

"How are the negotiations going?" Chantal rolled off Rolfe's spent body and peered down at him.

"Too slowly," Rolfe muttered. "Your husband's too damn cheap."

Her tongue flicked in and out of his ear. "It's a game. Your people set a ridiculously high price and his a ridiculously low one."

"Precisely."

"How far apart are you?" she asked casually.

"A lot."

"What's your real number?"

"If I tell you, you'll tell Hunt."

"No. I promise."

Coldly, calculatingly, he let her pry the number out of him.

* * * * *

Hunt stared blankly at the New York skyline, the phone receiver tight against his ear.

"I tell you, Bruce, my source is one hundred percent reliable," McCory repeated.

"And for two million goddamned bucks, you'll tell me Ritter's real price. Do you think I'm crazy?"

"What's a few bucks if I can save you a couple of hundred million?"

"Ah," Hunt said disgustedly. "All right."

* * * * *

"We're finished," Falkman announced to Rolfe at 1:15 A.M. from Bernstein's meeting room. "Mel and I are going home to sleep. The closing's at noon tomorrow, here. Hunt's going to lord it over you. Promise me you'll be humble and act like you've been out-negotiated."

* * * * *

"Unpack," Rolfe told Susan, who had been waiting for his call. "Tomorrow we sign."

It was early morning in London, and Momo would be awake, but he decided not to call her yet. After the papers had been finalized, he thought, anticipating the sublime pleasure of it. Then, I'll be free.

CHAPTER 53

2002

How long had he waited for this moment? Bruce Hunt sat in his library, sipping cognac and reveling in the fact that mattered above all others: Ritter was finished.

After all these years, the business demise of his adversary had been easy. Yes, a tricky negotiation—and to Ritter's credit, he got the highest possible price—but the speed of his change from buyer to seller showed him to be the cowardly worm he was. Why, that little shit Dutch hotelier's investment bankers and lawyers had practically caved in at every step of the way. In the end, the bastard didn't have the balls for a fight.

One more celebratory drink wouldn't hurt. But with his second cognac, his good mood vanished. Uncertainty took hold in his brain like a cancer and started to grow.

Ritter doesn't have any money. He's broke.

That terrible thought was followed by another: He never intended to buy Metropolitan. It was all a fake, a goddamned bluff, a means to bail him out.

Hunt's scream of rage shattered the quiet of the night.

* * * * *

"It was a good deal last night, and it's a good deal today," Bernstein argued at nine the next morning. "So what if it's what he wants? You get what you want as well."

"I know Ritter better than anyone else in the world. The scumbag tried to sucker us." He glared at Bernstein and Anderson sitting across from him in his office. "And you fell for it."

Bernstein's eyes flashed, but he maintained his outward serenity. "This is craziness. We've negotiated a good deal, the market will lap it up, you got rid of your foremost competitor, and no one will ever touch you again. Be satisfied. You've won."

Hunt shook his head. "If I sign this afternoon, he's won, and I swear by all that's holy, it isn't going to happen." He focused on Bernstein as though Anderson wasn't in the room.

"Last year, Ron Falkman had dinner with Norm to see if we'd be interested in buying Kestrel. Norm told Ritter that if he wanted to dump his stinking company at a below-market price, we'd accommodate him. Otherwise, he could rot in hell." Hunt allowed himself a smile at the memory. "And now he's suckered us into paying a premium price to achieve the same result."

Bernstein remained unflappable. "If that's the case, why don't we drop our price and buy his company cheaper?"

Another tight smile. "Because we can hurt him worse if we don't buy now, if we do nothing. Sooner or later, his investors will take control. When they do, they'll either sell us the whole company cheaply—or, better, break up Kestrel, and then we'll buy the pieces we want. Either way, Ritter's penniless."

"There's one problem," Norm Anderson said.

"What's that?"

"If we reject Kestrel's bid outright and don't offer any alternatives, the analysts will issue sell recommendations on your stock, and it'll drop like a brick. Your shareholders will go crazy. Do you want a slew of lawsuits?"

"I'll risk it. It'd take years, and by that time, Ritter's investors will have gained control, and we'll act. That'll stop any suits. The shareholders will be kissing my ass." He stood. "The signing's set for noon? How about we take in a movie instead."

* * * * *

"It's off?"

"So Anderson said." Falkman's expression was as dour as his employer's.

"I want his words exactly."

"'There's no price low enough to save Ritter's ass.'"

CHAPTER 54

2002

Rolfe's first thought, when he could think clearly enough to focus, was of Momo. After his euphoria of the night before, their future together now seemed void. There would be no trip to London, no reunion. Momo was unattainable. Once more, he was alone in the abyss.

Day and night melded. Rolfe shuffled listlessly around his apartment. Hardly sleeping or eating, he talked briefly to Susan—to tell her the dire news and to beg her not to contact him; when he was ready, he'd let her know his plans.

When he called Falkman, the banker had no solutions. "I'll call you if I come up with something," he said.

Rolfe wondered if he, like the others, would now betray him.

His mother called. "I read that the deal collapsed," she said. "Are you all right?"

She was weak, he knew, the spark gone out of her after Jan's death. He did not have the heart to tell her the humiliating truth. Maybe when he visited her...

"I'm fine," he managed. "There's a Plan B."

He had no inkling of what it might be.

* * * * *

He heard nothing from McCory or Popov, but each time he looked out the apartment windows, he saw the same black Mercedes parked beneath.

* * * * *

An insistent buzzing woke him. Dressed in the running shorts and a torn T-shirt that served as pajamas, he opened the door.

Susan barged in carrying two briefcases. "Jesus. You look like shit," she said, sniffing cheerfully. "And I don't know which smells worse, you or this apartment."

"Who asked you to come?" Rolfe grumbled, though he felt a stir of pleasure at her arrival. "I told you I didn't want to see anyone."

She ignored him. "I'm going to make coffee. Want some?"

"I suppose so."

"I've brought the mail from the office. In the brown briefcase."

He followed her to the kitchen. "Not interested."

"And I've got some news."

"If Hunt's changed his mind, tell me. Otherwise, I repeat: not interested."

"Oh, I think you will be. Remember Longstreet, the guy I hired to dig up material on Chantal and McCory?

He was interested. "Go on."

"I've had him dig deeper. His men kept the wiretaps on Chantal's line, for instance. On the day after the deal went under, they had her and McCory on a conference call. Guess who with?"

He accepted the steaming mug of coffee from her and sat at the kitchen table. "I'm not in the mood for quizzes."

"Your good friend Popov."

"What?"

"Yup. Popov. He and McCory were whining about how much they lost on Metropolitan stock—stock that you persuaded them to buy. They held it while it went downhill, because Chantal told them about Hunt's plan to buy out Kestrel. When he didn't, it slid to twelve dollars in a matter of hours. They blame you for it."

Rolfe shrugged. "Add it to the list."

"Most of all, they focused on what they were going to do to you personally and how they were going to get back their money you owe them for the casinos."

His brain, working for the first time in days, caught the inference. "You did say 'their' and 'them'?"

"Right. Our team tracked the profits on McCory's casinos from the Cayman Islands to Liechtenstein via Liberia, and then to Zurich in a cozy Swiss bank. Now tell me: Who else hides money in Switzerland?"

Of course! "Popov."

"Bingo. For the price of an envelope stuffed with cash, a Swiss bank clerk showed our man proof that all roads lead to your 'good friend' Popov."

Rolfe grimaced. "They've been together for years?"

"Ever since McCory involved you in the casinos. Chantal told McCory everything she learned from you, and he passed it on to Popov."

The impact of her words slammed into him. A memory flashed into his mind. "Oh, my God. After you and Josh told me how you'd emptied out all of the various accounts, I tried to discuss it with Ron, who didn't want to hear it. So I spent the night with Chantal—"

"And?"

"And I told her we'd done stuff I couldn't explain." He began to cry, the tears coming suddenly from the depth of realization. "It's my fault Josh is dead."

"Everything fits," Susan said remorselessly. "McCory and Popov had Josh tortured to find out what we'd done, and then had him murdered once they got what they wanted: information on you that they could use to get their money back. They figured they'd try that strong-arm stuff again. Hence, the attack in Berlin and the kidnapping of Pieter's kids."

"McCory and Popov," Rolfe breathed. "I'd have bet on Hunt or Steinmann."

"No, it was your so-called allies. Your 'friends.' But they've played you long enough. There's nothing more they can hope to get from you. They'll kill you, I'm sure of it."

He was sure, as well. "Let them. I deserve it. Retribution for Josh." The abyss was bottomless.

"You've got to run," she said. "You can't stay in Los Angeles."

He looked at her pale face and beseeching eyes, and felt a rush of love. "You run. You're the one with your bags packed. Take whatever money's left in the company and get out."

"There's no money left," she told him.

"No money? Then how could you pay Longstreet?"

"Simple. I followed your advice and pillaged the casinos and Popov's hotels' accounts."

"But that's suicide!"

"It'll take them a while to figure out what I've done. In the meantime, as I told you, I have my own money. Enough to get me away. Besides, it's you they want." She stood and walked with him back to the living room. "If you decide to elude them," she said, smiling wanly, "take a look in the black briefcase. There was money left after I paid Longstreet. Lots of it. It'll give you a head start."

With a cry, she flung herself into his arms. "For God's sake, at least try and save yourself," she sobbed. "Please, Rolfe. Promise me. Please."

Then she pushed him away and ran to the door, closing it noiselessly behind him.

Run? Where? Stay here and die? He wouldn't give them the satisfaction. Fight back? With what?

He opened the briefcase Susan had left and stared incredulously at bundles of hundred-dollar bills; he picked one up and counted it. Ten thousand dollars. The bundles were piled high in the briefcase. Half a million dollars at least, plenty for maneuverability. But maneuverability for what?

He was totally lost.

* * * * *

"Kenneth? It's Rolfe Ritter in Los Angeles."

Palmer's voice on the other end of the phone was chilly. "Yes, Rolfe. What can I do for you?"

"I need help. Now."

"What sort of help?"

"Our mutual acquaintance from Moscow and some of his friends are planning to kill me. I need to disappear."

"And you want me to arrange it?"

"Yes. You owe it to me."

"Why? You've made a fortune from our Moscow acquaintance, and as I remember, the last time you asked for something, I told you I was only doing it for Mike's sake. Besides, I asked you for a favor in Shanghai, and you blew me off."

"So you refuse me now?" He couldn't believe it.

"Mike's long dead," Palmer sighed. "You're on your own."

* * * * *

T-shirt soaked with sweat, Rolfe paced through his apartment, searching for a decision. I should have put that bullet in my head, he told himself, and, remembering his fear, knew he wouldn't try it again.

I won't do the job for them, he thought. If they want to kill me, let them find me. He stuffed a suitcase with his clothes; he'd take the cash with him in the black briefcase. He opened the safe and removed his ready cash, jewelry, the keys to his safe deposit boxes. He put the keys in an envelope addressed to Ron Falkman, along with a note: *Use these, you old rabbi. I hope what's in the boxes keeps you amused.* Paramount was his diary. When he got to his destination, wherever it might be, he'd start another.

He wrote to his mother, telling her not to try to contact him; he'd be in touch as soon as possible. Then he picked up his pen again:

My darling Momo,

By the time you get this, I'll be long gone from L.A., running like a hunted fox to God knows where.

Please know that I've always loved you. My heart was torn apart when I pushed your love away, but I did it for your safety and would do it again today. Without you, I would never have known love.

Rolfe

He made a quick tour of the apartment. The brown briefcase lay where Susan had left it, and he opened it more out of habit than interest. On top of a file of faxes, printouts of emails, and letters, Susan had left a list of messages. He scanned it quickly. Three jumped out: Bud McCory, Yevgeny Popov, and Sir Martin Treadwell, "urgent."

CHAPTER 55

2002

Treadwell flew in from London the next day, and the two men dined in his suite at the Loews Hotel in Santa Monica.

"I watched your bid for Metropolitan," Treadwell said. "Impressive. A bold move. When you have no defenses left, attack. Our bankers sent me a copy of the bid documents, and I read your plan for combining the two businesses. It made great sense."

"Thank you," Rolfe replied, not daring to hope. Where was this leading?

"Our first and only executive committee member had an idea I rather liked, and I want to try it out on you. You remember Momo Takenaka, don't you?"

Rolfe shifted to the edge of his seat. "What did she say?"

Treadwell pushed away from the table and casually crossed one Saville Row-tailored leg over the other. "She thinks we should buy Metropolitan."

Brilliant, Rolfe thought. Instant scale, distribution, and a faltering company to fix. Perfect for EUF. He applauded Momo's relentless logic. "What has this to do with me?" he asked.

Treadwell watched him closely. "You really don't get it, do you?"

Rolfe's emotions were frayed to their edges. "No, not really."

"We'll not only buy Metropolitan but also Kestrel and your investors' hotel and casino properties as well. Then, as EUF's deputy chairman, you'll implement your plan to combine both companies. With our capital and your expertise, we'll do exactly what your bid promised: create the world's largest—and the world's best—hotel company."

Staggering! Rolfe was dizzied by the audaciousness of it. "Buy Kestrel? What about all the things you said to me last time we met?"

"Things have changed since then, haven't they? The lodging industry's recovering from September 11ᵗʰ; in a year or so, business will be strong, with or without a war with Iraq. Lodging stocks have improved, with the exception of Hunt's, and you need a deal. Seems to me the timing is ideal."

Rolfe clutched the table to stop the dizziness. It took a few seconds to wrap his mind around this turn of events, to fully comprehend Treadwell's words. Was it true? Was he safe? Yes! he exalted. Momo, you saved me.

Instant elation, and then, almost immediately, profound sadness. The world's best hotel company, Treadwell had said. But EUF's. Not his. You failed, a voice inside him taunted, you failed. Your dream is shattered. You're a failure.

He swallowed hard, trying not to acknowledge that the voice was right. Slowly, Sir Martin's face swam back into focus, and his words became clear.

"Well? Yes or no?"

* * * * *

When he returned to his apartment, Rolfe barely registered the Louis Vuitton suitcases in his apartment foyer.

"Hello?" he called out.

"I had the doorman let me in." Margaret came down the hall from the living room. She was wearing a black dress with a diamond brooch, and her hair was in the familiar tight bun.

"I thought you wouldn't travel!"

She smiled. "Apparently I did. Are you glad to see me?"

"Of course." It was true. "But why are you here? Are you all right?"

"Fine." She looked old and tired. Lines around her mouth and eyes were deep, and the excess of rouge on her cheeks made him feel that he was standing too close to her. She'd be ashamed he'd seen her so wasted, he thought.

He took a step away. "Would you like some tea?" he asked. "Or a drink?"

"Tea would be nice."

She followed him into the kitchen and watched as he put a kettle on to boil. "That used to be my job," she said.

"Strange, isn't it?" he acknowledged. He poured tea for both of them and sat next to her at the kitchen table. "Now," he said. "Tell me why you came."

She took his hand. "Your bid for Metropolitan was a last-ditch effort to stave off disaster, wasn't it?" He shrugged an acknowledgement. "There never was a Plan B was there?" He shrugged again. "Anyway, I realized you were desperate, and I knew I had to be with you. I refused you help when you asked for it last time. I'm here to help you now if I can."

I've waited a lifetime for this, he thought. But no one can help. The Kestrel and the son of The Kestrel—ultimately, neither had met her vision. It was not his need that had brought her here, but hers, he realized. Maybe he could give her some of what she wanted.

"I'm not desperate any more," he assured his mother.

He told her what Treadwell had offered, and that by accepting it, he had accepted the limits of his flight. "The sun was too hot," he admitted, feeling a deep melancholy. "I had to come back to earth."

"Oh, I'm glad!" She was, for a moment, radiant, the way she was with his father. "It means we can spend more time together, be available to each other when troubles come."

Did he want that? Yes, to a degree. The wounds still smarted, he knew, in both their souls. It would be many years more before they would be fully healed, if ever. But her words were a balm, and he felt a gratitude that went far beyond this moment to the core of his life.

She sat with her eyes downcast, not daring to search his face for a response.

He raised her hand to his lips and kissed it with gallantry and love. "That will be nice," he said. "As a start, I remind you that I left home to be a chef. I got good at it. Let me cook you dinner so I can prove it."

* * * * *

"Fifteen dollars a share?" Hunt roared. "Pathetic. Norm, set a board call for this afternoon. I'll tell the directors to reject it."

Anderson looked at Mel Bernstein, and then at the floor—anyplace but at Hunt. "It's not your decision," he said.

"What are you talking about? Of course it's my decision."

"The board met without you this morning," Bernstein said. "I've been instructed to accept EUF's offer. They want you to meet with EUF's people this evening to arrange the transition."

Hunt's face was livid. "They can fuck themselves. This is my company!"

Anderson licked his dry lips. "Not any more, Bruce. Not any

more."

* * * * *

The deputy chairman of EUF stood quietly in the doorway of Mel Bernstein's conference room and watched a battered, old man wait alone for the arrival of the EUF team. Hunt wheeled to look at him.

"What are you doing here? Come to gloat?"

Rolfe had been looking forward to this moment—indeed, the anticipation was the only thing that gave him pleasure. But he was unable to summon up the joy he'd envisioned. Hunt had lost, but so had he.

"No. Not to gloat," he said.

"Then what?"

The words he'd rehearsed for a lifetime vanished, and he shook his head, feeling empty.

"Well?" Hunt growled.

Rolfe bent over, his face inches from Hunt's. He whispered two words into his lifetime enemy's ear.

"You're fired."

CHAPTER 56

2002

"I'm glad you came back," Rolfe said.

"Me too. Things were getting pretty dull in Perth."

Rolfe took Susan's hand. "It's over now. I signed the papers the day before yesterday. Can you believe it? I'm an employee."

"A wealthy one."

"Who's talking to a very rich woman."

They sat on the Malibu sand in front of Susan's home. Rolfe opened the bottle of Roederer Crystal champagne he'd been carrying in his backpack and poured two glasses.

"It's hard to grasp," Susan said. "After all the years of robbing Peter to pay Paul, all the lies, all the crises . . . it's finally finished. I can't help feeling sad. You too?"

"I'm bloody miserable. I failed, and that's the goddamned reality. Our hotels will still be called Kestrels, but the bird's been shot down."

"It'll fly again," Susan said. "This is only one more step in your journey."

Rolfe shook his head. "I don't know. Right now, the only good news is that McCory and Popov have been paid off, and we're all safe."

He stretched lazily. "By the way, I had a talk with Kenneth Palmer yesterday. He called to apologize for shutting the door in my face when I asked for help." He snorted. "The two-faced shit wants to be my best friend, now that I can be useful to him again. Anyway, I told him everything you'd found out about McCory, Popov, and Chantal."

Funny, her name evoked nothing in him. She belonged to a closed-down part of his life.

"What did Palmer say?" Susan asked.

"Something strange: 'That won't do at all.'"

"I wonder what he meant."

"I have no idea." He lay back on his elbows. "Tell me something: How did you cover up the money you took from the casinos?"

Her expression was one of bland innocence. "The books show it as a series of payments to Bud McCory for 'consultancy fees.'"

He sat up again. "Great!"

"I thought so. Sooner or later, Popov will find out and go nuts. But just to be sure, I called Chantal this morning to wish her and her husband good luck in his retirement."

He stared at her in amazement. "Oho!"

"Then I told her that not only had McCory been stealing money from the casinos, he also hadn't shared any of the proceeds with her. If I know her, she'll run straight to Popov and tell him everything."

"So I'm not the only one manipulating her," Rolfe said, impressed.

She smirked. "It gets better. I also showed the casino making half a dozen large payments to her for 'investor relations services.' That should really screw her up with your pal Yevgeny. By the way, she told me she's leaving Bruce, wants a divorce."

"Wants half the golden handshake EUF gave him." Rolfe laughed ruefully. "Well, I suppose she's earned it."

They sat silently for a while, before strolling back toward Susan's house, both experiencing the let-down revelers feel when a party is over.

"I want you to do something for me," he said.

"Of course."

"I haven't the heart to deal with the transition."

"And you want me to handle it."

"You got it."

"And what's next for you?"

"I've got something I need to do."

EPILOGUE

Remember the story of the Spanish prisoner. For
many years he was confined in a dungeon....One
day it occurred to him to push the door of his cell.
It was open; and it had never been locked.

Winston Spencer Churchill

2003

It was a different bench. Set in a garden overlooking the bay of Phuket's Audley resort, it provided anonymity, tranquility, peace. The woman by his side was so beautiful she seemed to be a splendid tile in the mosaic of trees and sunlight surrounding them.

But at the moment, Rolfe's attention was focused not on her but on an article in the *Asian Wall Street Journal*. "Union Leader Dies in Car Crash," the headline read; the article below it detailed how Bud McCory's car had veered out of control and smashed into the supporting column of an overpass in Summerlin, Las Vegas.

An accident? Rolfe wondered. Surely not. It sounded like Popov's handiwork. Yet, Susan had faxed him a *Time Magazine* article entitled "Putin Cleans Up," describing how Russia's president, continuing his onslaught on the corruption in big business, had arrested Yevgeny Popov on charges of embezzlement and fraud. So was it probable the Russian was behind McCory's death? Maybe Palmer had made a deal with his Russian counterparts for them to clean up the mess, Rolfe mused. Maybe it was an advance payment from Palmer so he could keep his hooks in me.

No matter. The sun was warm, a gentle breeze blew, a bird sang, and he was married to the vibrant woman beside him. He stretched out his hand to her. Momo grasped it and kissed his fingers.

* * * * *

After Momo had fallen asleep that night, Rolfe tiptoed to the sitting room of the suite and took out the files he'd hired Longstreet Investigations to produce. Each file had the name of one of EUF's directors printed in gold on its dark blue cover.

The thickest file of all read "Sir Martin Treadwell: Strictly Confidential." Rolfe opened it and began to read.

A long-unused mantra crept into his mind: *Information is key. Knowledge is power.*